DUBIN'S LIVES

Books by Bernard Malamud

DUBIN'S LIVES

REMBRANDT'S HAT

THE TENANTS

PICTURES OF FIDELMAN

THE FIXER

IDIOTS FIRST

A NEW LIFE

THE MAGIC BARREL

THE ASSISTANT

THE NATURAL

Bernard Malamud

DUBIN'S LIVES

Farrar Straus Giroux

New York

Copyright © 1977, 1979 by Bernard Malamud
All rights reserved
Third printing, 1979
Printed in the United States of America
Published simultaneously in Canada
by McGraw-Hill Ryerson Ltd., Toronto
Designed by Betty Crumley

Portions of this book originally appeared,
in somewhat different form, in *The New Yorker*,
The Atlantic, and *Playboy*

Library of Congress Cataloging in Publication Data
Malamud, Bernard.
Dubin's lives.
PZ4.M237Du 1979[PS3563.A4]   813'.5'4
78-23897

A limited first edition of this book
has been privately printed

Max and Bertha,
my father and mother

And for
Anna Fidelman

DUBIN'S LIVES

"What demon possessed me that I behaved so well?"

THOREAU

"Give me continence and chastity, but not yet."

AUGUSTINE

One

They sometimes met on country roads when there were flowers or snow. Greenfeld wandered on various roads. In winter, bundled up against the weather, Dubin, a five-foot-eleven grizzled man with thin legs, walked on ice and snow, holding a peeled birch limb. Greenfeld remembered him tramping along exhaling white breaths. Sometimes when one was going longitude and the other latitude they waved to each other across windswept snowy fields. He recalled Dubin's half-hidden face on freezing days when it was too cold to talk. Or they joked in passing. Had he heard the one about the rabbi, who when his sexton prayed aloud, "Dear God, I am nothing, You are every-thing," remarked, "Look who says he's nothing!" Dubin hoarsely laughed. Once, looking not at all well, he said, "This has to be the center of the universe, my friend." "Where?" "This road as we meet." He stamped his boot as he spoke. Once in passing he said, "Ach, it's a balancing act," then called back, "a lonely business." A minute later: "In essence I mean to say." There were times Dubin handed him a note he read later and perhaps filed. Once the flutist read the slip of paper on the road and tore it up. "What are you doing?" the other shouted. "This I've seen before." Afterward he asked, "Why don't you keep yourself a journal?" "Not for me," the biogra-pher replied. "None of this living for the gods."

They embraced after not meeting for months. Nor was Dubin afraid to kiss a man he felt affection for. Sometimes they wrote when either was abroad—a card might bring a letter, but otherwise now saw little of each other. Their wives weren't friends though they spoke at length when they met. There had been a time when both men drank together on winter nights, and though the talk satisfied, neither was able to work steadily or well the next morning. Eventually they stopped visiting one another and were the lonelier for it. Dubin, as time went by, found it hard to bear the other's growing quietude, and Greenfeld did not that much care for confession. Dubin could stand still, look you in the eye, and say some intimate things. Greenfeld liked not to know all.

Although it isn't yet end of summer, William Dubin in a moment of his walk into the country—rural into pastoral—beats his arms across chest and shoulders as though he had unexpectedly encountered cold, clouds have darkened, a snowstorm threatens. He had, in a way, been thinking of winter.

The biographer had left the house in late-afternoon warm sunshine and had casually walked himself, despite nature's beauty, into a small gloom. He imagined it had come from sensing change in the season, one day to the next. August was a masked month: it looked like summer and conspired with fall; like February it would attempt to hide what it was about. Dubin had uncovered bright-green shoots under dead leaves in February. In the woods today he had spied a flare of red in a broad maple. A sense of short season: Northeast cheat. The days had secretly cast off ballast and were drifting toward autumn. Cold air descended to the roots of trees. The leaves, if you touched, were drying. The noise of bees sucking pale flowers, of crickets rasping, seemed distant. Butterflies, flitting amid trees, flaunted their glad rags a moment before generating and expiring. Dubin felt change and could not bear it. He forbade his mind to run to tomorrow. Let winter stay in its white hole.

Beating his chest he flails at time. Time dances on. "Now I am ice, now I am sorrel." He shakes his useless fist.

Dubin, the biographer, a genial angular middle-aged type with a bulge of disciplined belly—thus far and no farther—and a grizzled head of hair, his head perhaps a half-size small for his height, walked briskly toward a dark-green covered bridge about a mile up the dirt road. His arms and legs were long; deep chest; shoulders, when he straightened himself, upright. He had gray-blue eyes, a slender long nose, relaxed mouth; he smiled now, touched by a pleasant thought. The mild existential gloom he had experienced in the woods had evaporated; he felt serene, doing his walk. Dubin had a way of breaking into a run when something intensive rose to think of. He was running —marvelous gait for a man of fifty-six. For a minute he shadow-boxed on the road, desisting when a woman in a passing car laughed aloud. He trotted on, enjoying the sweep of space in every direction. He loved the free pleasures of perspective. Fifty yards from the road, a narrow stream, turbulent and muddy after a heavy morning shower, wound through the pasture. To the east rose masses of green trees climbing New York hills; beyond were the looming low Vermont mountains in misty receding planes. Dubin remembered once, in approaching Capri in search of D. H. Lawrence, the hills like a big-breasted woman on her back, raising her head to kiss the sky.

Remembering his work, he unconsciously slowed to a brisk walk. He'd had thoughts while shaving that he ought to try developing a few notes for an autobiographical memoir—type a page or two to see if they came to life with texture, heft. Or do it the way Montaigne did—you start an essay and thus begin an examination of your life. "Reader, I am myself the subject of my book; you would be unreasonable to spend your leisure on so frivolous and vain a matter." His smile turned into snicker when he foresaw Kitty's judgment: "Why bother when there are so many unusual lives to write about?" She'd be right although any man speaking truthfully about his life should be worth reading. Still, no sense thinking about it until he had completed the Lawrence he was, after years of research, about to start writing. "My God, whatever brought me to him?" After several steps he ran on, a little in fright.

He was running lightly, forearms loosely lifted, watching a wheeling flight of birds—grackles?—when an orange VW with a battered door and a soiled cracked windshield—it looked as though it had passed through the bird flight —roared out of the covered bridge, came to a halt, abruptly started forward, at last pulled jerkily to a stop at Dubin's side. He felt a flash of recognition on beholding the driver but it came to nothing: she was a stranger.

The young woman begged his pardon in a voice he would surely have remembered, vaguely drawing down her skirt over bare thighs. She was braless, her face attractive; he had noticed a few darkish blond hairs on her chin. Her loose fair hair she wore long; the well-formed sturdy body was feminine, appealing. A half-eaten yellow pear lay on the seat beside her but if she had enjoyed the fruit it no longer showed. The girl's curious eyes, he thought, were uneasy, as if she was staring at last night's dream instead of only good-willed Dubin. She wore wire-framed blue-tinted glasses that muddied her green irises, he saw when she removed them. Her smile was nervous, mouth sour in repose. From habit he tried to imagine her past but made no headway. Her first glance at him had seemed tight, as though she was calculating whether his visible interest went beyond what the moment required; or she wanted not to be quickly read by anyone who could possibly read; then her focus shifted, gaze eased; she asked if she was on the right road to town. She had, out of the window, touched his arm.

Dubin, pleased by the gesture, pointed a helpful finger in the direction he had come. "Take the left of the fork."

The girl nodded. This was no comfortable lady despite nature's favor of an impressive body and on-the-verge-of-beautiful face. Whatever she had she seemed to want less of. He was about to walk on but she was still unsure where to go. Dubin gave her a good word: "A lovely day." He was a deep-voiced man with a tentative laugh.

"Some would say so."

"Not you?"

She did not reply.

"Be kind to yourself." He had stammered as a child, and the impulse to on occasion converted itself into a mild hoarseness of expression, sometimes a self-conscious laugh. Dubin cleared his throat.

She gave him an almost sullen look.

"Why do you say that?"

A man behind them, in an Oldsmobile with Jersey plates, honked to pass. "Whyn't you make love in bed?"

The girl burst into a nervous laugh.

Dubin told her he had no idea and hurried on.

It later occurred to him that the disquiet lady had been wearing a Star of David on a thin gold chain around her neck. If they had spoken names might they have touched lips?

Ah, Dubin, you meet a pretty girl on the road and are braced to hop on a horse in pursuit of youth.

There he stood by the tree that had wounded him.

The blow on the head and broken bones were not the wound; they had evoked the wound, he had thought a minute after his car had struck the tree —the aftermath when one cursed himself for suffering the wound. Dubin had tramped through the booming bridge, where the muddy stream turned west and he east, and was again at the point of the road he still shunned, twenty feet from the highway: it had iced up during a freezing late-fall rain last year and Dubin, on a trivial morning errand—a container of milk Kitty had forgotten to buy—slid into an accident. His thoughts had hardly changed. The car spun like an arrow on a board and the biographer—as if trying to foretell the future: what begins with a wound?—had struck a tree, the last lining the road—another foot and he'd have skidded to a stop in the dead grass.

He had not at first felt pain as blood streamed down his face. He had stumbled to the highway waving his left arm, the other cracked at the wrist, bloody nose broken, right knee cut. It had seemed to him hours before anyone stopped to pick him up. Three drivers had seen him and sped by—"Fools!" Dubin had cried in astonishment. She who had stopped for him was a girl in her late twenties in a red Pinto, on her way to work. He had felt ashamed to be bleeding in her car. It was years since he had seen his own blood flowing and he wondered if it was a portent; but nothing came of it except a week of pain and a mild depression for not being able to work.

Through his bleeding nose he could smell her incisive blooming perfume. Some responses have no respect for circumstances, characteristic of Dubin.

He told her his name. "I'm a biographer." And laughed embarrassedly. "Sorry to be messing your upholstery."

"It'll wash off—do you feel much pain?"

"Curiously not. I will, I'm sure."

"I'm Betsy Croy."

"Charmed. What do you do?" Dubin asked her, mopping with his handkerchief the blood dripping down his head. Better to talk.

"I bookkeep. What did you say you do?"

"Write lives—Mark Twain, Thoreau—others." He smiled foolishly; she didn't know the name.

Betsy drove awhile in concentrated silence, then said hesitantly, "I married this boy from my high school class when we graduated. Now he's twenty-eight and has got impotent."

"A shame," Dubin replied. "The composer Mahler was helped in similar circumstances by a long walk with Freud in Leiden—that's in Holland. If he hasn't already, your husband ought to talk to a doctor."

"He has but it did no good." She said nothing more.

Dubin was moved to offer his services but surely not now; he bled quietly.

Afterward he had stupidly forgotten to thank her, express heartfelt gratitude for her kindness; he had wanted to send her flowers. Dubin had visited the State Police, hoping her address might appear on the accident report. It did not. Occasionally he dreamed of her. He had for an instant thought this was she whom he had just met on the road; she was another.

The bark of the oak had been obscenely skinned for months after he had hit it. Although an accident on the road was sooner or later almost certain, given the hard wintry weather and frequency of mishap, Dubin had felt insulted by fate. A year later he would still not look at the tree as he walked or drove by.

He ran across the highway when traffic let up, wobbling as his arthritic knee tightened, and limped a minute after entering a theoretically hard-topped road—subject to winter potholes, spring mud—then went on with his country walk. Dubin thought of it as circular although it was in fact an irregular quadrilateral on the county map. He strode on at a steady pace, refreshing his lungs, exhaling with pleasure. He had put this walk together years ago—the long walk—and his route rarely varied. The short walk went to the bridge and back, about a mile each way. He left by the kitchen door; across the back lawn into a grove of tall gray-trunked silver maples with slender sharp-pointed leaves—gave the elegant effect of elms but less lyric, more grandeur—through a broad field with a pliant path he had worn into it; then, past the old barn, into the sunlit, still, pine-scented wood, drama of white birch with evergreen; in addition, sugar maples, aspen, ash. Kitty called it "Kitty's Wood" because she'd been in it first; explored it while he was unpacking his books after they'd moved into the house. And then up the road to the covered green bridge.

The walk he was into now Dubin estimated an additional four miles, the whole taking about an hour and a half or three quarters, unless he hurried. The way not to hurry—to enjoy nature, not suffer obsession—was to go the short walk; but sometimes he hurried the long. He felt he was taking his time today when he had the thought—sensation—that the road was coming at him counterclockwise—moving as though the journey hastened its end.

8

Dubin's mind ran ahead of itself. What's my hurry to get back? What must I do that I haven't done? The truth was he hadn't meant to take the long hike today and was probably hitting it up unconsciously; he had meant at the bridge to turn back but walked on remembering his accident. And Betsy Croy.

As he hastened on he warned himself to be attentive to what's present, namely nature. If you looked without seeing, the walk was more of the same —the same subjectivity. The good of it beyond exercise was that it changed the mind's scenery after a day's work. He felt uneasy when not observing— the big ones missed nothing, had eyes that remembered. Thoreau: "The perception of beauty is a moral test." More test than moral but one ought to look. The road came at him in slow motion—he tried to explain it but couldn't. What's happening today that hadn't yesterday? Only this moving road, a device of time hurrying me home. Dubin runs to do what's next. The way to counteract forgetting to look was to join up—take courage in both hands, move your ass off the confining road, be involved. Hop a wall; follow a stream through pasture—what's so sacred about private property when it's all God's earth? Walk up a hill; enter sunlit wood; swim bareass in a pond reflecting day's eye. Walk home wet in dry clothes.

When had such happened lately? He could count the times on one finger. I rarely leave this road. Now and then a picnic under Sunday-evening trees. Sometimes I cut in along an old path to the pond in the quarry. Wild flowers scattered in clusters along the way. Once, with Kitty, we climbed Mt. No Name with the kids—walked up the low north flank. They'd been summer people who had stayed on. City people—Dubin from Newark and Bronx tenements, Kitty originally from Montreal; she had also lived in Augusta, Maine, with her grandmother. Dubin, after a decade and a half in Center Campobello, could recognize and name about twenty trees, a half dozen bushes, fifteen wild flowers, a handful of birds. He followed the flight of a crow elated to know who was flying. He had slowly learned to look, name things of nature. When he passed a flower he told himself to take it all in. What he couldn't name, or when names slipped his mind, he asked Kitty. She saw the flower whole—corolla, stalk, the shape of its leaves. He felt for a moment bereft.

In sum, William Dubin, visitor to nature, had introduced himself along the way but did not intrude. He gazed from the road, kept his distance even when nature hallooed. Unlikely biographer of Henry David Thoreau—I more or less dared. Even in thought nature is moving. Hunger for Thoreau's experience asserted itself. Besides, great men are men; a genius in doubt is a man in doubt—I got close to his human nature. Thoreau gave an otherwise hidden passion and drew from woods and water the love affair with earth and sky he'd recorded in his journals. "All nature is my bride." His biographer-to-be had been knocked off his feet on first serious encounter with nature, a trip to the Adirondacks with a school friend when they were sixteen. Before that he had hungrily sought signs—promises?—of the natural world on city streets and found, in walks out of his neighborhood, private houses with flowers on lawns; hedges; trees; and the dead leaves he was surprised to find in summertime. As a young man he had lived much in public parks; had sought, if not his bride, his bride's cousin? The first time in the mountains had turned him on in the manner of the Wordsworthian youth in "Tintern Abbey": "The sounding cataract haunted me like a passion." Dubin, haunted, had been roused to awareness of self extended in nature, highest pitch of consciousness. He felt what made the self richer: who observes beauty contains it. One is stabbed by the miraculous creation and interwoven whole. He wanted nature to teach him—not sure what—perhaps to bring forth the self he sought—defined self, best self? Nature compelled him to feel what he hadn't felt so well before: "the shaping force," Hardy called it. He never forgot this although the experience, infrequently renewed, had diminished as youth had. My God, how nature moved me. Now "that time is past," as Wordsworth had felt it. Now, on the whole, in varying moods Dubin looked at scenery, and scenery, in varying moods, looked at him. But in his heart he still expected something he could not define. If you dared look you earned seeing. Dubin did his walks in nature's presence.

Still, what nature had meant to him, though not only nature, had inspired him to undertake and ultimately complete a fine life of H. D. Thoreau. In his mind he flipped through pages: close portrait of the solitary sensuous man, privately wounded, who lived on wonder, observed the bald fact and spun metaphor and myth out of nature. In his writing he celebrated his consciousness identified with the Absolute. *Walden* was a lied of death and song of resurrection: Thoreau had it both ways. Now and then someone argued the book was not literally true; it was fictitious: In truth, the man went home often to see his mama. If so, Dubin thought, it was nonetheless a masterpiece, nonetheless inspiring. It had stirred the imaginations of Proust and Yeats. How can it be less than it is? You write sentences and men are sensibly affected. Dubin, proud of the biography, contemplated with confidence his present work on D. H. Lawrence. Do the primitive labyrinth of the man, mystic flame-boiled essence, bloody simple human self.

He warned himself then as he often did, although it came to not much, that a good writer adventures beyond the uses of language, or what's there to put into words? Yet the truth is some do not: of them Dubin is one. As though to make up for his limitations, from his pants pocket he dug out one of his impulsive notes to himself: "Everybody's life is mine unlived. One writes lives he can't live. To live forever is a human hunger."

He was running. As the road dipped the hills rose. In spring light-green foliage raced up the rumpled hills and by June covered the scabrous shoulders of the mountains. Dubin trotted on the road going south. In the distance white clouds moving above patches of sunlight on the hills. The land sloped up to a line of trees advancing on him like a marauding army. For a while the wood rode on his head. Dubin rose on the road as the hills sank; he settled into a fast walk. A sparse quarter mile of old houses went by as on a rusty turntable, then broad fields with now and then a stark farmhouse, upright and spare to a point of principle—with weather-beaten barns, red or black silos, Angus and Herefords on cow paths in the pasture. Dubin liked to come by on rainy late-afternoons to see the steaming swollen-uddered cows lying in the wet waiting to be milked. When he passed in light fog, the ripe hot smell of cow dung from a barn nearby assailed him across the field—he knew where he was. One night, driving the road alone, he saw a cow cropping grass in moonlight. The farmland around gave pleasure: each neat walled field, each shifting shade of brown beige and green; furrowed, cultivated, harvested, plowed under: order of uses of men, animals, seasons eternal.

Robert Frost and his doomed brood had lived a summer on one of the farms not far away, and Dubin, long after the fact, had talked with his neighbors in Vermont and written an article: "Frost, the Season of His Wife's Death." The poet had been hard on her. His will, it had been said, could tolerate no other wills around. "Elinor has never been any earthly use to me." She had kept him from her bedside while she was dying. He waited in the corridor, saw her only when she was asleep, unconscious; dead. He'd had no last word from her. Her defense was silence. "She was not as original as I in thought but she dominated my art with the power of her character and nature." Dubin occasionally visited their anguished grave in a churchyard a dozen miles away. They were together now in the vault under the tombstone; their ashes were, with the remains of those of their children who were not buried elsewhere, although all their names were incised on the stone. "There's only one subject for a poem," Frost had said. Dubin had laid a small white stone on the marble tombstone.

The biographer had once wanted to do a full-length life of the poet and had written him a letter requesting a talk if he was interested. But the old man wrote back he had already chosen someone "to preserve my immortal remains." "I'd rather be in the hands of a man whose spit I'd seen." Dubin, after going through her papers in the N.Y. Public Library, had considered the life of Virginia Woolf, whose intelligent imagination and fragile self had drawn him to her; but her own nephew, Quentin Bell, was already into a biography of her. Dubin had then thought of D. H. Lawrence, a complex type with tormented inner life, if that's who you felt you had to get involved with.

Thinking of the biographies he had written, in particular *Short Lives* in a single volume, he felt a sadness come into him. Completed, most lives were alike in stages of living—joys, celebrations, crises, illusions, losses, sorrows. Some lives accomplished much, some very little. One learned, as he wrote, the arcs, forms, consequences of the flight of lives. One learns where life goes. In fact he led them there. When you know the end the rest moves up only too quickly. Therefore, Dubin, what's on your mind? That he was about to create a new life would in the end shorten his own? When the work was done he was that much older—more serious matter than a decade ago. He had sacrificed to his labors that many hours, that many years. Prufrock had measured out his life with measuring spoons; Dubin, in books resurrecting the lives of others. You lost as you gained; there's only one subject for a poem.

The last part of the country walk went west before it turned south again on an upward pitch to the highway, a length of solitary shaded road heavily wooded on both sides. Overhead, lightly laced branches touched and intertwined. The road was cool in the green shade, the air fragrant. Dubin breathed. He tramped on in the light-green dark. No sound except him walking along thinking his thoughts. At one place on the deserted road he broke into a run. He had more than once encountered a dog racing at him across a field, or bursting out of the woods, teeth bared, growling in its belly. His response was sternly to say, "Go home, boy," and hope for the best. Mostly they wandered away as he walked on; but he feared meeting an animal with no respect for human language. A black German shepherd had all but treed him once—his back against a tree, the hound snarling when Dubin attempted to inch forward. He'd been trapped a mad long time but kept the dog off by talking to it, his heart where it needn't be, telling it the story of his life. At last it yawned and trotted off. In afterthought it had seemed that a cardinal's shrill call, sounding much like a man whistling for his dog, had sent the animal on his way. Dubin waved to the invisible red bird in the trees. He's been set running by the thought of the dog and was running now. "Why, then, should man hasten as if anything less than an eternity were allotted for the least deed?" Who says?

As he ran, the road had stopped moving and he slowed to a walk. A reddish-brown bitch followed him, a shaggy Irish setter who sometimes appeared, a friend of the people. Ahead, where the bushes rose fifteen feet high on one side of the road, and the trees moved into the downsloping wood on the other, he observed a moving figure. It was Greenfeld in white cap and shirt, ambling along. He often carried his flute or recorder and would play as he walked. Dubin would hear a song in the trees. The flute got gut-close to primitive lament. "Ach, ich flöte." Greenfeld did one thing and did it well, not a bad way to live a life. Not now in a mood to listen or be listened to —he felt a hunger for solitude—the biographer stepped behind a tree until the flutist had passed by.

Some other time.

He was looking at a grove of evergreens below—a pleasure to gaze down at the pointed tops of trees—and a little farther on turned as the road grew level and approached the highway. Soon country merged into village, not a charming sight. After departing the highway Dubin walked north on an old sidewalk of broken slate. Center Campobello was a town of 4,601 souls in New York State, almost a mile from the Vermont border. He had lived there fifteen years, unknown to most: Wm. B. Dubin, who wrote lives, and who, it said in *Newsweek*, had once received a medal from President Johnson. There was a picture of them shaking hands. He recalled the clutch of the man's big paw. At the courthouse he turned and walked toward a crimson sunset until he came to the edge of town: his three-story yellow clapboard house with black shutters and wrought-iron widow's walk on the roof. A porch with white pillars ran half the length of the rear of the house. Dubin began his daily walk at the back door and returned from it, as from a journey, by the front.

He went around to the rear but Kitty was not in her garden. Dubin studied the dead elm coming down next week. And a skimpy-leaved maple was expiring—"maple decline" the tree man called it. "Save money cuttin' them both down the same time." Dubin thought he'd wait till the maple was properly dead. Emerson had counted one hundred and twenty-eight trees on his property, lamenting they must ultimately fall. Dubin had counted sixty-one on his nine acres. Emerson could name every one of his trees; not Dubin. The biographer entered the house, called his wife, and when there was no reply, walked up the stairs. He stood solemnly in Gerald's old room, then in Maud's. Later he heard Kitty come into the house and she called up that they had a new cleaning person. "That's what she calls herself. I advertised today and she phoned while you were on your walk. Would you like your supper hot or cold? I feel dreadfully hot."

Dubin, in his study, had picked up his marked copy of *Women in Love*. A wasted walk, he had wanted to work.

"Why do you berate yourself in the poor mirror?" Kitty had asked.

"Because I'm handsomer in my mind than when I look in the glass."

"Don't look," she had said.

Rubbing in shaving cream, he was this morning in the bathroom mirror a solemn gent earnestly expostulating. "Next time round I'll do a comic life. Mark Twain's wasn't all that funny."

"Shush," Dubin warned himself, then remembered Kitty had left their bed. He tried to hold down the talk when she was in the bedroom because —if she was awake or it woke her—it made her uneasy; still, after these many years. If you shouted, groaned, or muttered for no apparent reason, or gestured Up Yours in her presence, you were showing loose ends, reminding her of hers. She would rather not be reminded. Kitty, when Dubin rambled on, made clicking noises with her tongue. He would then shut up, though he had more than once reminded her that Montaigne himself used to groan "Confounded fool" in the morning mirror. And Dr. Samuel Johnson was a noisy beehive of crackpot mannerisms.

"I'm not married to them."

"Montaigne's motto was, 'What do I know?' He was a wise man. And Johnson—'winking and blinking,' Blake described him—though he looked like a mad hatter, inspired men to reason and courage. He had learned from life."

"It's your voice I hear, not theirs."

He beheld in the mirror, under stress of course—like this morning beginning a new biography—a flash of himself in his grave, and with a grimace clutched his gut where he had been stabbed. "Papa," he cried, wishing he had done things better, and made unhappy gestures of evasion and shame that irritated Kitty when she observed them. He would strike his chest with his fist, point at the sky; his nose twitched like a rabbit's. Or he would intone a single sentence like: "My daughter never learned to waltz." That, after six times, would awaken Kitty; she asked through the closed bathroom door what it meant. Dubin pooh-poohed it all. But here he was at it again—a relief this particular morning, conversing with himself at length, glad she had got up and gone out, rare thing for her to do this early in the day. Through the window he watched her contemplating her flowers in thinning mist on the ground. Kitty, wearing blue sneakers and faded pink straw gardening hat, though there was no sun to speak of, looked up and casually waved. The biographer lifted his razor like a sword in salute.

When he arose at seven, usually she slumbered on. Kitty slept raggedly and liked to pick up an hour or more at the morning end. Her sleep, after a fairly decent springtime interval, had got worse in summer. She slept deeply awhile, then was restlessly awake for hours; and slept again in the early morning before Dubin awoke. He left her lying on her stomach, wound in a sheer nightgown, the coffee au lait birthmark on her buttock a blemished island, visible when it was too hot for sheet or blanket. Though she tended to deny it—this depended on how well she was presently treating herself—her figure was good, despite large slender feet and thin shoulders. Kitty, brown hair fading, was still an attractive woman. She said she slept best mornings, when he was no longer in bed; and her most memorable dreams were morning dreams.

He had asked her recently what she thought about when she was awake and she said, "Lately the kids again—mostly. Sometimes silly things like a pair of shoes I paid too much for. Or a clerk who said something rude to me. Or I wish I had been born beautiful, or could lose weight. Some worthless things grind on all night." "Hemingway prayed when he couldn't sleep," Dubin said; "he fished and prayed." "If I prayed it would have been to be more purposeful, organized, kinder. One would have liked to do less harm." "To whom?" "Anyone. —To Gerald," Kitty confessed. He asked her if she thought of death. "I think of those who've died. I often play back my life." Sometimes she went downstairs to read if the house wasn't too cold. She'd rather not read because it woke her thoroughly and she could afterward not find her way back to sleep. She lay listening to the singing bird-world in the 5 a.m. trees. Or sometimes wept that she wasn't sleeping. Once in winter Dubin woke to soft stringed music and went downstairs to find her playing the harp in the dark.

Last night she'd waked him to say she had dreamed of Nathanael, her first husband. "This is the second time this month and I don't think I've dreamed of him in years. We were on our way somewhere, maybe to church to get married. He was young, about his age when I met him, and I was my age now. Somehow I was pregnant, though I couldn't tell whether it was with Gerald or Maud—that's what made the dream so weird. I wanted to say I couldn't go with him, I was living with you, but then I thought Nathanael's a doctor, he'll know. What a mishmash. What do you make of it?"

"What do you?"

"You're better at dreams."

"Did it frighten you?"

"Nathanael wouldn't frighten me."

"Then why wake me up? I've got to start my Lawrence this morning."

"I woke up, thought of the kids gone."

Dubin said that could be what it was about. "The kids are gone. You're floating around with time on your head. You want to be young again."

"People are always leaving," she yawned.

Irritated, he tried to sleep—the curse of an insomniac wife. Kitty crept close and held him; Dubin ultimately slept.

The house, she often complained, was all but empty. "Get some kind of work," he had advised, and now after months of unsatisfactory seeking she was reluctantly working as a volunteer in the town clerk's office. "I stop thinking when I go there." "You're overqualified," Dubin said. "I feel underqualified." She complained she had accomplished little in life. "I have no true talents, I've tried everything." He had given up arguing with her about her life.

Mornings she was active, sleep or no sleep, though she dawdled as she dressed. "Thank God, I have energy." Dubin, after half a night's loss of sleep, had to conserve his. Kitty went to the stores before noon, did her husband's errands, phoned friends—always Myra Wilson, an old widow on a farm in Vermont, a mile and a half up the road, whom Kitty shopped for—then she attended her house. She kept it well; sparsely furnished, suiting the cold climate. Center Campobello shrank, seemed to lose streets and people in wintertime. She was good with space, placed it where it showed. Each piece of furniture looked as though it had been set like a small sculpture. She hated accumulation, clutter; yet placed things around it was pleasant to discover: small antique bottles, oriental tiles, lacquered boxes and pieces of stained glass. Kitty was good with flower arrangements, although she mercifully picked them late and the flowers in her bowls and vases were often slightly wilted. She was strict with her cleaning women, yet patiently showed them how to do things she wanted done. Dubin appreciated the order of the household; it went with his work.

Outside, she was continually digging in her perennial border, pulling up bulbs and planting them elsewhere as though transposing the facts of her life. Dubin enjoyed the flowers brightening the back lawn, but when he complimented her on her garden Kitty said she had no real green thumb. He called it a light-green thumb. The biographer appreciated his wife's good taste. He admired her kind nature, her honesty, even when it hurt. Kitty was spontaneously generous; Dubin had to measure his out. She was empathic: a single string bean in the sink was "lonely" to her. One flower of ten, fallen from a vase, had immediately to be restored to its "home." When Dubin was thinking of the gains over losses in marriage, he felt he had honed his character on hers. In all she had helped stabilize and enlarge his life; but he was not so sure, after a generation of marriage, that he had done the same for her or why wasn't she at peace with herself? Though he thought he knew the answer he continued to ask the question.

Kitty, as he dried his razor by the sunlit window, seemed to be dancing on the lawn. The dance astonished Dubin although she had as a young woman thought of becoming a dancer; had taken lessons. Yet he had not seen her perform anything like this before, this flow of movement—giving herself to it so. Shows you can't know everything about those you know best. The soul has its mysteries. Kitty waved to Dubin, he waved back. It was a running dance, very expressive—fertility rite? Her straw hat flew off and she made no attempt to retrieve it. She ran with her arms raised toward the flowers, twirled and ran the other way; then again to the garden. Her arms moved like a bird's wings; she swooped, turned, now hopped sideways toward the trees. He thought she'd duck into the grove of silver maples and dance there—marvelous sight—but instead she ran toward the house.

"Happy," Kitty called.

He opened the window wide. "What?"

"Hap-pee!"

"Wonderful!"

She danced on the lawn, her body bent low, then rose tall, graceful, once more flapping her arms. He tried to figure out what the ceremonial meant: wounded bird, dying swan? My God, Dubin thought. He had seen her in some happy moments but nothing to dance to. He felt how strange life was, then began thinking of his *Passion of D. H. Lawrence: A Life*, before he realized Kitty was in the house, screaming as she sped up the stairs. Dubin opened the bathroom door as she rushed in, shouting to him, her face red, eyes angered, frightened.

"Why the hell didn't you come and help me?"

"What for?"

"A *bee*, William," she cried.

"My God, where?"

"In my blouse. It crawled up my sleeve. Help me!"

"Unbutton it," Dubin advised.

"I'm afraid, you do it."

He quickly unbuttoned her blouse. A dull buzz sounded as the bee flew forth, a fat black-and-yellow noisy bumblebee. It buzzed in the bathroom close to the ceiling. Dubin defensively seized his razor, waved the weapon. The droaning bee zoomed down on a course between his eyes, shot up, twice circled his head, and barreling down, struck him on the back of the neck.

He had expected it, he thought, but not, after her gasp and his grunt, Kitty's uninhibited laughter.

Not long after breakfast Dubin sat at his desk in his study about to begin. "What's my opening sentence going to be? Christ, it may point the way forever." Kitty, without knocking, entered quietly and handed him his mail. "It came early today." She read on a yellow slip of paper on his desk the daily list of things to do and quickly crumpled it. He pretended not to see. Kitty said she didn't think the cleaning person would work out. She was a college student who would stay on only till school reopened in September. "She's competent but I doubt her heart's in it. She's doing this to earn a buck and take off. I guess I'll have to advertise again."

On the way out she paused. "William, why do I have strange dreams of Nathanael at this time of my life?"

"You tell me."

She said she didn't know.

He impatiently begged off. Kitty stepped out of the room.

After calling up, "Goodbye," she left the house to go into town for her groceries, his newspaper. Dubin heard her back out of the driveway. He laid down his pen and waited with shut eyes two minutes till she had returned, easily imagining her strained face, compressed mouth, eyes mourning as she got out of the car. Kitty hastily reentered the house, hurried into the kitchen, fighting herself. Herself won. She approached the gas stove and drew long deep breaths over each of the four burners, as though after a time of drought she was taking in the salt breezes of the sea. She then pulled down the oven door and breathed in, as her chest passionately rose and fell. Slowly her body relaxed. There was no gas leak; there never was. Kitty then sang up, "Goodbye, dear," and Dubin once more picked up his pen. She swept out of the house, briskly, sensually, almost gaily, as he ravagely wrote down his opening sentence. The biographer was in business again, shaping, illumining lives.

He had seriously resisted Lawrence, so intricately involuted, self-contradictory, difficult a man. He had traveled so mercilessly, lived in so many out-of-the-way places; had written so well, so badly, so goddamned much; was so vastly written about—someone had said second to Shakespeare; or if not second, third, Samuel Johnson intervening—therefore who needs more by William Dubin? Who needs, specifically, yet another life of David Herbert Lawrence? Kitty, who had conscientiously traveled with her husband four summers as he had researched Lawrence's obsessive pilgrimages, had asked much the same question. But one fantastic day in Nottinghamshire Dubin had discovered, in an old miner's widowed daughter's slate-roofed attic, two dusty packets of Lawrence's unpublished correspondence: eleven impassioned notes to his mother—surly complaints against the father; and no fewer than twenty-six letters—once thought burned—to Jessie Chambers, his boyhood girl, whom he had ultimately rejected because she had too much the genteel spiritual and intellectual quality of the mother—vagina dentata, or so he thought; he had never visited her there. It was she, who by one means or another, became the Miriam of *Sons and Lovers*.

Later, in a London bookshop, Dubin had also found seventeen unpublished letters of Lawrence to J. Middleton Murry, loveless husband of Katherine Mansfield; there'd also been a strange love-hate relationship between the men. "Weasel," "dirty little worm," "rat," the novelist had called him, "I despise you"; and after breaking off their friendship, Murry, drawn to Lawrence and Frieda, time and again returned to try once more. Dubin's elation at his discoveries—extraordinary good luck—had at last resolved his doubts and hooked him firmly to the biography of Lawrence, at the same time apparently convincing Kitty. He had more new material than anyone in recent years and felt he could do a more subtle portrait of the man than had previously appeared. That was the true battleground for the biographer: the vast available documentation versus the intuition and limited experience of Wm. B. Dubin, formerly of Newark, New Jersey.

Sometimes he felt like an ant about to eat an oak tree. There were several million facts of Lawrence's short life and long work, of which Dubin might master a sufficient quantity. He'd weave them together and say what they meant—that was the daring thing. You assimilated another man's experience and tried to arrange it into "thoughtful centrality"—Samuel Johnson's expression. In order to do that honestly well, you had to anchor yourself in a place of perspective; you had as a strategy to imagine you were the one you were writing about, even though it meant laying illusion on illusion: pretense that he, Dubin, who knew himself passing well, knew, or might know, the life of D. H. Lawrence: who seemed not to have stepped beyond his mythic mask—explained himself without revealing himself; created an ur-blood mystique that helped hide who he ultimately was. Beyond that is more: no one, certainly no biographer, has the final word. Knowing, as they say, is itself a mystery that weaves itself as one unweaves it. And though the evidence pertains to Lawrence, the miner's son, how can it escape the taint, subjectivity, the existence of Willie Dubin, Charlie-the-waiter's son, via the contaminated language he chooses to put down as he eases his boy ever so gently into an imagined life? My life joining his with reservations. But the joining —the marriage?—has to be, or you can't stay on the vicarious track of his past or whatever "truth" you think you're tracking. The past exudes legend: one can't make pure clay of time's mud. There is no life that can be recaptured wholly; as it was. Which is to say that all biography is ultimately fiction. What does that tell you about the nature of life, and does one really want to know?

By mid-afternoon he had done two pages and was feeling good when Kitty returned from the town clerk's office to pay the cleaning person. Dubin was sitting in the living room with a drink. The bee sting no longer bothered. The girl had gone after slantedly writing her name and address on an old envelope on the kitchen counter.

"I'll mail her a check," Kitty said. "What do you think of her? The house is fairly clean. Should I keep her for a while or look for someone permanent?"

He had barely caught a glimpse of the girl but felt magnanimous. "What have you got to lose?"

The cleaning person—Fanny Bick—he had read her name on the envelope—who had appeared Tuesday morning, returned to work on Friday—resisting it all the way, Kitty said. Fanny, a nervously active girl, vacuumed and dusted, and was supposed to do a wash but hadn't got to it the first time. Kitty had done the wash on Thursday and had left a pile of Dubin's underwear, pajamas, socks, to be ironed—she had tried to talk him out of ironed socks but he liked them that way. As he worked that morning he was vaguely aware of the girl outside his door yanking the vacuum cleaner from room to room; and he later asked Kitty to tell her not to come into the study, because there were so many note cards laid out on the desk and worktable that he didn't want touched. She could clean his room next time, once he had the cards weighted down. He'd have lunch meanwhile or would read upstairs in Gerald's old room.

The girl had left before Dubin stopped working—he had eaten while she was in the master bedroom and as he went downstairs for coffee, had caught a look at her on hands and knees, shoving an aluminum hose under the double bed. But on the following Tuesday, when he left his study in mid-morning to visit the bathroom—he went sometimes to think a thought through—there she stood barefoot, a brush in her hand, grimly swabbing the toilet bowl.

Fanny sweated as Dubin apologized—he would use the downstairs toilet, no trouble at all. The biographer had recognized her; she seemed younger than he'd remembered, possibly because he now knew she was still in college. Or had he suddenly grown older? Her light hair hung loosely down her back, and he was again aware of the random bleached hairs under her chin—counted four or five and wondered why she hadn't had them removed, a matter of esthetics. Fanny wore a faded denim wraparound skirt and black shirt without bra. Her abundant body, though not voluptuous, clearly had a life of its own.

21

Dubin stood at the bathroom doorway. The girl had retreated to the tub, holding the brush behind her.

"I'm Fanny Bick," she said, in annoyance and embarrassment. "I'm helping your wife."

"She mentioned it. Glad to know you." He spoke gently, sorry for her unease, apparently a persistent quality of her.

Fanny explained her situation—after a moment seemed calmer—and he lingered to hear: that she was working in his house because there wasn't much else to do in town. "I tried the State Employment Office and all the guy there does is show you unemployment figures for the county and shakes his head. Makes you feel zonky."

"That so?"

"Twittery. So I bought the town gazette, or whatever you call it, and put together four mornings of work at three different houses—this and two others. I had no choice but I don't like cleaning." She made a face. "I do an absolute minimum for myself. I'm not a slob but I don't like housework."

He nodded seriously, not entirely approving.

She smiled dismally.

He clucked in sympathy. "You should have gone on to Winslow. It's a bigger town—more variety. You might have picked up something at the piano factory there."

"Not the way things have been going for me lately. My car pooped out after an accident. My fault, and all I carry is liability."

He shook his head at her luck.

She said with a tense laugh, "Please don't tell your wife I don't like this job. I wouldn't want to lose my two mornings here."

"Have no fear."

Her body eased and she brought forth the brush.

Fanny said she was broke and had to settle for whatever she could get. "I've had it with college and have just about made up my mind I'm not going back. Anyway, my father said he wouldn't support me any more, so I'm trying to put together enough to take me to the Big Apple."

"To do what?"

"Ask me when I get there."

"Haven't we met before?"

She regarded him with fresh interest. "On the road? I thought I'd got lost though I guess I hadn't. I was where I was looking for."

"You can't be much more than twenty-one or -two?"

Her glance was friendly yet reserved.

Dubin said lamely, "Maybe I'm intending to prove I know something about people your age?"

"Twenty-two," she said. "Yesterday, actually. My friends say I look older."

It struck him he had almost hoped so. Dubin said he was fifty-six and after a moment laughed huskily.

She mulled over the news, her face impassive.

"Don't cheat yourself on education," he advised. "College is limited but at least it's a beginning. That's what I told my daughter."

"Giving up college isn't giving up your education. Far from it."

"William James, the psychologist and pragmatist philosopher, reflecting on the social value of the college-bred, thought the major effect of a college education might be to help you recognize a good man when you saw one." Dubin laughed saying this; had often said it. I have a one-track mind.

He tightened his belt. "Here I am offering free advice again," he apologized. "I am a biographer is why. I often have this souped-up sense of other people's lives so that I don't always mind my business. Pardon me, I don't mean to offend."

"No sweat." Fanny was amiable. "You feel empathy for people?"

"That's putting it kindly."

He had noticed her Star of David. Nodding abruptly, Dubin broke off and returned to his study. He was surprised at the time he had given her; and it annoyed him a bit that he had felt her sexuality so keenly. It rose from her bare feet. She thus projects herself?—the feminine body—beautifully formed hefty hips, full bosom, nipples visible—can one see less with two eyes? Or simply his personal view of her?—male chauvinism: reacting reductively? What also ran through his mind was whether he had responded to her as his usual self, or as one presently steeped in Lawrence's sexual theories, odd as they were. He had thought much on the subject as he read the man's work. Despite his reservations it tended to charge him up some. Dubin counteracted the effect by recalling the continuous excitement of Thoreau, woodsy dybbuk, possessing him as he was writing his life. The biographer had for a time become the celibate nature lover, or so it had seemed.

He became aware he was leaving his study more often than usual; he would drift down into the kitchen to pour himself a cup of coffee. He'd be restless,

Dubin explained it to himself, well into beginning a work—it might take fifty, sixty pages before you were settled in, sure you were working right. He had the sense of having been more quickly into Thoreau, wasn't yet knee-deep in Lawrence. Once he was securely placed in the life he'd stick it out steadily—hours at his desk without a break, except for an occasional visit to the john. Holding cup on saucer he'd wander through the house, sipping absently, standing around thoughtful, probing his problems. If Fanny, on days she was there, happened to appear, Dubin nodded as though in thought and went on thinking.

Once when he lifted his coffee cup in greeting she said "Hi" cheerily and ducked out of the room.

"How come," Kitty inquired one morning, "you're drinking lots of coffee?" Years ago she had tried bringing up a cup of mid-morning broth to his study. This had soon come to an end: not really her style, not really his. It took time and added weight.

"Beginnings are tough."

"But you've begun."

One did not necessarily begin at the beginning, Dubin explained. "Beginnings may be more effective independent of strict chronology—where the dominant action of the life starts, the moment of insight, cohesion, decision. You can search that out or perhaps define a moment as a beginning and let what follows prove it. I'm not sure I'm there yet."

"You will be," Kitty said. "Don't strive for perfection right off."

He ignored the remark. They'd agreed she was not to advise him how to work unless he asked her.

She poured herself a sherry; it was near lunchtime. He was aware how well she looked this summer, her long body retaining its shape, if slightly heavier than last year. She looked younger than fifty-one, but if you said so she tittered, or sadly smiled at all you hadn't tallied.

"How's the girl working out?" He poured from the coffee pot.

"Not badly. She tries. I told you she's off to New York in September. I'll advertise then."

"Has she said anything about herself?" Kitty had long talks with people who worked for her.

"Not very much. She's intelligent, has a mind of her own and the usual dissatisfactions of someone her age, plus a few I can only guess at. Her old man's let her down, but I don't know how or why—the usual crise de confiance, I suppose. She's apparently decided to drop out of college, after a year in, two out, in again into her senior year and now wanting out for sure, she says."

"What brought her to Center Campobello?"

"She was living in an upstate commune, got fed up, and was on her way to New York City when she had an accident coming off the highway outside town. So she stopped off to earn some money to have her car repaired, et cetera. She's hinted some vague other reason, maybe looking up an old lover —I don't know. She's a mild depressive, I'd say."

Kitty analyzed people; she'd long ago been psychoanalyzed.

"She reminds me a little of Maud," Dubin said.

His wife was incredulous.

"Lots of vitality," he offered. "Direct too, wouldn't you say?"

"She's energetic enough when she wants to be, otherwise tends to droop."

"Seems to present herself as sexy?"

"I'd say so—does Maud?"

"Don't run it into the ground. Just an impression."

"Impressions either have or haven't validity."

Dubin was silent.

"She knows Roger Foster," Kitty said. "Apparently she applied for a job in the library but they had none. Now he calls for her after work—waits in his car in the driveway. I've asked him to come in but I think he's uneasy with you."

Dubin grunted.

"What more could you ask for a single attractive slightly blowsy girl who isn't your daughter, or for that matter much like her?" Kitty asked. "Fanny strikes me as not quite put together."

"Is Roger her lover?"

"How would I know?"

He'd never liked him, a sandy-haired large-shouldered insistent young man. When Roger was in college he'd worked one summer for Dubin, theoretically assisting a carpenter who was altering the barn Dubin was in part turning into an outside study that he had since then not much used. Roger hadn't worked well, goofed off. Lazy bastard.

"Maud never liked him either," Dubin said. "He hung around when she was barely fifteen. She had his number."

"With your assistance," Kitty said. "That was years ago. He's a serious man now and a really good librarian. Crawford isn't coming back and Roger, I hear, will replace him."

"He won't get my vote."

"He won't need it."

Dubin was uncomfortable with his judgment of Roger Foster, because he had disliked him on meeting him and forever thereafter. The biographer did not care to be the victim of that kind of response to people. It indicated objectivity missing, a quality he could not afford to be caught short of.

He glanced at his watch and whistled. "I've been talking to you for half an hour. Lawrence will fry me alive."

"Don't regret it," Kitty said. "I hardly see you once you're into a new biography."

"You see me forty times a day."

She wanted a hug before he left. "I've been feeling lonely."

They kissed affectionately as Fanny entered the room and at once headed out.

Dubin would wander through the house with his cold coffee cup, sipping from one room to another: a momentary break from work—he'd return refreshed. He enjoyed coming on Fanny in motion: forcefully stroking the rugs with the vacuum cleaner; the choreography with a mop over the kitchen floor; her intense private gestures of ironing; hurrying up and down the stairs. He enjoyed her hips in bloom, ample bosom—she wore a brassiere now after a glance or two by Kitty—everything in her figure more beautifully rounded because of the dramatic narrowing of waist between bust and bottom. She was gifted in femininity, Dubin had decided. Fanny wore miniskirts; on hot days she appeared in shorts and gauzy blouses—black, orange, yellow—her white or black bra visible through the garment.

Intermission, he called his viewing of her—the serious looking when she seemed inattentive yet had surely invited. Is she flirting with me? Whatever for—a man my age? When she bent it was a gracious act. A beautifully formed female figure suggested ideal form—her ass a bouquet of flowers. Ah, my dear, if I could paint you nude, if I could paint. Fanny as "sexual object" was balanced by the responding thought that he wouldn't mind being hers if she could imagine it. Is she really so tempting a dish, he asked himself, or am I beautifying every cubit of her according to my need? Women move me to deepest feeling, of pleasure and loss. As if they are eternally mine yet never belong to me. He felt at his thought, as it reverberated amid others, a mounting loneliness. Dubin waited till the feeling had passed. Afterward he reflected that this intense unexpected response to her had probably occurred at the thought she would soon be gone—in a few weeks to the omnivorous city. A momentary source of innocent pleasure lost—the beauty of a vital young woman. Too bad she'd never know. My God, how long does this romantic hunger—residue of old forms, habits, daydreams—haunt the blood?

Though he foresaw her departure he might as well enjoy the time she'd still be around. As for interrupted concentration, so long as he produced his daily two pages he had little to criticize himself for. But Fanny, as though to prove that his foreboding of an end was itself an ending, seemed to tire of the entertainment: his seeking her; her unwilling continuous performance. How juxtapositions distort intent, pleasure. She seemed all at once actively avoiding him. Dubin, concerned, looked less her way, would play no wolf to her harried Pamela. Once when he accidentally came upon her in the kitchen as she was ironing his underpants, Fanny's expression was grim. Both were embarrassed as their glances met. Dubin drained his coffee cup and hurried off.

Afterward she hid when he appeared, or attempted to, whatever his amiability or good intentions; she dropped what she was doing and walked off. Fanny ducked into the bathroom or hastened down the cellar stairs and in a few minutes the washing machine was rumbling. Or she slipped out on the porch and had a cigarette, leaning against a white pillar, staring at the old hills; the hills at least were eyeless. But the biographer enjoyed the sight of her: Susanna turned away from leering elder—lovely figure, something lonely about her. What sort of life does she have? Too bad she can't feel my admiration—as admiration—or perhaps she does and still would rather not. We can't all be friends and relatives as the world is; most of us have to be strangers—terrible construction, and here's Moses-Jesus preaching love thy neighbor as thyself. He went back to his study, dejected. Old billy goat— these feelings at fifty-six, disjunctions of an ordered life. We are all clowns.

Dubin resumed work with affection for it—truly working kept one from useless emotion—on keel, more or less content. The chapter was bestowing more, resisting less. The facts had been laid out easily enough though he wasn't satisfied with all they said or didn't say. But patience: good beginnings, those that assured the biographer they were right and so was he, blew in like spring winds; some like storms. Some you coaxed out of the blue. The sky was in the process of yielding. What grew word by word grew in value. The young Lawrence had appeared, his face in a pool, or the pool his face. That is to say, the boy, from the first, reflected himself. Double self—never, then, recognized as such? Was this one of the hidden keys of the life— explains the sexual things, never at peace—and his love of ideologized metaphor—double image defined as one? The essential broken self?—unity achieved only in the work, his rainbow? Dubin, concentrating sentence by sentence, no longer ventures out of his room when the girl's around. Were she clinging to his door, he'd hold his water.

Fanny, he thought, a foolish name.

Summer was ending.

Winter waits in the wings.

One morning in early September Dubin hurried downstairs for a cup of hot coffee to keep him awake. Kitty had slept badly and borne him along part of the ride. When he returned to the study he found Fanny there, gazing at the pictures and mementos on the wall; she was examining in particular a framed blue-and-white beribboned gold medal.

The girl was standing close by the wall. Nearsighted, he thought, yet she rarely wears glasses, terrible vanity. In any case she was reading the citation of the medal in the frame. Dubin knew it by heart: "Presented by Lyndon Baines Johnson, President of the United States of America; to William B. Dubin, for his achievement in the Art of Biography; at the White House, December, 1968."

"Medal of Freedom," Dubin explained; formal—would not impose.

"Far out," Fanny said, amiably turning to him. "I've seen it here but never read what it said because you like to get back into your room so fast. The reason I came in just now is the door was standing open and I thought you were reading in Gerald's room so I could dust here."

He set down the cup on his desk, trying to keep it from rattling. A puddle of coffee had formed in the saucer.

"It was presented to me after the publication of my *H. D. Thoreau*— you've heard of him?—American essayist, 1817–62, author of *Walden* and other works. He was a disciple and somewhat ambivalent friend of Emerson —idealized his wife Lidian, might have been in love with her but there's no impressive evidence. A biographer can't afford to lean toward guesses of that sort, no matter how sympathetic his nature."

"I've read *Walden*. Some chapters turn me on—the scenes in winter and at night."

"Wonderful." Dubin had been about to say they had much in common but caught himself.

"You may not think so but all my life I've wanted to live close to nature, except I've never figured out how."

She said she had joined a Buddhist commune near Tupper Lake that summer. "Which was to be no sex and very vegetarian, including growing your own lettuce and beans. I liked it at first but one of the swamis there, a secret acid tripper, got on my nerves, so I split."

The swami pursued her with his naked eye? Dubin felt drawn to the girl in a way that saddened him.

He pointed to a small photograph in a hand-carved frame on the wall. "That's Henry—he was called Davy when he was a boy—not exactly a handsome man but people liked his looks. Hawthorne said they became him more than beauty." He beamed at her.

Fanny looked closely at the picture

"Note the longish nose," Dubin observed. "Emerson said it reminded him of the prow of a ship. They say Thoreau would pretend to swallow it—tried to get his lower lip over it for laughs. He also tooted a flute as he danced with himself. In winter they skated on the frozen Concord, our boy waltzing like Bacchus on ice. Emerson leaned his ministerial face into the wind and self-reliantly shoved off. Hawthorne, his daughter Rose wrote, skated like a Greek statue on runners. Henry clowned on the ice. With luck he might have been a comedian. Mostly he settled for a solitary life in the woods—one makes his fate: he was there in every wind and weather. Some say eventually it undermined his health and shortened his life—but it's the old business of what for which. Out of this experience came his journal, where he appeared as a figment of his own imagination. And from which he extracted many treasures, including much of *Walden*. Or it might have worked the other way: he had started a journal on Emerson's say-so and went into the woods to let it find its world."

Fanny gave him the first warm smile he'd had from her.

Dubin went on, "He was ambitious to be great—become a major American artist. He is said to have felt a guilt-ridden desire to surpass at all costs and did so by turning nature into a personal possession. Perry Miller made him more conscious of every move toward his literary destiny than I. Not everybody knows what his personal metaphors mean or what he's secretly becoming, though one may sense it, of course. To my way of thinking his major concern, given who he assumed he was, was learning how to live his life. 'One doesn't soon learn the trade of life,' he said. He spent years trying, which is to say he lived to learn, to apprehend and control the forces that shaped him. He said he didn't want, when it came time to die, to discover he hadn't lived."

"Neither do I," said Fanny.

"Nor I," Dubin allowed. "Once he accidentally set fire to the Concord woods and burned up several hundred acres. The townspeople were furious. His behavior was strange: he watched the fire and made no attempt to help put it out. Death, one might expect, inhabited the journal. His brother John's short life was something he never ceased mourning. They'd been rivals for a young woman who turned them both down when each proposed marriage."

"I know he wasn't married. What did he do for sex?"

"Apparently he died chaste—as they say," the biographer soberly answered. "He's one of those people who live on sublimated sex. There are more around than one would think. You marry nature and live in solitude, having it both ways. But given how he lived, and considering what he accomplished, who's to say how much he missed, or that he missed much?" Dubin seemed to put it tentatively.

Fanny made a face. "I don't buy that. I don't care what he accomplished in his books, when you get right down to it he missed the most satisfying pleasure of life. I mean we're human, aren't we?"

His glance fell on her bosom. Dubin quickly looked up into her light-green eyes. Fanny observed him with nearsighted intensity. Her expression momentarily surprised.

"One of his best friends," he admitted, "said, 'No man had a better unfinished life.' I'm not attempting to justify his celibacy or whatever part of it he practiced, Fanny. I simply say he found his way. In essence, like many men of his type, he was a happy man. 'I love to live,' he said, and I believe him."

"Do you?" she asked.

He listened for mockery but heard none.

"Why do you ask?"

"Because I ask myself."

"What do you answer?"

"It's my question."

"Affirmative," Dubin replied.

Her eyes, he thought, reserved judgment.

"I have my doubts about how happy he was," Fanny said. "It must be a pretty dry lay, banging nature."

"There are many ways of love," he ventured.

"Not if you have to do it to a tree, Mr. Dubin."

He laughed warmly. "Please call me William."

"William."

To hold her there he went on concerning his medal: "I didn't want to accept it at first because I didn't like what Johnson had done to escalate and prolong the Vietnam War. But my wife said it wouldn't be courteous to turn the medal down if my country wanted to honor me and my book; so I took it."

Fanny mildly grunted.

"After dinner Johnson took me aside and asked me to write his 'truthful biography.' He held my hand in his big hand and said that Lady Bird had loved my book and there was no doubt in his mind that I could do a first-rate *Life of LBJ*. I said I was honored but couldn't accept his kind suggestion."

"Good for you."

"That's what my daughter said. Anyway, I backed off as best I could. I said that though I'd done a life of Lincoln, on the whole I preferred to work with literary figures. 'You son-of-a-bitch,' his eyes said, 'I'm a better man than you.' 'Yes,' I thought, 'I took your medal.' "

"Later he told my wife, 'No man worked harder for peace than I did.' And when we left he loaded us with presents. She got a green scarf with border designs of a million LBJs strung together, and a glass bowl embossed with the Presidential seal. He gave me a waterproof watch engraved, 'Do Unto Others As You Would Have Others Do Unto You.' The watch never kept good time but I had the medal framed and there it hangs on the wall—I feel a certain affection for it now—and here we are, you and I."

They were standing within inches of each other, Fanny leaning against the wall, breathing audibly, her pelvis casually thrust forward. She seemed relaxed, as if she'd forgiven him for having burdened her with his desire to know her. Now that she was about to quit working for them, perhaps she had decided that he had wanted not very much from her. She's sought after by men, Dubin thought; yet even in the best of circumstances he doubted he would have tried to entice her into bed. She was only a couple of years older than Maud and he sensed in himself something resembling incest taboo once removed—you don't bed down a girl your daughter's age—let alone other inhibitions. I like to look at pretty women, though in her case maybe I overdid it considering I had her cornered in the house.

"Here's a picture my wife snapped of Johnson handing me the medal."

Fanny examined it closely. "You look like a puppy dog who doesn't want to bite the bone."

"That's more or less the way I felt."

Neither of them spoke for a moment. He thought she was about to leave but she wasn't.

"What are you writing now?" Fanny asked, not at all concerned she wasn't doing her work; neither was Dubin.

He responded quickly: "A new life of D. H. Lawrence, English novelist, poet, prophet, superb letter writer, man of genius and rages. He lived almost forty-five years—from 1885 to 1930—just about as long as Thoreau. They both died of TB—short lives."

"Was he as important as Thoreau? I mean why did you pick him after the other one?"

"He'd been in and out of my mind for years," Dubin said, his voice grown gravelly. "One day I woke up in his presence. Not that he was actually there, you understand, but I couldn't put him aside in my thoughts. So far as I could remember I hadn't dreamed of him, yet I could not shake the sight of this fierce consumptive bright blue-eyed red-bearded man hectoring me. The experience was puzzling because, try as I would, I couldn't understand what he was saying. To answer your question, maybe I decided to write about him because I wanted to elucidate the mystery."

"Which one?"

"Are there two?"

"I wouldn't know," Fanny said.

Dubin said he had read nothing by Lawrence for years. "But he and Thoreau, though they led vastly different lives, had more in common—apart from being major writers—than is apparent. As writers their themes were alike—death and resurrection. As men both were oppressed by dominating possessive women. Both greatly loved and celebrated the natural world. Both were puritans. And both were less than fully heterosexual. Thoreau, as I said, sublimated his sexuality. Lawrence seemed never entirely at peace with his sexual nature. He felt he needed a man's love as well as a woman's to complete him, but he never seemed able—maybe he lacked the good fortune —to realize a bisexual relationship. He apparently proposed a blutbrüder- shaft to Middleton Murry, who though he seemed to be homoerotically inclined, was afraid of Lawrence. He grabbed his hat and ran. Lawrence once said that the idea of putting his arm around a woman's waist and dancing with her appalled him. If it weren't for Frieda, his sexually talented wife, he'd have been a lot more limited. She wrote someone that she had fought with Lawrence over his homosexual inclinations and had won—whatever that meant. She apparently could handle any kind of sexual experience. Ulti- mately he made a mystique of sex, preaching it as a dark force of blood- consciousness through which man experiences the primal mystery. It's a paradox that his theories occupied him, especially toward the end of his life, more than the physical sex that by then had failed him."

"What about *Lady Chatterley's Lover?* That had a lot of real live sex in it. Didn't he write that near the end of his life?"

"It too is ideologically charged, but you're right—his sensuous world is real, affecting, no matter what the theories come to."

Fanny, after a moment, wondered if Dubin's coffee was cold.

He thought it might be.

They gazed seriously at each other.

"You sure know a lot about him."

"I wish I knew more. I don't pretend to see him plain. For instance, in his letters he speaks as if he were telling the factual truth but one can't take him at face value—the letters give autobiographical information yet there is a sense of their belonging to his creative work. I hope to figure him out as I go deeper into the life."

"I was thinking what you said about sex failing him—"

"You understand, Fanny, he was never an exponent of free sex? He didn't like people aimlessly copulating. He said sex should come on us unaware, 'as a terrible thing of suffering and privilege and mystery.' "

The girl seemed, then, troubled. "I think we're entitled to have sexual pleasure any way we want. Not worried or afraid, I mean. Why should we be?"

"Why, indeed?"

"I'm not ashamed of the way I live my life, Mr. Dubin."

"William," he said.

"William."

"I should hope not— What I'm saying," he went on, "is that too many people think of Lawrence's sexual doctrine as exactly the opposite of what it was. Though an innovator in fiction, he was in many ways a conservative person. Marriage, for instance: his own with Frieda was rough-and-tumble —there was much they were at odds about, especially her desire to see her children. Katherine Mansfield saw bruises on her body when they went bathing together. In the presence of Frieda's daughter he threw a glass of wine in her mother's face. She once socked him with a stone plate across the skull. Yet, beyond question, it was a vital enduring relationship. A true marriage, he said, established an unconscious connection 'like a throbbing blood-circuit'; and he once wrote a correspondent something like this: 'Your most vital necessity in this life is that you should love your wife completely and explicitly in entire nakedness of body and spirit.' "

Fanny said she couldn't have guessed.

"On the other hand, despite her marriage to him, Frieda sought and had sexual experiences with other men. She thought of herself as a liberated woman. She told people she was close to, that Lawrence, who was always shaky in sex, was impotent at forty-one."

Fanny sighed. "It sort of wipes you out. I mean a man like that. You wouldn't think so."

"What stays with me most from the biographies I write," Dubin went on, "apart from what one learns about the map of human lives—the unexpected turns and dramatic twists they take—the joyous ways they do, and the tragic ways they don't, work out"—the biographer's eyes momentarily misted and he had to cough a huskiness out of his throat—"what stays with me most, is that life is forever fleeting, our fates juggled heartbreakingly by events we can't foresee or control and we are always pitifully vulnerable to what happens next. Therefore what the poets say about seizing the day, dear Fanny, is incredibly true. If you don't live life to the hilt, or haven't, for whatever reason, you will regret it—especially as you grow older—every day that follows."

"Do you regret it?" she serenely asked.

Dubin gazed at her gravely.

"I'd regret it beyond bearability if I were not involved in the lives of others."

"You mean in your books?"

"Largely so, but not only so."

"And that gives you your big charge? To me life is what you do. I want it to enjoy, and not make any kind of moral lesson or fairy tale out of it."

He felt momentarily let down, despondent.

She seemed, however, affected by him, her color heightened, and in her eyes something resembling affection seemed to show.

Dubin impulsively drew a book out of one of the shelves. "Accept," he said, handing it to her, "a copy of my earliest work: *Short Lives*. Nobody in it lives to forty."

After momentary hesitation she took the book and pressed it to her breast.

"You're beautiful, Fanny," Dubin whispered.

She touched his arm with four fingers.

Moved by her, though he told himself he had wooed her falsely with the business of his Medal of Freedom, his refusal to write President Johnson's life, his too long account of the lives of his betters, Dubin drew Fanny into his arms with immense relief. She rose to him on bare toes, with pointed breasts, forceful hips, hairy chin, hungry tongue. They kissed deeply.

They passed on the stairs as strangers—sometimes she brushed against him—he felt her hair graze his forearm. Dubin, returning to his study, forcefully concentrated; let her flow off in a flood of facts. Sometimes he sensed her presence outside his door but did not open it. He thought often of their embrace. It had caused Fanny to reverse direction, stop evading Dubin—gave him satisfaction: the small victories of life. But while he worked his study was a privileged place, really sanctum. He was headily into his chapter and feeling a long sense of future pleasure: savored the joys of accretion, of laboring and constructing order; appreciative of the self who served him best.

One early afternoon a few days after they had kissed, Fanny tapped on his door and Dubin opened it imagining she had finished *Short Lives* and would want to know if they could talk about it. But she apologized for not yet having read the book—had merely knocked to say hello. She seemed unsure of herself calling on him in his study. Her eyes were characteristically tense. Observing this, Dubin invited her in. He had known he would if she came to the door.

Fanny sat in his armchair, crossed her fine bare legs and smoked. Dubin lit a cheroot. She had washed her hair and it hung loose and light. Pendant silver hoops dangled from her ears, a fine touch while working. Dubin turned his chair to face Fanny. He regretted the menial work she did in the house. He knew she typed and had thought of asking her to type for him, but only Kitty typed for him.

Fanny wondered if she could borrow *Sons and Lovers* and Dubin, with a bound, got her his copy from the bookshelf. She said as she fingered the book that she had enjoyed their recent talk. "I also wanted to say—and I'm sorry if I'm taking your time but I don't know how else we can talk—I just wanted to say that the real truth about my own sexual experience, at least as I am now, is that I have become a better person because of it."

"I wish I were a better person," Dubin said.

He imagined she had felt a need to say this and might just as well to an older man. If you said it to a young man he would want to put you to bed to make you a better person.

"I'm not kidding," she said.

He acknowledged it with a nod. "You're gifted, Fanny."

"How do you mean that?"

"Truly. Some people are gifted in life."

Her body eased. She seemed about to reach out her hand but they weren't within touching distance.

Dubin then asked her why she had joined the meatless sexless commune on Tupper Lake.

"I like to try things."

The biographer, touched by her remark, said he wished he had her kind of freedom when he was her age.

"What kept you from having it?"

"I was a satisfied romantic—loved longing. It made an occasional poem for me."

"Did you have any affairs?"

"I enjoyed the presence of women—I'm describing an almost aesthetic need, not saying it was all."

He said that his mother had been a sick woman and he had no sisters. He had had a younger brother who had drowned when he was nine. His mother was a disturbed woman afterward. She had died when he was thirteen. Thereafter his only company at home was his father. "He never remarried and I missed a feminine presence in the house. I missed a woman. I tried to appease this lack by often falling in love."

"Did you sleep with any of them?"

"Not usually those I loved. Not often others. It was a different world in those days, Fanny, though perhaps I was not as daring as I might have been. There was much I missed."

"Not that different," Fanny said. "My father, who is about your age, screwed around a lot."

They were interrupted by Kitty. She had knocked once and walked in. "Oh, I beg your pardon, I had no idea you were talking."

Fanny got up quickly.

"Don't go, please," Kitty said.

"Your husband loaned me a book."

"We were chatting," Dubin explained.

Fanny left the room and, later, forgot the book she had come to borrow, when she went home for the day.

Dubin, that evening, had thoughts of asking her to go for a walk with him sometime, the short walk.

The next time Fanny was in the house Dubin spied her on the porch, taking time out for a cigarette. He went out with his coffee cup and sat on the bottom step as she sat behind him on a canvas chair. Fanny's legs were parted and her lemon underpants were visible at the crotch. Her feet were bare.

Dubin turned to the hills. To the north was the nameless mountain he looked at when he wanted to look at a mountain.

He asked Fanny what her plans were in New York.

She said she didn't know.

He talked facing the hills, his back warm in sunlight.

"Plans are not my strong point," Fanny said.

Dubin, after a moment, asked her where she had got her name.

"My name? My mother was the one who named me."

"After a relative, friend? Who?"

"No, she named me after Fanny Price in *Mansfield Park*. She was on a Jane Austen kick when she was pregnant."

"You don't say," said Dubin, turning to her. "Do you know Jane Austen had a favorite niece named Fanny Knight? She was charmed by the girl, reread her letters the day she was dying. The sad thing was that Fanny later

37

wrote her sister their Aunt Jane had lacked refinement. She was ashamed of her aunt and, in essence, betrayed her memory."

"I don't think my mother knew that," Fanny said.

She had made no attempt, as they talked, to bring her knees together. Dubin drank up his coffee and went upstairs.

A few minutes later he was jolted, at his desk, by a single swift knock on the door as the girl slipped into the room.

He was about to wave her out when she untied her wraparound skirt and whipped it off. Her blouse and underpants came off and she was naked.

Dubin was struck by her youthful beauty.

He mumbled his gratitude.

Fanny tossed her yellow underpants at him. He caught them and tossed them back. They struck her breasts and fell to the floor.

The girl studied him curiously, nervously.

"Whatever you're offering," Dubin said, "I regret I can't accept."

"Your wife went to the flower farm. It's an hour each way."

"This is her house."

"It's yours as well."

"Under the circumstances I can't accept."

Her face had reddened. She was angered. "All this beautiful bullshit about seize the day and what life is all about."

He hoarsely laughed at the jest.

Fanny pulled her clothes on in a grim instant and was gone. Nothing of her remained that he could find.

Dubin reached for his pen and after a while slowly began to write.

Fanny quit. She had told Kitty she was off to the city, although Kitty had heard she was still in town, living with Roger Foster. Dubin one day at lunch asked his wife what she had thought of the girl.

"She is sexy," Kitty said, "but I'm better proportioned."

Kitty had waked that morning saying she ought to go to Montreal to see her father's grave, then possibly her mother's in Augusta, on her way back.

"I owe him a visit. I've never really made my peace with him. Will you come with me, William? We could do it in a day there and one back."

"Is something bothering you?" When Kitty thought of visiting graves she was asking her life questions.

She seemed distracted. "I wish you'd come with me. I hate long drives alone.

"Why didn't you suggest it before I began my chapter?"

"It wasn't on my mind then."

Dubin said his work was going well. "It'll take me a week to get back into it if I go off with you now."

Kitty, as she dressed, thought it through at the bedroom window. He watched her watching a flicker in the chestnut. A maple, barely missing the house, had fallen in a storm shortly after they had moved in, and Kitty had planted a chestnut there, now a luxuriant tree.

"I guess it's something I'll have to do myself."

He tried to persuade himself to drop his work and take off with her. But the journey was to cemeteries and he wasn't in the mood. He had his own graves to visit, that he hadn't been to in years.

Kitty said, "I have to go, why am I lingering?"

After lunch she slipped on two silver bracelets and a large ring. She painted her toenails, packed an overnight bag, and drove off toward the Northway.

They had kissed at the door—goodbye, not for long. She squeezed his hand. He regretted he could not go with her. She asked him to check the burners and Dubin promised but forgot.

On occasion he liked eating a meal out of a can—spaghetti, baked beans, carry-over from boyhood, youth—eating alone; but he prepared instead a hamburger Kitty had left defrosting. The meat burned in the pan, so he called a cab and went downtown. Dubin ate a plate of soup and a roast-beef sandwich at a restaurant counter, and since light still glowed in the evening sky—early fall had run a cool hand through the air—walked home. The stars appeared in misty swarms, Dipper brilliant. The biographer pondered the mystery of north—direction of death—white, silent, frigid, sans soul. Where was Kitty now? He hoped she would not drive at night. The moon had not yet risen. Walking alone in the dark he felt sadness of a sort. He thought he would listen to Schubert lieder, then decided, forget it, I'll go to a movie. Schubert, dead at thirty-one, was the first life Dubin had written for *Short Lives*. No one had written a good long life of Schubert. He had lived long in music and short in life.

The house, once he was inside—he had hesitated at the door—was surprisingly empty. Dubin was staggered, as he entered, at the surge of loneliness he felt, like acid invading the bone. Ridiculous, he thought. Standing at the foot of the stairs the biographer, shaken, tried to puzzle out what was affecting him. As a rule he enjoyed solitude. Being away from home, or occasionally remaining alone there, awoke moods he rarely experienced when his life was geared with Kitty's. What he felt now was more than a melancholy sense of being alone, or perhaps remembrance of that feeling in the past; this seemed a spontaneous almost soiled awareness, more apparent than ever, of one's essential aloneness: the self's separate closed self-conscious subjectivity. Dubin defined it for all time, as previously defined: death's insistence of its presence in life, history, being. If so, nothing new but why once more at this moment?

What had set it off? The absence of his children, a constant remembrance? One day their childhood, and your enjoyment of it, was over. They take off as strangers, not confessing who they presently are. You tried to stay close, in touch, but they were other selves in other places. You could never recover the clear sight of yourself in their eyes. They had become, as though by need, or their own definition, distant relatives. Dubin thought he had got used to the thought. Therefore it must be mainly Kitty's unexpected going to her father's grave? Perhaps he should have gone with her? He switched on the light, waiting as if expecting more light, then trod up the stairs, uneasy still, as though he were a man with three legs who remembered having only two. He wandered in the silent empty house, avoiding his study. What was Lawrence up to when Dubin was away: magicked the circuits of his dark blood? The biographer went up to the third floor to Gerald's old room, sat on the boy's bed. The pall of loneliness hung close—negates the sufficient self. Who rides Dubin's back? It occurred to him it wasn't so much he was missing his wife as being oppressively aware of himself.

In Maud's room he put in a person-to-person call to Berkeley. She wasn't in; he left a call-back message. Dubin was looking up Gerry's number in Stockholm in Kitty's address book when the telephone shrilly rang—Maud returning his call?

It was Kitty saying she was in Philadelphia.

He listened very carefully. "Weren't you going to Montreal?"

"When I left the house I felt I wanted to see Nathanael's grave. I've not been there for years. I hope you don't mind?"

He didn't think there was any reason he'd mind.

"I honestly almost never think of him any more. But when I got to the highway I had the impulse to see his grave, and drove south instead of north."

"I don't mind."

"You're easier on me these days," Kitty said.

"One learns," Dubin said. Then he said, "One thinks he does."

"You sound constrained. Are you all right?"

He was fine.

"I'll go to the cemetery with some flowers in the morning, then drive home."

He said he was surprised to hear her in Philadelphia as he was thinking of her in Montreal.

"Your voice sounds distant. Has something happened?"

"I called Maud. I thought you were Maud calling back."

"Give her my love," said Kitty. "I wish they weren't so far away."

Dubin said he'd go out for a short walk before turning in, and Kitty said she was sorry she wasn't there to walk with him.

When he hung up she called back.

Dubin said he'd thought it was Maud again.

"I'm not Maud, I'm me. Please tell me what you're worried about. Is it the Lawrence?"

He said no.

"He's a hard person to love."

"I don't have to love him. I have to say truthfully who he was and what he accomplished. I've got to say it with grace."

"Then is something else worrying you—money, for instance?"

He confessed he worried about money.

"Are we spending too much?"

"We'll be all right for another year and then we may be tight."

Kitty said if she had to she would look for a paying job. "Good night, love, don't worry. I'll be home tomorrow." She was tender on the phone when either of them was away.

The night was dark deep and starlit, and Dubin walked longer than he thought he might. He was standing at the poster window of the Center Campobello Cinema when the last show broke and he saw, amid two dozen people straggling out, Fanny Bick in bluejeans and clogs, carrying a shoulder bag. She was wearing a white halter tied around the midriff, her hair bound with a red cord. Dubin sensed her before he saw her. He watched, thinking she would look up and see him but she didn't. She seemed to be still into the film, conscious of herself; he recognized the feeling. He had not expected to lay eyes on her again and now he felt he would have regretted not seeing her. Roger Foster was not in the crowd. To make sure he hadn't stopped in the men's room, Dubin crossed the street and let Fanny walk on; when he was sure she was alone he recrossed the street and followed her.

No more than a diversion, the biographer thought. He doubted he would talk to her; then he thought he *must* talk to her. His odd loneliness still rode him—a discomfort he wanted to be rid of, something from youth that no longer suited him. He felt a hunger to know the girl, could not bear to have her remain a stranger. The lonely feeling would ease, he imagined, if he knew more about her. Crazy thing to feel it so strongly, as though he'd earned the right to know. Here I am hurrying after her as if we are occupying the same dream.

Fanny sensed something. Her pace quickened, the clogs resounding in the shadowy lamplit street. At the next corner she nearsightedly glanced back nervously.

"Wait up, Fanny—it's William Dubin."

She waited, austerely, till he caught up with her. If she was relieved she hid it. But her face, pallid in the street light, and restless eyes, offered no welcome.

Dubin was about to tip his hat but had none. He hoped he hadn't frightened her by pursuing her.

Fanny denied the importance of it.

He explained, with a gesture alluding to the loveliness of the night, that he'd been out for a stroll before going to bed. He was, this evening, alone in the house. "I happened to see you leave the movie and thought I'd say hello. Do you mind if I walk with you?"

She said it was a free country.

"Come on, Fanny—you'll have to do better than that. I'm sure you know I enjoy your company."

She seemed to hesitate. "I don't mind if you don't, Mr. Dubin."

"Was it a good film you saw?"

"Good enough—sort of a love story."

"Anything I ought to see?"

They were walking together, her clogs setting the rhythm.

"It's better than nothing."

He laughed at that, felt awkward, as he had in his house when she was conscious of him observing her, imposing himself.

"I'm sorry you left without saying goodbye," Dubin said. "I'd bought you a copy of *Sons and Lovers*. Would you like me to bring it to you?"

"Thanks anyway."

"Where can I send it? I heard you were living with Roger Foster. He used to do odd jobs for me when he was in college. He wore a green sweater and his beard had a green cast. I confess I never liked him very much. Perhaps the fault is mine."

"Well, he has a blue sweater and a dark beard now and doesn't do odd jobs any more, and neither do I, certainly not house cleaning."

"It seemed to me a curious experience for somebody like you. I hope I conveyed my understanding, my respect. I regret we hadn't met under better circumstances."

"Who said I was living with Roger?"

Dubin cleared his throat. "My wife happened to mention it."

"She sure is all over the place. I live in a room in his house but not with him. His sister and brother in law live there too."

"Fanny, I'm sorry about the incident in my study," Dubin said. "I regret we couldn't be congenial."

She made no reply.

He asked her if she had left because of that.

"Not that I know. I just got awfully tired of the cleaning crap. I'll never do anything like that again."

He asked her if she had read *Short Lives*, the book he had given her.

Fanny said she hadn't.

"I've wondered," he remarked a moment later as they were walking along the store-darkened street—he had no idea where she lived—"why you wear that Star of David?"

"I wear it because I own it. A friend of mine gave it to me and I wear it when I think of him. I wear other things too." Then she asked, "Your wife isn't Jewish, is she?"

He said she wasn't.

"How did you happen to meet her?"

He said he'd tell her the story sometime.

"What was she doing when you met her?"

"She was a widow with a child."

"She sure is conscious of everything."

"She has a sensitive nature."

"So have I," Fanny said.

The stores were thinning and there were more private houses. At the corner she turned and he followed her into a short street. In mid-block an orange VW was parked in front of a dour narrow wooden house with a thin high gable. The two-story house was dark, its window shades drawn.

A bright half-moon shone through a copper beech on the lawn. The dark-green house in dappled moonlight looked like a piece of statuary, or an old painting of an old house. Dubin had on a light sweater and loafers, Fanny her jeans and white halter.

He told her D. H. Lawrence used to go wild in the glow of the full moon.

"I'll bet it doesn't do that to you."

"I'm a controlled type," he confessed.

She yawned.

Dubin pointed in the sky. "Look, Fanny, the Big Dipper. And that's Andromeda, really a galaxy, like ours heading into infinity—if there is an infinity and not just a finite wheel with no apparent end, if we crawl forever around its rim. In this universe, finite or infinite, man is alive amidst an explosion of gases that have become stars in flight, from one of which we have evolved. A marvelous privilege wouldn't you say?"

Fanny, momentarily silent, said she thought so too.

"Lawrence called it 'the great sky with its meaningful stars.' "

"Does he mean besides astrology?"

"Besides that."

"Does everything have to mean something?"

"Where there's mind there's meaning. I like the idea of the cosmic mystery living in our minds, and that enormous mystery reflecting our small biological and psychological ones. I like that combination of mysteries."

"Like our minds are the universe, sort of?" Fanny reflected.

"Yes," he told her. "Perhaps we were invented to see the stars and say they're there."

"That's not why I was invented."

"Tell me why."

"I wish I really knew. Why do you bring all that up now?"

"So that I shan't appear naked when we meet again."

She smiled dimly. "I guess I better go in now. Thanks for the astronomy lesson."

Dubin asked her when she would be leaving for New York.

"Next week I plan to go."

The biographer had had a thought: "I've got some research to do at the New York Public Library. Can I drive you down?"

Fanny said she'd be driving her own car. "Roger's going with me."

Dubin had to conceal his disappointment.

"He's coming for the ride and going back by bus. You can tell your wife I'm not living with him. He wants to marry me but I don't dig getting married just yet. I have other things to try out before I do."

"Marvelous. What sort of things?"

Fanny raised her arms in the moonlight. "I'm young yet. I don't do everything for a purpose. I do some things for fun."

"Fun is a purpose."

"It's a purpose that doesn't take away your fun."

"May I hope to see you in the city, Fanny? Couldn't we have dinner together?"

She gave it a moment's reflection. "That's fine with me."

"Good. Where shall we meet? Where will you be living in New York?"

"I don't know yet. I haven't looked for an apartment. Do you want me to come to the restaurant?"

"Would you care to meet me at my hotel?"

She said that was as good as any other place.

They arranged a meeting a week hence. Dubin said he would be at the Gansevoort. "That's Melville's mother's maiden name."

Fanny stifled a yawn. "This night makes me sleepy."

"I won't keep you," he said. "I'm happy we're going to meet again. I was inept the last time we were together. In afterthought I realized how kind you were being."

"Forget it."

"I don't think I want to."

They had parted friends, he hoped.

The house, when he returned, had lost its lonely quality, although Maud, if she had telephoned, did not call again.

Dubin, standing at the darkened bedroom window, looked up at the wash of stars in the night sky. In the universe even the dark is light. "Why should I feel lonely?" Thoreau had asked. "Is not our planet in the Milky Way?"

He would tell that to Fanny.

Dubin talks to his mirror: he weighs how some things happen to happen: Kitty's letter, many years ago, had crossed his desk shortly after he began a new job.

There were two handwritten letters in green ink, the second cancelling the first: "Please don't print my recent 'personals' note. I should have known not to write that kind of letter when I was feeling low. Could you kindly destroy this with the other I sent you?"

Having read it because someone had mistakenly laid it on his desk, Dubin searched through a folder in the next office for the first letter. It read, "Young woman, widowed, fairly attractive, seeks honest, responsible man as friend, one who, given mutuality of interests and regard, would tend to think of marriage. I have a child of three."

Dubin would tend to think of marriage.

After a night of peering into his life, of intense dreams; of being tempted to take a chance because the time had come to take a chance—he was past thirty and neither his vocation nor his relationship with women satisfied him —he wrote her in the morning: "My name is William Dubin. I'm an assistant editor at *The Nation*. Your letter happened to cross my desk. I've read it and would rather not destroy it."

He had had the job a week and had recently also been writing obituaries of literary figures, on assignment for the *Post*. Dubin told her he was thirty-one and unmarried. He'd been in the army two years. He was Jewish. He was responsible. He wrote that he had practiced law for a year, had finally, like Carlyle, decided it was not for him, and was no longer practicing. He said he loved law but not practicing it. His father had lamented his giving up his profession. He had for a while felt lost, a burden of loss. Wherever his life was going he did not seem to be going with it. "People ask me what I'm saving myself for. Whatever that may be—I want to change my life before it changes me in ways I don't want to be changed."

He said he had never written to anyone as he was writing to her now. "I am touched that only you and I know about the letter you sent and withdrew. I know something I have no right to know; in that respect I'm privileged.

46

I sense you understate yourself. You seem to be capable of a serious act of imagination: to be willing to love someone willing to love you. Plato in the *Republic* says that marriages between good people might reasonably be made by lot. I assume we're that kind of people. Obviously, for whatever reason, you've been flirting with the idea yourself. I have the feeling I've been predisposed to it all my life, although I can't say why. Your letters have excited me. Mayn't we meet?"

She wrote: "Dear Mr. Dubin, Yours disturbs me. It does because it moves me terribly. I am—at least at the moment—afraid to go further. Let me think about it. If you don't hear from me, please forgive me. It will be best not to have said no. Ever, Kitty Willis."

Another letter from her came in less than a month. He almost tore it apart as he tore it open.

"Dear Mr. Dubin, I am twenty-six, my little boy is three and a half. I wish I could believe I know what I'm doing. I thought I ought to say I don't think life will be easy for anyone living with me. I sleep poorly, fear cancer, worry too much about my health, my child, our future. I'm not a very focused person. It took my husband years to learn what I'm telling you in this short letter. I want at this point to get these things down: My father was a suicide when I was four. My mother went abroad with a lover when I was nine. She died in Paris of lung cancer and is buried in Maine. I was brought up by a loving grandmother—my rare good luck. My poor husband died of leukemia at forty. It's such a chronicle of woe I'm almost ashamed to write it."

"Of course I'm more than the sum of my hangups and traumas," she wrote. "Nathanael and I were reasonably happily married, and I ought to make someone a decent wife. I can't say my emotional season is spring but I love life. Fortunately, I have a strong reality element that keeps me balanced against some of my more neurotic inclinations. You have to know if we're going to be serious about each other. I had hoped to write earlier, but it took me some time to put my thoughts together. I don't want to ensnare you with my unhappy history, Mr. Dubin. I sense you lean to that tilt."

They had met at the Gansevoort bar. Each recognized the other. Kitty looked as though she was looking for him. She was a tallish slim-figured woman with bright brown hair and luminous dark eyes. Her eyes, as she greeted him, were contemplative, unsure, not very gay. She hadn't, Dubin thought, fully joined her resolution.

"I'm glad you came."

"I had to."

He agreed they had to.

"How serious we are," she said after a moment. Kitty laughed breathily. "I admit I ask myself why I'm here."

"What do you answer?"

She looked at him with a vague smile, shook her head.

He tried to tell her why, a way of telling himself.

She listened as though she had come to believe in him and all he had to say now was what he had already said in his letters.

This he managed to do.

They ordered drinks. It was not a bad meeting, though they were constrained. Kitty studied him, not seeming to care that he saw her studying him. Dubin was not at all sure of her, much more the gentile lady than he had supposed. Then he placed his hand on hers and Kitty did not withdraw it. She looked at him holding her hand, then withdrew it and pressed it to her cheek. He remembered that gesture for years. One night they went out and enjoyed themselves, enjoyed each other, gambled a kiss. She kissed with passionate intensity. They were hungry kisses he thought of many times. Not long afterward they agreed to be married.

"Let's be happy," she said.

He was willing.

"I hope you know what you're doing."

"Don't you?"

"I don't want you to be disappointed in your decision, or in me."

Dubin said he thought it would be a good life. He had gone through it often in his mind and thought they were doing the right thing. "All it takes is character."

"That's not all it takes."

"Whatever it takes I think we have."

She laughed as though he had said something very witty. Her dark clear eyes were eyes to dance to, he thought. Sometimes she looked older, less pretty. She sometimes looked as though she didn't want her looks to influence his decision.

"I trust you, I think," Kitty said. "You seem to say the right things. In a way you remind me of my husband."

He hoped not too much.

Her eyes grew anxious. "Let's not get married until we know and love each other."

"Let's get married and know and love each other." He said it with doubt like a cold stone in his gut, yet felt he had to say it.

"Where do you get your nerve or whatever it is?" she asked.

He said he had drifted enough in life.

They were married one cold day in spring. Dubin felt inspired. The bride wept at the wedding.

"That isn't how I remember it," Kitty said behind a yawn in the bedroom. "A lot happened that you've forgotten."

Dubin drove to New York with Evan Ondyk, the Center Campobello psychotherapist, who'd been practicing in town for two years. Ondyk had heard through a patient, a friend of Kitty's, that Dubin was driving to the city. He had called him to ask for a ride. His Buick was in the garage for a new transmission. The biographer respected Ondyk's poker playing but not his mechanistic judgments of people, as though possibility did not go beyond Freud. On the other hand he read a lot and talked well about books.

"Why did you pick D. H. Lawrence to write about?" Whoever knew Dubin sooner or later sprang that question.

"Someday he'll tell me."

"Why didn't you try Freud?" Ondyk asked. "We could use a good biography of the man—nobody's done very much past Ernest Jones unless he goes at Freud to attack psychoanalysis. It would be useful, for instance, if someone could find out how he felt about analyzing his daughter Anna. Or from her how it went. Also what his relationship was to his wife's sister. That's ambiguous territory. Jung, in an interview, is on record as saying Minna told him that she and Freud were intimate. Freud himself said—I think to Fliess —that he was forty-one when he gave up sex with his wife. Why, if true? It would be interesting to know."

"I was considering Chekhov," Dubin replied. "He died at Lawrence's age of the same disease, tuberculosis. There were other similarities: problems of loving, impotency, what-all."

"Why didn't you do him instead of Lawrence? He's a much more sympathetic person."

Dubin said he didn't read Russian.

He pondered Ondyk, wondered about his judgment of him. Is there more to him than I think? One has so few facts to go by. He had the reputation of being a good practitioner. He was a deliberate effective card player, peering over his hand to psych out who was holding what. He often called when Dubin bluffed. Eyeball to eyeball, who would best understand the other? the biographer wondered. Someone said Ondyk was not content in his marriage and went off periodically to the city for his sexual pleasure.

Dubin would have liked to be alone but the ride was pleasant. It was a fine autumn day. His vision was stereoscopically sharp, his heart light. A resurgence of sadness had occurred and gone. Here I am, a single man on a date. He felt at peace, serene, had in the mirror that morning looked youthful. He hadn't talked to himself. Fanny had been in his thoughts. It was early October and on the Taconic many of the sun-filled trees, although in high color in the hills above Center Campobello, were yellow-green and growing greener as they drove south. This was a rented car because Kitty needed theirs. She'd been surprised that he had not asked her to go with him but Dubin reminded her how rarely he got out of the house alone. "Being married doesn't mean being tied like cats by our tails." Afterward he recalled the simile was Montaigne's; and Kitty reminded him that lately he'd been making remarks about marriage. "Have I?" Dubin asked. He explained he liked a long drive alone once in a while and she said she understood. He wore tartan slacks and a blue blazer, and in his briefcase carried a bottle of perfume and a Schubert record as presents for Fanny.

"Well, have a good time," Ondyk said. "What are you here for?"

Dubin said he hoped to relax a little from work.

"How's it going?"

"Not badly."

"How's Kitty?"

"She's well," said Dubin.

"Attractive woman," Ondyk said.

He didn't say what he was in the city for.

After Dubin had left the psychotherapist at his hotel and checked into his own, it seemed to him he could use a brighter tie so he went out and bought a yellow one, and while he was at it, a new belt with a heavy silver buckle. He had got to the Gansevoort shortly after three. At four he showered, changing into fresh underwear although he had changed into fresh underwear that morning; and he dressed again. Dubin imagined Fanny would appear at about five. He would order drinks sent up—no, it might be better if they went down to the bar. Afterward he would invite her up and she could say yes or she could say no. They'd go to bed, have dinner late, and let the evening find its way. They would not have to decide one minute what they were going to do the next. If Fanny liked, they could either go for a walk along Fifth Avenue or see a movie. It would be a nice thing to do between twice in bed.

It was a long wait doing nothing, so Dubin unlocked his briefcase and read several of his notes about Lawrence and Jessie Chambers, a good companion but bookish and apparently not much interested in sex. It was a stillborn affair, hard on them both. Lawrence had wanted to love her but couldn't. It was said she reminded him of his mother. The girl had a broad tremulous mouth and uneasy eyes. "I could never love you as a husband should love his wife," he had frankly told her. Lawrence never kept bad news from anyone. The letters Dubin had discovered showed him at his hardest to her.

The biographer thought it must be close to five when he discovered it was close to six. He hurried down to the lobby to see if Fanny was there. Dubin waited for her amid a crowd of new arrivals. He had not waited for her before; it was difficult to say how late she was when she was late. The lobby was afloat with men, single and married, meeting pretty women in bright dresses and pants suits, single and married. Dubin admired an Indian stewardess in a golden-red sari, standing with a white-turbaned bearded Sikh pilot; they were waiting for a limousine to the airport. In the bar the pianist was playing an aria from Puccini. The lobby stirred with expectancy—a sense of adventure, sexuality—Faust ascending, but no Fanny. Fearing he had missed her— perhaps she had gone up as he was coming down, Dubin entered an elevator and rode up to his floor; but she was not in the corridor by his room, nor had he expected she might be. The years I've wasted being on time.

He descended in the elevator, then stood for a while in front of the hotel, trying not to dislike the girl for desiring her. At seven he waited outside till eight. Dubin felt his age. When one is my age the old and maimed stand out in a crowd. One recovers of youth only what he can borrow from the young. Perhaps this is not my privilege. It was a pleasant evening. He eyed passing couples, young with young; and young women with older men— these he envied most—looking as though they had been intimate or were about to be. The young ones did not look at him. Those his age knew whom he was waiting for. Waiting Dubin thought he did comparatively well. It was a matter of temperament, perhaps. He waited not so well for the small things of life but better for the important. Some wait badly. Kitty waited badly. "Un bel di vedremo," the Puccini went in the bar. Puccini, the cantor of longing. Kitty sometimes plucked the aria on her harp. But waiting in expectation is easier than waiting in doubt. It was easier to wait for one who was coming than one who was not.

At nine Dubin ordered a roast-beef sandwich on rye and a bottle of ale sent to his room. If she still came the long wait would have been worth it. He had decided that Fanny had planned not to come because he had not taken her when she had offered herself. There are some things one ought not to do. There are some chances one ought to take.

Looking in the mirror over the bathroom sink, Dubin disliked the yellow tie he had bought. He changed it for a purple one before going down to the bar. He washed his hands and face and went downstairs.

At the bar Nixon was lying on television. His expression was sincere as he sincerely lied.

Dubin ordered a brandy, sipping as he observed the middle-aged bartender.

He told the bartender he seemed sad.

"You look kinda wiped out yourself."

The biographer confessed his lonely nature.

"I have my daughter dead about a year," said the bartender. "She took an overdose when she was twenty."

Dubin was sorry to hear it. "I have a daughter myself."

After a while he said, "Mark Twain lived in heartbreak after his daughter Susy died: 'The mind has a dumb sense of vast loss—that is all.' "

"They stay in your thoughts," said the bartender, rubbing the wood with his cloth.

Dubin in his heart of hearts mourns Dubin.

Two

A light fog lay on Venice that end-of-October late afternoon they arrived via an hour in Rome where it had been sunny and warm. Dubin and Fanny after debarking the vaporetto—terribly slow but he was eager to point out hazy sights, mist-enshrouded palazzi—were following a porter wheeling their luggage up a narrow calle. There, as the mist thinned and they could see others approaching, it seemed to the biographer that a red-haired girl clinging to the arm of a gray-haired man—both backed against the wall to let the newcomers and their baggage go by, Fanny and the elderly gent momentarily stood between Dubin and the redhead half hidden from him—was his daughter Maud. He, startled, his legs beginning to tremble, had been about to cry out her name, but the need for concealment was inexorable so he turned from her, pulling his hat brim low over his eyes, and when, no more than a minute later, he gazed back at the couple they were shadows in the fog. The bronze hair had disappeared like the flaming sun sinking in a cloud-massed charcoal sunset.

Anguished, regretful, feeling imperiled—Dubin had the impulse to chase after them to determine if she was indeed Maud, but how could it be during the academic term at Berkeley where he had telephoned and talked with her only a few nights ago? He was surely mistaken, had more than once confused

Maud with another redheaded girl nearby. One is struck by the color and recognizes someone who isn't there. Fanny, wearing her blue shades, had noticed nothing and chattered amiably. The porter pushed ahead with the bags. Dubin was still shaken though he had for the most part recovered his calm when they entered the courtyard of the Hotel Contessa. Behind them the setting sun appeared as a fiery half disk in the silvery fog and the evening promised pleasure.

"What's the weather saying for tomorrow?" he asked the black-suited segretario at the desk as he examined their passports.

"Improving, professore." His nose had twitched: that swinging single with this ambitious vecchio? Dubin felt he must look older with her than when alone.

"I have no university connection. I'm a professional biographer."

"Please pardon me, I meant as compleement."

He nodded genially, not altogether displeased by the man's curiosity nor by the aura of expectancy Fanny stirred up around her wherever she appeared. He'd been mildly surprised by her unseasonable getup—a voluminous violet dress, not her best color, and a wide-brimmed straw hat—though summer, although it could be said to be lingering in Rome, had departed Venice. She wore her wire-framed dark glasses, jade earrings, and a small gold crucifix in place of her Star of David.

"For the fun of it," Fanny had said. "I like to feel at home where I am."

"Will you feel at home with yourself?"

"Some people are freer than others."

That, Dubin granted. Fanny on holiday surprised, had overturned his expectations. She'd be a beautiful woman if she saw herself as one. This is she, Dubin reflected. Let her be.

With her unfurled by his side who would have noticed him in a foggy Venetian street? He was certain it hadn't been Maud they had passed yet wondered: if I was hiding, was she?

The portiere beckoned two bellmen. One, a vital youth, gathered Fanny's three bags as if by instinct, none of which he would yield to an older man who lugged Dubin's worn suitcase; and together with the assistant secretary, they all rose slowly in the wire-doored wood-paneled lift.

The assistant secretary, a closely shaved and powdered man with a sculptured black mustache, led them twice to a wrong room before leading them to the right one. "I deed not recognize eef it was a three or a seven on my paper."

"It's on the key," said Dubin. "But you are absolutely right," said the astonished young man, his eyes mostly on Fanny. They had entered an attractive double room through an adjoining single that Dubin wanted locked on their side. The assistant secretary offered to return immediately with the key but Dubin said he would ask the maid to take care of it in the morning. The man unhappily assented, though a thousand-lire note seemed to settle his nerves.

Their room on the top floor of the Contessa was a magnificent high ornate-ceilinged one with French doors leading to a small balcony overlooking the Grand Canal. The fog had lifted and the view before them—Venice afloat in a rising sea on a serene late-October early evening—and the anticipation of his amorous adventure, filled Dubin with satisfaction at the rightness of his decision to do what he was presently doing.

They had met by chance, after the Big Apple fizzle, on Grand Street in Center Campobello. Dubin, at the tail end of his country walk, had intended to slip past her; but Fanny, approaching as he hesitated, abruptly explained she had returned to pick up a lamp she had bought but hadn't been able to carry in her overloaded VW.

"I was hoping I would see you. I lost the name of the hotel I wrote on a piece of paper, and you weren't registered in the two others I tried."

"Which did you try?"

"I went to the Brevoort, also the Plaza."

"I was registered at the Gansevoort. Why didn't you telephone or at least drop me a line afterward?"

"It was on my mind," Fanny said, "but I thought your wife mightn't like it. Also I was annoyed at myself for losing the name of the place."

Dubin said his wife didn't open his mail. He searched her eyes, she seemed contrite.

Two days later he telephoned Fanny in New York and proposed a week in Italy.

"Why not," she said after momentary hesitation. "I haven't found a job yet so it's okay with me, if you can make it."

On the plane he had asked himself, "What am I doing here, a man my age with a young woman hers?" The answer came easily and happily: "Enjoying myself. I have it coming to me."

Fanny was affectionate, buoyant; they joked. She sat snuggled close, straw hat on her lap, head against his shoulder, her hair spread like a flag across his chest. She had shown nervousness before the flight, which had disappeared after they had ascended. Dubin's difficulty was afterthought: he regretted deceiving Kitty. There ought to be a better way. He recalled Lawrence's remark: "Honesty is more important than marital fidelity."

"—Kitty, I'm going off with a chick for a week. A night out in life. I want the experience before I'm too old to have it. Don't fret, I'll be back soon as good as new and as loyal as ever."

Fat chance. She'd probably have told him she'd be elsewhere when he returned. Kitty was vulnerable, why upset her? He had lied to protect her.

Fanny and he embraced on the Venetian balcony, Dubin nuzzling her neck. Her hot floral breath drew his mouth to hers.

"In a little while," she murmured after a long kiss. "We've been traveling all day and I could use a bath."

"Should we get into the tub together?"

"I'll be out in a sec, lover."

While she was bathing Dubin tried on a pair of striped pajamas Kitty had not long ago bought him. After a moment of reflection in a closet-door mirror he removed them and changed into fresh underwear. He did not admire his girth in boxer shorts, or his thin legs, so he drew on trousers and buttoned up his shirt.

Fanny, as the tub gurgled and toilet flushed, stepped out of the bathroom in a short white nightgown. Her body glowed. She had brushed her hair full and bright. Dubin, like a man about to be dubbed knight, sank to his knees, his arms clasping her legs as he pressed his nose into her navel.

She reacted in surprise, momentarily stiffening, then with affection ran her hand through his hair.

"I have my suitcase stuff all over the bed so I'd better finish unpacking like I see you have."

"I thought I'd get my things out of the way."

"So will I. It won't take long."

" 'Had we but world enough and time,' dear Fanny," Dubin, rising, sighed.

"We have all week."

"You're a practical type."

"I'm not romantic, if that's what you mean, though sometimes I have romantic thoughts."

"It lingers in me, perhaps it's my generation."

"Forget your generation. Even if you are older than I you act young when you want to."

"L'chayim," said Dubin, holding aloft an imaginary glass.

"It's cool," she laughed.

She was sorting the contents of a small store: casual clothing—piles of it —and plastic containers of creams, lotions, deodorants. This consumer's side of her was new to him—he barely knew the girl—and he wondered how it squared away with her abstemious stay in a Buddhist commune.

"It's no ripoff. I happen to have this uncle who owns a drugstore. And my mother sends me clothes she doesn't want."

Amid her possessions he noticed a rubber diaphragm in a worn plastic case.

"Don't you use the pill?"

"My uncle says it can give you breast cancer."

"My wife never approved it."

Fanny also carried a traveling iron and portable clothesline she could rig up in any bathroom. "Anything you want to hang on the clothesline, please do it, Bill."

He was helping her put away things into drawers and the medicine cabinet.

"Why don't you call me William, Fanny?"

"I don't like to call you what your wife does."

That hadn't occurred to him, but he preferred William to Bill.

She fell, with a comic groan, into an armchair, her nightie billowing.

"What do you say we get into bed, Fanny?"

"If you wish, Will-yam."

"Call me Bill if you like. What do *you* wish?"

"Are you worried I might call you Bill and your wife would hear it?"

He was startled, could not foresee circumstances in which Kitty and Fanny were likely to meet. Don't consider yourself her equal, Dubin thought.

She regarded him cunningly. "Is something bothering you?"

"My mood at the moment is, as they say, macho, but you are being coy."

"No, I'm not. What did you tell your wife was the reason you were going away for a week?"

"I indicated I had some unexpected bits of research to do in Italy to settle a few things on my mind. But since she knows I'm presently working on Lawrence's early life, she may have wondered whether I wanted to get away for some other reason—possibly so I could see my work in perspective."

"Will she believe what you said—about going to Italy?"

"She believes me," Dubin said soberly.

"This isn't your first affair since you were married, is it, William? I wouldn't think so."

He thanked her for saying his name. "No, but it is with someone—if you'll pardon the expression—as young as you, a long trip involved, and some elaborate deception. Kitty happens to be easy to lie to, which makes it harder to do. I don't like not to be honest with her."

"Sometimes you sound innocent."

"I'm not innocent though my experience is limited."

"Like to some one-night lays with older-type ladies?"

"Not exactly grandmothers."

"How many?" she asked curiously.

"A few affairs—none prolonged."

"In how long a time?"

"I've been married twenty-five years and have been adulterous the last twelve."

"Adulterous? What were you afraid of?"

"There was no special fear. I was largely satisfied as things were. I was married after thirty and had for years too much to do to go actively looking for extramarital sexual experiences. I was working well and had a family to take care of."

"But nobody has to go actively looking—it's there. It always is."

"It may be there but in a way I wasn't," Dubin explained. "I'm only recently a visitor to the new sexual freedom. How many affairs have you had, Fanny?"

She started at the question. "I never counted."

"Often with married men?"

She nodded. "I was into that a lot for a while but less so lately."

"Good," said Dubin, noting a contradiction.

"Why did you pick me to go away with?"

He asked her if she was looking for compliments.

"Not really but I am kind of curious, William."

"Your warmth," he said, "—good looks, womanliness, openness. Because you touch my arm with your fingers when we talk. You're a little larger than life, Fanny. I mean you make life seem larger. I felt that before you tossed your underpants at me."

"What about your wife? I never really got to figure her out."

"What about her?"

"She looks sexy for her age but is she? My mother does but is limp as a rag."

"Fanny, ask anything you please about me and I'll answer, but let's not talk about my wife—she wouldn't like it."

"What is she—the Queen of Sheba? Are you afraid of her?"

"There's no reason to say that. Kitty's a private person with a complicated personal history. That's her business."

"I'll bet she worries a lot."

Dubin admitted it. "The night before I was to leave she asked me to call the trip off. She felt she didn't want to be alone in the house for a week. I said I wouldn't go if she felt that way in the morning. But by morning she had changed her mind: 'You've got to go,' so I went."

"What's her real problem?"

Dubin hesitated. "Let's say she's going through a prolonged glandular thing. That's as much as I intend to say about her."

"You don't have to tell me any more—I don't want to know," Fanny said, drawing up her legs and clasping them with both arms. "Just do you love her?"

Between her ankles her blond pelt was visible. As his eyes rose to hers she lowered her legs.

"I loved her," the biographer responded. "I love her still but differently. Time passes, needs and feelings change. One tries, with others, to recover past pleasures, past privileges. One looks for diversion."

"Is that what I am to you?"

"What would you want to be?" Dubin asked.

"I am not a hooker."

"My God, why should I have thought so?"

"Attitudes don't always need words."

"What attitudes? I assure you of my respect, Fanny."

"How much respect does a diversion get?"

"Forgive the word, I might have chosen better. In any case there are always possibilities. The course of a relationship is unpredictable."

"Well, what is possible?"

"I suppose it's possible to love one woman one way and another another."

"Which way do you think you could love me?" Fanny then asked.

He answered slowly: "I am drawn to you. Surely that's obvious? Anyway, it's as much as I want to think of or define just now. Let's stop analyzing our relationship, dear Fanny, and get into bed. An act defines itself."

"I would really like to," Fanny answered, "but my stomach is rumbling like ape. When I am this hungry I can't concentrate on anything, not even going to bed with someone. But I will if you want me to."

"Let's eat," Dubin said.

Fanny pulled off her short nightgown—her breasts were beautifully formed. She wiggled into black bikini underpants, then drew on a short deep-pink minidress. Her hair she wore attractively up and slightly messy, though the effect was splendid. Her nipples were imprinted on the dress. He considered asking her to put on a bra but didn't. Fanny then draped on the small gold crucifix and slipped on her blue glasses.

"Do you have to wear those?"

"Don't you like them?"

"They blank your face."

"I hate the glare," Fanny said.

"You are the glare."

She liked that, laughed.

When Fanny, in her fuchsia dress—not Dubin in his silk suit—appeared in the Contessa dining room, it burst into life. The vast elegant room, with gold-decorated white walls and a flight of cherubim in blue tones across the ceiling, fronted the dark canal. Before them, as they entered, a multitude of tables draped in white cloths extended into semi-darkness. Only a brightly lit rectangular section under two crystal chandeliers was roped off with a thick white silk rope and lavishly set for dinner. Into this dining area of about two dozen tables, none presently occupied, Fanny and Dubin were led and courteously seated by the maitre d'hôtel.

"I guess we're early," said Dubin.

He had seen the man's discreet yet momentarily stunned glance at Fanny and had noticed that the four waiters who had been standing impassively at the doors had stirred and risen, if not to military attention at least to animated interest in her. Though her young legs were outstanding in short dresses, Dubin, if he had had his wits upstairs, would have suggested a more discreet garment for the dining room.

"Not at all, sir," the maitre d' responded. "The season is at the end. Only a few guests stay."

He was a handsome heavy-eyed man who, as Fanny smiled and he bowed to her, let his eyes rest fleetingly on her bosom; he lingered on the crucifix and recommended the pesce. Dubin felt a stirring of mild jealousy but kept it down. The reaction surprised him.

After studying the menu Fanny ordered brains and Dubin bass. She had shrimp and he melon with prosciutto. Fanny had turned down a drink—too many on the planes—and Dubin signaled the steward and ordered a bottle of wine.

He urged her to remove her sunglasses. "They put you at a distance."

"I'll come nearer." Fanny dropped them into her stuffed purse. He had noticed she had tucked her diaphragm box into the bag before they left the room.

"What for?" Dubin had asked.

"Just a habit."

As he pondered her reply she gazed around the room, her eyes alert, comfortable, eyebrows slightly ragged. The nails of Fanny's efficient plain hands were bitten to the quick. When the wine was poured she gulped it as if it were water. She was affectionate, chummy. "What were you saying when I was in the bathroom? You were saying something."

"Encouraging myself."

"Do you have to?"

"More or less, when I'm away from home and operating adventurously."

"Once you said you would tell me how you met your wife."

How she harps on my wife. "I told you she was a widow then," he said. "She was married to a doctor who died young. He was apparently an unusual man who influenced her strongly. I had trouble competing with him in her memory but that changed after the birth of our daughter."

Fanny, listening with interest, chewed absently.

Dubin then said, "I'm sure you understand, Fanny—I won't bring this up again—that she mustn't know about us, not have the remotest suspicion. Her life hasn't been easy. I wouldn't want to hurt her."

"Would you hurt me, William?"

He swore no. "I feel tender to you, Fanny, and hope you feel something similar for me."

She felt she did. Her wine-flushed face was lovely. Her eyes, more intensely green, looked gently at him. Dubin was enjoying the food and liked the half-hidden glances of the waiters and the concern of the heavy-eyed maitre d', who came by often to see how things were progressing.

"What about you?" he asked: "For instance, what does your father do?"

"He imports," she said doubtfully.

"You don't get along with him?"

"It's very mutual."

"May I ask why?"

"He's self-centered and doesn't have much respect for me or my mother though he gets along with my sister. My mother is a gutsy lady but I don't want to talk about her either. I'm enjoying this meal."

He lifted his glass in agreement. Dubin drank wine freely and loved the evening. Fanny relished the brains. One or another of the young waiters appeared from time to time, ostensibly to replenish bread or pour wine. All, Dubin thought, came to view Fanny up close, who seemed to radiate nudity and was, she confessed, very happy. Dubin felt she was one of those gifted people who give public pleasure, not a bad thing in life.

As they were waiting for dessert, the biographer felt a hand on his knee, then as it slowly traveled up his thigh, decided he was dealing with Fanny's foot. She had removed her shoe and was caressing him under the table.

"You make my foot warm."

"Warm or cold, it's a marvelous instrument. Is this what is called footsie?"

She smiled affectionately. "Do you like it?"

"Won't the waiters know what we're doing?"

"They don't give a shit. It goes on forever in restaurants."

"I should be more observant."

He poured the last of the wine as Fanny, her face composed as she stroked his leg, after a paradise of expectation touched his aroused organ. Dubin made no objection. This was Venice, this was Italy. This, according to the arts and humanities, was what it was all about.

He felt in his pleasure a loosening of ties, concerns, restrictions—a sense of trumpets blaring in the woody distance. Here's William the Bold, with upraised sword on a black charger, galloping onward under the bright blue sky. Stepping out of his shoe he began gently to move up Fanny's calf with his adventurous right foot. Deadpan above table, impassioned below, he felt her thighs yield to his insistent gentle probing. Fanny gazed at him dreamily as at last he pressed the soft flesh under her bikini panties. Dubin experienced a desire to pull off his black sock but the perspiring maitre d' fortunately came by, inquiring if they had enjoyed the meal. The biographer, with dignity, said they had indeed, and could he have his check. Fanny nodded. Dubin felt drunk and embarrassed as they got up and walked past the waiters at the French doors, all silently aware of them, one regarding him with a connoisseur's approval; but other patrons were coming in and it was not too bad. Yet he felt he had overeaten and overdrunk, the weight of food and wine antipathic to self and spirit.

"I like you," she said in their room. "Can we go out tonight, William?" Her things were still strewn all over. He felt he knew her well.

"Where for instance?"

"Someplace lively, where we can dance."

"This is off-season," he told her. "There are no night clubs in Venice. We can look for a movie, if you like."

"Let's have some real fun."

"What about a walk in St. Mark's?"

"Could we go to Harry's Bar?"

Dubin agreed. "Put on something warm."

The night was dark, damp, the streets still. Houselights went on as they walked up XXII Marzo. Fanny touched his arm and they stopped in midstreet. He put his mouth on hers. They kissed with wine-soaked tongues.

"I'm wet through my pants," she said. "Let's go home."

"Wonderful," Dubin said.

In their room he undressed her, brief episode—fuchsia dress, underpants, shoes.

Fanny had trouble getting his undershirt over his head.

"Why do you bother wearing them?"

"My wife buys them."

"Tell her not to."

"They help in wintertime. She shops for me, I hate to."

"I wish you wouldn't praise her to me—"

"I wasn't aware I was—"

"Lift your arms."

She drew the undershirt over his head.

"Pardon this bit of belly. You wouldn't think I exercise."

"You wouldn't have the belly if you stood straight."

"Exactly what Kitty says."

"I really don't care what she says. Step out of your shoes."

"I wish I were younger for you."

"Fuck your age."

"Well put," Dubin laughed.

When she bent to remove his socks there was a tearing noise.

"What was that?"

Fanny laughed wildly. "I farted." She ran with a sob into the bathroom, flushed the bowl.

After five minutes, when she failed to answer his inquiring knock, Dubin turned the knob and cautiously looked into the bathroom.

"Are you all right, Fanny?"

She was standing at the toilet bowl, retching, a blob of diarrhea dribbling down her leg.

Afterward she was sick, vomited raucously, spilling her supper, spitting, weeping.

"I feel awful."

"Poor baby, what can I do for you?"

"I also feel I am tripping. 'Seize the day,' hump your lay."

After he had cleaned her with paper, when after sobbing awhile she lay asleep, her mouth open, breathing noisily, Dubin washed her legs and buttocks with a warm soaped cloth but could not wholly remove the odor of her illness.

The biographer recalled Yeats on love's mansion in the place of excrement; but not much came of it.

As he was falling asleep Maud appeared in his mind; Dubin awoke. Was it she he had seen in the fog with a man old enough, ironically, to be older than her father? Whoever he was had seemed past sixty. "My daughter is not for thee": Brabantio. Yet, could Dubin despise an aging man who desired the company of a young woman—endless insistent hunger? The old gent, he guessed, would have to be one of her teachers—maybe someone from her Mexican dig last summer? So soon out of the crib, so quickly grown—bleeding, breasted, gone—lost to me. Out of the house at eighteen; at nineteen as deeply as he into amorous intrigue? How is it possible—the

hunger to adventure in contravention of time's good sense? He figured her age
with her friend's would average a good forty; his with Fanny's, less. Himself
less culpable—if one were to use the word—than Maud's male friend—if it
was Maud—because Fanny was three years older than his daughter and no
innocent. Life responds to one's moves with comic counterinventions.

He dressed in the dark so as not to awaken the girl.

"I don't want to die," Fanny moaned in her sleep.

A universal lament.

Dubin went down in the cage elevator and through the dimly lit lobby,
though it was not much past eleven, into the street. Where does a concerned
father seek his erring daughter? The sky was clouded, no sign of moon, the
night air hazy, cool; he crossed a stone bridge over a narrow canal exuding
mist. In an alley he passed a blind black man touching the wall with his fingers.
The biographer drifted through a maze of crooked streets around La Fenice,
peering into lit places, staring at elderly men with young women. Though his
search, if it was one, came to nothing, he fantasied meeting Maud—she
wandering alone wanting to find him—their encounter, embrace. Afterward
they'd walk together. He wanted to tell her why he was in Venice though she'd
probably not want to know. Perhaps they had experienced similar disappoint-
ments and might, tomorrow morning, leave together for the States. Dubin
doubted it in afterthought. He doubted Maud was in Venice.

Entering Harry's Bar he sat at a table in a corner. An old waiter with long
gray sideburns brought him a brandy. Dubin was moved to speak to the man
but did not. He sipped his brandy, watching those at the bar and tables,
smart-looking men and sensuous women, even when oddly dressed, beautifully dressed. He sought among them a woman with a sense of past: past
time, past pain, awareness of the difficulty of loving. Only the young, the raw
young, were present. He did not want to be among them.

Dubin wandered into St. Mark's Square, through the piazzetta to the water.
It was a square walk he was making in a circle. There were a few tables in front
of Florian's—three or four people sitting quietly in the dark. The other cafés
were closed, their tables set top on top, chairs stacked in columns. Some of the
summer tables were piled up under the gallery arches. On the embankment by
the mooring poles several gondolas lay like dead fish out of water, to be
stripped and stored in back canals and there await the end of winter. Two
gondolas were still moored in the dark water. The tide was rising and the
undulating water slapped the boats and sucked at them. A narrow plank

boardwalk on carpenter's horses had been laid across the piazza for the winter floods.

Over the water the night was starless. A string of dim lights ran along the misty shore of the Giudecca. Behind the shore lights rose a dark mass of houses, lit windows here and there in a sparse ascending diagonal. Behind this island other islands floated in the sea. An island is a mystery, he thought. A man is an island in the only sense that matters, not an easy way to be. We live in mystery, a cosmos of separate lonely bodies, men, insects, stars. It is all a loneliness and men know it best.

Dubin stood at the low wall overlooking the water in front of the small tufted umbrella pines in the giardinetta. A half dozen starved cats were consuming the remains of somebody's spaghetti supper on a spread newspaper. An old man in a light coat approached and asked him for a cigarette.

"I have forgotten my own," he said.

Dubin thought it was the waiter he had seen at the bar but this was another man. He handed him his pack of cigarillos.

"Thank you, signore."

"For not much. They're bad for your health."

"I have no health." The old man touched his hat and walked slowly along the embankment. He crossed the steps of the small stone bridge and disappeared.

The biographer thought of that other waiter, his father, who had waited all his years for life to catch up with him. He was waiting when he died. He died waiting.

Papa, his son said, you died before much had happened with me. I wasn't married. You only once met my future wife, never saw your granddaughter. I am a biographer. I want you to know that President Johnson—he was also after your time—gave me a medal for a book I wrote about someone called Henry Thoreau, a large-souled man in the natural world. That's what I do: write books about the lives of men.

He looked at his hands as he spoke. They were his father's.

What do you know about people's lives? said the waiter.

I'm not a kid any more, Papa. Some things I know.

So what kind of a medal you got?

It's called Medal of Freedom—an award for accomplishment.

It would be better if it was from President Roosevelt.

I was only a child then.

66

Believe me, if I could write a book it would be a wonderful book. I saw a lot in my time. I'm not a waiter thirty years for nothing.

I wish you'd been alive when they gave me the medal. There was a dinner in the White House.

This I would enjoy. I would also donate my services if they needed an extra waiter.

I hoped you would live till I began to earn some money. I wanted to make your life easier.

A living I always made. Not much a living but I made a living. Enough to take care of your mother.

I wish she had lived.

In good health, said the waiter.

He was a round-shouldered man of medium height with purple-veined legs and an overly patient nature. Waiting was congenial to him; not much changed as you waited. He had wet blue eyes and a puffy pinkish face. His eyelids itched and he rubbed salve on them. At work he wore an alpaca jacket whose stains he rubbed out by brushing them with a rag dipped in hot coffee; a daily washed white shirt, snap-on bow tie, black wool trousers. He wore white cotton socks he changed twice a day and knobbed ankle-length shined black shoes. The shoes, when at last he abandoned them, looked like misshapen baking potatoes. He carried a yellow pencil stub on his right ear and worked mostly in Jewish dairy restaurants.

Charlie Dubin was an infinitely patient man, not known for his humor. He did not endear himself to his customers as other waiters did, with their bantering, wisecracks, jokes. He did not do as well with tips as some of the other men. The bosses said you could depend on Charlie but he made no great effort to make those he served happy.

I give good service, said Charlie Dubin. Let the food make the customer happy.

While his customers were eating he withdrew to the coatracks and waited. He waited earnestly, attentively, patiently.

Whyn't you crack a smile once in a big while? a patron asked.

Give me your order and I will deliver to you right away, Charlie said. Smiles I am not serving.

The man left a nickel.

One boss said he depressed the place, the customers complained.

Mr. Goldfein, said Dubin, I am a good waiter. I write down right the order and deliver quick from the kitchen. I don't want to be a vaudeville entertainer. Don't ask me I should be Pat Rooney or Smith and Dale. If the customer wants vaudeville let him go to RKO.

Take a walk, said the boss.

Charlie Dubin took another walk. A month later he was working elsewhere. But he told no jokes, seemed to know none. His life had made him a deadly serious man. He had seemed to want little, made do, lived a meager life. All he knew was being a waiter. When he was a boy William had found it hard to approve him. He gave me all he could, more than I wanted of his: an inclination to a confined lonely life. It was mine before I knew it; for years I held it against him.

Charlie winked at him.

Hannah Dubin, a thin small once redheaded whispering woman, cracked her knuckles against her breast, whispering, Siz mir nisht gut. She had, in her late thirties, not long after the death of her nine-year-old son, become mentally ill. She was afraid of the white window shades and of the long dark hallway of the railroad flat. She was afraid of footsteps on the stairs in the hall. She hid in the back bedroom, coming out to clean; or cook a chicken, then hid in the bedroom. Her face tightened against old friends visiting. The waiter feared sending her to a hospital; he feared she would suffer there. The doctor who had talked to her told Charlie Dubin that keeping her home wouldn't help; still she might recover, remissions were possible.

One winter morning, alone in the house, she swallowed half a bottle of disinfectant, and William, sent home from school because he was running a fever, came upon her lying on the clean kitchen floor, the acrid-smelling uncapped bottle of CN sitting in her shoe. He rushed downstairs to the drugstore and afterward induced vomiting by getting her to swallow the contents of a bottle of citrate of magnesia he had bought in panic.

Yes, she whispered, yes, yes. She drank from the bottle as though famished, as though she had wanted all her life to drink the miraculous potion he served her. It would make her sane again, healthy, young—would restore her chance to have everything she hadn't had in her life. She drank her own everlasting hunger. When she recovered, her graying hair coiled in braids on her head, she promised she would never—never again.

Willie, don't tell Papa I am crazy.

Mama, don't say that.

She warned him: Don't go in the rain, Willie, not in the rain. You will catch a cold, the doctor will come, you will get pneumonia. Don't go, Willie, out in the rain.

Hannah sat in the darkened bedroom, shades drawn, whispering to herself. She was meek in the house but when she ventured into the street to buy something to eat she shouted at those she said were following her.

The steak is in the bathtub, she whispered in the dark.

The doctor thought she ought to go to the hospital but Charlie, waiting for her to get better, cooked, and cleaned when he could and talked to her in whispers. Hannah, he said, get better or your whole life will be wasted. When her eyes were wet she lifted her skirt and wiped them with her cotton petticoat.

Look how clean she is, the waiter said to his son.

She was dead at forty, of pleurisy and anguish. She did not thank her husband for waiting for her to get better; she did not thank her son for having kept her from taking her life.

He hid from his memories of her.

William and Charlie Dubin lived alone in the house.

After William had met Kitty he told his father about her, and the old man said miserably, Why do you want to marry a goyish widow with a goyish child that he will someday call you names? She won't be comfortable with you.

Dubin said he would take his chances.

William, said the waiter passionately, you know what we went through with Hitler. Don't marry somebody that she will take you away from the Jewish people.

He wrote his father a note: Dear Papa, How can a man be a Jew if he isn't a man? How can he be a man if he gives up the woman he wants to marry?

His father kept his letter in his pants pocket and Dubin found it there when Charlie died. He tried to have him buried in a grave near his wife's but there were no plots, so they lay in different cemeteries.

"Go look for your daughter," the waiter's voice said.

In a street near the embankment a long-faced girl in sweater and jeans sat on a stool bowing a cello clasped between her legs. The music she played was from a Bach suite for cello unaccompanied. Dubin had the record but stayed to listen. He listened, standing to the side, not to distract the girl. It was late. On the ground lay a small cardboard box with a few lire in it. The girl did not play all that well but he listened till the end of the movement. Dubin liked the harsh-sweet gutty bowing. He liked the sensuous dignity of J. S.

Bach, husband of two wives and father of twenty children, jigging in a state of grace, his music flowing like water falling in an iron fountain. The pouring fountain was the music. The cellist was not a beautiful girl—her face was long and her figure meager; but she looked handsome playing the cello in the Venetian night and Dubin felt he loved her.

In the morning Fanny said she was so much better, though her gut felt tender. "It was all the wine that did it. I always overreact to wine." Dubin had hovered over her like a mother duck. He had given her a pill that stopped diarrhea and another that diminished nausea. They were pills that Kitty brought along when they traveled. He fed Fanny dry toast with sugarless tea. She was hungrier than she had any right to be but he wouldn't let her have more food. "I'm dying of hunger," Fanny complained. She still felt queasy and had cramps but they weren't bad and she was decently comfortable and even "cozy."

It was raining on the canals. They watched the rain through the window, Fanny lying propped against two pillows in their double bed, her legs covered with a blanket. She wore a light black nightgown. She was reading *Sons and Lovers* and said she liked it.

"I'm up to here," she read aloud: " 'He only knew she loved him. He was afraid of her love for him. It was too good for him, and he was inadequate. His own love was at fault, not hers.' Why is he such a shnook?"

"She reminds him of his mother. He senses it."

"Don't tell me the end, I don't want to know."

"The end is there already."

"I don't want to know it." For a while she stopped reading, seemed depressed.

"Anything the matter?" Dubin asked.

"I was thinking about myself. I'm not the world's most stable woman."

He said, after a moment, that the feeling was not an unnatural one at her age.

"Yes, but why now?"

"You tell me."

"Just a mood, I'm tired of being in bed." Sighing, she went back to her reading as he flipped through a guidebook of Venice. He felt close to her, easy in his mind—at home; he was glad he had suppressed his doubts and gone off with her.

She told him about her life—the usual happy unhappiness of childhood. She had an older sister she called a bitch and a father who thought of Fanny as one. "My mother is the only friend I've got."

"You've got me."

Playing with her long hair, she observed him. "I like to be with you, William. I also like the vibes you have with what you're doing. I wish I could do more with my life."

"More what?"

"More good," she said hostilely.

He said he had often had the same thought.

Dubin got up and kissed her dry lips, and her ears and eyes. She pressed his hand to her breast.

She had tossed her blanket aside and lay in bed in a nightgown that touched her body like an enduring kiss. Extraordinary the grace a bit of draping gives nudity. Her every casual movement stirred him.

"But I still have cramps that come and go," Fanny said.

Dubin went into the bathroom and briskly brushed his teeth.

She said she could eat half a horse and, when he advised her nothing solid yet, said she would settle for some ginger ale. "Ginger ale is what my mother used to spoon us after an upset stomach."

There was nothing in the midget-refrigerator in the room but hard liquor and mineral water. Dubin called down for a bottle of ginger ale but the waiter offered only Pepsi. Fanny made a face: she had this thing about cola drinks —they gave her hives. Dubin said he would hunt up a bottle of ginger ale. He put on his raincoat and borrowed an umbrella from the porter.

He walked in steady rain from their hotel to the Rialto before he was able to find the soda. He was happy he had found it for Fanny. He imagined her saying, when he returned, that she had bathed and wanted him to undress and get into bed with her.

"I think you'll feel better after we make love," Dubin, speaking to himself, said to her.

When he returned to their room she was lying in bed wearing sunglasses. "Jesus, William, I thought you were dead and gone." She said she had ordered a sliced chicken sandwich because she was painfully famished, had eaten every bit of it, and held it down.

He was happy to hear it. He thought he'd take a shower.

She came into the bathroom as he was standing in the shower and retching, threw up the bread and chicken into the toilet bowl; her diarrhea returned; and hours later he began to spoon-feed her some warmish ginger ale, which, by God's grace—if not her own—she was able to retain. Fanny promised not to do anything equally stupid. "Please don't hold it against me."

Before falling asleep she whispered, "Tomorrow, William, I promise."

Tomorrow appeared exquisite—warm, clear—"inspiring," Dubin said. Fanny awoke glum, as though she'd long worried in her sleep; but after chancing—against his solemn advice—a continental breakfast without suffering consequences, she took a bath with salts, vigorously shampooed her hair, opened windows and doors to air the room, and though still pale, was energetic, vitalized.

"Let's zap out and see the sights."

He readily agreed. She put on the crucifix, then removed it and dropped it in the drawer. Fanny took it out again and draped it around her neck.

He felt at times he would like to be rid of her.

They hurried to St. Mark's, she—after shedding a cardigan because of "the heat"—in white jersey over black bra and in denim swing skirt, carrying her suede shoulder bag. Though she wore heavy-heeled shoes there was a ripple in her walk and people on the street seemed to like to watch her go by.

Fanny and Dubin hurried on in the brilliant sunlight, she keeping pace with his practiced long strides. The biographer wore his blue blazer, with flared reddish plaid slacks, and blue striped shirt with watermelon-pink tie. He was growing longer sideburns whose dominant color was gray. Dubin had occasional thoughts of dyeing his hair. Venice, absolved of fog and rain, had let a golden day rise like a balloon over its annealed islets. The sky floated azure over the green canals of antiquity. The effect was of island, plage, seashore—once more of holiday.

"Fanny," Dubin advised, "take those silly glasses off and look around. Some extraordinary painters took their light from this sky."

She blew a kiss to the sky, removed the glasses and slipped them into her bag. She walked close to Dubin, their bodies touching. He had never felt younger.

Pigeons rose, wheeling, fluttering over them in the Piazza San Marco. There were a dozen tourists on the Square. Dubin, showing the girl around, pointed out artifacts, objects of interest in and around the Cathedral, reading to her from his guidebook what had been plundered when and where. She listened, looked where he pointed, walked on.

Kitty, on first seeing the Cathedral, had cried out in delight. Coming to a new city, she walked on air through its streets. Fanny gazed around almost without curiosity, looking back as though she did not trust either what she saw or her response. He was not dissatisfied. She would learn; he enjoyed her company. Fanny liked to lock fingers as they walked—what pleasure the simple gesture gave, what a compliment, flesh on flesh.

She had a Kodak in her bag and pulled it out to snap his picture. Dubin threw a hand up before his face.

"Oh, come on—what's a picture?"

"Let's take yours." He snatched the camera and snapped one of Fanny, her knees bent, extending a palm to a curious pigeon. Another alighted on her head. "Get off me, you shitty bird." She swatted at it, laughed in embarrassment as the pigeon fluttered away.

A priest in skirts and biretta, carrying a briefcase and rolled umbrella, perhaps noticing Fanny's crucifix if not her vital good looks, inclined his head in courteous greeting.

He offered to take a picture of them with his Polaroid.

"Let's, William—"

Dubin thanked the priest, said it wasn't necessary. "Are you from the States, Father?"

"Newark, New Jersey."

"Small world, I was born there."

"I was born in Trenton," said Fanny.

"Were you?" Dubin asked in surprise. "We're all from the Garden State —maybe the same garden."

The three laughed.

"Where was your wife born?" she asked.

"Montreal," he answered, clearing his throat.

The priest tipped his biretta. "Blessings on you, my child," he said to Fanny.

Later she squeezed Dubin's hand.

"What made you ask about my wife just then?"

"Just then I wanted to know where she was born."

They wandered on the Piazza, along the galleries toward the Campanile.

He asked her impression. "Does this city get to you? Some who see it for the first time wonder if they're the victims of their imagination."

"I like it all right though it isn't Fat City. I can smell smog. It's like a whiff of L.A., only oilier."

"That's from the mainland. Still, not everybody loves the Square or Venice itself. Montaigne did but thought it stank. So did Lawrence. In a letter he called it écoeuré—without heart; in a poem he speaks of it as 'the abhorrent green slippery city of Venice.' "

"Then why have we come here?"

"To be together."

"But why here?"

"I thought it might rouse up a bit of magic and blow it around."

"Did your wife like Venice?"

"Encore my wife?"

"It's an honest question."

"She loves it, although we've never been here but a short time before something nasty happens."

"What did?"

"Once I had a manuscript stolen out of my suitcase. I got it back a year later. It was mailed to me in the States and when I reread it I was glad I had lost it."

"Why?"

"It wasn't a good piece of work—a blow to my pride."

"Did anything else happen?"

"Kitty got awfully sick here."

"Like me—the trots?"

"She ran a high fever—she almost never does—and wanted to leave. She was afraid the plague was back for a visit, but as soon as we were on the plane she recovered and that was that."

"What bugs her? Why does she go around sniffing the gas?"

"It's not important."

"Man, it's weird."

"Forget it. Anyway, here we are together."

She said she wished they had stayed in Rome.

"We'll be back in a day or two. I wanted to scoot up to see if Venice affected you as it does me. Obviously it doesn't."

She momentarily rested her head on his shoulder.

They had stopped in front of a small jewelry shop. Dubin, noticing something in the window, asked her to excuse him.

"Can't I go in with you?"

"It won't take more than a minute. I'll be right out."

When he came out of the jeweler's a moment later, Fanny was earnestly engaged in conversation with a taut-bottomed erect red-haired young man in front of a lavish glass shop a few doors down.

"This is Amadeo Rossini. He wants us to ride in his gondola," she said to Dubin.

"I thought they were mostly stacked away till spring," he said genially.

"Not his," Fanny said.

"I am steel een my beezinez, signore," the young gondolier said. He resembled a matador in black T-shirt and jeans. His pants were tight, buttocks elegant.

"Care for a ride, Fanny?"

"I wouldn't mind."

The gondolier led them, Dubin carrying Fanny's cardigan, up a narrow street to a mooring pole where a single battered gondola, its prow spotted with bird droppings—the boat looked as though it had barely escaped a drastic fate—lay in the green water at the dock, lapped by ripples a parting vaporetto made.

After assisting his two passengers into the bulky boat—he seemed charmed by the vision of Fanny's black bra through her jersey—Amadeo, wearing his professional red-ribboned yellow straw hat, pushed off with a long oar and the ride began pleasantly in the warmish early-November sun. Fanny, her color restored, lifted her face to the light. If there were Indians in Italy this was an Indian summer's day.

Amid the decay what beauty! Many of the palazzi were façade-eroded yet stately, graceful, despite asymmetry of windows and columns. Some houses were boarded up—pigeons nesting in the grillwork—in need of restoration; but their shimmering reflections in the greenish water—salmon, orange, aquamarine—excited Dubin. He lit a cigarillo and smoked contentedly, at times beset by thoughts of Venice subsiding in brackish water at the sea's bottom to be nibbled at into eternity by bony pale fish. The gondola was gliding toward Ponte Accademia and as he watched the reflections in the water it was no great effort to think himself afloat in an insubstantial world. With open eyes Dubin dreamed of passionate love in a fantastic city.

The gondolier broke into song. In a pleasant high tenor he celebrated love in a gondola. His eyes, when Dubin turned to look, were anchored on Fanny. Hers, dear girl, were shut as she listened. Perhaps he was singing to her black brassiere? Or was it her gold crucifix that had inspired his song? No doubt simply Fanny herself, sexy Pippa passes. Dubin experienced no jealousy. What he felt in her presence no doubt the young gondolier also felt, but me first by prior contract. I met her once on a country road, wooed her by wanting, flew away with her over the sea. She's with me—my girl. No point feeling sorry for the gondolier. He has youth; I am momentarily graced by her presence. Next week it's into my long work again.

"Two bits for your thoughts," he remarked to Fanny musing as she watched the water.

She smiled affectionately, pinched his nose. He bent to her. They kissed in the gondola as the youth sang. She lightly ran her fingers up the inside of Dubin's thigh.

"We're highly visible, should we go elsewhere?"

"I dig this ride," she softly sighed.

The battered gondola with blue seats and faded green carpet glided on, the youth singing still, confessing passion and pain to an unknown ear, Trident maybe? Though he did not understand the Venetian dialect, Dubin made out "jealous husband" in "Le bele toseta ga el mario gelosa," and was tempted to advise the young man to rest his voice but refrained.

The boat was in mid-canal after rounding the bend toward the Rialto before he noticed people staring at them from palazzi windows; others from small craft on the canal. It then occurred to Dubin that theirs was the only tourist gondola out that morning. The Venetians were, from old, commercial types, but he beheld no other sightseers around and felt momentary apprehension which he ridiculed but it was there. Had the gondolier on his fat nerve taken them out at a forbidden time? He had waked that morning short of cash and decided it was still summer? So he hauls his banged-up boat from a back canal and goes hunting for belated tourists? Summer anyone? Fanny with Dubin had walked into his practical needs? What a nuisance if they were stopped by the police motoscafo. He looked around and saw the municipal garbage scow, trailed by floating lettuce leaves and a few boiled onions bobbing in the wavy water.

There was also a sand barge and a variety of rowboats, blunt- and sharp-nosed, plus assorted topi delivering produce, meat, cases of beer, even a small coffin for a child or midget.

A hairy-chested man called to them from a barge filled with gray sand. "What's he saying?" Fanny asked.

"Get off the canal, they need the water."

"Va fan'gulo," chanted the gondolier.

The hairy bargeman cupped his palm over his upper arm, thrusting the free fist into the air.

Unaffected, Amadeo went on singing his love songs. Now he celebrated a petite blonde in a gondola, who out of exquisite pleasure went to sleep as the gondolier rowed. Dubin had asked him what the song was about. To what end he did not sing. A few people crossing the outer stairs of the Rialto stopped to look at the boat. A woman with flowers waved at them. Dubin, facing an audience, felt self-conscious: glad-ragged goat of fifty-six courting a chick of twenty-two who'd be better served, at least in appearance, by the youth who rowed them. I should be rowing them.

Why, he asked himself, didn't this happen to me when I was twenty-five and had less to be self-conscious about? Why was I studying law when I should by some miracle have been in Venice? He felt false and hungered for privacy.

"Pull over," he said to the gondolier. "We want to get off."

"Oh, not yet, please," Fanny said.

"Pull over to the dock," Dubin said. "If the police come we may be ordered off the canal."

"You mak' meestake, signore," the gondolier replied, angered. "No one 'as the right to tell me when I weel work or what to do, if ees summer or weenter."

But Dubin, still uncomfortable, insisted and paid him off; to placate Fanny he included a healthy tip over an exorbitant fee. The handsome gondolier lifted his straw hat, bowing stiffly. His copper head of hair remained an enduring vision.

"I wish you hadn't done that, William," Fanny said on the embankment, her face tense. "So what if the guy was singing at me? It did no harm."

Dubin denied the singing had bothered him. He said he was restless. "There's so much to see in the city. We'll do better on foot. Distances are deceptive here."

He insisted on showing her where some extraordinary people had lived and worked. Close by, near the Goldoni Campo where Venetians gather in talky droves each evening, he pointed out the cortile where Marco Polo's house was supposed to have stood.

"He left Venice when he was a kid of seventeen for a fabulous journey throughout the East that ended a generation, plus a Venetian war, later, in a dank prison in Genoa. There he dictated a book of his travels, which is, among other things, a masterpiece of observation of an anthropological sort. In folklore he's become Marco Millioni, the comic liar, but in truth he said what he saw in a precise Venetian way, without poetry or passion, yet he saw well and kept the Asian world in his head until he was able to record it on paper, via the help of a literary hack he discovered in his cell. Two centuries later Christopher Columbus read the book and had one more reason to take off for what was to be the new world. Isn't it marvelous, Fanny, the way things tie up and turn out?"

"I read about it when I was a kid."

They then hurried, by ways Dubin knew, over stone bridges arching quiet canals, to the Moorish neighborhood where Tintoretto had lived and painted. Fanny and Dubin entered the church of Madonna dell'Orto to see his frescoes. Tintoretto was buried by the side of his favorite daughter Marieta. The biographer told Fanny about the painter—a self-educated imaginative man of genius.

"Some say he painted too much and wasn't as good as the Venetian best, but many of his pictures knock me cold. His miracles have the mysterious force of the miraculous. Marieta was herself a fine portrait painter who used to help in his studio dressed in the then equivalent of dungarees. She died young, at thirty, and he mourned her the short rest of his life. There's a legend that he painted her portrait as she lay dead."

"Didn't he paint her when she was alive?"

"Probably. This was something else—a last act of love." Dubin, as he talked, perspired.

"Maybe he flipped," Fanny said.

Reversing direction when they were once more outside, Dubin led her back to St. Mark's and then along the embankment to the Chiesa S. Maria della Pietà. Fanny was showing fatigue. He asked her if she wanted to rest but she said she would stay with it if this was the last of the sightseeing that morning. Dubin assured her it was.

In the church he said: "Here once stood a church orphanage with a music chapel for girl foundlings. Rousseau said there wasn't one of them without some considerable blemish but when they played their beautiful music he saw less and heard more. Vivaldi was known as 'il prete rosso'—he had auburn hair; he taught them to fiddle and sing, and confessed himself in waterfalls of stringed music. He worked there, off and on, for forty years, composed in a hurry, and earned thousands of ducats. Kings came to hear his concerts but in the end he ran afoul of the Pope's nuncio and fell out of favor, presumably for neglecting to say Mass; not to speak of his friendship with a singer and her sister who had traveled with him for fourteen years. He spent money like water and died a pauper. Like Mozart's, his grave has vanished, but given his music who needs it?"

Her face was weary. "Jesus, all you think about is biography."

"Not all," he said with a light laugh.

Dubin explained that since they were so near where men of this kind had lived it was only right to stop by and pay their respects. "I get this mind-blowing sense—as you say—of their lives and quality. I'm taken by those who celebrate life by making much of their own. It's a subtle altruism."

"If genius is your bag."

Dubin thought their genius made their humanity more clearly apparent. "One learns easily from their ordinary lives."

"I've got my own to live."

"To live it well—"

Though her mouth drooped, Fanny assented.

She said she was dead tired and could they now go home? "At least in the gondola it was a ride."

Dubin led her by short cuts back to the Hotel Contessa, but not before he had stopped off at the jeweler's he had visited earlier, to pick up a bracelet for Fanny, a twenty-two-carat gold band overlaid with a spiraling coil, which surprised and delighted her. She kissed him warmly as she admired the handsome bracelet on her extended arm. "I am really genuinely happy."

After a light lunch at the hotel, spaghetti al burro with a small bottle of non-gaseous mineral water for her; fettucine with red wine for Dubin, they went out again. Fanny, after the meal, had complained of cramps but they quickly disappeared. The day's beauty persisted: the flawless sky flared blue; canals encrusted with green sparkling light; and aura of Venice: expansive, enlivened—sense of island, sense of sea, of voyage.

To Dubin's surprise, though not Fanny's, a small fleet of pleasure gondolas appeared on the Grand Canal as though a carnival had been declared. Dubin offered to make restitution for the aborted ride of that morning by taking her out again but she, after seriously surveying the scene, shook her head. He suggested, if her cramps were gone entirely and she felt refreshed, the Accademia Gallery so she could see some paintings of Tintoretto's after the frescoes of that morning. But Fanny wanted to do some shopping first and Dubin went with her. She bought discreetly—a few modest presents for friends, which he offered to pay for because she had only fifty dollars with her. She would not accept.

Wherever they went she cast occasional glances behind. Dubin, looking where she had looked, saw bright sunlight between palazzi. If you saw through dark glasses would that people the world? Fanny removed her shades only to examine the colors of objects in the shops.

"You feel all right, Fanny?"

"I guess so. I guess what's on my mind is that I better have a bath and get some rest instead of tracking along with you to the museum. That is, if you expect me to have energy for this afternoon." She smiled affectionately.

"In that case do rest, my dear."

She asked him not to stay too long, and Dubin promised to be back at five.

He took the gallery picture by picture at first, viewing slowly; yet not always seeing: thinking of Fanny as Venus bathing, Venus revived. He stayed until half-past four and considered remaining longer to give her more time to herself—he had thoughtlessly worn her out with walking that morning; but Dubin hadn't the serenity to wait longer. He left the gallery and as he was recrossing the Accademia bridge, observed below, in a long black gondola on the sunlit canal, an auburn-haired girl with a gray-haired man, his arm draped around her shoulders. They were sitting with their backs to him, the girl resting her bronze head against the old man's breast. Dubin, watching in a confusion of emotion, called down from the bridge, "Maud—it's your father! Maud, it's me!" She did not turn. He hurried down fifty steps and ran, as Venetians watched, across the Campi Morosini and S. Angelo, then into Calle de la Mandola toward the water. After ten minutes he emerged at the Grand Canal close by the Rialto. Dubin arrived before the gondola and waited, winded—not sure what he could say or do or not do—for the boat to catch up with him. But when it floated toward the bridge, the gondola had in it only the gondolier poling it. Could this be the one he had seen? Another that followed contained two young women and a boy. Dubin looked into the distance and beheld no others.

He called in Italian to the gondolier: "Where are your passengers?"

The man blew his nose in the water and waved vaguely with his hand: "Al sinistro."

Dubin went hastily up the bridge steps and down the other side into the market streets. He hurried through crowds and on the first side street spied a red-haired girl about a block before him, but not the man. Was it his daughter? Though now fatigued Dubin hastened toward her. When he reached the corner she had disappeared, but the first house as he turned into the street was a pension, and he was convinced that was where she was. He thought of entering and seeking her out, then decided not to. If it was Maud it would be wise to talk to her alone. The last thing he needed was to confront his daughter in the presence of her lover—who else?

Seeing a bakery across the street, Dubin went in, tempting the reluctant baker with a thousand lire to produce a telephone book; then he called the pension number.

"Is there a signorina Maud Dubin registered there?"

The padrone wasn't sure and who was calling?

"Tell her her father, William Dubin."

"I can't tell her a thing if you're really her father because there's nobody here by that name."

"She's red-haired," Dubin explained, and the padrone laughed and said, "We've got two different redheads this week. Eh, signore, they're a deceptive lot. You can't tell what they really are until you've looked up their legs."

"I'm much obliged." Dubin lingered at the corner to see if either of the women came out and in less than thirty minutes both did; one a girl with hair dyed orange, the other a strawberry blonde with a middle-aged spectacled escort, neither so much as resembling Maud. Dubin, relieved, though irritated with himself for wasting time he could have used to better purpose, hurried back to the Rialto; since a vaporetto was about to depart and he was weary, he hastened up the gangplank.

It was an interminable trip. He arrived at San Marco at close to seven and broke into a hurried run. What a stupid waste, he thought in anger.

Dubin absently got off the elevator at the fourth floor and ran up to the next flight. Fanny was not in their room. He began to undress for a shower when it occurred to him that the adjoining room was giving off percussive sighs. As he tried the door it easily opened: the bed was made and unoccupied; but not the floor.

On the rug, crouched on hands and knees was the red-haired Amadeo, his fiery hairy ass not so handsome as it had seemed in tight Levi's; and under him, alas, lay Fanny. Dubin observed her gold-braceleted arm around the young man's strong back. Her eyes were shut, her face drawn; she looked, he thought, before slamming the door, like a woman of fifty.

The biographer felt as though he had wasted every cent of a large investment and stood on the verge of desolation. Afterward, when he forced himself to go back to the hotel room late that night, Fanny, in a man's workshirt and denim pants, taut-eyed, pale, her expression ill at ease, fearful, said she had waited hours for him to return, had got anxious, and decided he was simply not interested in her, when the gondolier knocked on the door.

"Why didn't you tell him to go fuck himself?" Dubin shouted. "Why did you so quickly and easily demean us?"

"Don't think you own me because you brought me to this phony city," she wept. "I did it because I was sorry for him. Because he's young," she said cruelly, "and I like his ass. And because you don't deserve me."

She accused him of loving his wife. "Why do I always get hooked with these married shmucks?"

After a dismal night when he woke often—listened for sobbing, a voice begging forgiveness, but heard silence, her breathing—hungry to embrace her, to blot out betrayal by making passionate love, Dubin slept as though awake and woke early. What will it profit me to fuck her in anguish? Fanny, her face in a pool of moist hair on her pillow, lay heavily asleep. In sleep her expression was dull, the face and aspect of a stranger. And what, my God, am I doing in the same bed with her, back to back, four thousand miles from home and work? He detested himself for falling into the hands of a child. Dubin felt in himself a weight of mourning he could not shove aside, or otherwise diminish. He was, he thought, ashamed at having offered himself to her to betray. He sensed a more intense commitment to the girl than he had guessed, or perhaps permitted, and wondered if he had been almost in love with her—sad pattern of long past. If that's so I'm glad to be done with it. Love—given who she is—given her promiscuity and my bad judgment—

would have led to something enduringly miserable. Better momentary pain than long heartbreak.

She woke as he was dressing, looked at him with one eye and reached for her tights. "I am," Fanny said, "just as moral as you."

"How would that work?"

"Don't give me that apeshit sarcasm."

He said he had asked an honest question.

"He needed me more than you ever did."

"His needs, assuming you're right, hardly constitute a requisite of morality."

"I have no obligations to you."

"Maybe you should have thought you had. Listen, Fanny," Dubin asserted, "I'm going out for a walk to air my brain. I'll have your breakfast sent up. You needn't get up yet, it's early. Maybe you ought to think a bit about yourself."

"All you wanted was cunt."

"If that's all I wanted I deserved what I got."

"What else did you want?"

"Passion, beauty—I want the world," Dubin shouted.

She fell back in bed and wept.

When he returned after two hours of aimless walking, aimless thought—not much relieved, conscious once more of his years, appearance, pain—Fanny had eaten and was reading in bed.

"What will you do?" he asked her dully.

"What do you mean?" Though her face was calm her voice wavered.

"What are your plans?"

She studied him unhappily. "I think I want to go to Rome and maybe Naples but all I have on me is less than fifty in traveler's checks and about ten in bills and change."

"And your air ticket home." He handed it to her.

"And my air ticket home."

"I've packed," Dubin told her, "and we're checked out. Why don't you dress and meet me across the street in Alitalia at eleven? I'm told there are two flights to Rome today."

"What time is the first?"

"I think at noon. If you decide not to go there you can have your ticket changed to the Air France late-afternoon flight to Paris and from there to New York."

"I have to see a friend in Rome." She said it as though the friend was female but he suspected a man.

He said he would meet her at eleven.

She arrived at eleven-fifteen in a tight black dressy dress and black pumps —a stunning woman, or so it seemed. Dubin resisted a resurgence of desire —"Carmen, il est temps encore"— born of frustration, the overthrow of his late happy adventure.

They greeted one another courteously. Fanny, before looking at him, glanced at the floor. Dubin nodded formally. She had on her blue glasses reflecting ceiling lights, and her Star of David—Jewish type she was meeting in Rome?—and still wore Dubin's handsome bracelet. Her hair was full, thick; to his surprise she had plucked the offending blond hairs on her chin. The girl could not have looked more attractive, or more innocent. Why? My need to absolve her? He was moved to say: "Let's forget it, Fanny—a serious mistake, no doubt of it, but not fatal. The moment's mistake; not for all time. Let's talk it over and maybe stay together the rest of the week? Perhaps there's something for us both to recover."

But he couldn't bring himself to say it. Pain is divisive. It spoke one word: shmuck.

At my age, Dubin modified it, all young women are desirable. I will keep it in mind and not hastily forgive her.

She paid for her ticket to Rome but the biographer insisted she accept a hundred in cash. "It isn't much, still if you're careful you can make it last a week. I suggest you not track around without money."

"You don't owe me anything."

He said he owed himself.

"Do you want the bracelet back?" She had slipped it off her wrist.

Dubin with a flip of his fingers refused to have it. "It's yours. I bought it for you with pleasure. Do what you please with it."

"You could give it to Maud."

"Maud will have to inspire her own bracelets."

"Do I deserve it?"

He laughed hoarsely.

"Are you punishing me with kindness?" she asked bitterly.

"That wouldn't be kind."

"I did it to hurt you," Fanny confessed.

"You hurt me."

She slipped her hand through the gold band. Fanny dug into her suede bag and returned *Sons and Lovers*. He accepted the book.

The baggage porter wheeled her suitcases to the dock on the canal. Dubin waited with her for the water taxi to return. It was another beautiful day, sky and water combining light; in the lagoon a scattering of islands they had planned to visit but never would. If one could embrace the day.

"You'll like Rome," he said.

"Where are you headed?"

He wasn't sure.

"I'll bet you hate me?"

"I wish we had done it differently."

"It was your fault as well as mine." Her mouth was firm.

He nodded gravely. "What will you do when you get back to the States?"

"I don't know. I might get married, maybe not."

"What do you believe in, Fanny?"

She reddened. "Do you mean do I believe in God?—I do."

"Do you believe in yourself?"

"I try."

Dubin, after a moment, advised her to go on with her studies.

She said they didn't teach in college what she wanted to learn.

"What do you want to learn?"

"I'm not sure."

"I see." He saw nothing.

The motoscafo was approaching.

"Take care, Fanny."

"Ciao. I appreciate what you did the night I got sick."

After hesitation they kissed lightly. Not better than nothing.

The motorboat slowly docked backward, piloted by a young capitano in lavender pants.

He wore a damp cigarette in the corner of his mouth and a white French sailor's cap with a red pompon. With gallant care the capitano assisted Fanny and her luggage into the chugging boat and seated her on a bench behind the wheel outside the cabin. There were no other passengers. He raised the accelerator, twirled the wheel, and at once they were off in the water in a wide churning arc.

When the boat hit mid-canal, Fanny, her hair flying around her shoulders, light in the sun, turned to wave goodbye to Dubin—to Venice? He lifted his hat, feeling as he did, glad at last to be alone, and had then his moment of elation.

Three

Q. What makes a clown sad?
A. Other clowns.

Dubin waits in the Swedish rain.

Marriage was his Walden—act to change his life; and what's past but
persists. Change you change your past, they say. I was the waiter's true
son, shared his inertia, fear, living fate—out of habit, compassion, im-
pure love.
Who am I, Pa?
What do you mean who you are? You are an educated boy.
Years after Hannah Dubin's death he seemed not to know what to do with
himself. If your train's on the wrong track every station you come to is the
wrong station. The wrong stops, year after year, were vocation and women
he couldn't make it with. It seemed to William Dubin he was not prepared
to invest a self in a better self—give up solitude, false dreams, the hold of
the past. The train chugged on: the wrong train.
In his twenties he was a half-reclusive too subjective romantic youth; yet
fed up with self-indulgent falling in love, living in reverie, trafficking in

heartache; worn out by what didn't happen: what he could not, or dared not, make happen.

Q. Why did it happen?
A. Who knows for sure? One day I took a chance, made a move, got involved. Life is to invest in life.

Dubin hadn't intended to fly to Stockholm. He'd been there with Kitty after Gerald had deserted the army in West Germany, and had fled to Sweden two years ago. After Venice the biographer had wanted nothing more than to take himself home and immerse his head in work; but that he was in Europe with Gerald nearby—a few hours into Scandinavia—made him want to see his adoptive son. Dubin had loved him as a child; he had intensely returned affection. The death of his father showed; the mother trying to be father had trouble being mother. It wasn't hard for her new husband to imagine himself the child. That was the first step to father. He had rescheduled his flight home and in a little more than five hours, shortly after an astonished view of Norway's fjords, had registered in a small Swedish hotel on the Skeppsbron, at the edge of the blue cold Baltic.

Strangers approaching each other in simple good faith: an act of trust was the imagined beginning. Though neither considered her/himself adventurous, each adventured. Kitty had invented a self-advertisement; and Dubin, though it was none of his business, had imaginatively responded. To that extent it was an arranged marriage: they had arranged it—he to escape his rooming-house existence, repetitive experience, boredom; he was thirty-one with little to show but fingers crossed, a self-critical Bronx Jew with no vocation he was pledged to. She was a troubled lonely ex-Episcopalian lady, a once and former doctor's wife, wanting a husband and protector of her child.
That's not all I want. I want joy, I want to live.
William Dubin promised life.

They promised love.
Kitty came to him with more than modest beauty; it was beauty she qualified. And the clinging remnants of trauma: modified mourning for the young dead, her ongoing burden, derived from a father a suicide at thirty-

four, and a husband in his fortieth year destroyed by leukemia—informed in September, buried before Christmas. Kitty, telling herself it needn't be, feared more of the same. She feared her son's imagined fate; soon the child held it against her. Against the will she taught him how to miss a dead father.

Let's call it half a widow she still was when I met her. She had shed deep mourning but mourning lingered where it knew the ground. And there's a presence besides the self, the self that opposes the self: she forgets where she is. Or what's to be done next. She unwinds very slowly from sleep or lack of sleep. Her level of frustration is low: she stamps her foot in a high wind. Or at a sudden blast of an automobile horn. Sometimes at a missed stitch in her knitting; or when she's misplaced her purse again. And laughs when she finds it. And praises her humor as though to defend it: You can tell from the way Gerald laughs that there's fun in me. She laughs at that; and laughs when she is embarrassed. Watching a movie she laughs twice to Dubin's once.

I took the chance. She took hers with me: an oldish youth in his long letters—man of appetites and hungers, yet the stranger who had responded I was, to her surprise, in her cast of characters.

Kitty said she trusted him but feared the future—nothing personal. The day before their wedding they walked in silence in Central Park. Searching his eyes at parting she said, I hope we aren't making a serious mistake. It isn't hard to.

Simply mistake would be serious enough.

Marriages can be difficult.

Was yours?

I was in love then.

Love is in life, in living, the bridegroom hopefully says. One gets in marriage, I imagine, what he earns.

Do you think so?

If she had asked out he thought he'd have let her go.

They were married in her best friend's living room; the bride, laughing breathlessly, wore a Mexican dress with flounced sleeves, pearls in her ears, and a gauzy rose shawl on her shoulders. It was a cold spring day.

Do you think I can wear a white sweater, I feel shivery?

Would you want a drink?

Later, I think.

She held in her hand a bouquet of white violets and wept silently during the ceremony, performed by her friend's father, an amiable judge. Kitty told Dubin afterward she always wept at weddings. Tears fill her eyes on ceremonial occasions. And when people go forth to distant places. Everyone's loss of someone's presence, significant or small, wakens a sense of prior loss.

Q. How did you feel?

A. Inspired.

Q. In truth?

A. I could come up with no other feeling.

Q. I'm sure. What of afterward, what we used to call the honeymoon?

A. We spent the first week moving into a new apartment. She had asked me to consider living in hers and I thought it was better not to: Let's both start with something new.

Not long before the wedding Dubin had made the acquaintance of her obsolete birthmark: for a while appeased, revived for him as a living fact. Kitty permitted, suppressing apology, yet managing to suggest damaged goods—if not impaired passion. He accepted the given.

As she undressed, she confessed the blemish: a dark skin discoloration that runs up my left inner thigh and spills out on my buttock.

Why do you call it blemish?

Birthmark, she said, with half a smile. It inhibited me sexually when I was young.

Does it now?

Not since Nathanael. He ridiculed me for making so much of it, called it an error in pigmentation. Inverse pride to make much of it. He told me to walk around naked in the bedroom with the shades up. When I wouldn't he pulled my underpants off. I was as angry as relief let me be. Once when we were alone on a beach in Maine he asked me to strip off my bathing suit, and eventually I did.

Dubin said it was a birthmark, not the Scarlet Letter. Why should you think you had earned it?

It's my nature. I don't understand why it should bother me in your presence, William, but it seems to. I have to tell you. They kissed and slid into bed. After a while Kitty said she didn't think she could come. Dubin held on. She begged him to satisfy himself; then cried, Harder, William, I'm coming.

The waterfront, through his hotel window, was lined with white craft: sailboats, sightseeing launches, a two-masted schooner; an ice-breaker waiting for winter. A smoking one-stack steamer was leaving for Finland. The whistle boomed.

How easy it is to go away. He watched the boat move slowly out to sea. What would I do alone in a foreign country?

Dialing Gerry to say he was in Stockholm, he got back a high-pitched busy signal; so he slipped on his raincoat and walked out into the narrow high-walled streets of the Old Town. The biographer asked at the address of a Mrs. Linder for Gerald Dubin and was told no one by that name lived there. There had been a Gerry Willis.

"That's his name," Dubin told her. "Willis was his father's name—he's entitled to it. I'm his adoptive father, William Dubin, a biographer."

The Swedish lady had begun speaking English at his approach; she said Gerry Willis had moved out a month ago. Her daughter might have his address. She might not. He could try returning at seven, when she came home from work. The lady shrugged. Would he excuse her now? She had supper to prepare.

Did she know whether Gerry was short of funds? "Was that why he moved?"

"I can't say if this is true. I think he likes to move, he has that nature. Our socialist government provides well the American deserters. It comes from our taxes."

He lifted his hat in apology. Dubin said he would return at seven and went back to the hotel.

Restless in his chilly small room, he went again into the city. Stockholm, where he explored, exhibited an austere dignity of space and proportion. He liked the well-formed stately buildings of past centuries. He liked the broad clean canals between sections of the city connected by street-level causeways and bridges. Dubin felt the melancholy of the gray-blue mid-autumn sky, as though some hidden Norse God, if not Ingmar Bergman, pointed eternally to winter, warning Swede and stranger it was more than a season; it was a domain.

Having little to do but wait and think more than he cared to, the biographer embarked on an hour's excursion by launch on the waterways. The boat passed along canals, under bridges, sailed by villas close to the water, old red-brick factories, parks lined with yellow-leaved maples and yellowing pines.

He had been idly watching a man and woman a few rows in front of him in the all but empty motor launch. The man was a middle-aged Indian sitting with a long-faced attractive white girl of twenty-three or so. She might be English, a darkish blonde, motionless, reflective, as though she might think them into an embrace. They looked at each other and looked away. He seemed self-conscious, shy. The girl smiled gently. Neither moved close to the other though their feeling was intense. They talked in whispers, then sat silent. The biographer watched until it grew dark and raindrops splashed on the window of the launch. It seemed to Dubin that there were only three on the boat, the shy couple and himself. They hadn't touched though they wanted to. When the boat docked he left quickly.

Once she went to Montreal to visit a friend hurt in a ski accident. Kitty traveled by train and when she returned Dubin was waiting for her at Grand Central. Coming up the ramp, she walked right at him, yet passed without seeing him. Angered, he called her name. It took her fifteen seconds to recognize her husband. I'm sorry, I got very little sleep on the train. They kissed formally.

Dubin, carrying her bag, asked her if she knew she was married. How can I forget? she said, and laughed. They stopped to kiss.

He asked her to sew a button on his trench coat. Kitty took the button and put it in her plastic button box. She said she would sew it on one morning if he left the coat home. Dubin left it there for two weeks, then wore it without the button.

She quietly talked of her first husband in a seemingly detached way. In Gerald's room there was a picture of Nathanael taken by a *Daily News* photographer: of an intern in an oilskin raincoat attending a man lying on his back after an accident in a wet street.

That was taken years before I met him. In college I cut my leg in a fall off a bike and he stitched and bandaged it. I still have the scar. I was an undergraduate when we were married. Nathanael knew a lot and taught me to think a little. I'm naturally skeptical and he helped me to a more solid intellectual base. He had me reading philosophy for a while; he used to read it the way I read fiction. Though I loved him I wasn't sure about getting married at twenty. I married him, a pretty uncertain woman, but he helped focus me. I wish he had encouraged me to do something serious about a vocation.

I had Gerald when we were three years married. I was nervous with a baby, but it wasn't hard to calm down with a doctor around. Afterward there was a time I thought the marriage was on the rocks. We were both irritable and I felt I was a bad mother. Then we got along well and I was not a bad mother. You can imagine how I felt when he died at forty. I know I've told you this often, but every time I tell you I have to.

Dubin said he was listening.

One rainy morning he shouted, Why the hell don't you sew the button on my coat? If you can't, or don't want to, bring it to a tailor.

Her eyes were shut as though she was concentrating on the button. I have it in my button box. I *will* sew it on. But she didn't.

One winter's night Gerald was sick with the flu; his temperature hit 105° and Kitty was frantic. She telephoned the doctor but couldn't reach him. Fearing the child would go into a convulsion, she ran with him from one room to another. Dubin, also made anxious by the illness of children, said they ought to call an ambulance. Kitty thought it would take too long to come. She wanted to wrap the child in a blanket and get him to the hospital in a taxi. Dubin then looked up fever in a medical adviser she had bought after her husband's death, and began to rub the shrieking child's naked body with alcohol. Kitty held her hands over her ears. Within minutes Gerald's temperature had dropped. Kitty sewed on Dubin's button.

In sex she needed, Kitty said, a man of patience. He provided, plus whatever other talents a man like Dubin had. They were both limited sexually; so apparently had Nathanael been. What she had solved with him she had to resolve with Dubin. There were times he lived on little and ate desire. What she missed seemed not to rankle her.

In bed one night Kitty said, You mean a lot to me, William.

How much?

Because I haven't put Nathanael out of my mind doesn't diminish my feeling for you.

Is it love?

That was the wrong question: She said, I'm not sure what or how much of something is something, philosophically speaking.

Speaking simply, like now in bed?

She admitted she couldn't say she loved anybody without qualification. One had to be honest.

When she asked him, Dubin said he loved her.

Without qualification?

With love.

Sometimes as she was saying one thing he knew from the way she looked at him that she was reflecting on another.

Dubin waited in the small hotel lobby until ten to seven, then walked back into the Old Town and got Gerry's address from his former landlady's plain and distant daughter. He went in the rain to the number she had given him, also in the Old Town, a heavy-shuttered stone house in a curved badly lit cobblestone-paved alley; though he rang repeatedly and rapped on the heavy wooden door, no one responded. He vainly called Gerry's name. He called for Gerry Willis and Gerald Dubin and got no one. Dubin waited in the low wet dripping doorway for someone to come into the alley. He watched the water pour out of the iron downspout of the house and run along a stone drain into the street.

There were better nights for waiting, yet he felt not bad about it. Here he was with nothing else to do. If he gave time generously maybe the waiting would end well. He'd been thinking of Gerald as a child, their mutual need: he needed a father, I wanted a son. Dubin nostalgically remembered their affection. He wondered if Gerry did. But what can he know of me as I am now, or I of him? One guesses at essences—identities. Maybe love is a means of making a useful assumption about another person. Yet once I was his father; he let me be.

He rang, listening in the drumming rain to silence within, then left the alley and sought a telephone in a bar. Dubin opened his address book and dialed the American Deserters Committee. The secretary, a Texan, answered. He looked up Gerald Dubin and said he was registered but hadn't visited the office for a year. "He wrote and asked us to stop sendin the newsletter."

"Any address for Gerry Willis?"

"Not that I have iny record of. Some men get depressed here," the Texan said. "They hate the cold climate and the cold Swedes, not to mintion the government bureaucracy that has you fillin out forms every time you want to pee or lose a pound of weight."

The man said that not everybody got acclimatized to Sweden. Some could not get used to the weather, or the language, or find a satisfactory job, or get on with their education. "They git druggy or go ape and are locked up in prison. I tell them if they can't make it here they sure as hell aren't goin to make it in the U.S. of A."

"You don't remember Gerry?"

"I honestly wish I could."

Dubin returned to the shuttered house, rang again, and waited until he was tired of waiting. He slipped a damp note under the door and left the alley.

The rain had turned into a cold drizzle. The biographer momentarily removed his hat to feel the wet on his face. If he doesn't call tonight I'll try again in the morning.

He felt he hadn't minded not seeing Gerry tonight; he was not much in a mood to. Dubin wondered if he had come to see the boy so he could tell Kitty he had stopped off in Stockholm to visit him. He wanted her to be grateful to him before he lied to her about Venice.

She woke him to explain herself: her father had killed himself when she was a child—after his wife had betrayed him. Yet I loved her till she deserted me for a lover she went to Europe with. I could no more do that to a child than I could destroy it. My grandmother disliked her. I've only once been to her grave. I want you to know what my young life was like. There's a gap in me I will never fill. I've never slept well since I was little. Either a gene is missing or I'm afraid to for understandable reasons. But the world is very real to me and I don't want to make it seem unreal. I've always been honest with myself. What you won't admit, you never understand.

Nathanael loved me more than anyone else ever has.
Including your grandmother?
You know what I mean.

Q. She mythologized him?
A. Whatever it was, there were times I felt I had married him.

Mimosa, she said, is always the beginning of spring.
One spring morning she suffered a miscarriage.
My dear baby, Kitty wept.
It was a fetus, he said, astonished by the depth of her grief, guilt, mourning.

95

No more death, *please*, no more.

He did not ask her to define death but promised no more. Nathanael packed his suitcase and moved down the street. She spoke of him rarely now, perhaps to make a point about a short life, or something about the nature of marriage. Simply a sufficient time had passed.

A year later Maud was born; Kitty was very happy to have a girl yet promised Dubin a boy of his own. He said he thought of Gerry as his son. She said she believed him.

He delighted in his daughter. Went often to look at her as she slept in her room; enjoyed her childhood. She called for him when she had had a nightmare. He pressed her warm shivering body to him. He kissed her head; she kissed his lips. He read to her; loved her red hair, often combed it.

Kitty slept better. The house was in order. There were parties, house guests, visitors. She was good with the kids: sewed their clothes and knitted them woolen hats. She lived easily in their world. And she baked, made jellies, put clothes in garment bags, watered the house plants, nightly wiped a round oak table with soaped sponge to give it a driftwood quality.

Having a family satisfied a harsh hunger in Dubin. He relished his wife's warm womanly body. And Kitty played the harp for him. She drew it down on her shoulder and with dancing movements of the arms plucked the strings.

Though she said she hardly had time to think of herself, she kept herself informed, judged public events well. She defined things accurately—Nathanael had insisted on careful definitions. She was analytic, skeptical— questioned what Dubin too easily accepted or inaccurately explicated. She hated obfuscation, hypocrisy, ignorance. She praised clear thinking and tested his thought the way Nathanael had tested hers. She analyzed Dubin's behavior aloud as Nathanael had analyzed hers.

Q. You resented him?

A. I resented her.

She lived with her fears—could not live without them—lived above them. She did not indulge in self-pity. What she had to do, ultimately she did. He gave her credit. Kitty wished she was a braver person; he said she was brave enough. That day she deposited what remained of Nathanael's life insurance in their joint savings account. Dubin said he didn't want Nathanael's money there. She withdrew it.

One morning she was formal with him, caught in uncertainty, trying to be calm. Kitty stood by the bedroom window in her nightgown.

He asked her what was the matter.

She smiled no smile to speak of, looked at him as if she weren't seeing him. It took her a while to reply in a strained voice. William, you have to palpate my breast; I think I felt a lump.

She slid into bed, drawing her nightgown over her chest, and he, trying not to think of it as a momentous act, pressed his fingers into her left breast, then gently into the right. He did not like to be doing this.

What am I supposed to feel?

A hard little lump the size of a pea.

Is that what you felt?

I thought so.

Kitty shut her eyes as he tried again to locate the lump, then, without expression, watched his face. Dubin dipped his fingers into her flesh, his eyes growing wet at the thought of the fragility of life. After a while he had found no lumps.

She then felt both breasts carefully; her mouth trembled in relief. Thank you.

He shaved with a mild erection.

At night as they lay together after making love, Kitty confessed her life with Nathanael hadn't gone all that well. He could be very hard on me.

Dubin said he had understood that; had put it together from things she had told him about Nathanael.

Once he hit me, she confessed; he said he hadn't meant to.

Dubin muffled a laugh.

Would you hit me, William?

If you hit me.

Kitty, laughing, later whispered, Don't ever leave me.

Q. It was about this time you got into biography?

A. He was still doing obituaries for the *Post* and book reviews for *The Nation*. He was tired of the obits but stayed with them because he liked summarizing people's lives. The editor had asked him to emphasize successful careers but he sometimes managed to slip in a failed life.

After Maud was born Dubin had to make a better living. Kitty, concerned about their finances, suggested he go back to practicing law. He felt it made her nervous to think her husband had given up his profession. He'd consider it, he said, if he could be in law without being a lawyer. She then suggested teaching. He doubted he knew enough to face serious students.

One morning as he was typing out the obituary of a poet who had killed himself by jumping from the George Washington Bridge into the icy Hudson—a fragment of ice floe, like a bloody raft, carried his body down the river—Dubin felt as he wrote that the piece had taken on unexpected urgency. The dead poet was terribly real. He felt an imperious need to state his sorrow, understanding, pity—wanted with all his heart to preserve the man from extinction. Dubin, you can't relight lives but you can re-create them. In biographies the dead become alive, or seem to. He was moved, tormented, inspirited; his heart beat like a tin clock, his head aching as though struggling to pop through the neck of a bottle in which it had been enclosed, imprisoned. He felt for a brilliant moment as though he had freed himself forever.

Afterward Dubin knew he had discovered—affirmed—his vocation: the lives of others, there was no end to them. He sensed a more vital relation between books and life than he had allowed himself to feel in the past. He felt that the pieces of his own poor life could be annealed into a unity. He would understand better, be forewarned. He felt he had deepened, extended his life; had become Dubin the biographer.

A month later he showed Kitty his short life of Schubert. She said it was a moving piece of writing but oh so sad. Dubin told her Schubert had once said he didn't know any cheerful music. He wasn't listening, Kitty said. A short life is a short life. He was dead at thirty-one. I'd rather not think of it, she said.

He searched for a restaurant amid a block of stores along a sidewalk that ran level, as the cobblestone street sank in a slant below the sidewalk. Dubin, thinking his thoughts, failed to notice he had to go down a double step before crossing the street. On the unexpected step he lost his footing, groped in the air, fell in disbelief; therefore with a semblance of calm. As he lay in the wet gutter the pain rose so thickly he had to struggle to keep from passing out. He had hit the cobblestones with his knees before pitching forward. Through the nausea and dry retching Dubin felt he had broken both legs. He lay in the street shivering and writhing. If someone had touched him he would have shrieked.

It seemed to him a man appeared in the rain, staring distantly at him, then walked off.

"Gerald," he called.

The man did not look back.

"Help me, I'm in pain."

"Who are you?" someone said in Swedish but did not wait for an answer. In a moment he had vanished. No one assisted him. He wasn't sure anyone had gone by. Dubin lay in the street until the cold wet penetrated his clothes. Fearing he would be run over, he managed to pull himself up. His trousers were shredded, knees dripping blood. He got up the steps, limped into a bar and found the men's room. There, after removing his soiled raincoat and torn pants, Dubin cleaned himself as best he could. He felt depleted, dizzy. In the mirror he beheld a stone-gray face disgusted with him for having fallen; for being in Stockholm rather than home; for having gone through the waste of Venice.

Kitty had said the city was no place to bring up children. When Dubin received an advance for *Short Lives* she added to it from Nathanael's insurance and they put down earnest money on the house in Center Campobello. She had for years wanted to go back to living in the country. Dubin hadn't wanted to leave the city but afterward felt he ought to shake up his life— get out of New York and do differently with the self. Afterward he became a good husbandman: cleaned, painted, repaired. Once he kicked the dead furnace into life; Dubin Prometheus, bringer of heat in a cold house.

There were weekend drives with the kids into small towns in the Adirondacks, around sunlit dark forests. They crossed Lake Champlain by ferry, into Vermont, and rode through quiet country towns with slender white-spired churches. Dubin enjoyed the sight of white rocks scattered in the beds of swift-flowing mountain streams. On secondary roads they passed long grasslands, dairy farms, groves of sugar maples. Once they drove to the top of a lookout mountain and beheld around them clusters of ancient mountains boiled up all over the state. Present at the creation, said Dubin. I love to see these sights with you, Kitty said.

At home the children were into physical lives, she called it. Their schooling could be better but they read at home and didn't seem to be missing much. Dubin's work went well; he was earning a living. He was glad they had left the city, felt he had played it right: a marriage could start anywhere and grow into a marriage. They talked in bed in the winter dark, confiding to each their lives. They embraced in the house when they chanced up on one another. He was at peace in his mirror.

There were, on the other hand, serious differences of temperament, reaction, rhythm: Dubin's wife could be overly intense, reserved, impatient under stress, punitive, too often anxious. He could be egoistic, time-bound, impulsive, defensive, too often anxious. Though they were alike in more ways than they had guessed; or grew to be alike; often the unmatched elements of their temperaments and tastes—disjunctions, he called them—caused tension, disagreements, quarrels. Her senses were highly charged conductors. She knew before she knew; he got the message more slowly.

Another self, a different self: unexpected noises irritated her. Kitty could hear water dripping in nearby rooms through locked doors and thick walls. In an unfamiliar house or hotel room she would lie awake listening to sounds that had waked her. Sometimes her restlessness woke Dubin and he joined her in the long trek to daylight. She shifted to the edge of the bed and lay still as he lamented his loss of precious sleep, then his fate. She sweated in mild heat and shivered in mild cold. An eyelash she could not quickly pick off her tongue would make her momentarily desperate. She was assailed by the smell of decaying things: food in the refrigerator, old shoes, old clothes, old closets. A close room compelled her, gasping, to throw open a window. A whiff of cheap perfume in a crowd set her teeth on edge. Kitty disliked body odors—abolished her own, kept Dubin informed of his. She passed gas immaculately; after an emission by him she sincerely asked what the smell was. Nathanael, he imagined, had never farted. She was touchy when her vitality was low, the biographer, when his biography was failing him. Her fears diffused her energy, scattered purpose. She regretted a lifetime of part-time jobs. Diligently she smelled the burners, complaining that the gas dried out her throat.

Don't smell them, for Christ's sake.

I can't help it. Don't humiliate me.

Her familiar insecurities made him impatient, preachy; Dubin's incensed her. They argued about taste, habit, idiosyncrasy. Both guarded their defenses. There were differences concerning timing, efficiency, sex. Don't explain sex to me, Kitty cried. Then explain it to me, Dubin shouted. Don't be hysterical, she said. He felt confined by her limitations; she was diminished by his smallnesses.

You yell so you don't have to reason.

You listen with your tongue.

You have a tin ear. You keep your mind in your pocket.

You talk like a bitch.

I'm glad, I always wanted to be a bitch.

When he nitpicked past the point of no return she smashed a dish on the kitchen counter and stalked out of the room. Dubin slammed doors. She repaid slow burn with cutting silence. Once she flung a small flower pot at him, a single geranium. It broke against the wall and the pink flower landed on his hat on a chair. Both laughed at the sight. After he had taught her the magic language Nathanael had failed to teach her, she stopped throwing things: they could swear at each other. Don't give me that shit, Kitty cried. If he swore she stamped her foot. You're alienating the children.

When she explained him to himself Dubin would yawp. Nor did Kitty want to hear who she was as he saw her. What may have begun as a disagreement became a quarrel. They sometimes tore into each other, going farther than they wanted. Each, then, suffered.

More or less, they educated one another concerning their natures. As a rule, not always, their arguments ended with apologies. He had a sense of not having been wise, of having stupidly got into a useless situation. Apology was a continent Dubin slowly explored. Kitty apologized more rarely: he made more mistakes.

As time went by he persuaded himself not to feel excessive guilt for not feeling total affection for her in every circumstance; and he taught himself, after an argument, to recover affection more quickly than he had in the past; she could be persuaded by a show of feeling. He had noticed she recovered evenness of temper faster than he: when Kitty had thought through a quarrel —understood cause and effect—she communicated by quietly asking what he wanted for supper. Or asked his opinion about something. Each learned to skirt the other's more touchy sensitivities. Dubin studied what most upset her and gave up attempting to justify himself under certain circumstances. The key to a quick end to a quarrel was to cut out accusation. He taught himself to accept her as she was; she lived according to her construction. He grew better at making peace after he began writing his biographies. Kitty characterized their marriage as "fairly good." He did not ask her to say how good it had been with Nathanael.

Whatever concessions she made about the quality of their relationship she went on defending "the real"—said she had to, as though a false fact was a poisonous snake in the living room. She still had to define, delineate, measure, weigh the truth of idea, issue, experience. She pointed at inexactness as though unmasking an illusion—a monster—seemed at times the undying foe of metaphor: I can't help it, have to say a thing's a thing. For her Dubin learned to count accurately, tell the time right, recall a number nearly correctly. If he slipped—if he said, Today I saw an eight-foot sailor, she nervously countered: *I* never saw one—as though her statement eliminated a threat to existence. Now the stars would not fall. From time to time she defined the true nature of their relationship, still regretting—five, ten, or more years after their marriage—that she hadn't been in love with him when they were first married—not *truly* in love. If they had been in love, certain things would have been easier, might have gone better. There would have been fewer spats—bad for the children. We would have been gayer, certainly less tense. I was gayer with Nathanael. And more carefree in sex.

Dubin doubted it: Love, once you have it, whether it comes with intensity and stays, or in slow building and stays, is love. He said he hadn't much use for the kind of honesty that crapped on experience because it had occurred one way and not another.

Kitty's color deepened. I say how I see things. Nathanael appreciated my honesty.

I wish to hell he'd stay in his grave.

She strode out of the room.

Later she returned, distraught. Forgive me, Kitty said, slipping her arms around him—I love only you. Do you love me?

Q. You felt it was love?
A. I loved her, or thought I did. In any case I felt I had become the kind of man who could love her.
Q. A self-flagellating type?
A. I'm speaking of love.
Q. That you can't swear was there?
A. Nothing is ever always or entirely there.

Q. You sound like Kitty.

A. She taught me.

In her middle age, when the children had departed the house, Kitty Dubin was an attractive woman with good features, a slender slightly heavy body, the flesh on her belly striated by three pregnancies. Her slim legs were veined, the long feet still elegant. She painted her toenails. Her dark hair was lightened by strands of gray. After wearing a topknot for years she cut her hair short, often talked of touching it up but never did. That seemed pretense to her. Her voice had dropped an octave. Her eyes were spirited, the left more reflective; the right more uncertain. She drank more freely than she had as a young woman, and was less concerned about the use of four-letter words. He had hoped she would kick smelling the gas burners, but she hadn't. She doubted she would. Kitty regretted growing older, and though she was not unreasonably pessimistic about life, seemed not unhappy. She would touch a handkerchief to her eyes when she looked at old snapshots of the children. Apropos of nothing, or seemingly so, she said to Dubin, I'll never forget how unhappy I was as a widow. Do you consider yourself happily married? he asked. More so than many; not as happy as some, was her judgment. She predicted she would die before him and Dubin vehemently denied it.

He swallowed a brandy and left the bar. Sickened by his fall, he wanted nothing to eat. This is not my night. Dubin thought he would go to the hotel, smear ointment on his knees, get into bed. No taxis were visible as he limped down the dark street. Approaching the alley where Gerry lived, Dubin saw a man in a long army coat emerge in the rain; he wore a flat-topped wide-brimmed hat and heavy shoes. The biographer thought he recognized the stride but couldn't believe the hat and long hair tied in a ponytail. The man stepped into a darkened shop doorway to light a cigarette and Dubin was at once moved by him: it was Gerald. His face uneven, eyes deep-set, dampened by life. The back of his neck had been scarred by boils when he was a boy. Kitty said Gerald resembled her, but Dubin couldn't see it. Whoever he looked like it wasn't William Dubin. They had drifted apart. I wasn't as attentive as I should have been.

At twelve, as though he'd had a prevision of the complexity of life, Gerald had become quiet and secretive. He had grown up a loner, not much responding to those who tried to tempt him into sociability. What have I done to that child? Kitty wanted to know. What have I done to him? I wanted him to be a man before he was out of diapers. Because of me too much of his childhood was a time of mourning. I dealt with him with a self I had little sense of. How selfish I was, how inconsiderate.

She blamed fate that she and Dubin were both without parents, relatives —a family to be part of. The children had no grandparents to visit, confide in, learn from; no cousins to play with, or remember. My grandmother meant the world to me. She made the difference.

They had no religion in common. Dubin said they had. I don't mean humanism, Kitty answered. That's not enough for kids. God is for those who find him, Dubin said. No, he has to be taught. Some people have to be helped to religious discovery. Gerald is one.

Q. Tell me, Dubin, what did the boy really mean to you?

A. I saw myself, in his eyes—a fatherly type. He seemed to trust me. I taught him to play chess. We walked together. He fed me mathematics, I described the new astronomy, as much as I knew it. He listened to every sentence. I told him jokes. I sometimes thought I had taught him to laugh. He was a tall boy with a well-formed head and uneasy thoughtful eyes. One day he asked me to adopt him and we kissed. His name was legally changed to Gerald Dubin. Kitty approved but I worried about it. He was so much his father it may have seemed like betrayal.

Will the earth explode, William?

We won't be around if it does.

I'm afraid to die, aren't you?

Dubin said he wanted his allotted time.

Do you love me? the boy asked.

Yes. You must know that.

As much as Maud?

Yes.

He seemed to doubt it.

Does Mother love me as much as Maud?

Yes.

He seemed to doubt it.

One day when he was fifteen Gerald accused them of not understanding him: I'm different than you think.

Why don't you explain yourself to us?

I try but can't.

You can't explain?

You don't understand.

He seemed fearful after he had said it, ran up to his room; stayed there much of the time. When Dubin came up to talk with him, he listened in silence, staring out of the window, then formally thanked him for coming.

He needed a lot more time than I gave him.

Q. Dedication makes displacement?

A. Important things to do, especially in work, reduce or nullify others. I tried to balance things off—father with children, my needs with Kitty's, not always well done. You think you have three balls in the air but when you count there's one.

Kitty criticized him for withholding himself from them. Every time I suggest something to do you resent breaking away from work. I'm not so sure you want a family.

He swore he wanted a family.

Maybe you oughtn't to have got married, so you could give your life to your biographies.

Marriage was his constitutional right.

We hardly talk any more.

They talked at long length in the dead of night.

Don't be sarcastic. You're obsessed with work.

Better than with alcohol.

When will you take time to live?

Writing is a mode of being. If I write I live.

Hemingway at least fished after he wrote.

I walk.

Why can't we all walk together?

We can on Sundays.

You don't have to work so hard or long, Kitty argued. I doubt you really enjoy being with people. I have needs other than solitude, certainly the kids have. You're either reading or writing biographies, or thinking your biographical thoughts.

The kids know their father loves them.

Love is being there; it means giving affection.

Much of his past had been badly used, Dubin often had to explain. Don't begrudge my taking time to do difficult work. To do it well one has to do it many times. You have to make time or steal it.

You steal it from us all.

He read her a note about Thomas Carlyle from a biography he was reading. His wife, Jane Welsh Carlyle, wrote to a friend: "All he asked, was, simply, that his wishes come first, his comfort be put before all else, the household so arranged that his sleeping, walks, hours of work or reverie should be when and how he wanted them." Think of that when you criticize me.

What a disgusting man, said Kitty.

Then there was Gustav Mahler.

She covered her ears with her hands: I don't want to hear.

She complained there was little conversation at the table unless she initiated it. You can listen to us speak and hear nothing. I can tell from your eyes you've gone for a walk in your book.

He mistreated holidays, she said. After Christmas-morning exchange of presents—Christmas was for Gerald and Channukah for Maud; Kitty said she wanted her to be a Jewish child out of respect for her father—Dubin went back to his desk to work.

He wrote a note to himself: I do few things perhaps to do one thing well.

Gerald kept a loose-leaf diary whose pages he occasionally tore out and burned in the fireplace. Once he handed Kitty a poem and she wept to be given the gift. He never gave her another.

He fed his words into the fire, telling his parents little or nothing of what he was thinking or doing; as though, if he did, he had betrayed himself.

But he talked to Maud, who kept his secrets. When they were talking together they stopped at Dubin's approach. Maud, he wanted to say, don't be corrupted by him. I am your loving father.

Yet there were times when Gerry seemed to want an adult to talk to. He would appear in Dubin's study before going to school, his book bag strapped to his shoulders, to say why last night's TV news had sickened him. Not why his flight had begun and where it was taking him.

If Dubin spoke about himself as a boy Gerry would listen and leave without comment. One lonely youth was all he could abide.

Dubin asked him to say what was troubling him. He wouldn't say why he didn't say.

We were once close—tell me what happened?

The boy stood stiffly silent, the back of his neck inflamed. With impassioned silence he answered nothing.

If we don't talk I can't tell you what I know, Dubin said. What good is my experience if you won't let me share it with you?

That's your problem. I don't have any interest in autobiography.

That's your problem.

If Dubin extended his hand, Gerald stepped back.

He had unwillingly become distant to the boy, matching a distance equal to his own from Dubin; as if he had held up a mirror to a mile and made it two between them.

I overdid mourning, Kitty lamented. He backed away from me. And from you because of me. I know he loves you, William, but I can't explain the change in him, except that at a certain point the person I was—I am—weighed too heavily on him. You're your screwy self a day too long and one or another of your kids takes off without telling you why or waving goodbye. Once he began to change he changed as though he was pursued by change.

Dubin, standing silent on the stairs, overheard her talking to Gerald in his room when he was home from college at Thanksgiving, during his freshman year.

She was asking him in a loud whisper to trust her, confide what ailed him.

My pain in the gut, Gerald replied. I hate the stupid war. I know I'll have to fight in it sooner or later. I hate the goddamned stupid military. I hate how America is destroying the world.

Things will improve, Kitty pleaded. Don't take everything so brutally hard. One must live, the world goes on. A man should enjoy his life or what's it for? Please, Gerald.

He rushed down the stairs.

Dubin, embarrassed to be standing there, stepped to the wall as he ran by.

You've got to live, Kitty, leaning over the banister, shouted after her son.

At lunch she smiled at Gerald, her lips compressed, eyes uneasy. He dipped chunks of bread into the soup and sucked them. Dubin, peacemaker, rattled on about the miserable youth of Edgar Allan Poe; his mother had died young. Kitty asked him to change the subject.

My son the stepson, early exile from self. He is contemptuous of war but won't, after quitting graduate school, register as a conscientious objector, because he can't define himself as one. He insists on accuracy of definition.

You're close to one in spirit, his mother says. You certainly are in principle.

Close enough is not good enough, says the honest lad. Dubin dislikes the mother for her son's passionate honesty.

Gerry considers flight to Canada as a war resister but decides against it. He is drafted and shipped to West Germany for training prior to Vietnam. He is kept on in Germany as a Signal Corps instructor. Three months before his term of enlistment is over, the night before he's due to be flown in an army transport to a jungle in Southeast Asia, he goes AWOL in a Cessna to Sweden.

Whose fate is he running after?

Gerald Willis stepped out of the dripping doorway, exhaling wet smoke. He was a broad-shouldered tall man who walked with a heavy-footed tread. Dubin had last seen him still wearing part of his army uniform and a short haircut going to seed. After crossing the narrow street walled by old houses, the biographer followed him a few paces along a thin strip of sidewalk, then called his name.

The youth swung around in alarm as Dubin, his arm extended, hastened forward. Gerald peered at him in disbelief. "Jesus, William, is it really you?"

"Who else?" He offered his hand. Gerald shook it vaguely and Dubin pumped his. The youth, in his odd hat and long hair, looked like no one he knew.

"What are you here for? What do you want?" His voice had the tone of a man objecting.

Dubin said he had flown in from Venice a few hours ago and had been looking for him since.

"What for?"

"What for, he says." He tried to laugh.

"Sweden isn't next door to Italy. It touches the North Pole. What's on your mind, William?"

"Not much. I was in the vicinity, you might say, and decided to come to see you."

"Why didn't you wire? I might have been in Lapland."

Dubin explained he had come on impulse.

"Is my mother with you?"

"Not this time."

"Anything wrong?"

He didn't think so.

Gerald, working his shoulders, blew his white breath on his wet hands. They stared at one another. Dubin asked him if he wanted a drink. Gerald shook his head. "You look like hell."

Dubin described the spill he had taken near a square with a church. "I missed my step and hit the street on both knees and my belly. I'm not comfortable. Is there somewhere we can sit? Have you eaten yet?"

He knew the question was useless: Gerry would not sit and talk. With him he felt as he often had: a man trying to finish a puzzle with a piece that never fitted. Here was this haunted house needing a door or window and the last piece he had was a hand holding a wilted flower.

"I have to do something. Give me your number, I'll call in the morning."

Dubin said what had to be done had to be done. "Did you find my note under your door?"

Gerald shook his head.

"I see by your nameplate that you've changed your name."

"It's my name." He seemed not to be sure. His breath misted, vanished.

"I wish you the best, whatever the name. I'm not taking offense. I consider you my son, or why did I adopt you when you were a kid?"

He felt off-balance, annoyed with his defensive tone. If I have any eloquence, in his presence I lose it. Those who don't approve me diminish me.

He diminished those who diminished him.

"I'll walk over to your hotel in the morning," Gerald said.

"Fine. I'm at the Skeppsbron. But why not take another minute to tell me what you're into these days. I'll probably be telephoning your mother and would like to say I saw you."

"You can say it."

Dubin said last time they were there Gerald had talked of taking some courses in biology and maybe going to med school.

The youth shot his lit butt into the gutter. "I don't think of that as a viable alternative any more."

"Alternative to what?"

"Other alternatives."

"Why don't you name one?"

He said nothing.

"How's your Swedish coming?"

"On stilts, on little cat stilts."

"You were considering studying Russian."

"I'm still considering it."

"Are you still working on the docks?"

He said he wasn't working.

"I'm sorry. Could you use some money? I have some traveler's checks I can cash."

Gerald shook his head.

"Are you living alone?"

"Alone." The word tolled.

Dubin compulsively went on: "I gather you're not much satisfied here?"

"You've gathered what there is to gather." From under his dripping hat he stared at his adoptive father. His eyes were expectant, expecting nothing.

Someday he'll change, Dubin thought. We'll sit together and talk with ease.

"Have you heard from Maud recently?"

"A card I couldn't read."

"Where was it from?"

"Ask Maud."

"Not from Italy?"

"Ask her."

"If you answered a letter once in a while," Dubin said testily, "it'd be easier on both of us than standing in the rain in a foreign city, asking and not answering questions."

"Neither of you approved of what I did when I screwed the army, so I don't care to inform you what I am doing."

"We didn't agree with your timing. You were about to escape the army if you had just been patient."

"It was my own fucking timing."

"Let's walk," Dubin said. "We may be going in the same direction."

Gerald bolted off. Dubin followed him.

The hazy wet street sloped down to the Baltic. Dubin talked to the youth's back and Gerald talked to the night.

"What we didn't like was your going AWOL three months before you were due for discharge. That wasn't a rational thing."

"The army's no place to be rational," Gerald said to the night. "If I had stayed in it another month I'd have killed somebody, not necessarily a Viet Cong."

"You'd have been free in a few short months."

"The months were short in your head, not mine."

Dubin said it was possible there'd be some sort of amnesty soon. "Congress is talking about it. Nixon will have to go along."

"It's bullshit."

"Some deserters are already coming home. They are making deals with the government."

"That's bullshit. It's handcuffs at the airport, court-martial, Leavenworth. I'm not going to prison."

"Where do you think you are?" Dubin asked Gerald's back.

"I am where I choose to be."

They trudged on in silence, singly, along the narrow sidewalk.

Dubin said he hadn't meant the prison thing the way he had said it.

"That's the way I heard it."

"Gerry, a father is a man who treats you like a son. At least walk with me. I'm the only father you've got "

The youth took off in a heavy-footed run.

Dubin awkwardly trotted after him.

At the Skeppsbron bridge Gerald slowed to a fast walk. The biographer limped along behind him. It was a bleak night, the lights of the long bridge glowing foggily in the freezing drizzle.

"Wait up, Gerry. I can't go fast."

Gerald told Dubin he had passed his hotel a block back.

I have to follow him, the father thought. It's the only way to be with him.

On the bridge a man with a soaking burlap sack on his head was fishing at the rail. Nearby stood a girl in a white cloth coat with a hood, yellow shoes, and a soggy yellow muff.

"Ett nyp?" she said to the biographer as he limped by.

"I beg your pardon?"

"Lof?" she asked him.

Dubin followed his son across the bridge, haranguing his back, and for a while the girl in the yellow shoes followed him.

Four

On the road a jogger trotted toward him, a man with a blue band around his head.

He slowed down as Dubin halted.

"What are you running for?" the biographer asked him.

"All I can't stand to do. What about you?"

"Broken heart, I think."

"Ah, too bad for that."

They trotted in opposing directions.

Dubin dropped his bag and embraced his wife. His arms stiffened as it seemed to him hers did. Kitty was nothing if not intuitive, sensed change of emotional weather before it was weather. He had considered telling her he had holed up for a few nights with a young woman in Venice—wouldn't say who because it would humiliate, wound her, more than if it had been someone other than Fanny Bick—anyway, it had come to nothing, if not less.

Kitty seemed constrained, preoccupied. He wondered whether she sensed something not quite right, off-balance—something wrong? Dubin said nothing about the trip, wouldn't unless she asked, would then say the necessary lies. It was painful not to be honest with a woman who did not lie. He was, on arrival, heavyhearted.

"You're late," she said. "Let's eat, I'm ravenous."

He unlocked his bag and produced a sculptured silver bracelet he had bought her in Stockholm. As she admired it, after a moment of hesitation he unwrapped a pair of antique gold earrings he had chosen for Maud and handed them to Kitty. She inspected the bracelet and earrings with interest. "They're beautiful, William, but one or the other would have been enough. Do you mind if I keep the bracelet and give the earrings to Maud?"

"Suit yourself."

They kissed affectionately, sat down for a drink, enjoyed dinner. She had prepared a tasty coq-au-vin. Kitty had the wishbone and when they broke it she won the wish.

"For Gerry?"

"For your new biography, and I guess for him too."

Dubin thanked her.

"How was he?"

He told her in detail; said Gerald had changed his name back to Willis.

She shook her head, eyes distant. "You were so loving to him. It was thoughtful of you to go see him; thank you."

He asked her not to thank him.

He built a fire in the living-room fireplace and they talked as they sipped coffee. The worst is over, Dubin thought, sitting by the fire, looking forward to his work in the morning. Kitty played the harp, some songs by Mahler. She sang in a small sweet voice.

Dubin woke that night relieved to be rid of Fanny. The week abroad had seemed a year. He sensed his wife was awake and drew her to him. Soon they made love. He would not admit the girl to his mind.

Before she slept he asked Kitty how she had fared while he was away.

"Not badly. I kept busy. The house behaved."

"You weren't afraid to be alone at night?"

She said she was.

"Why didn't you sleep at Myra's?"

"It doesn't bother her to be alone day or night. I want her to respect me."

"She respects you."

"I want her to."

"Well, I'm home now," Dubin said. He asked her if Maud had called.

"I called her. She had a nasty cold but is back in class now."

"Anything new with her?"

"Not with her but there is with me," Kitty said in the dark bedroom. "I've been working part-time in the library. Mrs. Eliscu is sick and Roger Foster rang me up the day you left to help him out. At least I get paid for work I do. I put in four weekday mornings and one afternoon. I'd prefer afternoons, but they need me most in the morning. I hope you don't mind? I can do your errands after lunch. I'll bring back the paper when I come home at one. Roger asked me to work a full day, but I said I simply couldn't."

"Let's get back to sleep, we both have to work in the morning."

"When we were first married I always got up with you."

Dubin remembered.

After flipping through a folder full of outlines the biographer began his working day. Rereading what he had written before he took off with Fanny, he was satisfied although a mild sense of waste lingered. Now he felt he'd soon complete the opening chapter and wrote well all morning. Dubin wrote listening to Lawrence's high-pitched insistent voice in his ear, to some degree resisting what he passed on as truth. He had to distance himself from the man to see what he must see. Lawrence wore a coat of many colors, pretending to wear nothing.

Dubin liked what he was writing. Nothing like interrupting the course of daily life to get the mind flowing, enjoying. At least he'd been to another country and had gone through something intense and different; now he lived his life writing another's. He felt for his wife a rush of affection.

On the Saturday morning following the Monday of Dubin's arrival from Sweden, Kitty came upstairs with an airmail letter. "From Italy." He went on with his typing. "Thanks." After a minute she left.

He thought he would finish the page.

When he had completed it, Dubin reached for the letter. It was addressed, as he had guessed—his thoughts of her already were fatiguing—in Fanny's large open slanted writing. Dubin's impulse, after a flash of self-disgust, sadness, remembrance of desire, was to destroy her letter without reading it. He had sensed he would hear from her, although not so soon. Standing apart from himself he tore open the envelope to get it over with so he could go on with his work.

The girl wrote: "I'm in Murano now with the capitano of the motorboat you waited for with me. I changed my mind about going to Rome. I'm writing this after midnight. The stars are out. I love the late hours when nobody but me is awake—feel closer to myself. I'm smoking as I look out of Arnaldo's window across the lagoon where Venice is. I like it a lot more than when you and I first came here, have got used to it.

"William, I've been thinking of you a lot and just got out of bed to write to you. I'm wearing the black nightie you liked me in. Over that I have on Arnaldo's sweater. He isn't a bad guy. He has a sense of humor and makes me laugh. He also cooks for us and I don't have to do very much although I wouldn't mind. Anyway, I had this urge to write you. Try not to think too badly of me if you can. Though we aren't the same kind of people in some ways, I think we are alike in others. I wear your bracelet even in bed. Maybe it will bring me luck. I hope you are less angry now—not that you don't deserve to be—and will write me sometimes. William, I would honestly like to hear from you. I remember some of our nice talks. I'm sorry it ended the way it did. Kind regards, Fanny B."

Dubin, as he tore the letter up, felt a punitive sense of disgust. From the gondolier to capitano in a short hop over his head. Another promiscuous lover to make her a better person. "I wear your bracelet even in bed."

Curbing an impulse to lay on sarcastically, the biographer typed out a plainspoken note. "You're right, Fanny, we have fundamental differences of values, not to speak of simple taste. Life is cheapened when there is no basic consideration by people of others. You've cheapened and shamed me. Please don't bother writing again. Yours most sincerely, William B. Dubin."

He tore her letter to shreds and burned the mound of paper in an ashtray.

In the afternoon he walked with Kitty to the green bridge.

The weekend was pleasant—unexpected visitors from New York City, an old law-school friend with his wife. They drove to Great Barrington to see a mutual friend.

On Monday morning, after quickly putting down a solid paragraph, Dubin felt as though he had walked into a wall. His thoughts were scattered. He felt vapid, vague, something pecking at the back of his mind, as though he'd forgotten to do what he had meant to. Nothing he could think of except to be joyfully into his biography. After a half hour of trying to concentrate he realized there'd be no second paragraph, good or bad, that day. It was a darkish November morning. Dubin turned on the desk lamp but that didn't help. He set aside his notes and spent the rest of the morning on business correspondence.

In the afternoon he went for his walk and after returning got into the car and slowly drove the same route, as though searching for something he had lost on the road.

"You look like someone holding his breath underwater," Kitty said as she came down the stairs. "Would you like me to fix you a drink?"

"Too early." Dubin remarked he'd had a poor day.

"They come and they go," she said.

"They come and they go."

"Sometimes I feel I'd like to see you give up that freaky D. H. Lawrence."

Dubin said he couldn't, had invested years in him. His voice sounded throaty.

Kitty, at the window, cheerfully said it was beginning to blizzard. She called any snowstorm a blizzard.

Fanny beats my brains, he said to his looking glass.

Mad, this reaction. He recalled her for the thousandth time in her black dress and pumps of that last unhappy morning together. She had been at her most desirable—why not if what you're playing with is loss?—as if she had finally become focused as a beautiful woman, defined in a way that had evaded her until the last moment. How else defined? As a bitch? Or a woman who had made a serious mistake and perhaps regretted it? Otherwise promiscuity is narcissism; identity lacking, probably something to do with her ungiving father. I would have been good for her. No use thinking these things, Dubin thought: they took you nowhere. Nowhere was an intensity of not having.

He stood at the bathroom window, staring at the mist-streaked distant mountains. The Vermont mountains, tying up with others in flanking ranges in New York, ran in a broken semicircle creating small valleys, one of which contained Center Campobello. Lawrence hadn't cared for mountains "intruding" through his window. Dubin liked them drawing his gaze into the distance; he made no symbol of them. The nearest peak was due north, a scraggy mass of twenty-eight hundred feet, in summertime covered with pines up its low sloping left flank. It had no name he could locate on the map and he called it Mt. No Name. The first snowfall of November had

116

amounted to a thin inch. Most of it had melted. No Name wore on its pate a crooked white crown. The wooded New York hills were dusted with snow —the woods in their winter underwear. He had to tell himself to quit looking. What a fool I was, when it was going well, to take that little hooker to Venice.

For two days the sunlit study resounded with the pounding of his machine as he retyped his opening chapter. Now I'm traveling again. He felt at the same time wild little thoughts, small fires of Fanny he managed to damp down: Dubin outthought them. After he had stacked twenty-three newly typed pages he consulted his notes and wrote a fine paragraph; but when he reread it twenty minutes later the paragraph grinned through broken teeth. Lawrence was a stiff boy, walked on stilts. His phallic mother was stiffly withdrawn. Who's the problem, him or me? The way I work or how he evades me? Dubin felt like a sculptor working with hardened clay.

Why the foreboding? He hadn't for years felt himself at fate's mercy but here she was doing her belly dance. A thoughtless girl, careless of him, had made a jackass of Dubin, shamed him as he hadn't ever been. During which time—before and after—almost anything I say to Kitty as truth is a lie: "Did you miss me in Italy, William?" she asks at breakfast. "Yes and no," I say, and she laughs at something she isn't laughing at. Then with a reflective look she says, "I sometimes have the feeling you'd get along well without me." "Yes, but why would I want to?" "I don't know," she says. He felt himself cut down a bloody inch. Doubt Dubin, doubt the biographer. Diminish the man, the writing suffers. He felt short of something he had had before he took off on a wild-goose chase for experience with Fanny.

Trotting downstairs later to heat the coffeepot, he took a minute to listen to the news on the radio: Nixon in press conference. Dubin shut it off in embarrassment.

He recalled Emerson's remark: "All that is clearly due today is not to lie." Emerson, liar? Everyone lies. Why am I making so much of it? Bad business, tying up behavior with writing biography.

After pouring his coffee he telephoned Kitty at the library. "Aren't you working?" she asked.

He understood the anxious question. If your husband or children ducked duty her boat rocked.

"You know the answer before you ask the question."

"You never call me in the morning," she explained.

"I'll see you at lunch, my coffee's cold," Dubin said. "Don't forget the paper."

"I almost never do." She hung up.

Kitty rang back. "I didn't mean to be impatient. If something's wrong, for Pete's sake, tell me. Was there anything in the mail that bothered you?"

"No. You know how it is at the beginning of a long work."

"You began months ago."

"It's a long beginning."

He awoke the next day in unease. As Dubin shaved he considered calling Maud but it was 4 a.m. in California.

He wished Kitty were staying home; they'd talk. What would he tell her? Not that he had had the girl but she had had him. Why bother telling her anything if there are no laughs in the story? What good will it do either of us if I make myself, in her eyes, a rare ass?

At breakfast he suggested he might want the car. "Roger will drive you home, I'm sure."

"I can call a taxi." Her eyes were tired. After sipping her coffee she asked, "Are you still having trouble?"

"Everyone's accounted for but isn't particularly present."

He thought of telling her truly about Fanny—get himself balanced again. No, he thought, if the writing were going well my conscience would be calm.

"Maybe you're pressing too hard?" she asked.

"Maybe."

"Shouldn't you try working before giving up for the day?"

"Please don't tell me when to work."

"Would you like me to read the chapter and give you my opinion?"

He said he would not.

Kitty examined her eyes in a pocket mirror. She had on the blue batik dress she had just bought and an attractive pair of black single-strap shoes.

"I could call Roger and say I wasn't coming in," she suggested. "We could drive into the Berkshires for the day?"

But Dubin thought she was right: he ought to reassess his priorities.

"Which ones?"

"I might give up on Lawrence. If the book's wrong for me, it's wrong."

Kitty set down her coffee cup and studied him. She got up, rinsed a dish, put it away, sat down. Her expression was calm, her voice even.

"William, don't make so much of this. You've had dry periods before and you'll have them again. I'll tell you what: let's goof off. I can ask for Monday off. We'll drive to Lake Champlain, and if we feel like it, go on up to Quebec City for the weekend."

He said, after a long moment, he wouldn't know what to do with himself once he got there.

"Is that how you feel?"

As of now it was how he felt.

She took a last quick swallow of coffee, rinsed her cup and placed it in the dishwasher. "I'm late. Do you want to drive me to work? I really don't mind if you go for a ride by yourself."

But Dubin said she could have the car.

Kitty buttoned her coat and tied on a head scarf. "Please air the kitchen if you think of it. The house is smelly."

"What does it smell of?"

"Burnt toast."

"I think it smells of us."

She drove off. He realized she hadn't returned to breathe at the burners.

Moved by a variety of useless impulses, he went through the house listing things that needed tending to. You skip work, trivialities assail you. Still, any activity is better than none. Dubin aired the kitchen. He went through the refrigerator—threw out two rotting lemons, moldy butter, cheese rinds. Sometimes she didn't know what the hell she had there. He arranged bottles, like with like, and separated butter bars from margarine.

In the cellar he discovered a puddle under the hot-water tank and phoned the plumber. He swept the cellar floor, emptied the kitchen garbage container into the can outside. He tried reading a detective story but couldn't stay with it. Dubin plucked at the strings of Kitty's harp.

In his study he thumbed through his second-chapter notes, looking for a compelling opening idea. If he found one he'd write a sentence. Sentences bred sentences. But the notes tensed him: they were only notes, separate, discrete, like seashells in a box. It was stupid, he thought, to try to work when the idea was not to; to give the brain a rest.

On a card he read, D. H. Lawrence had said to his girl: "I don't believe in the idea of one man for one woman, do you? I mean, there just isn't one woman and one only that a man can marry." Cunning question, foreshadowing the brushoff; she never got over him.

119

Dubin climbed the stairs to the third-floor unfinished room they called the attic, where the kids had often played. He flicked on the light, moved by a sense of past time rooted in his children's childhood, and poked around in their abandoned toys, books, folders of drawings and correspondence Kitty had saved. She tore up letters she answered but those she saved were from the children and Dubin. That made family history. He had never been able to find Nathanael's letters.

On an impulse he searched in a footlocker for Maud's white wool hat with blue band. Was it still alive or had it been given away? He could not find it, nor any of the dolls she had played with. He remembered a valentine she'd drawn and searched for it. Dubin found the one he'd had in mind, a red-crayoned heart addressed to "Willyam, Be My Valentine," but it was signed "Gerald" in black letters. In apology he touched the paper to his lips.

He kept hunting for something of Maud's, perhaps a note from summer camp when she was nine or ten. Maud still wrote rarely, once in a while a satisfying letter, then months of titbit phone calls. Some were talky calls, others little more than formalities: she was checking in, and what she really said was what she didn't say. She didn't say what most affected her. That ran in the family, began with his mother. Dubin left the attic room. He had wanted one of Maud's affectionate notes as a child to keep in his pocket. The uses of the dwindling past.

The biographer walked downtown in his galoshes, mackinaw, long tan-and-black scarf Kitty had knitted him; took her a year to do the thing. The day was crisp, the wind whipping by, snow flurries scattered through the leafless trees all morning. After withdrawing cash from the bank, having nothing better to do he crossed the street and paid the gas bill, groaning inwardly at the uselessness of the act on a perfectly good day. Since it was already close to one, he thought he'd stop off at the library and let Kitty drive him home. As he came up the street he saw her standing with Roger on the library steps; Dubin could tell as she spoke—the way her body moved—that she was emotional. Roger, since Dubin had last seen him, wore an Edwardian haircut with long sideburns. The biographer considered turning quickly and walking back before they spotted him. Kitty seemed troubled. Dubin worried that Roger, having heard from his friend Fanny about the asinine Venetian adventure, had told his wife the happy news.

But they had seen him and instantly stopped talking. Dubin had paused to retie his shoelaces and pull up his socks. He approached with tight gut, concerned that he had lost first chance to tell her himself; that the librarian, whose business it was not, had informed her in his place. Roger thrust forth his hand and Dubin unwillingly took it.

"Kitty said you've been abroad, Mr. Dubin."

"For a week. What else have you heard?"

Kitty gazed at him with surprised wet eyes. Before he could speak again—to utter what idiocy?—she broke in: "Mrs. Eliscu has cancer of the breast. Roger heard from her husband a half hour ago. They have three small children."

With a hidden sigh Dubin expressed regret. He also regretted his stupid remark to Roger but no one had made anything of it.

"Have a good time?" Roger asked. He'd never been comfortable with Dubin, and wasn't now, in his green suit, blue tie, field boots. Roger rarely wore an overcoat. He had hot blood, he had once told Dubin. Where? Dubin had almost asked. With a nod, Roger walked down the steps to his car at the curb.

"Anybody I can give a lift to?"

Dubin said Kitty had their car.

"He knows," she said impatiently.

"Then why did he ask?"

Roger waved and drove off.

"Why aren't you nice to him?" Kitty asked.

He said he had nothing against Roger. I feel like a jackass and he acts like one. Kitty seemed apart from, almost uncomfortable with him.

If they weren't talking about Fanny, I ought to be, he thought.

"What brought you here?" Kitty asked as though expecting bad news.

He said he had walked into town to get some cash.

"I could have done that easily."

"I needed something to do."

"Are you giving up on your book?"

"Not as of right now."

They kissed as though greeting, then got into the car and drove to the supermarket. Twice, as they walked the long grocery aisles, Kitty dropped a can he had picked off the shelves.

"My hands are small," she explained to her husband.

They hadn't for years shopped together for groceries, and Dubin enjoyed it despite the wasted day.

Though the biographer felt he was dealing with a literary as well as a psychological problem, obviously one tied up to the other. There were too many reverberations of Fanny, too much static in his head, too much guilt. He had reacted as though his character had failed him; the true failure was one of judgment. Dubin wanted to put his thoughts in order by getting to work and doing it well. To not work regularly was to fall into the condition he was out to avoid: purpose sidetracked, the mind adrift; Dubin left on the pier, the ship gone. Montaigne had believed his effective judgment was instrumental in keeping him in good physical health.

He had returned heavier than he'd left, as though misery had paid interest in flesh. He disliked the bounce of his belly as he briskly walked or ran. He disliked the naked sight of himself in the closet-door mirror; pictured youthful slimness, not impossible. He figured he'd cut out brandy after dinner—drink less wine at the dinner table, eat smaller portions. Kitty had a booklet of low-calorie foods; he'd ask her to watch his intake. To get himself effectively together he had to put himself in shape. In fooling with Fanny he'd allowed desire to overflow the workaday life. A pipe had broken, the psyche was flooded. He must rid himself of his ongoing half-jealous thoughts of the girl—these irritating intrusive two-bit emotions—make the floodwaters of the unconscious recede. He had once more to be the man he'd been; *who Dubin was.*

Besides starving his belly he wrestled it off. From youth he had exercised daily—shades of Gatsby—his personal need, in accord with controlling, shaping. But after Maud was born, though Kitty approved calisthenics, he performed superficially—too much to do to earn a living. And he was walking more after they had moved into the country; had invented his long course in nature, part of which he trotted. Now Dubin revived the old setting-up exercises, not easy to go back to at age fifty-six: pushups, bending, pedaling, pulling his knees into the offending gut. In his striped shorts he danced around Maud's room as Kitty slept, the floorboards creaking, a squeak for each shift. He worked resolutely a half hour each morning, protesting in the pit of the self at the effort one had to make, the inertial strain of fabricating monotonous movement, as though he were dragging a carcass of himself back and forth across the floor, frightful bore if present necessity. Indeed necessity. Dubin fought the possessed self.

Afterward, although Kitty was rising early, for her, to go to the library, he had breakfast alone. He'd got into the habit when Maud was an infant and Kitty, when she could, slept later. Dubin liked being alone at that hour, enjoying morning light, morning quiet, thinking whatever thought; relaxed. Now breakfast, given diet, was a chore. He kept the repast simple: fruit followed by sugarless black coffee, with half a slice of bread. For lunch the food made little difference; he ate minuscule portions. Kitty shook her head. But dinner, in principle, satisfied—if that was the word—where there wasn't that much satisfaction. Kitty broiled fish or lean meat, served one green or yellow vegetable, offered sugarless dessert. She clicked her tongue at his modest helpings. Dubin finished the meal hungry—praise moderation, though little after not much all day was hard to bear.

It wasn't easy, after rising from the table, not to dip his fingers into a Swiss chocolate bar he had hidden in a desk drawer; but if he went quickly upstairs and brushed his teeth he brushed away the compelling hunger. He learned to eat slowly, let each forkful of food, each permitted sip of wine, ride the length of the tongue. He savored well the little he ate; and still smoked an occasional cigarillo though he'd given up serious smoking long ago.

Kitty, although friendlier to less rather than more, disliked seeing him at diet's mercy.

At his own mercy, he insisted.

"But isn't the diet what you went on mainly because of your trouble working?"

He more or less nodded.

She said no more; nor did he.

The day's work, if it comes to something, burns out night's dross; night craps in your pants. For the investment the biographer makes in gathering himself together on cold hard mornings, in coming drearily to life, he expects some accomplishment during the day—a good deed, it helps. Dubin felt he was getting nothing much. But though change took its time he daily expected signs of a forthcoming visit. He watched for it out of his better eye, two might scare it away. After Thanksgiving, when winter set in with a wind and a bang, he sat regularly at his desk, promising himself he would stay with it if something good evolved; but day after day very little did—an aimless page or two; so he went—after three prescribed working hours—for a routine walk in any weather, the next sequential imposition on the poor self; a man had to conjure up some relief from nothing much achieved.

Work generally pulls me out of the clutch of the subjective self; but since

I'm not working well I have to spring myself another way, if I know another way. S. Johnson, unable to work, would walk twenty-six miles to Birmingham, to shake himself into shape. Dubin was not prodigal with miles, limited himself to four or five each day. "The safe and general antidote against sorrow is employment," Johnson said. Dubin hopes to find an antidote growing in nature.

In December he switched to walking after breakfast, then trying to initiate prose after pouring out on paper a bag of thoughts gathered on the road. He entered his study at about ten and stayed for two and a half hours, his pen at the ready; then lingered at the window, staring at the unnamed mountain; or read and reread his meager mail. Or paced back and forth in the room to shake things in his head into place. At length he laid out a page of notes, concentrating on surprise in arrangement, but too often settling merely for changing the language of the initial note, not going far beyond that; and felt textual thinness, that he was adding little to the naked facts. Go, Dubin, back to obituaries. How can my small brain light up the dark forest of D. H. Lawrence's psyche? He felt distant from the action, from growth of character, inner motivation; sat peering at young Lawrence, handsome youth, floating off in pale water amid lily pads; or trotting into the white-flowered bushes with his mum as pale-faced Jessie peeks through the leaves; Dubin, secondary voyeur, not really knowing what they were up to, barely able to guess. He was not with it, whatever it was. It was—whatever—with Fanny. He lived on memories of her; Lawrence would have scorned him for the little he'd had yet lived on.

Among other cures he added hydrotherapy: re Carlyle, daily on arising— his wife's advice—dumping a bucket of cold water on his head. In Dubin's case a cold shower in winter, hot turning gasping cold—each morning, to get him up and onto the daily merry-go-round; the icy water beating blood into his dull brain as he snorted and pranced in the tub. And at night hot to tepid water to ease a bit, he hoped, a deepening frustration. Though he slept during long intervals of night—vaguely sensing Kitty's controlled restlessness—he dreamed he wasn't asleep, hadn't dared to sink into deep sleep, as though he might be murdered there; Dubin awoke fatigued. His sleep pretended sleep, cheated itself. Some mornings he stayed forty minutes in the hot shower before he could bring himself to turn the cold knob; or if he dared not, to step out of the tub, get into underwear and begin exercise. And if the long day was especially long, therefore especially unproductive—too many hours to count the ways—he went to bed directly after supper.

"I've never seen you this way," Kitty worried.

He had had bad times before, Dubin says.

"Never quite like this. You managed always to do something you liked. At least a little." She looked at him with feeling. "Would it help if we got into bed and kept ourselves company?"

He doubted it; thanked her.

"Sleep well, darling."

Dubin left her sitting in the living room with yesterday's newspaper and a handbook of psychiatry Nathanael had owned. She also consulted a medical adviser.

He got into his pajamas and hurried to sleep. He slept quickly, trying to dawdle. When he went to bed this early he was up at five and fought to sleep again—on principle—but couldn't. Sleep had for a few hours possessed him, not he it. Dubin tossed aside his blankets and staggered in the dark to the shower. Afterward as he diddled with breakfast, the sheer stretch of morning ahead weighed heavily on his imagination. He left the house early, earlier after each early bedtime, to lose himself out of doors; to not think despite the turgid flow of thought: how to get back to productive work, without which his ego was more savagely self-obsessed.

He went through the bare pewter-trunked silver maples, away from the house—sometimes whistling, pretending God's not too far off his heaven, in case anyone's listening—then hurried through Kitty's silent wood, trotting now, the will rampant. Dubin jogged the short walk to the bridge but if it brought no relief—there were times it did—he traveled the long route. Nothing like a little "agitation," Johnson had said, to escape misery. He ran from his gross belly, from Fanny in all her guises, naked to not quite. She flung her underpants at him for the thousandth time; tempting him, betraying him. He ran from heartbreak revived, his dreary discipline, loyal wife, depression afflicting him. Sometimes his legs went faster than his body cared to go.

What a miserable price to pay for unpleasure! My God, whatever hit me so hard? She meant at first not much to me—almost nothing; she gave me little, only what I took, why do I so unwillingly mourn her? Now he regretted his stiff-assed frigid letter to her basically warm one; considered writing another canceling the intent of the first, but would not. He felt—shame on Dubin—jealous of her jape of a lover who had wooed and won her with his red-pompommed sailor's cap and lavender pants, fifteen minutes after he had handed her into his motor taxi on a Venetian canal. The capitano had driven his passenger to Murano, put her safely to bed, and banged her madly. The gondolier had taken her fancy the day before with his manly ass and a lilting love song; the capitano, a day later with his pompommed pitch in a splashing speedboat. For shame, Fanny, what are you doing to yourself? She had canceled out Rome and settled for amiable fornication on an isle of glass. That Dubin would so often replay his humiliation with her was an astonishment to him. It's she who sent me into this tailspin, though not only she. I blame me for offering myself as victim. What was he doing to himself?

Kitty had her theory: "You hit the jackpot with *H. D. Thoreau.* You want, naturally, to repeat with D. H. Lawrence. It's inhibiting—you're afraid you won't. You must think of yourself as being off the Rock Candy Mountain, plodding along a plateau, hunting another mountain. What an honor it was that night, not to mention President Johnson asking you to write his life. God, I wish you had. I'll bet you could have said anything you felt you had to about him. After that a letdown was bound to occur, William, and you'll have to ride it out. Patiently, I hope." She laughed breathily. "Don't you think so?"

Dubin nodded. What she said was true enough, yet not the truth. At meals he sat opposite her, looking out of the window behind her, saying little, agreeing with her, pretending things might be worse; wearing a mask. Nietzsche had said the profound man is he who needs a mask. Dubin, if not profound, was profoundly disgusted with Wm. Dubin, which calls for a small disguise in the presence of your believing wife. Kitty now got out of bed after he had done exercising, drew on her black and burgundy African robe, and yawning, followed her husband downstairs to prepare breakfast as she had used to almost every day when the kids were young. She kept him company, a gracious gesture, for which he saw her plain.

He plunged into the snowy woods. The bleak landscape gave forth bleakness; he gave it back. Though his flesh diminished the paunch persisted.

In the evening, after a long day and subdued supper, unless she could persuade him to go out with her to see a movie, or turn on TV, they sat in silence in opposing armchairs, Kitty knitting as she talked from one thought to another, or sat regarding him above her slightly lowered newspaper as he pretended to be reading a book. I am in my thoughts a detached lonely man, my nature subdued by how I've lived and the lives I've written; subdued by the dyer's bloodless hand.

Dubin was fifty-seven on the twenty-seventh of December, 1973, and the last thing he wanted, or needed, was to celebrate the dismal occasion, but Kitty had urged, insisted. "William, let's get out of the rut we're in. We haven't had a dinner party since before you went off to Italy." He was born in a cold season yet liked to think he had been conceived in spring. Dubin dragged his feet because he had forgotten Kitty's birthday, last April, and wanted her to forget his.

Kitty, who had been a poor cook for her first husband, was an excellent one for her second. She roasted two ducks, produced three bottles of Cabernet Sauvignon and five of Lanson champagne, and arranged masses of red and lavender anemones and bronze chrysanthemum daisies in white vases. He decided her favorite color was white.

She had invited, for this festive occasion, the Greenfelds, Ondyks, Habershams, and, of course, Myra Wilson. The Habershams were old friends, Fred, an activist civil-rights attorney; his wife, Ursula, also a lawyer, was a Vermont Senator, one of three women in the legislature. The Ondyks came, Evan, the psychotherapist, and his wife, Marisa, an insecure lady with a nervous nose she often blew and lips drawn at the corners. If you kissed her on the cheek she said, "Mmmuh," meaning a passionate kiss in return. Her passion was a play-reading group she had formed that Kitty sometimes attended. Marisa preferred tragic roles; Kitty read comic ones.

She and Flora were currently amiable and though they were never entirely at ease with each other—one coveted "more," one "less"—greeted the other cordially. It was, through the years, an ambivalent relationship. Flora was an animated woman of regal bearing, a violinist without professional career or children. Kitty pitied her for not having children, not because she hadn't had them, but because she had wanted them and Oscar hadn't. Dubin had always responded to Flora; they kissed on meeting. Kitty called her "born dissatisfied."

"She pretends, hides so much. When you talk to her you can sense all she's holding back."

"We all hide," Dubin confessed.

"Obviously," she said sadly.

"Then why blame her?"

"She pretends not to."

Myra Wilson, at seventy-eight, was a still vital self-reliant white-haired farmer's widow. Living alone had not soured or scared her. She lived competently and said little about her ailments, poor circulation, arthritic pains in shoulders and neck. "So long as I have my bottle of aspirins." Kitty admired her independence and invited the old woman to her dinner parties; she almost daily attended her. They talked often and at length on the phone. Kitty was genuinely fond of old people, perhaps women more than men: she had been brought up, she often said, by a loving grandmother. Dubin, for this birthday and this mood, would have wanted some young people around, but only Flora was younger than fifty. Not that much younger. But she was womanly and attractive in a low-cut black dress. She was the one woman Dubin was drawn to that night.

"We hardly ever see you, William," Flora said. "Oscar says he meets you on his walk once in a while. I hear you're into your new biography?"

"Deeply," he sighed.

Oscar Greenfeld and the biographer embraced after skirting each other during drinks.

"What's wrong, old boy," Oscar asked.

"Does it show?"

"A strained swimming against the stream."

"My work, I guess."

"Not going well?"

"No."

"If I'd known I'd've brought my pipe to flute you up."

"Too bad you didn't," said Dubin.

He went through the evening with a show of having a good time. Knowing he wasn't, he ate too much too quickly, tasted little, shoveled down more food, grew irritated with himself. He hurried upstairs to brush his teeth, then flung the brush into the sink bowl.

Dubin slogged through the night in a saddened mood. There he was, not being who he was or felt like. Kitty, taken in by his pretense—mask?—seemed to assume the party was working for him. For dessert she sailed in with a birthday cake she had baked from scratch, lit with a flickering white candle; and the guests toasted the biographer with champagne as he smiled with his head bowed.

Kitty would not play the harp when Flora asked her to, despite the applause of her dinner guests. "No, no," she laughed and almost cried, "I'd spoil the fun."

"Oh, come on," said Flora.

"Let her alone," said Greenfeld.

Afterward Maud called. Dubin, sitting in the downstairs bathroom that morning, had heard Kitty dial Maud and quietly ask her to remember to telephone her father that night. He assumed Kitty had also called Gerald but doubted she'd been able to persuade him to put in a collect call.

"Hi, Papa," Maud said, "happy birthday."

Dubin said he missed her and was counting on her coming home for the winter vacation.

"I miss you too. I will if I can."

As he sat at the phone in the hallway he was watching Kitty in the kitchen by the sink, both faucets running, talking seriously with Ondyk.

If she's consulting him about me, I'll break her ass, Dubin thought.

Maud said she'd be home in early February. "I'd like to take off a few days after finals. I hate to leave the sun."

"It would help me to see you," he told her.

Her voice grew serious. "Is something the matter?"

"I like to look at you," he said. "I like you around."

"Don't put more pressure on me, Pa. I'm taking five exams."

He said there'd be no pressure and felt low. She had changed. If a man needs his daughter so much, Dubin thought, maybe he needs somebody else more.

Maud's voice was tender when she said goodbye.

In their bedroom, later, Dubin thanked Kitty for the party.

She was sitting in a chair, her skirt hiked up over her knees, legs raised, looking long at them.

"I have pretty good legs," she said. "Not bad for my age."

Dubin agreed.

"Did you like the evening?"

"Yes. Thanks for going to all the trouble."

She got up to undress. "I don't think of it as trouble, but you don't look very happy."

"I haven't pretended to be," he said, though he had.

Kitty asked whether he might care to talk to Evan Ondyk. She said it doubtfully.

"Were you talking to him about me?"

"No. About myself."

"What would you like me to say to him?"

"Stop being ironic. He might be able to help you pinpoint what's bothering you—to figure out where you stand."

"I know where I stand. He doesn't know. I doubt he knows where he stands."

"I know people he's helped. He's an excellent psychotherapist."

"I don't need his advice. His view of life is reductive. With him a lot more is determined than with me. I know how free I am. I've picked the horse I ride."

"Never mind the horse. How free do you feel?"

"Once I asked him his interpretation of Thoreau and he came up with the usual can of oedipal worms. There's that but there's more."

"He's not a literary critic."

"He's not wise."

"Neither are you," said Kitty.

"That's true," Dubin answered after a pause, "but I know as much about life as he does. Once I didn't, now I do."

"No, you don't. Maybe you do about the careers of certain accomplished literary figures, but not necessarily about yourself and not necessarily about the unconscious."

"Biography—literary or otherwise—teaches you the conduct of life. Those who write about life reflect about life. The unconscious is mirrored in a man's acts and words. If he watches and listens to himself, sooner or later he begins to see the contours of the unconscious self. If you know your defenses you pretty much understand what it's about. In my work I've discovered how to discover. You see in others who you are."

"Mirrored is right. You ought to hear yourself in the bathroom."

"I hear, I listen. That's the point I'm making. I've lived fifty-eight years."

"Fifty-seven."

"Fifty-seven. I think I know myself reasonably well. No one knows himself entirely. There's a mystery in knowing. The big thing is what you do with what you know."

"You exercise? You lose weight?"

"Right now I'm saying to myself that I *can* exercise and lose weight."

"Where will it get you?" Kitty asked. "You're still a depressed man who has trouble working. William, I feel there's more to this than either you know or have said."

She's clever, he thought, but I won't clobber her with honesty—not hers or mine.

He said he had real literary problems with his book. "So far it's a dry piece of work, a compilation of facts rather than a living life—it reads like de La Grange's *Mahler* or Blotner's *Faulkner*. I want the juices of life in it. My reaction to it is not, simply, neurosis."

Kitty had never said it was. "I feel in the dark," she said, her voice strained. "In the dark I'm afraid. I feel you can't work well for a reason, William. If you know what it is please tell me. Don't keep me in the dark."

Dubin told her he would tell her when he knew.

"Losing weight won't do it," Kitty said, looking· at him with moist dark eyes. "Nor what you think you know about life because you write biographies. Working it out with someone usually helps. If you don't want to talk to Evan, why don't you go see Dr. Selensaal in Winslow? I hear he's very good."

"I haven't got that kind of time. Winslow is seventy miles one way and seventy back. It'll kill a day to go there."

"Go once and talk to him instead of frittering the morning away getting nothing done."

"Once leads to twice, then twice a week. I haven't got that kind of time."

"Stop yakking about time, for Christ's sake. You're not doing much with it."

"Life is what I'm thinking of," Dubin said. "I know its structure and spin and many of its ways of surprise, if not total pattern or order. I know enough, in other words, to take my chances. I want to run my life my own way, not like yours or Nathanael's. I don't want to go on sharing with you to my dying day the benefits of your previous marriage."

"That's cruel."

Kitty drew her dress over her head. He looked away from the mark on her buttock through her white underpants. When he looked again she was slipping on a nightgown.

"Don't be so fucking proud," Kitty said in bed.

My pain is tolerable, Dubin thought. All I can not do is work.

He fought winter as if it were the true enemy: if he tore into it the freeze would vanish, his ills be gone, his life, his work, fall into place. He would overcome belly, mood, joyless labor—lust for Fanny, the burden of his unhappy experience with her. Dubin assailed winter by daily testing himself: running through its icy womb to demonstrate he was not afraid of the dead season. Not fearing it, he would fear less the dysfunctioning self—what was or was not happening. He ran in rain, slush, in end-of-December fog—to show weather, winter staring at him as he went by, the quality of Dubin's self, his premise, the thought he ran by. As a youth he would hold a burning match till the flame touched his fingertips: if you held the glowing matchstick until the very end, the girl you loved would love you.

It was as hard a winter as Dubin feared it would be. He had to force himself, after breakfast, to open the kitchen door and step into the frozen morning, facing his icy breath. The cold struck him like a blow of a fist. His face tightened; he could tell every stroke he had shaved—a cut on his chin burned like acid. Dubin walked three steps and broke into a run, his spine touched by chill; across the inert grass, through light snow, along the solitary path of the icy-damp morning wood. Thoreau had called winter a resonant instrument that twanged its own music. Dubin, as he ran, heard branches creak in the cold; once on an icy day a dead tree exploded. The listening wood, animistic, druidic, recalled Stonehenge. Occasionally he saw a small animal stirring, rat or weasel scuttering through the brush; or a dark bird in flight, unrecognizable. Dubin thumped alone along the path in the wood.

He left the trees, trotting on the dirt road to the bridge, the stream misting by his side, his breath flowing behind him. If a car appeared this early in the morning, neither jogger nor driver dared look at the other. He slowed down at the bridge, limped through the booming snow-covered construction, crossed the highway, and at the fork relentlessly ran into the long route. There were times he turned back at the wooden bridge: temporary cure: felt he could get into writing if he tried. Dubin turned back rarely. He went on if when he thought of himself it touched pain. The trick was to get into the winter world and out of within—shift the weight of inner conflict to outside. The cock's tail turns where the cock's head had been. His thoughts therefore were images of gnarled broken-fingered oaks, naked birches—imagine a white tree! And there were more winter birds around than he had guessed —the flyways were overpopulated, the South crowded; some birds remained in the snow. And the frozen circular road.

It took him a half hour to turn the shivery clinging cold in his clothes to warmth gained in running. He slowed to a fast walk, past farmhouses with monumental barns looking like forever; cows in winter pasture as still as statues, their breaths flags in motion; frozen fields undulating up the mist-streaked hills. He pushed on in winter silence, every step striding against the force of nothing, aware of roadside mustard-yellow willows, their long yellow strings limply dancing in the cutting wind. He plodded breathlessly up the road, conscious of the weight of ascent, dismal cold, the unhappy task he had set himself. Walking uphill, Dubin stared at his feet lest the hike to the top slay him. Trotting down, he kept his eyes on the beckoning distance. The ascents were endless. Segments of the road he had once thought level, he realized, were pitched up from five to ten degrees. He tried not to stop on the walk up; it was hard to get started again. Ravenous for summer, for an end to the barren season, he hurried on thinking of the next rise or bend. He felt with each step resistance of the long long walk-run, monotony of self-inflicted cure. Climbing is not ascending. My will is my enemy. It restoreth not my soul. Yet he stayed with it. if he overslept he ran faster.

The flutist remembered him at this time as a strained, almost haggard man in motion, heavily bundled up, a grim-faced man who had lost weight, or might, without knowing it, be ill. He wore a red wool hat his wife had knitted, a long striped scarf his wife had knitted, galoshes with unbuckled buckles that clinked as he ran, and a poplin fleece-lined coat with a brown fur collar. Dubin ran slowly, heavily, in snow or slush, as if his boots were lead and each step an ordeal, his sober inward grayish-blue eyes set dimly in the distance. What he saw there Greenfeld hesitated to guess. When they met, although the biographer appeared to be drowning in all there was to say, he was mute. Sometimes in passing he would stammer half a sentence, break off, and hurry on.

William, Oscar cried, let's not forget our friendship. William, it's a lonely world!

Greenfeld was haunted by the expression of Dubin's eyes as he looked back —embittered?—as though the fault was the flutist's that he did not then know what his friend was living through.

When he had returned to the house, after resting awhile he sat at his desk. Dubin never did not work though he stayed with it for shorter intervals of time, down to an hour and a half each morning. He wrote long swirling sentences on sheets of yellow foolscap and reflected on each. Kitty, one Saturday morning, brought up a cup of consommé. He took a grateful sip and thanked her but did not finish it.

"Don't you like it?"

"Warming—after that long haul."

"Why don't you eat the rest?"

He did not want to eat between meals.

"You're mad," she said.

After she left he went back to his tortuous sentences. It was a bright sunny day after the New Year. Later she brought up the mail. Kitty bent to kiss him as she handed him an airmail letter.

Fanny hoped to hear from him.

"It isn't easy to write to someone who won't answer you. I know you're there, William, because my letters aren't returned to me. At least your first letter, I had the pleasure of opening it before it hit me in the face like a bucket of ice.

"As you can see by the postmark I have left Murano. Arnaldo wasn't easy to get along with. He was good in bed though not much more than that. When I said I was leaving he begged me to stay. He wanted to marry me but I don't want to be married yet. He got awfully angry, beat his stringy cock on the table. I felt terribly depressed. I hate myself for this kind of thing —I mean going to bed with the nearest guy when I am anxious. In my mind I don't seem to be that kind of person. In my mind you are my friend.

"I am now in Rome, staying with this old friend of mine I mentioned to you that day we broke up. Harvey says I am genuine, whatever mistakes I make. I'm the only woman he knows who can be easy with him when he is impotent. He's sixty-two and was once a singer. He knew my father in L.A. and didn't much care for him. My father used to say I was oversexed and I used to feel awful until one day I realized what *his* problems are.

"Recently, when Harvey and I were standing in a movie line I passed out. In the hospital I thought I was pregnant—that Arnaldo had knocked me up, but it turned out I had developed a cyst in a fallopian tube because of the IUD I had changed to. I hate the Pill because it makes me bleed. Anyway, I was operated on and lost a tube. I felt deathly depressed until the doctor said I could still have children. Harvey has been kind to me. He says I am independent and enjoy life, which is partly true.

"I've been thinking of going back to the States to find some sort of steady work—don't ask me what. I have ideas about what I ought to be doing but am afraid of the next move. I don't want to get into something I can't get out of if I make the wrong choice. Or into something that won't come to much, and will make me feel, again, that I am up Shit Creek in a leaky rowboat. William, please advise me about my life. I like the way you talk to me about myself.

"I wish you would sometime write me a letter saying things I could think about. What happened at the Hotel Contessa between us wasn't all my fault, if you've stopped to think about it. You were kind in your way but your mind wasn't really on me. And not everybody can be lovers —I'm sure you'll agree with that. But I have the feeling we could have been good friends. Could you specifically say what I ought to be thinking about in the way of a job or career, or recommend books that might be helpful? Or give me the names of courses I could take when I get back to New York City?

"I'd like to be better organized and enjoy my life more, but Harvey isn't that well put together and has problems that remind me of my own, so I don't think I ought to stay here. I don't think I'm so good for him either. I'm afraid of my day-to-day life. A day scares me more than a week or month. But the truth of it is I want to be responsible, to work my life out decently. Couldn't we at least talk about that? Affectionately, Fanny B.

"P.S. This is my last letter unless you answer it, gently."

Dubin burned the letter.

She wrote once after that: "I'm not writing to humiliate myself but to show you I have respect for you though you don't seem to have much for me. F."

He kept this letter, her last. She had enclosed a snapshot of herself in jeans, sneakers, and embroidered blue blouse, her long hair stringy, her sad face plain. She was not an ideal woman. Why was he so drawn to her?

In the woods, later, he thought if he had had her in Venice he might not have wanted her afterward. Yet he thought he wanted more than just wanting her.

Dubin awoke in moonlight, unhappy to wake. He'd gone to bed after supper, too intent on sleep to draw the shades. What was that song of Schubert's about a man who was awakened by starlight? It was late January and the ground was covered with snow. Kitty had been sleeping in Maud's bed, not to disturb him. Dubin, moonlight spilling on his face, thought he ought to get up and draw the shade. He lay there, trying to rouse himself. At last he flung the blanket aside. At the window the moon was full, the somber hills bathed in a darkish bronze glow. He stared at his wristwatch on the night table: it wasn't ten yet. He looked again in disbelief, watched the second hand move. He had slept a few hours and now it felt as though today was tomorrow. He felt a sadness of waste. Dubin dressed and went down the stairs.

Kitty, reading in bed, called to him through Maud's closed door. "Is there something you need, William?"

"I waked and can't sleep. I'm going out for a short walk. It's a full moon."

After a minute Kitty asked, "Would you want company? I'll get dressed."

He didn't think so.

Dubin drew on his overcoat and wool hat and buckled on his galoshes. He took along a thick stick that had once belonged to Gerald. Maybe he would go to the bridge.

"It's a freezing night," she said through the door, "don't go far."

He didn't think he would.

He was at first afraid to enter the wood. Then he went through it, dimly lit trees casting shadows on the darkly lit snow.

At the road he turned left instead of right toward the bridge. A few fleecy clouds floated in the night-blue winter sky. After some minutes of careful walking on and off the snowy road he passed the Wilson farmhouse, a narrow two-story white frame house with a sloping addition on the left side. It lay off the road about two hundred feet. An orange light burned in the upstairs darkened bedroom. It was Myra's night light, an old woman alone in a farmhouse in the dead of winter. He imagined her sleeping in a bed she had lain in with her husband for fifty years. Ben, the dog, growled as Dubin went by. He gripped his stick.

Oscar Greenfeld's house was a half mile farther up the road, a two-story spacious red clapboard with a large lawn. Dubin thought of their friendship with regret. How strange to love a man and rarely see him. Dubin had enjoyed coming to Oscar's house in the past—walking along this road in summer, driving the front way through the streets in winter. They played chess, talked and drank. The flutist had come less often to Dubin. He never came with Flora. If you're not alone with a friend there's no friendship, he said. In his company Dubin drank more than he was used to, and Kitty worried when he got into the car at one or half past one a.m. to drive Oscar home. The flutist didn't drive. Flora drove him there but wouldn't call for him that late at night, though she stayed up waiting. That was one of the things about her that antagonized Kitty: Kitty went for Dubin when she had to. Neither of them cared for the drinking, and driving on icy streets. Oscar Greenfeld stopped coming to Dubin's house; then Dubin stopped going to him. After an evening together hitting the brandy bottle, Oscar when he woke the next morning could reach for his flute and move to Mozart on the music stand. With Mozart dealing out the notes Oscar could toot away most of his hangover. Dubin, working with words, felt he was pushing rocks with his nose, so he stopped visiting the flutist although they talked on the phone. But a telephone conversation now and then could not be called friendship.

He drank, Oscar told Dubin, because he was not a better flutist.

"You're one of the best, Oscar."

"Not in my ears."

"Rampal says so."

"Not in my ears."

"That's not the only reason you drink," the biographer said.

"I never said so."

As Dubin entered the driveway he heard Oscar's flute, clearly, limpidly, deep within the house. He listened: Schubert's "Serenade." Lately Oscar had been transcribing lieder into flute songs. The song was like a lit candle in the night. In his "Short Life of Schubert" the biographer had written that the composer, on hearing the song sung at a concert, was supposed to have said, "You know, I never remembered it was so beautiful." How moving a simple song is, Dubin thought. How often they go to sadness. It's as though the sad song was the natural one, the primal song. Someone sings without knowing why and it's a song expressing hunger for love, regret for life unlived, sorrow for the shortness of life. Even some of the joyful songs evoke memories of something lost that one hopes endures.

The moon bathed the birch trees on the lawn in liquid light. There were several white trees in an irregular circle, inclined in different directions, looking like white-clad dancers in the snow. Oscar had written a flute song called, "The Birch Dancers." He said he wrote it one night when he couldn't sleep, after looking out the window at the white trees.

Listening to the serenade, this lied of yearning, he reflected that Schubert had often intertwined themes of love and death. In a certain time of his life the two experiences had become one. He had died of typhus at thirty-one. A few years before, at twenty-six or -seven, he had been infected with syphilis. "Each night when I go to sleep," he wrote to a friend, "I hope I won't wake again; and each morning reminds me of yesterday's misery." Love, he told his friend, offered only pain. The doppelgänger seeks the mystical fusion of love and death.

Dubin did not go into the house. When the song had ended he left the driveway and walked toward town.

in diesem Hause wohnte mein Schatz;
sie hat schon längst die Stadt verlassen,
doch steht noch das Haus auf demselben Platz. -

It looked in the garish moonlight like a piece of stark statuary, or an old painting of an old house. Ah, Fanny, what if you had found me in the Gansevoort that night in the city, would a different beginning have made a happy end?

A window went up with a rasp on the top floor of the house under the high-gabled roof, and Dubin was too surprised to duck into the shadow of the beech tree. A naked large-shouldered man leaned out into the wintry night and stared down at the astonished biographer. This was not the Eve of St. Agnes, nor was Dubin Porphyrio, so he could not have expected to be gazing at Fanny, naked or clothed; but it was a strange surprise, and not unrelated to his mood, to behold Roger Foster's bare curly-haired chest and moonlit thick-sideburned handsome face.

"Good Christ, Mr. Dubin, is that you down there?" the librarian said in surprise.

On a freezing night in January he talks to you naked from his window without a shiver.

"I'm afraid so."

"Anyone in particular you're looking for?"

Dubin calmly replied, "Nobody in particular. I couldn't sleep and am out for a short walk."

"Sorry about that. Anything I can do for you? Would you care to come in for a drink or maybe a cup of hot coffee?"

"Thank you, no."

He wanted to ask about Fanny but dared not.

"How are things going, Roger?"

"Pretty good. All's well at the library, what with the help of your kind wife."

"Wonderful," said Dubin.

"Has anybody heard anything from Fanny?" Roger asked.

"She's in Rome, I believe. Haven't you heard from her?"

"Just a postcard a couple of weeks ago, that she was in Venice having herself a ball."

"You don't say," said Dubin.

"She sure gets around."

"She seems to."

"You know, Mr. Dubin," Roger then said, "someday I hope we get to understand each other better. We have things in common—bookwise, I mean to say. We keep your biographies, every one of them, on our shelves. I know you've never liked me all that well but I'm not such a bad egg, if you ask around, and I hope to accomplish more than you might think."

"You put it well, Roger, I wish you luck."

"And I wish *you* luck, Mr. Dubin."

He breathed in the cold air, exhaling his steamy breath.

"Well, good night now, it's getting chilly."

Roger shut the window and pulled down the shade.

Dubin waited a minute perhaps for Fanny to peek through a slit in the drawn window shade. She did not.

After walking home he listened to a recording of "Death and the Maiden." It was after midnight. Kitty came down in her robe and had a drink as she listened.

They went to sleep in the same bed, Kitty wearing a black chiffon nightgown. She offered herself and he accepted. Afterward she changed into a white flannel nightgown and got back into their double bed.

"I want to travel again soon," Kitty said. "There's so much of the world we haven't seen, so much that's varied and beautiful. Let's have more fun than we've been having. When do you think we'll travel again?"

Dubin didn't know.

It seemed to him he'd been sleeping deeply when he heard a shrill ring and sat stiffly upright in bed. At first he thought the doorbell had sounded and was about to run down the stairs when it shot through him that the phone had rung piercingly once and stopped.

No one answered his insistent hellos.

"Maybe it was Maud," Kitty said. "Or Gerald."

If it was Fanny calling from Rome he was glad she had rung off.

Kitty had snuggled close and fallen asleep.

Dubin lay awake.

Middle age, he thought, is when you pay for what you didn't have or couldn't do when you were young.

The man trudged diagonally across the snowy field to the slushy road. Dubin watched him as he came, listing to the left. He seemed insufficiently dressed for the cold—had on a ragged jacket, thin pants, wet boots. He wore no hat, his thin black eyes expressionless. He was a burly man with heavy ears and small features, face unshaved. He waited in the road till Dubin had caught up with him without trying, and then walked along at the biographer's side.

"Good morning," Dubin said.

The man grunted. Once he hawked up a gob of phlegm and spat at the snow. Every so often, as they went on, he lifted his arms as if pointing a shotgun at a sparrow flying overhead. "Bang bang." The bird flew off. The man lowered his arms and trudged on with Dubin.

Who the hell is he? Does he think he knows me because he's seen me walking here? They were alone on the road and he was uneasy with the stranger.

"You live nearby?"

The man barely nodded.

They walked on, saying nothing. Dubin, after a while, would point at something in the distance and say what it was: "Frost's farmhouse one summer—the poet. His daughter Irma went crazy that year."

The man trudged along with him, scanning the sky. Is he an escaped convict, Dubin worried, or just some poor bastard looking for company?

Suppose he knifes me? He saw himself lying dead in a pool of blood in the frozen snow. There's Dubin lying in the road with a gaping wound in his chest, his gray-blue eyes staring at the gray-blue sky. It's a long hard winter.

The man hung close by, their arms bumping as they walked. Dubin reconciled himself to his company. After all, it's a public road. He's picked me to walk with, though who he is he's not about to say.

"Neither am I," he said aloud.

The stranger, tight-eyed, scanned the sky.

Suppose a man like him clings to you forever? You try to shake him and he follows you home. You have him arrested and he convinces the judge he's your uncle and moves in. Suppose, by one means or another, he stays forever? Who is he to you then? Dubin talked to himself sub voce.

As he was experiencing these thoughts two crows flew overhead in the white sky. The man dropped to his knee with a grunt and raised his arms as though sighting up a gun barrel

"Boom boom." To Dubin's astonishment one of the black birds wavered in flight and plummeted to the ground. The stranger let out a hoarse shout and plunged into the white field to retrieve the crow. Holding it up for Dubin to see, he pressed the dead bird to his chest and awkwardly ran, kicking up snow, diagonally across the field in the direction he had come.

Can a crow have a heart attack?

One of us is mad, the biographer thought.

Dubin ran in his rectangular circle.

He remembered, when he was twelve, one day walking home from school with his seventh-grade teacher, a broken-nosed knowing nasally talkative young man. As they were walking, this strange reddish-haired woman wearing a green hat trimmed with brown felt flowers approached in excitement from down the block. When William saw his insane mother coming toward them he said goodbye in the middle of somebody's sentence and hurried across the street. When he looked back she was standing alone on the sidewalk, sobbing, crazily waving her fist.

"In diesem Wetter, in diesem Braus, nie nätt' ich gesendet die Kinder hinaus!" Kitty sang at her harp.

As Samuel Johnson, at the top of the stairs, was turning the key of his chamber at Pembroke College, he heard his mother distinctly call, "Sam!"
Willie.
Leo!
The child had been sucked by the waves beyond the ropes. Willie screamed at the lifeguard who jumped into the boat and rowed in the choppy green water to where the child had drowned.
Leo, she called, Willie.
Willie, she wailed, *Leo.*

Q. Why don't you keep a journal?
A. I'm afraid what it might say.
At night they sat in opposing armchairs, hers a wingback against possible drafts, reading in separate pools of light. He had offered to build a fire, but she said she felt hot. He watched her pulse beat on her neck.
"This is one of those nights I keep sweating, then getting cold."
"Don't open the window."
"I will if I want to."
As they were reading, Kitty, a day behind with the day's news, read him humorous snippets from yesterday's papers.
"Don't," Dubin said. "I find it hard to concentrate."
"Why bother?"
Afterward she said, "We used to talk about everything in the world. We talk about nothing now."
He got up to put on a record, not because he wanted to listen to it, but because he must think of Fanny. His thoughts of the girl were a gluey collage representing an unalterable desire to be with her.
Why don't I tell my wife and maybe the misery will yield?
It seemed to him he had not told her because Fanny was still possible. If he answered her letter they might meet.
Mad, Dubin thought, after the treatment she had dished out in Venice. What can I anticipate, given who she is, but more of the same? What fantasy am I living? What imbecility?
He was, in his thoughts, living with Fanny, living it as they hadn't before.

Dubin was in Rome with her, in the same rooms, eating with Fanny, enjoying her, enjoying life. They walked through the Borghese Gardens in winter sunlight; wherever he turned he felt her warmhearted embrace. Before his eyes the girl changed: had become loving, loyal, protective, kind. She loved Dubin and he, in his right mind, loved her.

"Tell me about Lawrence," Kitty sometimes said as they sat alone in the room, and Dubin would make the effort to relate episodes of the man's life.

"You tell it so interestingly. Why is it so hard to write?"

"It resists the pen. The second thought hides from the first."

"Why don't you try dictating?"

"That's not for me."

"Why not?"

"I've tried it," Dubin said. He was on the verge of shouting.

"I feel cold. Is there a draft?" she asked, looking around.

"It's you, the house is warm."

Shivering, she tried to read. She glanced at the book she had opened, took in a few sentences, then stole a look at him, or looked away. She read slowly, every word of every sentence. She wanted to know in toto what each sentence said. He knew what book she was reading.

She had suggested cards but he had declined. He had never felt, he thought, this much apart from her. There were two houses and she was in the other. Kitty sat huddled in the Queen Anne chair, wearing pants and two sweaters, a rose cardigan over a black pullover. She's hurt by what she doesn't know.

From behind his book, held to his face, he reflected on his silence. He had nothing to say because he hadn't said it when it was his to say. What you don't say grows into not saying. A locked house is full of locked rooms.

He was, in his silence, elsewhere. He was not who she thought he was. Whoever he was, wearied by sticky fantasies, he wanted escape from his dream-drugged existence. He did not forever want to go on dreaming of Fanny Bick as she wasn't now and never would be. Dubin waited for his drawn-out steamy reverie at last to come to an end. He waited for it to wither, die in the mind. Until it died he was separate, alone, a small fog in a chair, pretending to read. He chilled the room with his presence. Kitty hugged herself against the cold.

At ten o'clock she glanced at her wristwatch, yawned, and shut the fat book.

"You've been whispering to yourself all night, William. Why don't you let me in on it?"

"What have I been saying?"

"I wish I knew. Will it help," she asked, her hands clasped white between her knees, "if I were to stay home mornings—I mean from the library?"

God, no, he thought.

He didn't think so, Dubin said. He wanted not to say it. He tried to say he needed her but felt no need.

"Is there something I can do for you? Some other way I can help?"

He said he was grateful for her patience.

"Patience is minimal. I'd like to do more for you if you'd let me."

Only patience, he urged. The misery could not go on forever.

She spoke firmly: "You're splendid with your gymnastics, William. You take brave walks in every weather. You diet as planned—I give you credit, though I'd go mad if I had to do it if I were feeling like you. You do what you've set yourself to, although I don't know what it comes to except you've lost weight, your clothes droop, your face is strained. You're out on your private little black sailboat in the rough green sea and here I am alone on a dreary lava-like shore. I don't know how to comfort you. I've never seen you so low so long. It has me frightened."

He asked her not to be.

"I can't help it," her voice wavered.

He spoke these words: "I've lost weight and move more easily. I feel lighter, a change at least. Something good may be happening. One day you wake and whatever it was that was sitting on your head has flown off. You feel yourself again."

"I hope so." She seemed doubtful. "Nathanael wasn't a psychiatrist—he almost became one but wouldn't because he enjoyed physical medicine. But he read a lot in psychotherapy, possibly because of me. I remember his saying that a sudden depression usually had a specific cause—you lost a job or love object—some specific disappointment or loss would set it off. William, did anything unusual happen to you while you were abroad?"

Dubin thought, Right here I could get off the train. I could walk out from under the pile of rocks I wear as a hat.

"I saw Gerald," he said. "It wasn't a happy time."

The train chugged on. There was no station. He had not got off.

"I don't mean Gerald. I mean something in Italy."

His eyes would not meet hers. "Why Italy?" he asked irritably, not wanting her to guess what was his to say.

"Just a feeling I have."

He said, believing it, the trouble was his work. If he solved that he'd solve everything.

She vehemently denied it. "It isn't your work that's doing this to you. It's you doing something to your work. I know your doubts about Lawrence as subject but you had similar doubts about Thoreau. You always have doubts at this stage. Please don't put it ass-backwards. It's not your work that hurts your work, it's you."

"Why would I need Evan Ondyk if I have you?"

"I'm not trying to sell you anything," Kitty said with hauteur. "But I think you need help."

He said he was not a child any more. "I don't deny I could have been helped by analysis once but I've lived my life without it. Now I have to go on what I know."

"I've been reading about depression and I think you've had it more often than you think, sometimes simply as lack of joie de vivre—"

"Does the book explain why you sometimes lack joie de vivre?"

"Not as much as you. Sometimes I think you've never felt young in your life; you've almost always interpreted it as obligation or lost opportunity. I'm basically a more carefree happier person than you."

He hoarsely denied it.

"There are times your nature dampens mine," she said.

"That works both ways."

"Let's drop it," Kitty said. "Forget the joie de vivre. I know you know a lot about people, William, because of the way you contemplate human lives, but I'm saying you could cut out a lot of unnecessary suffering if you consulted with someone. The will isn't everything."

"It keeps me going," the biographer shouted.

"If you know what's wrong with you," she said, her voice thickening, "for Christ's sake, tell me."

He said things changed in time; he needed time.

"But what about me while you're dieting and exercising for wisdom? I feel like shit when you want nothing I have to give."

"I want everything," Dubin shouted, waving his arms.

"You seem to want nothing *I* have to give. You hide your life, whispering what I can't hear. You're not affectionate. We never really talk to each other."

"What the hell are we doing now?"

"We aren't talking. You're yelling, we are not talking."

"You have no confidence in me. You insult me by giving me psychiatric advice. Spare me Nathanael's textbooks. I don't want to be his posthumous patient. I don't want to be yours."

Grabbing her *Handbook of Psychiatry*, Kitty ran up the stairs.

To quiet his self-disgust for renewing, replenishing the deceit, Dubin sniffed the gas burners for her.

He found the brandy bottle and poured himself a glassful.

He drank with his hat on in the cold house, his coat draped on his shoulders. The wind clattered down from the mountains. He drank, listening to the roaring wind blowing snowflakes through the straining groaning cracking branches of trees. After midnight he felt himself go to bed in a blizzard. Dubin wound the clock gloomily, unable to look it in the face. The wind wailing around the house seeped in through storm windows. He felt it like a live presence in the room. Undressing, he got into the lonely bed, compounded by two. Kitty slept soundly at first, her breathing heavy. Dubin lay awake listening to the storm: primordial blast blowing from the beginning of the world. If it could only change a man's life. Snowflakes spat at the windows. He slept and woke heavily, resisting waking. The drinking had added to the weight of the heaviness. It was a black heaviness, iron on the soul. Or you were drowning in nothing and this stone arm forced your head under; the arm was your own.

He rose in the live morning dark and stumbled groggily, step by step, through the brutal routine of the day. I must go through it. It is to show the depression it is not all. It is to show I fear it only so much, only so far. It is depression, an entity, it is not all. I know its black heaviness. I must be detached. I will not lock hands with it so that it becomes an adversary, another self; an ax to strike me with. I will wait for it to go its way. If I daily do what I have to, go through the motions, it will leave the house. It wants me to be its love, fuck it, marry it, but I won't. I welcome the white blizzard. It is a thing to think of, to be in other than depression. Thoreau was wrong in saying nature doesn't sympathize with sorrow. It does because it interrupts; it flings its frozen self at you, assails the plots and conjurations of my bleak brain.

He was old in the bathroom mirror. Dubin was afraid not to shave. He told himself not to but didn't know what else to do. This was the wrong day not to shave. He had rarely not shaved when he wasn't sick in bed.

In the lusterless mirror his left eye was fixed, distant, cold; contemplating his frightened right eye.

Dubin felt himself groan.

"Hush," said Kitty from the bedroom. "It never ends."

"Stupid bastard," Dubin groaned.

"Who?" she wanted to know.

He groaned in silence.

"Be silent," Carlyle writes himself in his journal, "be calm, be not mad."

Dubin tries to get a religious thought going.

"Love," Lawrence wrote, "is a thing to be learned through centuries of patient effort."

Where can I find the time?

"Please come out of the bathroom."

She was up early, dressed, studying herself in the long mirror. A night's decent sleep had helped her mood, looks; had brightened her eyes, quickened last night's lank hair.

"I wouldn't go on the long walk if I were you. It's going to blizzard."

"I thought it was."

"So far it's been only the wind with snow flurries. The radio says a blizzard is coming."

"I thought it had begun."

"That was the wind," Kitty said.

He'd come back to the house if it snowed heavily, Dubin said.

"No further than to the green bridge," she cautioned. "And put on long johns and your wool socks or you'll catch cold."

He looked away from her. They ate breakfast in silence. He listened to her chew her crisp toast.

Kitty left for the library. She returned to sniff the gas burners. "Ta ta," she called as she left.

He looked at his work, tried not to think how he felt. He held the misery off, kept it at bay with a stiletto as he wrote out his long yellow page of snaky

147

sentences, reflecting on each, trying to connect them; by some act of grace to weave a tapestry, a life, a biography. Then on a white page he wrote a dozen new sentences and read them with care to see what they said; to find out if they were taking him seriously. He read them with dignity to show the sentences he had written and respected them, and must himself be respected. They were not to crawl or slither or flop around. They must go somewhere seriously into the life of Lawrence, revive, re-create, illumine it. But the last sentence, when he read it, said, "I am trapped." Dubin with a cry flung his pen against the wall. Disgust rose to his gorge and he fought the approach of panic. I've got to get out of here. I've got to get away from my fucking mind.

He left the kitchen door and ran through the trees into the field. Here the wind leapt at him, struck him, clawed his face. He gasped, choked, stood immobilized by the wind. His eyes teared, breath ached, as he tried to push on. The wind was a gorgon with an armlock on his stone head.

He retreated into the house, waited shivering in the kitchen, to recover his strength. He wanted not to go anywhere, to stand there till the weather abated, winter disappeared, the world changed. But he was afraid, if he stayed, of nothing, heavy, painted black. He was afraid of the silence ticking. After endless minutes he went out the front door, stumbled down the steps, hurried along the street. A heavy wind tore through the tops of moaning trees. He made his way downtown, icy snowflakes stinging his face.

Dubin hurried to the library. If he bought a newspaper he could read it there, forget himself; he dared not return to the empty house. Could he sit in the library reading the paper? Not with Kitty around, concerned to see him there. It was best not to buy a paper. He'd be better off into his routine, part of it rather than nothing. Not doing what he had to added to the misery of not doing. He would walk in the weather rather than do nothing.

Dubin went slowly in the falling snow to the outskirts of town, past the thermometer-assembly plant, the auto graveyard, two gas stations, then a motel and a tourist house. Along the wet highway he trod, approaching the long route by the back way. He had never walked it this way before. If Kitty asked why he had taken the long walk after all, he would say he had never done it this backwards way before.

Whatever diverts the mind from itself may help. What else is there to do? The wind-driven snow was now falling heavily. Dubin tramped on quickly a quarter of a mile in a world growing white, then had to tell himself it was no use, to turn back. For a while the wind had been thrusting him forward and it was no great trouble plodding on. Now it shifted, blew at him from the east. The wind, wailing, blew the coarse snow in blasts across the field, assailing him like a cluster of arrows, as though he was its only target. His field of vision was luminously white. He had turned tail and had trouble walking back to the highway. He inched on, stopping every several steps to discover if he knew where he was. When the blustery freezing wind momentarily died down and the snow thinned he was able to stride along. Once he beheld in the distance winter fields growing white, a wall of whitening black trees, and beyond, the misted fields flanking the snow-laced hills. Extraordinary sight: he felt a moment of elation before it vanished in the snow. Dubin peered around for a shelter but saw none. Most of the houses were behind him, toward the mid-point of the long road. He expected he would soon reach the highway. The wavering wind came at him again. He stiffened, staggered forward, then realized the ground had softened; the earth had roughened, he was no longer on the road. The snow, blowing in veiled gusty waves across the uneven fields, had wiped out every sign of the familiar road.

He felt fright, an old fear: his mother frightened by winter; himself stranger, where he oughtn't to be. Dubin found himself moving on a slope propelled downward. With fear in his gut he then diagonally ascended the incline, following his tracks disappearing as he sought them. The snow came down momentarily slowly, the flakes hanging in air before touching earth. He was standing in a hollow in an unknown field. As he tried to think which way to go he saw a rabbit skittering through the snow pursued by a dog; Dubin realized it was a fox. The rabbit slid up against a rock. The fox pounced on it and in a moment tore the screeching creature apart. The snow was covered with blood. Dubin stumbled away. The wild begins where you least expect it, one step off your daily course. A foot past the road and you're fighting with death. He had changed his black inner world for the white outer, equally perilous—man's fate in varying degrees; though some were more fated than others. Those who were concerned with fate were fated. He struck his boot against the dazzling white ground to get a fix on where he was but could not tell one part of the frozen earth from another. Dubin could see nothing in the distance, had no understanding of direction. Then he kicked up some threads of dead grass and knew he was still far off the road.

He waited for the wind to die down so he could see more than snow whirling around him. But the blustery wind continued to blow strongly.

Pushing into it, assuming it was coming from the east and he had probably gone off the western side of the road because he had not been walking facing traffic, he wandered amid ridges that rose at last to a level surface. Dubin, in gasping relief, stumbled onto the road. He chose, after a moment, what he thought was the direction to the highway and plodded on, holding his arm above his eyes, trying to see the way ahead. Now and then he could make out a utility pole streaked with snow, and overhead, glimpse the white-coated thick utility wire. Lowering his head against the wind he pushed on, stopping often to peer around through his snow-encrusted eyes. The snow snowed in his ears. He brushed it off his face with his wet mitten. He had gone perhaps an eighth of a mile farther when he felt his galoshes sink into soft snow as a grove of trees opened before him. Disheartened, he knew he had lost the road again.

Panic went through him in a lightning flash. He pictured himself running in circles, but managed to bring himself under control. Dubin stood motionless, breathing heavily, trying to work out where he was. The woods opened upon the light. No tracks of his own he could see beyond ten feet. Probably the road had turned, though not he with it. He must be somewhere near it, surely not far from the highway. Backtracking, he was once more in the open. He thought for a moment he knew where he was: the road had curved to the right as he had walked on level ground straight ahead, gone into the trees. If he had turned with the road and stayed with it he'd soon have got to the highway. After about a mile, possibly via a ride he might hitch in a passing truck—if there was a truck in this wild weather—he'd be safely into Center Campobello.

To find his way he had to make the right next move. Dubin trudged along, stopping at intervals to listen for traffic sounds in the distance; or perhaps a car on the road he'd been walking. Sooner or later a clanking snowplow would come by; sooner on the highway, later on this country road. He heard only the soughing wind. The storm was increasing in intensity, the wind blowing flowing sheets of snow over the road. Dubin turned from the wind. Snow crackled on his clothes. He heard a shrieking bird but could not see it. He thought of running but dared not—would break his leg if he stepped into a hole. A moment later overhead became strangely light but there was no sky. The wind abated. He pushed on. Why haven't I learned more about nature? Which way is north? He had seen moss on all sides of a tree. How can I keep from walking in circles? You can't if you live in them. He felt a chill of fear, an icy trickle on his head, his brain pierced by cold. With a cry Dubin tore off his hat and slapped it savagely on his arm, beating off the wet snow. The red wool hat in his hand startled him.

He was tired. Coming to a low stone wall—would it be bounding a road or dividing a field?—farmers sold their fields with walls running through them—Dubin climbed over it, following until the snow-covered wall ended in a spill of rocks amid trees; then he slowly traced it back the other way. The wind had decreased in force but the coarse wet flakes were falling so rapidly he could barely see five feet ahead of him. He thought he might follow the wall, touching it with his hand; but it was not there to be touched. He was into a grove of sparse trees once more. The woods were gusty with wind, impossible to go through. Now I am really lost. Should he cry for help? Who would hear him in the wailing wind? If a car passed nearby its windows would surely be shut. Who could hear his shouts?

As Dubin came out of the trees he pictured an abandoned house. He pictured the kind of hut children built and left in the fields. After walking up the long flank of a rise and then down, he was again at a gray lichen-covered stone wall—the same?—another? He must stay with it, see where it led. The wall crumbled as he climbed it. Dubin, after a while, got up, brushed off his pants, limped on. He went through a grove of knee-high pines, then beheld a stand of tall whitened Norway pines. Where were these trees? He was almost certain he had seen them close to the road before the bend to the highway where the road sloped on the right. But there was no downward slope he could feel, let alone see. Are these pines where I think they are? Am I where I think I am? What a mad thing not to have stayed home with my small stationary miseries. Now I risk my life. He thought he ought not move until he could think of something sensible to do next. How few choices there are when the weather is white, wind fierce, snow thick. I am mad to be here. He jabbed a finger at the sky. There was a man in his mind wandering forever in deep snow. Dubin beat his breast. He heard his mother's voice. *Leo*, she called. I could drown here as my brother did in the ocean.

Exhausted, he sank to the ground and crawled under the branches of a spruce. Here was room to sit, perhaps rest. Above, the drooping branches were heavy with snow, the lower ones dry tufts of green. The beige spruce needles that covered the ground between trees were dusted with patches of white. He sat with his back to the broad spruce tree, waiting for fatigue to ease, trying to restrain fear, to stay alert.

It was quiet where Dubin sat, though he could hear the wind still groaning in the swaying trees, and every once in a while a clump of snow fell, sifting like mist through the spruce. He would wait till he had recovered his strength to get up and go on being lost. His lungs seared his chest. He could feel his mouth trembling. Despite the cold he felt sweaty; he felt his age. It was easy enough to sit under a tree but he feared the woods filling with snow. He saw himself buried amid trees in snow up to his neck. Embarrassing to die so close to the road; like drowning in a bathtub. Dubin let out a shout for help but the strange cry frightened him, so he sat with hard pounding heart, silent in the still spruce grove. He whispered to himself.

What a mad thing to happen. What a fool I am. It was the having I wanted more than the girl. Who is she to me? She doesn't deserve the feeling I give her. See what I've done to myself. I'm like a broken clock—works, time, mangled. What is life trying to teach me?

The woods were growing dark. He sat unable to decide whether to stay longer under the trees; wait the storm out. Suppose it snowed till nightfall and throughout the night until morning—Dubin frozen stiff, snowman. Death's scarecrow. He heard a sudden heavy plop in the branches overhead and cried out as lumps of snow showered on him. His first wild fear was that a bobcat had seen and leapt at him. But when the powdery mist settled he beheld a hook-nosed white owl perched on a swaying branch over his head staring at him through the leathery slits of its cold blinking eyes. But the owl as if frightened by Dubin flew off into the wind-driven snow with a hoot and great flapping of its long wings. It disappeared into the trees. Dubin rose to his knees, crawled out from under the spruce, walked into an open field.

The wind had quietened, the snow falling silently. It was now more than a foot deep, deeper in drifts. He floundered around the fringe of a stand of bleak ash trees. Two of them had fallen. Dubin picked his way over the fallen trees. Through the brush ahead he made out a snow-covered stone wall about a foot higher than those he had already encountered. Separating him from what fate? He was cruelly fatigued; could barely keep his eyes open. He saw himself lying in the snow. Then he climbed the wall because it was the next thing to do. Dubin lifted himself over the rock wall. He found himself wandering on the recognizable road; assumed he had crossed and recrossed it.

The narrow road had been plowed, plowed narrowly, though he hadn't heard the truck go by. Since then another two inches of snow had fallen, but there were earth-streaked mounds of plowed-up snow banking both sides of the road, and he felt with relief that he could easily follow it. Yet snowflakes continued to pelt him thickly so that he could still not tell direction; was still not sure which was the way to go. It begins again: which is the nearest way to the highway? What side of the road did I go off? Where did I come out of the field? Did I cross the road without knowing it? Why is it I don't remember the high stone wall I just climbed? Has it always been there and I have never noticed, or have I seen it but am too frightened to remember? Is this the long hard-topped road I usually walk, or have I gone somewhere I have never been before? It must be more than a secondary road or they wouldn't have plowed it so soon. Unless a farmer cleared his own access road and I am on it? If so where does it go? Is there a farmhouse or barn nearby? He saw no light. Now how shall I go? Am I already into the turn of the road, therefore head west, then south and I hit the highway? Or should I go north and if I'm lucky I ought to sight a house in twenty minutes; unless I don't.

Dubin turned left where he had been standing at the wall and after tedious and forgetful walking, as dusk grew darker, he was convinced he was on the right road plodding the long but wrong way back. Wrong because long. He stopped, deathly wearied, trying again to decide whether to go the other possibly shorter way. He was dully cold, his clothes wet, face stiff, hands and feet freezing. His back teeth ached with cold. The wind had died down and it was beginning to rain as well as snow. He could feel the icy rain through his soaking hat and see it snowing. Dubin trudged on. After a white wet timeless time it seemed to him something was approaching, a truck, or car, its wheels churning in the slush, brights on, wipers flapping as it loomed up like a locomotive out of the raining snow. The biographer flailed both arms, frantically waved his red hat as he stumbled toward the slowly moving vehicle. It then shot through his frozen head that the white-faced woman, her head wrapped in a black shawl, who sat stiffly behind the wheel, peering nearsightedly through the fogged windshield; frightened, perhaps already mourning, was his wife.

Kitty held the door open as Dubin numbly got in beside her.

"I saw a white owl."

Crying silently, she drove him home.

Five

Kitty's old friend, Myra Wilson, died in her farmhouse of heart failure. She knew she was dying but would not be moved to a hospital. She died a week after her seventy-ninth birthday, a woman more vital than her body permitted. She had rarely mentioned her age or ailments. In her presence Kitty spoke little of hers. Myra would kiss Dubin mouth to mouth when they met, a way she saw herself. Kitty had wired her daughter that her mother was dying and wired again the next morning to say she was dead. Mrs. Meyer flew in from Milwaukee late in the afternoon. With Kitty's help she completed the funeral arrangements.

Mrs. Meyer was a restrained bulky woman in a brown felt hat and black cloth coat. She was about Kitty's age but looked older. Her right eye was tearing—the effect, she said, of a cold. She stayed with the Dubins for two nights and was restless to be home with her family. "Mr. Meyer said Mama could live with us," she told them. "She had her choice." Her youngest child was a boy of thirteen. The girls were nineteen and twenty-four. "My daughter is nineteen," Dubin told her. "Twenty," Kitty said. "She was twenty in October." Dubin felt he had misplaced a year of Maud's life.

There were eight at the graveside: the Methodist minister; Kitty and Dubin; Flora Greenfeld, moody handsome lady—Oscar was on a concert tour in Australia; Ursula and Fred Habersham; Craig Bosell, carpenter and handyman, who had looked after the house and barn for Mrs. Wilson; and there was Mrs. Meyer facing a leafless elm, holding the family Bible. It snowed at the graveside. It snowed lightly into the open grave. As the casket was lowered and the prayers recited, Kitty wept brokenly. Mrs. Meyer darted her a startled glance and wiped her wet eye with a handkerchief. Kitty tried to suppress her sobs, squirmed, bit her lip, but couldn't stop. She walked away from the grave and sat in the car. Dubin, when the ceremony was over, drove her home.

"I couldn't help it," Kitty said.

Mrs. Meyer telephoned them from the Wilson farmhouse. She was shutting up the place and would return in the spring.

"Your mother was a courageous woman living alone in that big house, I couldn't have done it," Kitty said.

"She didn't have to but that's the nature she had."

Mrs. Meyer delivered the farmhouse keys to Kitty in case someone had to get in. "Bosell is closing the house," she said. "He's drained the pipes and when the company takes out the phone he'll lock the doors and shutters. There's no stock left in the barn or henhouse and the dog she had ran away."

Kitty regretted it. "I should have remembered Ben."

"When I come back in the spring I'll put the place up for sale. We sold off seventy acres after Pa died. Now there are twenty-four left, and the house, barn and henhouse. Thanks kindly for your kindness and consideration to Mama and me."

"Myra was a favorite of mine." Kitty quickly turned away.

Mrs. Meyer left for Milwaukee.

"Why am I always crying?" Kitty asked Dubin. He praised her generous nature while disliking her for outdoing Mrs. Meyer at the graveside.

Kitty, after mulling it awhile, had quit her job at the library. Dubin had urged her not to, but she said she had to think of Roger Foster: he needed a professional librarian who could work full-time. "I'm no great help to him."

"That wasn't what he said to me."

"What did he say to you? When did he say it?"

"He said you were doing a very good job or words to that effect. I met him by chance on a walk in town."

"What else did he say?" she spoke casually, studying him.

Had Roger mentioned Fanny? Was Kitty alluding to her? "Nothing I can recall," Dubin said.

"I quit because the work was becoming a bore," Kitty said, looking bored. "I'd rather give you the time I gave them."

Dubin said she gave him as much time as he needed. He spoke gently and she was gentle with him.

Her first morning as housewife resumed she spent showing the new cleaning woman, a bulky French-Canadian of fifty-five, how she liked things done. Kitty also sewed on the sewing machine, typed and filed recipes she had torn out of newspapers and magazines, arranged and catalogued their old travel slides—Dubin often studied the villas and farmhouses Lawrence and Frieda had lived in—and energetically wrote letter after letter, some of which she tore up and at once rewrote. "I owe to everybody, especially the kids."

She started something new with a burst of energy. She had begun a reading project: to read a book on contemporary philosophy and all of Jane Austen. She had never read Lawrence's poetry or Thoreau's *Cape Cod*, which she thought she would do.

Shortly after leaving the library she suffered a spell of indigestion and for a while was worried about her health. "I've not been feeling well. My color has been poor for weeks. You don't think there's anything wrong, do you?" She was nervous and pale, her eyes troubled.

He didn't think so. "You're on edge about something. Just watch your diet. That usually does it for you."

She said she would. When the indigestion disappeared so did her worries about cancer. She kept busy and had few complaints.

Once more Kitty slept late to make up for weary periods of wakefulness in the pit of night, but she would come down in her robe for coffee with Dubin if she was not sleeping when he rose at some outrageously early hour.

Afterward she got back into bed. She still experienced flashes of feeling hot and cold. When she was hot her face looked as though she had just stepped out of a hot shower, or was deeply blushing. She blushed scarlet; so did Maud. When Kitty felt cold she raised the thermostat and went to her dresser for a sweater.

She was not content when she looked at herself in the mirror. Recently while standing without clothes in front of the full-length glass in the bedroom, she had touched her hair, then lifted her breasts and said, "Don't you think I look reasonably young for my age?" She confessed, "I'm mourning my losses. If only one could get used to it. But one doesn't. I see it so clearly, the loss of my looks."

"Du bist noch die alte Marschallin?"

"I wish I were, she was thirty-eight."

"You don't look your age. You'd easily pass for forty-five."

"I wouldn't," she said. "I don't think I would. I'm fifty-one and look every bit of it."

He left her standing sadly naked before the glass.

It was a long white winter—leaden skies broke, spilling snow endlessly on snow. Sometimes it snowed lazily half the day, sometimes savagely for a day or two in flowing waves of white. The biographer stood at his window watching the snowflakes flying, white curtain lowered, ending no play, beginning none. When it stopped snowing for several days, or a week, the scene, the drama, was the endless white world mournfully searched by an eyeless wailing white wind. The monochrome white dulled the mind, restricted movement, experience. Yet the roads were continually plowed, salted, sanded; and Dubin, heavily coated, scarved, booted, against the weather, walked, the one man in town visible on the snow-rutted roads. The temperature rarely rose above zero. The stringy willows in the dead fields were a greenish mustard-yellow. Pines and bent spruce bristled with icicled snow. Once as he tediously walked—it seemed to him nowhere—he plunged into a snowy field up to his gut and waited for his life to change.

The long walk-run was still routine. He had fitted himself for the task: you did it daily and therefore could do it. The experience proved you could. He was compelling a willed experience to contend with another, unwilled, that lingered. But as soon as it became easier to do, the wind, freezing cold, and the icy earth, made it harder to do. If you stopped for a single day, much you had accomplished—at last got used to—you had to accomplish again. For two days at the end of the month the temperature rose and it rained steadily, drearily, foggily; then the weather again turned frigid, the snow stiffened, slush froze; the roads were inches thick with ice. There was a week of twenty below, two awesome days of thirty below. The rumbling clanking snowplows only thinly shaved the stony ice-ruts on the road. Dubin gave up the long walk, against the insatiable will. Now when he left the house he picked his way along the glistening slippery ice only to the covered bridge and back. Even a mile seemed a mad thing to do. People offered rides and shook their heads when he waved them off. They sensed his creation: his trial.

The radio called it a hard winter. It was desolate; and in his study the windows were frozen over. Icicles hung from the deep eaves of the roof and grew thick and long. One long icicle was a four-foot spear before it broke in sunlight and crashed below.

Kitty was sick of being housebound. "Let's, for God's sake, get away to a warm place. We've never been to the Caribbean. What have you got against a warmer climate?"

He offered to let her go alone.

"I don't want to go alone, don't ask me to. Let's both go for a week. I'm married to you, not your book. I want to be free of it."

"You are free of it."

"I want you to be."

He had to hang in. She thought, he guessed, that he might be getting back to work and said no more about going away. Dubin kept to his room for long hours each day, letting her think what she might be thinking. He let her think so but sat at the desk reading. He read one biography after another, famished for lives.

From his window he watched the sunset reflected on the nearby hills. As the winter sky darkened the hills were suffused in rose, lilac, mauve, and these colors, in contrast to freezing daylight, seemed warm, warming the bluish-gray outcroppings on Mt. No Name. One evening the icy mountain blazed in rose flame. From this illusion of warmth he traveled to another: the rosy winter sunset was the promise of spring. Hadn't Thoreau said the mind was the only stronghold against winter: it could, at least, anticipate spring. Good, but not if spring held out to the end of spring: it shunned the anticipating mind. The outside thermometer read six below and winter had far to go before it yielded to reason or mercy—or to the thunder of the wheeling earth: through February and March into the teeth of cold April. In the Northeast, at the thin edge of New England, it sometimes snowed on the flowers of May. If spring comes can spring be far behind? Anticipation admits there is tomorrow, not much more.

Kitty, nursing a cold, was too restless to stay in bed. She wandered in the house, straightening things: ashtrays, vases, flowers. She wiped her oak table. "When I have nothing to do I do everything." She wore a voluminous robe over her bed jacket and nightgown, and a pair of Dubin's black socks he hated to see on her, to keep her feet warm. In another mood she wore a brown housecoat and silver slender mules; and a kerchief to warm her head.

Her hair fell in strands on her shoulders. Colds, she complained, made her hair lank and darkened her complexion. Her nose ran, her eyes were rheumy; she was like a small animal he couldn't name. Kitty pulled up the living-room window and poured sunflower seeds on the bird-feeder shelf, then sat sniffling, sneezing, waiting for a winter bird to appear. After an hour a blue jay landed on the feeder with a thump, saw her watching, and flew off scattering sun seeds.

She sat in the kitchen, grooming her housecoat, picking off long hairs. "I seem to be shedding." She jumped when Dubin coughed, then apologized for being startled. She sighed restlessly, seemed someone's lost self—his fault, he thought. Dubin was burdened by his lack of affection; knew she felt it.

The telephone rang. When she picked up the receiver a boy's voice said, "Why don't you go get yourself fucked?" Kitty flung the phone against the wall.

Sometimes when she answered the ring the telephone clicked off. She gave up a call reluctantly. "Hello, hello," she called. "Hello!—Hello!" she insisted to the telephone.

"Who are you trying to hear from?"

"That's a stupid thing to say."

One night she waked from a dream and woke Dubin to tell it to him. She said she would not have minded his waking her.

"I dreamed I was menstruating again. I was flowing profusely and was frightened. I said in my dream, 'William, what shall I do, I'm bleeding so heavily?' And you impatiently said, 'Cut it out!' "

"I apologize," said Dubin. "Now let me sleep."

"I'm burning tonight," Kitty sighed five minutes later. "Is the house overheated?"

"No. Don't open the window or the wind will blast us out of bed."

She turned on her bed lamp and changed, panting, from a white flannel nightgown to a pink sheer sleeveless one; then fell instantly asleep, while he remained awake thinking useless thoughts until the alarm rang in the dark and he groped his way to the shower.

"Drop dead!"

She woke. "Who?"

"Nobody you know."

"I'll bet I do."

"I spoke to the mirror, don't take credit."

160

"Jesus, Mary, and Joseph, the goddamned things you say."

In the bathroom she gargled loudly, ferociously cleared her throat, coughed on and on. He could hear her in his study. She discovered a large black moth on the wall and socked it relentlessly with a rolled-up towel.

Kitty misplaced her diary and asked Dubin whether he had seen it. It was an on-and-off affair in a spiral notebook, rebegun recently in black ink. When they were first married her diary was written in green ink and he occasionally glanced into it when she wasn't around. He felt she left it in sight so he could read what she wanted him to know, but would rather not talk about. A diary was a punitive instrument.

She had begun a book on modern philosophy and after twenty pages set it aside. That afternoon she drove to Winslow to shop for a dress. She couldn't find one she wanted and drove to Albany. There she bought a pair of shoes and a green dress. She returned the dress the next morning. "Green offends me," she said to Dubin. He had said he didn't care for the dress. She kept the cross-strap elegant black shoes. She had also tried on several hats, but none suited her. Sometimes she bought things to return them.

That night she informed Dubin she had been seeing Evan Ondyk. "Not about you," she said uneasily. "About myself."

He knew why but asked anyway.

She said nothing, then went to the bird-feeder window and looked out as she talked. "Since Myra's funeral I haven't felt right. You remember I couldn't stop crying at the cemetery? A sense of loss has stayed with me."

Dubin remembered.

"Since then I've been thinking of my life—with you, and with Nathanael. That seems to be starting again, though I haven't done it in years."

"You were dreaming of him last summer."

"Not as often as I used to. I have no intense feelings about him, but he's still a familiar stranger who keeps standing on the street corner, expecting me to come over and say hello. I remember the most trivial things of our life together, for instance buying him a pair of tennis sneakers one Saturday afternoon while we were out wheeling Gerald in his carriage. Isn't it strange the way we're constituted—I mean about the past? Jesus, why are we?"

He felt again as though he had married her marriage.

Once when she used to talk about Nathanael, herself, Gerry as a baby, Dubin had felt a sense of being out of it; he no longer felt that.

"Don't make too much of it," he said.

"I honestly don't want to, but certain things keep bothering me. I don't mean Nathanael. Now I think of Myra alone in that empty farmhouse and I scarcely gave her the time of day."

He reminded her she had visited the old woman almost daily. "When you couldn't you telephoned. Sometimes you'd shop for her in the morning and also call at night."

"I could have done more for her when she was sick. She was alone too often. And I feel terrible about Ben running away. I should have paid attention to him."

Dubin thought it might have been better if she hadn't given up the library job. "At least it got you out of the house half the day."

"Lay off about that job," Kitty said in irritation. "I think you'd like it if I was never in the house."

He denied it.

"All you want is to be alone. If I died you'd get along very well without me."

"I'd want you to get along without me."

"I hate your beastly love of solitude."

She had again been playing the harp. Kitty pulled the gilded frame down on her shoulder, pressed her feet on the pedals, and began to pluck the strings, her hands moving like birds flying at each other. When she sang in a soft mezzo her singing voice was small. One day she played for hours and whatever she played—Chopin, Schumann, Hugo Wolf—sounded lonely. The next day she played as though she were in love or wanted to be; and wanted him to know.

He heard the harp as he sat upstairs at his desk, and found it impossible to read. She never played while he was at work. Dubin was angered, then thought she must be certain he wasn't writing. Yet as he listened to her playing he felt the possibility of life with feeling. He thought, as he listened, of meeting someone with whom he might fall in love, a woman of thirty perhaps. He wanted another chance in marriage; he could do it better than he had done it. And he'd be his bride's first husband.

Kitty tore the strings into a reverberant jangle, then went out for a drive.

When she returned she gaily told Dubin that a young man had tried to pick her up in the parking lot of the supermarket when she came out with her bundle of groceries. "He had a heavy mustache and wore bell-bottom trousers. He looked like a New York actor," she laughed.

"What did he say?"

"He called me Cutie and asked me to come for a ride. I said I had a ride and took off. He knew I could see through him."

She then regretted her nature. "I should have flirted with him." And said she had frittered away much of her life. "I find it distressing not to be better pulled together at this time of my life. I should have done more for myself and not depended so much on my husbands. I'm upset about your problems and the way we are. I'm also upset because I feel I've been a lousy mother, or my kids would write once in a while. I'm tense about Maud coming home —if she ever does."

She approached a mirror to look at herself and turned quickly away. She went into the kitchen to brew herself a cup of tea and deeply breathed above the burners before setting down a pot and lighting the gas.

The next morning she misplaced her wedding ring. "I can't find it anywhere, it's lost." It was an inexpensive thin band. She had always liked its design, its simplicity. Kitty could not find it after taking her shower and spent the morning grimly going from room to room—unmaking beds to hunt for it. She pulled up rugs, opened drawers, stood on chairs searching closet shelves, feeling along every inch. In the afternoon when after an hour's restless rest she went on relentlessly looking, Dubin offered to buy her a new wedding ring if this didn't turn up.

"I want my old ring," said Kitty. "It took you a month to find the one you wanted. It was your first real present to me."

She went on vigorously searching and at last found the ring in a plastic glass in the bathroom.

"Bravo," said Dubin.

They faced each other in hatred.

Maud Dubin, who had come home only for short stays last year, appeared at the house in early February, her beautiful long red hair shorn and dyed black. Her brows were lined black. Her light eyes seemed to have darkened. "Maud, for God's sake!" Dubin cried. Her eyes appealed to him not to say more. He momentarily turned away, then put his arms around her, kissing the cheek she offered, and after an attempt at casual talk, trotted up the stairs. For a while he stood at his study window watching the leafless swaying trees in the windswept field near the side of the old barn. In ten minutes he trotted down once more to greet his daughter, but

Maud had called a friend and had driven off in Kitty's car. Dubin stared out of his window.

She'd kissed full on the lips as a child, it was her way. She gave feeling so naturally he thought he had earned it. Maud had a raucous laugh and high voice and seemed a little girl until she opened her mouth and spoke in full sentences. She grew according to his vision of what she must ultimately be. Maud resembled Kitty more than Dubin although her red hair derived from his mother, whom he rarely remembered as other than gray-haired. Charlie had told him that as a girl she had a deep-red head of hair. "So people came miles to look on her." Maud's bronze hair had hung thickly down her back. Kitty had knitted her a white wool hat with a blue band that she wore for years in and out of the house. One night Dubin entered her room as she slept wearing her hat. As he tried to remove it she had lifted her warm arms and held him in sleep.

At fifteen Maud plaited her long hair into a pigtail; and when her father heard the front door shut in the morning he would put down his razor and go to the bedroom window so he could watch her on the back lawn striding along in brown boots, white hat, blue coat, the wooden-barretted pigtail swinging as she sturdily walked toward the woods on the way to the bus stop at the covered bridge.

He would sometimes stand in her room after she had left for school, or was away for the summer, to reflect in it, reflect on her. He would look over her books, surprised by some he had given her. He liked the many volumes of poetry she had collected; her small desk; the flowered coverlet on her prim bed in a soft-yellow room; throw rug on the floor; colored pictures of savage and saint taped on the wall above her head. Dubin looked out of her windows to see what she saw. She was a handsome lanky active girl—swam, backpacked, skied—with a slender firm body that grew lovely, after a crisis of fat, as she matured. She had a quiet handsome face with light-blue eyes, uneven lips—they were Dubin's—and a small bony chin. Maud had unexpected qualities and did unexpected things. By Kitty's edict she was Jewish and she called herself a Jew. Kitty had said, "There are only five in town and no house of worship, how can she learn?" but Dubin said, "If she thinks of herself as Jewish let's see what she makes of it."

Her parents' marriage had been best to her teens; she knew when it was at its less than best. Though Gerry, in his private world, had given her short shrift, she spoke up passionately for his rights. Among her own, apparently, was a curious impatience with childhood. She seemed to want to live life in contravention of time—before it permitted. Whatever you're running after, her father thought, wait a bit, it'll catch up with you.

"What's her hurry for experience?" he asked his wife.

"I was never like that," Kitty said. "I played with dolls long past the time she'd given them up. Maybe she's read *Short Lives?*"

She had, in fact, years ago.

Maud had departed her room and house in what had hardly seemed sufficient time. After going away to Berkeley she returned comparatively infrequently. She had spent one summer on a dig in Mexico. Another, she worked as a professor's research assistant. She preferred to work when she could, earn part of her keep. "Not that I don't miss you but there's a lot to see and get done."

Dubin saw the connection with himself yet could not fully comprehend it. "Why should you be gone so long so often?"

"It's not as though I'd left the house, if I keep coming back." She said in afterthought: "I think of you both a lot." Perhaps she shared his hunger to live many lives? In imagination he lived hers. She had eased in him a wanting of much he hadn't had as boy and youth. Kitty, it seemed to him, had loved him in part for his love of the girl.

Dubin was disheartened that he had only this ragged self to offer on her short visit home. And that Maud had appeared almost unrecognizable, the fiery flame of her dyed black. She had walked into the house masked. What is she hiding? Had she seen him, after all, with Fanny in Venice? Had it been she in the gondola with the old man? Who is she, nervously clumping around in boots and poncho, who comes as my child, though I can hardly recognize her? What have we become to each other, who were once so much more than we presently are?

When they were alone during the evening after her arrival, Dubin asked his daughter why she had dyed her hair black.

She answered, "Because I'm me"; then said, "I wanted to see how I look in black hair, I know how I look in red."

"How do you look in black?"

She was for a moment uneasy. "Pretty much as I expected."

"Couldn't you have imagined it?"

"I'm not good in imagining. I'm good in seeing."

He said he sensed a symbol in her mask. "This sort of thing a bit extended could hurt you."

She was annoyed. "Please don't read symbols in everything I do, Papa. I'm not a book. And if I'm masked I'm not the only one."

"Am I?"

"Maybe. Anyway, let's not go ape on this. Everybody overanalyzes in this house."

He called it an occupational problem.

"If you want a symbol, be satisfied with something simpler—maybe somebody looking for herself."

Dubin therefore apologized.

He recalled, the week she was there, other dissatisfactions of hers: she had, for instance, from childhood, complained about her name. Kitty had suggested her own grandmother's name—Christina—for her, which Dubin had doubted. After considering Crystal they had settled on Maud, later discovered it derived from Magdalene; but Maud was by then Maud. Her middle name was his mother's, Hannah. Who's in a name?

"Maud, Maud, the birds cawed," she had parodied Tennyson when she was in high school. "Boy, what a jackass name."

"On you it sounds good."

"It sounds like a cow call. I'm maudlin is what it amounts to. In grade school the kids made it 'Muddy' and now all I hear is 'Moody.' What a shitty thing to do to your little girl." She laughed at that.

Once as he followed her on a trail in the woods, she complained, "Too many of my habits are like yours."

Dubin would not apologize.

"You were always yawking about work, going to bed early so you could be early to work—all that sort of thing, and it took me years before I stopped being afraid to waste time."

"Waste what you want," he said. "I do what I have to. If Mark Twain had applied himself to his writing instead of piddling time away trying to make money on things that didn't work, he'd have been a greater writer. F. Scott Fitzgerald, before he caught himself near the end, had wasted much of his talent. I'm telling you what I learned from their lives."

She laughed scornfully. "Why didn't you learn about some of the fun they had, especially Fitzgerald?"

"Someone once said, no valuable work is accomplished except at the expense of a life."

Maud bet it was Thoreau. "I'm sick of him. Also it depends what you mean by valuable."

Dubin said one had to make choices.

"I'm trying to," she shouted.

He remembered having run over her black-and-white cat in the driveway and hastily burying the animal before she could see its maimed body. When he told her later what he had done she was inconsolable he hadn't given her the kitty to bury. He sometimes felt she had never forgiven him.

One day she had accused him of having favored Gerald over her.

He told her not to believe it.

She reddened, yet insisted it was true. "He was the interesting one you were always going up to talk to, and I was fluff and yum-yum." She complained he had never really understood her. Dubin looked at her to see if she was kidding; she wasn't. It hurt. He thought he had communicated with her better than with almost anyone. Another illusion. When she was fifteen he had sensed a growth of antagonism in her without being able to define it more than generally. Perhaps she had changed faster than he had imagined? It happens so quickly with kids. While I was out for a walk she became someone else.

"You were a good enough father," she once defined it, not noticing the tense or qualifier. "You cared and provided but we could have been closer as a family."

"Propaganda—we were close and attentive to each other."

"Not that close."

Who remembered better? Close? He sometimes thought his life had pressed hers too strongly. He was too intensely aware of Maud, had made her self-conscious.

He wondered what kind of father he had been. A decent one, Dubin had thought, but who was he to say? God, the impression one made without knowing it. What had he ultimately given them? —Much willingly but they made unconscious choices from his daily offerings—or non-offerings, simply being who or what he was. Some take from that what they will never be able to use. The father of Maud's childhood and Gerald's, being in essence little known to them, ultimately a mystery because other—love to the contrary notwithstanding—had left his mark as mythological father; but the historical Papa they had discovered and felt some affection for as they grew was, as self, recognizable, measurable, predictable, vulnerable. They knew reasonably well his strengths and limitations and sensed how they themselves were bound by them. By definition he was as parent—more than Kitty—the opposing self; and in subtle ways they opposed him. They opposed him best by changing. —Ah, fooled you! Overnight, it had seemed, they had changed and gone, each to pursue an unpredictable destiny. —Who would have thought so, contemplating them as kids? Yes, you said love, they said love, but each lived a world apart. They saw him differently as they changed, and against the will he was a changed man. Dubin felt, as much as he could, that he had been himself to them, defined himself as he was; and they would therefore, sooner or later, return to claim his friendship. But either they hadn't listened, or had and forgot; or hadn't he spoken?

Yet every so often the father had the feeling he had lost or misplaced his daughter at a specific time in another country, a foreign experience. Had he, indeed, lost her in Venice, although he did not, in truth, know whether she'd ever been there?

Kitty, after a quiet devastation over the dyed hair, had revived her good spirits in Maud's presence. "She's home rarely, let's not be so critical of what she did. She's been a good kid." She and Maud had got along well. Kitty admired her good looks, independence, sense of adventure; she wished she had been similarly endowed. Maud respected her mother's taste and strength. Kitty pooh-poohed "strength" but the girl insisted. "You do what you have to even with your doubts." Kitty looked emotionally away.

Now they were shopping together, Maud mostly to please her mother because she wanted no more than a pair of bluejeans and two pairs of socks. And Kitty loved cooking for Maud though she had asked her to go easy. "I'm into organic foods and brought a batch with me." "Then let's cook them up," said Kitty. Maud laughed till it hurt.

About her dyed hair Kitty said to Dubin, "It's not forever, the black will grow out."

"What have you told her about me?" he asked. "I'd rather she didn't know what a mean winter I've had."

"She always complained we keep secrets from them."

"There are some things I'm entitled to keep private."

"I've told her nothing she wouldn't guess on laying eyes on you."

He asked her what.

"I said you were having some trouble with Lawrence. I also said you had lost twelve pounds on your diet—was that all right?"

He thanked her.

Maud went to see a high school friend living with an unemployed mechanic in a shack up the side of Mt. No Name. They had rapped about Eastern religions. She had also cross-country skied with Roger Foster—Kitty's dubious arrangement; Dubin had, as usual, his doubts about the librarian. And Maud was restless, prowled around the house; tightened water taps; lowered the thermostat if Kitty permitted; convinced her mother to use cloth napkins instead of paper. "We have got to save trees, Mother." She spent hours looking through things in the attic, searching for something she couldn't find.

One morning when Dubin came downstairs, Maud was eating a granola she had mixed of rolled oats, wheat germ, sesame seeds, other ingredients. Formerly she had eaten a soft-boiled egg almost every morning of her life. The world had changed. He pictured her with red hair.

She studied him as he sipped his coffee. When he looked at her her gaze shifted.

Dubin asked her if she had heard from Gerry lately.

"A card. He's working on an excursion boat. He's moved, I think."

"Again?"

"He can move if he wants." Her voice wavered angrily.

"What's with you?"

She filled her teacup. "Why did you walk away from me the minute I came into the house, Papa?"

He said her black hair had upset him. "I sensed you had changed in a way that excluded me. I guess I didn't want you to see how bad I felt."

"Are you used to me now?"

He said a stupidity had got into him; he regretted it.

She rose, washed the cup and cereal bowl in the sink, then sat down and lit a cigarette. She eats health foods then smokes, Dubin thought.

"Just one," Maud said. "It's snowing," she said, looking out of the window. "I love winter. I don't think I want to spend my life in California."

That seemed good news. Dubin imagined her home again: they were sitting at this table talking and Maud had red hair.

"You haven't said what's been happening to you."

"Not much." She listened to herself say that, then put out her cigarette and said, "Not very much." After a moment Maud asked him if he would like her to recite a poem. She often recited to him poems she had learned. Once she had tried to write verse but had given it up, though he had asked her not to. She said they weren't very good poems; and sounded like Kitty.

Maud recited gravely, her voice expressive, face softened, seriousness deepened:

> O Thou whose face hath felt the Winter's Wind,
> Whose eye has seen the snow-clouds hung in mist,
> And the black elm-tops 'mong freezing stars,
> To thee the spring will be a harvest time.

Moved, Dubin said, "Keats."
She went on, ending: " 'To thee the spring shall be a triple morn.' "
He thanked her for her kindness.
"Do you remember reading me 'Bright Star' after I had read about Keats in *Short Lives?*"
He remembered. Keats spoke in youth's voice and Dubin had listened with youth's ear.
She seemed gently embarrassed.
Each then left the room. Dubin worked upstairs for a while. The snow had stopped and it was white and still outside. He knocked on Maud's door and asked her to walk to the bridge with him. They trudged along the snowy road, Maud in ski pants and boots, wearing a white padded parka. Dubin had on his black galoshes and red wool hat.
As they stood under the snow-covered bridge, resting, their white breaths intermingling, Maud quietly began another sonnet of Keats'. It was "To Fanny." She spoke the poem feelingfully.

> That warm, white, lucent, million-pleasured breast,—
> Yourself—your soul—in pity give me all,
> Withhold no atom's atom or I die,
> Or living on perhaps, your wretched thrall,
> Forget, in midst of idle misery,
> Life's purposes,—the palate of my mind
> Losing its gust, and my ambition blind!

His voice was heavy when he asked her why she had recited that particular poem.

"I loved it when I was sixteen."

"So you recite it now?"

"I just thought you might be in a mood to hear it; I am."

"It's appropriate," he offered. "It helps."

"Helps what?"

"My mood." He thanked her for the poem.

"Mother says you're having trouble with your work?"

Dubin confessed he had been writing without authority.

"Do you really like Lawrence? You're not much like him."

"I like him well enough; he's an interesting man. Not all his books are good, some are very good. He had genius. I doubt he loved mankind but he relished life though he explained it insufficiently."

"But isn't it hard for somebody like you to write about somebody like him?"

"Nobody I've written about is like me though they all are."

"Aren't some more congenial than others? I don't think you had much trouble with Thoreau."

"He came at a better time."

"Why did you pick Lawrence to write on?"

"He picked me. There's something he wants me to know."

After studying him a minute, she said, "You've had bad periods before. You'll soon be back into your rhythm of work."

"It's been a long time."

The next morning at breakfast Maud said she had learned her first poem by D. H. Lawrence. She recited it with eyes closed.

Desire may be dead
and still a man can be
a meeting place for sun and rain
wonder outwaiting pain
as in a wintry tree.

She treats me with poetry, he thought. "Bravo," Dubin said.
Maud reddened.

He worked in his study later in a calm mood.

On Friday of the week Maud was home, as they were again returning from the short walk, he considered telling her what had happened to him in Venice. He had wanted to all week. Dubin said his trouble with work had started after an experience there.

"What kind of experience?"

"Unexpected. I thought I was fairly good facing up to what happens unexpectedly, but apparently less than I thought."

He did not elaborate; she didn't ask him to.

As he was following her along the path through Kitty's Wood Dubin stopped and said, "Maud, I love you."

She turned to him. "I love you."

"I love you more than anyone."

"Papa," Maud said, "I'm not your wife."

Dubin said he hadn't asked her to be.

"You neglect Mother. She's lonely."

"It's a long story," he said, "but I'm addressing you. You're my daughter, I need you. Let's stay more closely in touch."

"You have me."

They embraced on the path in the white wood. Maud kissed him quickly.

Though he had warned himself not to, Dubin asked her if it was she he had seen with an old man in Venice.

"Please don't ask me questions like that."

The next day Maud flew back to California.

One freezing night Dubin drove through the white silent streets to Oscar Greenfeld's. He had had to get out of the house, could not stand being alone with Kitty.

Flora had called a week ago. She said she had wanted to talk with him about a book she was reading, but they had never got to it. On the phone Dubin wasn't sure what they were talking about. Oscar was in Europe.

"Are you all right?" he had asked Flora.

"More or less. Listen, William," she said with mellifluous intensity, "you and I ought to be better friends."

"How would that work?"

Flora hung up on him.

"Who was that?" Kitty had asked. She'd been in the bathroom. Dubin rarely answered the telephone; it was her instrument.

"Flora."

"What did she want?"

"She wanted to talk about a book she was reading."

"What book?"

He said he had forgotten to ask.

"I think she's been lonely since she's given up traveling with Oscar," Kitty said. "I had that feeling when I saw her at Myra's burial."

"Should we invite her over?"

"If you want."

"You don't want?"

"God knows I've tried, but I simply don't take to her."

That very cold night, a week after Flora's call, Dubin parked his car in the driveway by the birch trees, and rang her bell.

"What a nice thing to do," Flora said.

"This isn't the wrong time to come?"

She insisted it wasn't. Flora was wearing a tight pleated white blouse and a long burgundy skirt. Her voice was chesty, throaty, musical. She said Oscar was in Prague.

"Are you dressed to go out?"

"I dress to practice." She took up her bow and went on with a Bach violin sonata. She played zestfully, a little wildly, her body swaying. The Bach was lively, vibrant, earthy. He had heard her say Bach should not be played like Bach. "He should be played like a gypsy."

Flora then went into the first movement of a Vivaldi violin concerto, playing him like a gypsy.

Afterward they sat in silence, he in a rocker by the fireplace, Flora on the sofa.

"Were you angry when I hung up on you?"

Dubin said he wasn't.

She laughed throatily. "Dear William, how little surprises you. Your understanding surpasseth surprise. Don't you sometimes feel cheated?"

He said he sometimes did.

"You look low," Flora said sympathetically. "You looked like hell at your birthday party."

173

"It was Kitty's party."

"It certainly wasn't yours."

"How long has Oscar been gone?"

"Three weeks tomorrow. He'll be back in a week."

"Why don't you travel with him any more?"

"Travel keeps me on edge. Besides he's happy to go alone."

She gazed into the fire. Dubin watched the small flames along the glowing log.

"Would you like a drink or what would you like?"

He asked for brandy. Flora poured herself a full glass of red wine.

"I hear Maud was home."

"For five days."

"What is she up to besides her Spanish?"

"She didn't say."

"I wish I had a daughter," Flora said. "I'd call her every night."

"No you wouldn't," Dubin told her.

"The music was lively, the talk is sad," Flora said. "Let's not talk sad, William. Let's surprise each other joyfully."

She went to her bedroom and returned in a white flowing caftan and jeweled sandals. She had pinned up her hair and her neck was long and lovely. She had light hair and high cheekbones.

"Do you know what we're doing?" Dubin asked her.

"Don't you?"

"You're my friend's wife."

"Your friend is away more than he's home. We've not been getting along well. Oscar is an egoist. And I'm honestly hard up."

"We've been good friends for years."

"You're not that much friends nowadays and I've never been friends with your wife. Come, we're not children. You and I have touched looks and fingers in many homes. We've loved each other lightly. Somewhere in a lifetime that calls for a consummation." She held out her hand.

Dubin rose. "Not in his bedroom."

Flora led him up to a guest room on the second floor. She removed her caftan and underpants and slid into the bed. Dubin undressed and got in beside her.

Flora's eyes were wet as they kissed. "Bodies are kind, other bodies. Passion is priceless."

Dubin said she was kind.

Afterward in the quiet dark she asked what he was thinking about.

"Oscar. Kitty a little."

"Think of me," Flora said. "I'm fifty today."

Dubin, at fourteen, would cross off on the stiff little calendars his father brought home from the Waiters Union the days and weeks of winter. He crossed off the dark days, slush, freeze, rain/snow, wind wailing. One by one he crossed off the icy mornings he dressed in the cold. His mother filled the kitchen stove with balls of newspaper and strips of wood from egg crates Charlie Dubin had got from the grocer on the corner; and when they were lit, spread on them small shovelfuls of pea coal from the pail on the floor. He would dress fast in front of the tepid stove. As a youth he crossed off loneliness. When will winter end? When will it go where winters go? He breathed the January wind, testing it for change, mildness, promise of spring. He was moved by the sight of dead leaves caught in the branches of leafless bushes. He crossed off the cold season as though he were crossing off an unworthy life. In his room he wrote, many times, a single word: "Will i am."

Now, in Center Campobello, he crossed off nothing. If you mangle time it mangles you. Winter, ancient operator, deaf and blind to his mood, lingered long after Maud had gone. The white sky reflected the white landscape. He hungered for change, change of him. But the iron season would not budge. Mornings were still dishearteningly cold. It snowed almost daily in March, a half inch, quarter inch at a time; the snow melted for a day or so, then it snowed again although rows of maples along the road already wore spigots over metal buckets, and the sugar house near the bridge was pouring white clouds of sweetish steam from its roof vents. There had been a momentary scent of sap and spring. The snow turned heavy-wet, melting as it touched ground. One day when Dubin awoke it was gone. The next morning it covered woods, hilltops, earth.

Again the snow receded, left soiled streaks of white on the hard ground. Except for evergreens the massed bare-branched trees were still winter-gray. The melting snow uncovered meadows wet with grass in soggy clumps and swaths, as though the earth was strewn with soaking rags of brown, yellow, faded-green. After a long rain the bare tree trunks turned brown or black. When the sun reappeared through morning mist some trees flushed rose, some shone an opalescent green. The silver maples, after rain, looked as though they were wrapped in wet brown blankets. Willows were suffused in bright yellow-green. At the end of the month there were tiny seed clusters on maple branches, but no leaves. It was gently snowing.

March he had given up to winter—who claimed choice?—but a wintry April tormented him. Yet the frozen dancer invisibly danced. One day he discovered snowdrops amid traces of snow in the woods. The snow vanished in the sun; earth dried or tried to; it got to be mud season later than last year. The sun grew stronger daily. On the long walk Dubin saw a darkly plowed field that shone with a greenish cast to its turned soil. Birds appeared in clusters on Kitty's feeder—jays, robins, house sparrows, starlings Dubin recognized; now and then a purple finch. And when they had flown off a mysterious black-masked loner, a crested red cardinal who had been in and out all winter, popped its beak at grains of corn, stopping as it ate to stare at invisible presences. When a sudden shower struck the earth the birds burst off the ground, flying in crazy arcs. Minutes later they were pecking in greener grass in a soft rain. Then from nowhere—from its grave—a mournful dark wind arose trailing bleak streamers of snow. Moments later the sun flared in the bright blue sky. Dubin, on Thoreau's advice, stopped loitering in winter and called the season spring.

He felt, oppressively, the need of an action to take. To do something differently—create a change that would lead to others. Why hadn't he moved beyond the weight of winter? He was bored sick with expecting something to happen. He felt a hungry need to simplify his life, to see what he could do differently. He felt, before long, the need of a new place to be, observe from, reflect in—after the gloom of these past months and his uneasy compromises with Lawrence. Dubin at length decided to move his study from house to small barn, where years ago he had built a room to work in, and for one or another reason never furnished or occupied it. Kitty had liked the idea of his having another place to work nearby. She had foreseen a time when Maud and Gerald would come for summer visits with their children, who would not have to be quiet, because Dubin was out of the house.

When the biographer inspected the study in the barn one day in early April it was damp—smelled distantly of silage and manure; and was abuzz with green-bellied flies that had hatched in the walls. The roof had dripped under the stress of heavy snowfalls, and several feet of top bookshelf were discolored. The smell was dank—winter's corpse. But the electric heat

176

worked and soon baked out dampness and attendant odors. A roofer replaced a section of cracked rotting shingles. Dubin killed off the green flies with a spray gun although Kitty had offered to shoo them with a newspaper. He had bought a rectangular pine table for a desk and transported two chairs from the attic room. Kitty gave him a floor lamp she had got as a wedding present when she married Nathanael; and Dubin bought a sofa that converted into a bed in case he felt like sleeping out in the heat of summer. She suggested putting in a phone but he resisted: "It costs money."

"Suppose I need you in a hurry?"

"When have you since the kids grew up?"

There was no telephone.

Before installing himself Dubin went to the barn in work clothes and galoshes. He swept the study floor and with rags wiped everything within reach. Kitty offered to help but he said he had been wanting for months to do something with his hands. The study was a walled-off quarter of the rear of the barn, a two-windowed room with a long interior wall of shelves halfway to the slanted ceiling. A lavatory with bowl, sink, and a small window had been put in. Dubin lugged boxloads of books across the field in Kitty's garden wheelbarrow. He enjoyed arranging the books, packets of note cards, folders full of manuscript pages, typed and retyped, on the shelves, carefully putting things in place after the disorder of the winter. He hung his picture of Thoreau on the wall by the window where the pine table stood, and near the picture, his Medal of Freedom.

Kitty hoped he wouldn't think of this room as his permanent place to work, though she conceded a change might be helpful now; and Dubin did not tell her that the move had seemed a little like permanently leaving the house.

The morning he tried to work he was assailed by the shrilling of birds in the barn. Dubin knew that a family of starlings had been in the eaves inside the barn but there were no signs of nests. They had got in through a missing windowpane, and when he was cleaning the study he drove them out simply by appearing in the barn. He had opened the double doors and the birds rose with short frantic whistlings and whirring of wings, and flew out into the trees. They sat in the high branches shrilling raucously at him. Dubin replaced the pane and kept the barn doors shut. But the birds slithered in through a two-inch gap under one of the doors; he heard their noisy chirping when he sat down the next morning. He then nailed a long board to the bottom of the barn door. The starlings, after being driven out again, hung around complaining in nearby trees, then, in a week, disappeared.

Kitty called him heartless.

It had led to an argument about his character, their life together, who had failed whom.

Ten days ago they had been to the Wilson farmhouse with Mrs. Meyer, who had come from Milwaukee to clear out her mother's effects and put the farm up for sale. Mrs. Meyer had seemed stricken at all that had to be done and Kitty did much of it. She had asked Dubin to go along. While Kitty, in head scarf and coat, and Mrs. Meyer, in her black overcoat and brown hat, in the cold farmhouse, were sorting out and packing into small cartons the old woman's house dresses, faded underwear and worn shoes, Dubin went through the trunks in the attic.

In one old trunk he found a half-dozen jars of petrified seed, a shoebox full of family photographs, and two bundles of letters, of James to Myra Wilson, and Myra to James, dated around the First World War. Dubin read several of the letters by candlelight. None could be called a love letter. Through the years of marriage they were pretty much the sparse same; little changed, little grew, little was revealed. Contemplating them Dubin felt tired of marriage, wanted to be alone. Solitude was a clean state of being. He wished he'd had less of it when he was young and more now. He thought Kitty and he would have got along better if they were with each other less often. They were too intent on what each did and said. Even when they spoke lightly each heard more than was said. Even when you were not saying it you were saying it. You sat there with the self your wife saw, not necessarily the self you were into; more comfortable with. He felt the long wear and tear and was glad he had decided to work in the barn, where he was away from her. One thing that wore on Dubin was the eternal domesticity of Lawrence and his wife. They were almost always together unless Frieda went to England to see her children; or detoured to indulge in a short affair. They rarely stopped traveling. Their way was to rent a villa or cottage for a season or two, move in, wash it down, paint where necessary; and live tightly and inseparably together. Lawrence cooked, scrubbed floors, sewed if he had to. Describing his intense domestic life wore on Dubin.

He brought the letters downstairs to Mrs. Meyer. Kitty, after reading two, asked if she could have them if Mrs. Meyer didn't want them; and she, with a little laugh, handed both bundles to Kitty.

The visit to the farmhouse, especially packing Myra's clothes, affected Kitty for days after Mrs. Meyer had gone. She was down again, she confessed. "I still feel bad that I wasn't able to do more for her when she was dying." Dubin said, "There are some things one has to forget."

"I can't forget. I regret what I should have done and didn't do. And I have the feeling that in her death I am diminished. I'm afraid I won't easily get over this. Oh, why did you ever marry me?"

He advised her to skip that one.

"It's the same useless guilt," Kitty confessed, "and it bores me stiff. If Myra is in my thoughts, along comes Nathanael to join us. 'Ah, Nathanael,' I say, 'why don't you go see someone else, please? My name is Kitty Dubin and I've been remarried for years to a man who writes biographies, so please leave me alone.' But he looks at me with his trusting intelligent eyes, the true color of which I am no longer sure of, and seems terribly alone. Then I think of his vulnerable son, far away somewhere in Sweden, doing his thing alone, never writing a word, never getting in touch, and I feel a failure at the way I handled him. If I could only shove him up and make him over."

"The same water under the same bridge. Why do you bother?"

"Because I am Kitty Tully Willis Dubin. Because of my stupid nature. Because you know very well why and keep asking me the same stupid questions. Because I feel you don't love me."

"Resist—fight it, for Christ's sake!" Dubin was waving his arms.

She said quietly, "I do, I am." Kitty looked into the distance through the window. She seemed someone on an island with no boat nearby. "I'm seeing Evan," she said. "He's helping me." She began to cry. Dubin put his arm around her and she wept briefly, her head pressed to his shoulder.

Let her go to Ondyk, he thought. I've done what I can.

Kitty blew her nose and nasally said thanks.

The next morning, with a last wheelbarrow-load of books, Dubin completed his move from the house to the barn.

He had set his writing table at a window that looked out on a mountain ash. Kitty had offered to make curtains for the windows but he wanted none. As he sat at his table he could see on his left Kitty's Wood, ragged and sparse after winter, just beginning to be green in spring. He sat alone in the silence

179

of the barn and the surrounding land. It was at first oppressive: he did not want this much quiet, so much space for thought. Then he began to enjoy it. And he was on the move again in his work, perhaps even on track; certainly on the move.

Dubin had at last completed the opening section of the biography, to the death by cancer of Lawrence's mother, and his own illness a year or so after that; and apparent recovery. Then came the watershed year for him, 1912, when in a burst of creativity, among other things he eloped with Frieda Weekley. He had come to consult his French professor; she was his wife, mother of three. Lawrence arrived to have lunch, "a long thin figure," she thought, "quick straight legs, light sure movements," and in a sense he never left.

They took off for the Continent together. David Garnett described him as "a slightly-built, narrow-chested man, thin and tall with mud-colored hair, a small moustache and a hairpin chin." Frieda was "a noble and splendid animal," a tall woman, blond, with high cheekbones and gold-flecked green eyes. Her movements made you think of a lioness. She had never lived, she once said, before living with Lawrence. She had abandoned husband and children. They fled to Germany and later lived in Italy. But she mourned her children; it enraged him. If she loved them she was not in love with him. He wrote a poem, "Misery." Frieda was happy and miserable, vivacious and gloomy. "She has blues enough to repave the floor of heaven." "Nevertheless, the curse against you is still in my heart / like a deep deep burn / The curse against all mothers." But she was present, day and night, and he woke to the beauty of her body and the sensuous delight and self-celebration it roused in him. "She stoops to sponge, and her swung breasts / Sway like full blown yellow / Gloire de Dijon roses." He wrote poem after poem and also finished *Sons and Lovers*. "My detachment leaves me and I know I love only you." "Frieda and I have struggled through some bad times into a wonderful naked intimacy all kindled with warmth that I know at last is love." "Look, we have come through!" They were "two stars in balanced conjunction." They had lived it well and Dubin was writing it well.

Kitty came over to see the furnished study. "It's grand. Is there some way I can help you—research, type, anything at all?"

He said he would let her know when there was. She then went home, pausing to ask if he wanted the mail brought over when it came, and Dubin said no.

"You used to love to have the mail the minute it came."

"I no longer do."

"I guess I think of the past."

When he was through for the morning she had a light lunch waiting and afterward went to Ondyk, or to work in the Youth Opportunity program in town. Ondyk wanted her to keep busy and had persuaded Kitty to take on a voluntary job three afternoons a week.

"All I do is type. I wish I could counsel, but I can't. Still the cases are interesting. The youth are the maimed."

"What about the middle-aged?"

"The middle-aged are the maimed," she said.

At home she pottered around, played the harp, tried to organize her reading. She had started Thoreau's *Cape Cod*. She had dipped into Lawrence's poems but had found the early ones not to her liking; she liked some of the love poems, "though it's his love mostly." She was occasionally in her garden. The weather was cold. She got down on her hands and knees and weeded a section of the perennial border. Kitty read the newspapers for hours. They went out to dinner to celebrate her fifty-second birthday.

The birds, given cold spring, sang in cold trees. Dubin knew the phoebe's call—it sounded like "see-bee"; blue jay's aggressive scream; "tisk" of cardinal, its near voice. He sometimes spied the red bird in the mountain ash. It stayed a minute and flew off. He could afterward hear its shrill whistle, its other voice, in the distance. The cardinal appeared in the mountain ash, barely showing itself, hiding its presence as it hopped on the branch, tisking, trying to have a look at him. Whatever he was doing or not doing, whenever the bird lit on a white-blossomed branch of the tree Dubin sensed it was there.

One morning he laid out some sunflower seeds, from Kitty's feeder, on the ledge of the window in front of him. But only when he left the table and stood elsewhere in the room would the cardinal float down. It pecked at the seeds, then flicked its head up, its beady eye watching, until it flew off. Once when Dubin was at work, to his surprise the cardinal flashed down from the tree to peck at the seeds on the window ledge. For an instant he was caught by the bird's eye, black, mysterious. He marveled at its immaculate beauty.

Where had it come from? Why is it so magnificent? To civilize man to protect the bird? "Don't ever die," Dubin said. The cardinal flew off and he listened for its distant song. He pictured it hidden in the tree in mid-summer when the berries of the mountain ash had turned orange-red.

Dubin became aware of a presence, something within or close by, like a disturbing memory waiting to occur. Was the red-bearded ghost of D. H. Lawrence, risen in contempt of the biographer's desecrations of his life, haunting the place to revenge himself? One day the feeling grew so oppressive he was drawn into the barn to look around. The old barn was dark, gloomy, wet-cold. Dubin, picking up a hammer handle from the floor, went cautiously among the boxes, garden tools and machines, fertilizer bags, the furniture junk there. He found nothing unusual and was about to return to the study when he was struck by the sight of a pair of glowing eyes. He heard a thud and the eyes disappeared. The biographer was momentarily fright-ened—had a wild animal got into the barn? After a minute of frozen silence he decided it wasn't likely; yet it could be a stray dog or raccoon. He hoped it was not a skunk. As he approached the corner of the barn, still grasping the hammer handle, an animal hissed. Dubin raised his arm protectively. Behind a barrel he beheld a long black cat lying on a moldy burlap sack. The cat hissed thickly, then mournfully yowled, but was too sick to move.
   He considered prodding the animal with the hammer handle, to force it out of the barn.
   You mean bastard, he thought, the cat's sick.
   The black cat got to its feet, its yellow eyes glaring. It snarled weirdly, its matted soiled fur thickened by fear. The cat stank of shit. Bile leaked from its mouth.
   Dubin went back to his table, found he could do nothing, then left the study, walking across the field to the house. He thumbed through the yellow pages of the phone book and called a vet. He said he had a poisoned cat in his barn. "What can I do for him?"
   "If it's poison," the vet said, "not much, depending what poisoned him and when."
   "Would you want to see the animal if I can get him to you? Could you pump its stomach?"
   "No, I handle horses and cows. We had a small-animal man in town but he died last year."

Dubin hung up. What was he doing this for? He had to work.

Going back to the barn he poured some water into the tin top of a jar he found. The cat, yowling low in its throat, let him approach but made no attempt to take the water. It coughed sickly, then tried a few licks. The cat choked, coughed hoarsely, then began to vomit, moving backwards as it regurgitated part of a rabbit or bloody rat. Dubin later flashed a light on the mess; the cat had gorged itself sick.

The next morning he went with Kitty to the barn. The black cat was better and lapped a little of the water she gave it. "Don't feed it anything, William. I'm pretty sure it will get better by itself and then I'll hose it to get rid of the smell."

Squatting, she patted the cat's head. He recalled how she had handled the kids when they were sick. She was affectionate and competent and tried not to be anxious.

The next day she arrived with some milk in a glass, and a saucer, and brought a box of dry cat food. The black cat lapped up the milk and chewed a little of the dry food.

In a week it had recovered. It was a long-bodied lithe almost lynx-like male, with an upright head and twitching tail. Kitty thought they ought to take it to the house. Their old cat had died, but Dubin wanted this one for the barn.

He called the cat Lorenzo. At first it showed no affection for him, then began to rub its head against his legs. Sometimes it jumped up and lay in his lap as he sat on the sofa reading. It's become my cat. He thought of the cats that had come and gone in the family.

Lorenzo lived in the barn and roamed the fields. One day it scratched at the study door, and when Dubin opened it, to his disgust the black cat held a broken-winged bloody cardinal in its mouth.

"You bastard." He tore the red bird from the cat's jaws. But the cardinal was dead. Dubin drove Lorenzo away.

An hour later he went searching for the animal far into his neighbor's field.

Kitty said she had liked helping him with the cat in the barn. "We do so little together." Dinner was quiet. She seemed like a clock listening to itself.

"What would you like us to do that we aren't?"

"I'd like you to respond to more than my voice. Why do you never think of putting your arms around me without my having to ask?"

"Other than that?"

"Other than that, I'm alone in the house. You live by yourself in the barn."

"I don't live there. I'm sorry you feel lonely. It doesn't raise my spirits, but at least you're seeing Ondyk. I'm glad of that."

"Are you?"

"If you are."

"I'm tired of 'seeing' someone. I'd like not to have to. I'd like my life to take over."

"Give it time."

"I have. Something's wrong with the way we live. We take no joy in each other."

"I like the way you look," Dubin said, trying to take joy. "Often I look at you and like the way you look."

"Thank you. You know what I mean."

"My work is mainly what's wrong. But I'm having better days. It's not easy to see Lawrence whole, but I'm closer to it. You can't explain him till you see him whole. It's hard to do that, but there are good signs."

"I'm glad of that. I'm glad something is good."

Dubin said he was reading a new biography of Freud. "This seems to get closer to the man than any I've read, with his neurotic qualities—hypochondria, constipation, anxiety, bladder difficulty. I've told you about his fainting, usually in Jung's presence. He was tied for half his life in an unexplained triangle with his wife and sister-in-law. But the neurosis, such as it was, led in part to his own self-analysis and thus to his life's accomplishment. His work shrived him."

"I'll bet you like that thought."

"Don't you?"

She admitted she did. "I wish I could work steadily at something I liked."

"Why don't you?"

"Because I never could."

"Don't blame yourself," Dubin said.

"For years I never did, now I do. Being home when the children needed me was a time of privilege and grace. Now that they're grown I wish I had some useful work to do."

After they had gone to bed she was still restless. "Listen to that wind, you'd think it was early March."

"April is March." He tried to sleep but couldn't and felt himself grow worried. Then for a few minutes he fell heavily asleep against Kitty's warm scented back until she moved restlessly and woke him.

The wind had died down. Kitty was sleeping. Dubin, worried about being able to work in the morning if he did not sleep well, got up and dressed in the dark. He wanted a cigarillo but had none and was unable to find Kitty's cigarettes. From the linen closet he got two sheets and a blanket. Then he returned to the bedroom for a flashlight.

Kitty awoke and switched on the bed lamp. She sat up.

"What are you doing with those sheets and blanket?"

"I'm going to the barn."

"What for?"

"To get to sleep so I can work in the morning. I've got a lot to make up. I need every bit of my energy to be sharp. You can do only so much on your nerve."

"I promise to lie very still," Kitty said. "Or you can go up to Gerald's room or sleep in Maud's. Please don't go to the barn. I won't sleep a wink with you gone."

Dubin said it would be best if he went.

"Why?" Kitty asked. She was on her knees in bed, in a flowered night-gown.

"To be alone—I have things to think of."

"I thought you wanted to sleep?"

"That's what I want to do first."

She said, "I don't know why you ever got married."

"You know why I got married," Dubin said.

He zipped up his windbreaker, went downstairs, and left the house. The spring night was austerely cold, and the sky, like a lit ceiling that had been lowered, teemed with jeweled stars. It had been a long time since he had seen so many bright stars so low in the sky.

Dubin dropped the sheets and blanket on the sofa. He got out the bag of kibbles and fed Lorenzo, then gave him some water. The cat wanted to stay but he tossed him out and shut the study door. He unfolded the sofa into a double bed and covered it with the sheets and blanket. He had forgotten a pillow and pajamas and lay on his back in his underwear, relieved to be alone. The cat scratched on the door, then gave up.

Dubin lay in the dark thinking what he would do in the morning. As he was dozing off, a tapping on the window woke him. He listened, wide awake, knew who it was and rose, angered.

He flicked on the light. From the sofa he could see her at the window, peering in, her eyes searching, face strained, white. Under his anger he felt concern for her.

Dubin got up and let her in, irritated by her appearance, by her constant interference in whatever he planned, whatever he did. Kitty had no flashlight. She had found her way to the barn by the light of his toilet window until she had got halfway across the field; then it had gone off. She had fallen once. She was wearing Maud's old hooded yellow oilskin over her flowered nightdress, wet below the knees. Her bed slippers were soaked by the wet grass. When, after she had tapped on the glass, his light went on, she had looked as though she hadn't expected it to. She acted now as if she had never been in this room before.

He gave her a towel to wipe her legs.

"I had to come," Kitty said. "The house was beginning to go at me."

He told her to get warm in bed. "I'm going back to the house."

Kitty looked at him vacantly. "You don't have to," she said. "I'll go back after I tell you what I have to. William, I've been holding back something I feel guilty about, not because of what it came to, which was zilch, but you probably sensed something and it might have made things harder for you than they should have been. I feel ashamed and sorry."

He asked her what she was talking about. Her eyes were restless, dark. her fists tight.

"While you were in Italy that week in the fall I had a sudden very brief and unexpected involvement with Roger. I was involved, not he. I think I was momentarily in love with him. I don't know what else to call it though it came to nothing—and I never told him how I felt. If it sounds slightly crazy that's what it was."

"Roger Foster?" Dubin said in disbelief.

"It was a crazy thing to happen. He's only a year or two older than Gerald. I felt tender to him. I also felt as though my wits were leaving me. When you came home I wanted to tell you but was too embarrassed. In the winter, when you were depressed, I felt awful. I imagined you had sensed a change in me and were let down—perhaps I was foolish, I don't know. I asked Evan what to do and though he said I wasn't what had caused your overwhelming change of mood, my guilt was like salt corroding my thoughts and I knew

I would have to tell you. I held back until now because the whole thing was senseless and trivial, and I didn't want you to lose respect for me."

"Did you want to sleep with him?"

"I would have."

"But he wouldn't oblige?"

"I hate the way you distance yourself from me," Kitty said bitterly. "Why do you put it so meanly? I said nothing came of it. I told you he never knew how I felt."

"Maybe you should have told him."

Kitty looked at him coldly. "If I should have I didn't. I'm sorry to say I couldn't arrange it. I wasn't about to begin an affair with someone twenty years younger than I by apologizing for the birthmark on my ass and my flabby breasts."

"Did he ever show in any way that he was interested in you?"

"That's my business." Her voice wavered. She wasn't crying but she looked as though she had cried. One sensed old tears. He thought of his bad time in Venice and felt compassion for her.

Dubin then began a story of his own.

"Kitty," he said, "Don't blame yourself for what happened to me. I made my own misery. I had a girl with me in Venice and it turned out badly. I give her little, she gave me less. There was more feeling in the aftermath. When I came home I wanted to tell you but couldn't, partly because I didn't want to hurt you, partly because I was unable to say—out of pride—what a beating I had taken because I had done it badly, or she had done it badly and I let her."

"I'm sorry, terribly sorry." Her eyes were lit with feeling. "I knew something was troubling you but thought I was wrong—mixing up my sense of you with what *I* was feeling. It took me a while to understand how unhappy *you* were."

They went to each other and kissed.

"Please let me stay with you tonight, William."

"Stay with me."

"My nightgown is wet."

"Take it off, wear my shirt."

In bed they forgave themselves; had done it before. That he had told her what had happened in Venice only after she had confessed her feeling for Roger did not seem to bother Kitty, but Dubin regretted he hadn't told her long ago. They talked into the night, watching the low stars out of the window.

"I feel as though we were away somewhere, don't you?" Kitty said. "I feel like a young bride snug in bed with her husband in a faraway country, with cables of stars glowing in the sky. I feel so much relieved."

Dubin said he felt better.

"You're the one I really love," Kitty said, "though I sometimes feel you ought to have married a different kind of woman—someone closer to you in temperament, who might have given you more than I seem to be able to give. Someone less concerned with keeping her own life together."

He said he had never had a better friend. "You don't always give me what I want but you give."

She laughed embarrassedly. "I wish I had given you more. I wish you had given me what I wanted when I wanted it. Sometimes I wish I could have met you before—I mean, instead of—Nathanael."

Dubin thanked her. "But I don't think you would have married me if you hadn't been married to him first. You had to have at least a touch of marriage, perhaps with someone like him, before I could mean something to you."

"What you have to know before you *know* is hard to understand," Kitty said. "Maybe I shouldn't have said that about Nathanael."

"Thanks for thinking it."

They then made love and slept heavily. Dubin felt eased, the self annealed, until he thought of Flora in his sleep and awoke. He felt he oughtn't to tell Kitty about her. He would hold it for another time, for Flora's sake as well as his.

Kitty, moving spasmodically in her sleep, opened her eyes. "What do you think was the happiest time of our lives?"

"When we began to know each other, when we were secure in our trust of each other."

"When the kids were young and needed us. I felt used, useful."

"I was completing *Short Lives* and then did *Lincoln* and *Mark Twain*. I was content, and even the lousy things that happened seemed to fit harmoniously into life. I went to sleep wanting it to be tomorrow."

"That's the time I most remember."

But after lunch that day, perhaps because Kitty had asked him who the girl in Venice was and he hadn't answered, Dubin told her he had once slept with Flora; and Kitty, trying to master it in her thoughts, passed out.

One Sunday morning in late April Dubin was in a stationery store on Grand Street, picking up his newspaper. As he was fingering an adventurous cigar at the counter, through the window he saw—peace to the day—Fanny Bick as large as life and enjoying it, across the street with Roger. He had had a recent card from her: the fountains of Rome: "Hi." The girl, in morning sunlight, was vivid, familiar, as though he'd been with her yesterday, a sad blow to experience. She had cut her hair; it fell barely to the shoulders. Dubin saw her without desire or regret, yet envied her and her friend their youth. So what else is new?

Thinking they might be coming in for a paper, he retreated to the phone on the wall in the rear of the store.

But they did not come into the place, had better to do than waste a Sunday morning reading the newspaper. He felt a saddened pleasure in thinking of her. She had joined the mythological types who lived in his mind: she who had deceived his desire, more than desire, a sort of belle dame sans merci, invention of the self intending to treat itself badly. No, he thought, I'm off that kick. No more slogging in the mud of jealousy; let me act the age I've earned. He was well rid of her. After remaining several more minutes at the phone with the receiver held protectively against the ear, Dubin left the store with his newspaper, got into his car at the curb, and lighting the cigar he had bought, drove off.

He drove a roundabout way home but to his startled surprise got onto the highway going the wrong way and was forced, amid visions of disaster, to crawl in embarrassment along the outer lane for half a mile, his brights on, horn blasting as the drivers in oncoming cars rushed at him in contempt, fury, or glee, before swerving to the next lane; until Dubin, ashamed, could at last make a turn between dividers and swing around to the other side of the highway.

He went to the barn to calm down before Kitty saw him. He decided he would stay out of downtown until he could be reasonably sure Fanny had left.

Before returning to the house he wrote to each of his children.

"Dear Gerry, we miss you, talk of you often. The amnesty issue is coming up in Congress soon. Where mercy arises in society I can't say, but there are good signs. It wouldn't at all surprise me if an offer of conditional amnesty is made to deserters. If the situation changes, as it may overnight, and you can leave Sweden, why don't you come here and stay with us until you decide your next move? We'd all like to see you. I know our relationship is difficult, sometimes no relationship at all, but that can change with good will if we stay in touch. Yesterday needn't be tomorrow. I wish I knew more about your nature but the key to mine, so far as you're concerned, is that I love you as I did when you were a boy. Your father, William Dubin."

A month later Gerry wrote on a postcard that the U.S. knew where it could shove conditional amnesty. He wanted unconditional amnesty and a public apology.

"As for who loved who and when, I never think of it."

Dubin also wrote to Maud. In the late spring she returned home and stayed the summer, a surprise to all.

Spring defined itself: present against odds. April rained in May; the early days poured. On the twelfth of May snow fell on white tulips. Kitty could not get into the soggy garden she had unveiled on a hopefully sunny April day. A flock of glistening wet crows, each a foot long, jabbed at the wet grass. One huge beast flew from a redwing blackbird circling in pursuit in the rain —to account for what crow-crime? A jay, screeching, hit Kitty's feeder with a seed-scattering bump, scaring flickers, two robins, a grackle. Lorenzo, watching from inside, threw up his breakfast. After mid-month the rain rained lightly. May showers brought May flowers: yellow troilius, feather-cusped red tulips, iris, white and purple; dandelions were scattered in the fields, buttercups; a blue haze of forget-me-nots; golden mustard in the green grass. In Kitty's Wood there were violets. The grass, come to life, thickened quickly. Dubin raked away last year's dead leaves from under trees and bushes. The new leaves had, on the thirtieth of April, burst forth like light-green lace on bony fingers. The green spoke a dozen green tongues, foliage covering hills and rising in lighter shades on the stony shoulders of Mt. No Name. In the morning, mist lay like a deep sea on the hills, their tops breaking through like green islands in white water. Sometimes clouds in gray and black masses were piled above the distant mountains, towering like Alps into the sky, a line of golden flame burning at the highest edges.

He welcomed the softened warming days; broke out the tractor mower on Saturday afternoons and drove himself in narrowing circles over the front and back lawns as Kitty sunned herself in a one-piece bathing suit on a strawberry beach towel in the grass. She wore her straw hat and sunglasses and read *Cape Cod* when she wasn't napping in the sun. Or she watched the flowers in her garden. They drove into small towns in the Berkshires, walked in each, sometimes picnicked on roadside tables. They played shuttlecock on Sunday mornings; once in a while tennis. Kitty disliked the game. Evenings they went more often to visit friends, driving with the Habershams or other couples to restaurants in nearby towns. After returning from his latest trip abroad, Oscar Greenfeld called and asked them to come for drinks. Kitty nervously begged off and Dubin, of two minds, wouldn't in the end go without her.

During the week, one afternoon she wasn't working he asked her to go along on his long walk and Kitty, after changing into sneakers, walked with him

"We haven't done the long walk for a long time."

At the end of the walk, close to where he had been lost in the snow, Dubin felt an urge to leave the road and attempt to retrace his circular wandering, wherever it had been; but one stone wall looked like another; and the woods were full of green trees and flowering bushes, the farmland growing grains and grasses. Where he had been was in truth no longer there.

"What are you thinking of?" she asked and he answered: "D. H. Lawrence."

"Why did I ask? I was thinking of you."

She had given up Ondyk with Ondyk's blessing.

"So long as we have each other."

He told her he had been working well. "I think it will be a good biography."

One morning Dubin, slim man—he had stopped dieting—instead of cutting an orange in quarters and eating it at the breakfast table, peeled it, and stood at the morning-blue kitchen window chewing it in pulpy sections. He sucked each juicy piece. He enjoyed fresh coffee, putting on a clean shirt, listening to Kitty playing her harp. That night he was struck by the splendor of the spring sunset bathing the hills brightly crimson, then mauve. The biographer determined to be kinder to his life.

Now as he briskly strode along the road it was May-become-June, a touch of summer in the mild breeze, nice reversal of running time. If you're into something—this lovely day—you're in it, not longing for it. Dubin wore buff cords, striped T-shirt, blue sneakers with loose white laces: he had been shopping; Kitty had said he needed summer things. He bowed to an ash tree, slender, virginal, but didn't linger. Its young leaves were light-green, seed pockets lavender, like a girl's spring dress. In the fall it bloomed green-gold; then the windy rain came and it was bare, broke the heart. The biographer hurried on. It could get dangerous loving trees, drive you wild. H.D.T. had wanted to embrace a scrub oak "with its scanty garment of leaves rising above the snow . . ." Lush fields were sprinkled with wild flowers; shrubs in bloom. The maples were dropping spinning white seeds into the breeze. Poplars reflected changing sunlight. The lyric greens of first spring had darkened and sights of field and wood enticed the eye: meadows sloping upward toward a descending line of trees; and above sprawling woods upland fields rose to groves of evergreens surging over the hills. Mt. No Name, behind him, was covered with foliage except its stony top. The day was broken by patches of bright blue sky through gaps in cottony clouds sailing like slow ships. At intervals the sun, looking through, lit the landscape. Dubin loved what he observed: nature rather than scene. For nature he *felt*—had earned in winter this beauty of late spring.

A new world, he sighed. In a new world he looked for a friend—scanned the road for Oscar Greenfeld—but the flutist, when you wanted him most, was elsewhere fluting. Dubin had regrets about his affair with Flora.

A white Volvo passed from behind, swerved suddenly—it had drifted too close to the walker's side of the road. Gave Dubin a turn; sped on in the risen dust.

Ten minutes later, as he was inhaling lungfuls of air at the verge of the road, the white car, long past its prime, drove by a second time, skirting the opposite shoulder of the road. It slowed down and, a hundred feet on, parked in the grass. Tourist stopping to view the view? She seemed to hesitate, head bent as though considering the odds, then opened the door, set a doubtful foot down and came toward him. Dubin knew the slender-waisted abundant body, her sturdy stride, female presence. He reflected it was inevitable they would meet again. He knows life.

Fanny, wearing sunglasses—he remembered the short denim skirt, her bare legs in sandals—walked toward him in deep focus, on her face an apprehensive smile. She was in no great hurry, taking her time, might never make it. Perhaps she didn't want to. People do impulsive things they immediately regret, Dubin for one. He might have trotted off the other way; she'd never have caught up once he was on the run—as if to prove he lived in his era, she in another. But here we both are. He'd give her short shrift.

Fanny smiled amiably, or tried to; obviously there were difficult emotions to contend with; maybe she was groping for one he couldn't match. The man had learned his lesson.

Now they touched hands, Dubin lightly.

"I thought it was you but wasn't sure," she said breathily, as though surprised.

"How are you, Fanny?" His voice was subdued, manner polite. Dubin saw clearly what she had and what she lacked; was unmoved by her. She lacked, he thought, experience of a necessary sort; certain mistakes are wrong to make.

"I hope you don't mind me stopping to say hello."

"Hardly." Why would he mind?

"I'll bet you thought you'd never see me again?"

"There were times I hoped so."

She paused to breathe, her lips moving as if she was searching for a new way not to wince. Fanny looked down, then directly at him, her pupils tight, mouth toward sour. He remembered the expression, tried to remember less, remembered all. Dubin was tempted to say a quick goodbye but after a momentarily shaky sense of wasted effort, a feeling quickly banished, objectivity returned. Mustn't make any more of the experience.

Neither spoke for a minute, he observing the small locket she wore, a gold heart with red ruby at its center. Gone six-pointed star and/or naked crucifix, whatever they had signified. Here was another sign. She looked sensibly older although less than a year had gone by since they had first met. She would be, he remembered, twenty-three come August.

A child, he reflected, recalling her face in sleep. Mad he had felt so much for her all winter. A sort of love; he knew the feeling, an old one, indulged in often in youth. Kept one young, he supposed. But how could I put my fate in her hands? Dubin wondered what she had learned from the experience. It seemed to him a commentary on himself that he expected her to have learned something.

"I finally had electrolysis done on my chin," Fanny explained as though he had asked. "One morning in Rome I waked up anxious and made an appointment. The creep used an unsterilized needle and my face blew up but after a week I was okay."

"You've cut your hair?"

"Don't you like it?"

Dubin thought it looked fine. "Visiting Center Campobello?"

She examined him vaguely. "Only for a week to take it easy, but I'm driving back tomorrow. Roger invited me up when I got back from Rome and I came up for the day about a month ago. This time I was here a little longer."

"Thinking of getting married?" he courteously inquired.

She shook her head. "We're friends—as my mother says— Platonically; I don't sleep with him."

He nodded politely.

"I'm capable of it."

"Is Roger?"

"He's really a great guy."

"How was Rome?"

"Not that good, in fact flaky. My friend who I wrote you about—Harvey —died."

Dubin grimaced sympathetically. Fanny sadly smoothed the road with her sandal.

"And I told you about my operation—the cyst I had?"

"Yes, I'm sorry." He remembered she could still have children and tried to think of her as a mother but it came to nothing.

"My father's been sick. I visited him last week in L.A. Otherwise I'm still living in New York. I had a job for a month that I lost when I went to California. And I take an evening course at the New School."

Dubin approved.

"How are you doing?" Fanny wanted to know.

"Fine, now, after a difficult winter."

She was for a moment neither here nor there, then said, "I'm sorry for whatever of it was my fault."

Fanny had hesitantly raised her hand as if to sympathize with at least his bare arm but Dubin had instinctively stepped back. She was again uneasy.

He spoke kindly. He had, now they had talked again, nothing against the girl. She was who she was, no doubt her own worst enemy. Caveat emptor, or words to that effect.

"No need to be," he finally replied. "We make our own fates."

"That might be, still people hurt each other without wanting to. Could I give you a ride somewhere?"

"Thanks, I'm on my walk."

She remembered, with a smile.

Dubin, after gazing in the distance as though estimating tomorrow's weather, after a confident minute of self-scrutiny, remarked, "Care to walk a little instead?"

If the invitation surprised her it didn't surprise him—normalizing things. For his sake if not hers: helped put the past in place. Calm now made experience then easier to live with. What still rankled still hurt. Better seeing in perspective, not always possible, but where it seemed to be occurring, let it. He didn't want the girl to be uncomfortable—scared of him. Suppose something similar—he doubted it—happened to Maud?

Fanny said she wouldn't mind. "Just let me get my bag out of the car. It's got everything I own."

She reached into the Volvo for her shoulder bag and car keys. He noticed a bit-into peach on the front seat.

Dubin advised her to lock the car; Fanny did.

They strolled in the direction he had been going. The afternoon sun, having escaped the steamy clouds, was now in full bloom.

"Why don't we get off this road and walk in the grass? I dig that."

Fanny stepped up on a stone wall and before Dubin could warn against it had hopped off on the other side.

"Private property," he said.

"I don't think anyone's going to arrest us for walking in the grass. There's endless miles of it."

Dubin stepped up on the wall and jumped down.

Fanny removed her sandals and dropped them and her glasses into her bag, swinging it back on her shoulder.

"Careful of poison ivy."

"I've never stepped in any that I know of, though I guess I've stepped in everything. I don't even know what it looks like, do you?"

He told her the plant had three shiny leaves.

For a moment Fanny proceeded cautiously, then walked on without concern.

It occurred to him he was more a comic type with her. With Kitty, their anxieties meshed, highlighting the serious life. That's the way it is: you marry a serious woman the chances are increased of a serious fate; a lighter type laughs every ten minutes and takes you with her.

He said he knew a better way to walk, led her diagonally across the field. A brown cow wandered in their direction. Fanny quickly moved toward Dubin, who shooed the animal away.

"At first I thought it was a bull."

"With those teats?"

"I'm not wearing my contacts."

They climbed over another low wall into county property, walking along an overgrown broad path, remnant of a former road. Nearby a narrow brook flowed through the matted grass, turning where some two-trunked silver beeches grew. Fanny thought it would be fun–following the water; Dubin said if it was water she liked there was a pond in a quarry not too far from there. Beyond those trees he pointed to.

It seemed, she thought, a good way to go.

Fanny, as they were walking amid a scattering of bushes and small trees on the overgrown path, as if they were now far enough away from Europe to talk about their late mutual misadventure, asked, "Why didn't you answer my letters? I honestly regretted what happened and said I respected you but the letter you sent me was a mean son-of-a-bitch."

"Mean was how I felt and the winter was freezing. I was in no mood to correspond with you."

"Is that the way you still feel?"

"Detached," Dubin told her solemnly. "I think I've earned it." He said he hadn't felt too bad when he. had left Italy but once he was home self-disgust came down hard on him. "After your letter, and for other reasons I won't go into, I was depressed and couldn't work. I've never lived through a worse winter."

"I said I was sorry," she said sullenly. "I did a stupid thing but a lot that led to it was your own stupid fault."

"In Venice you said you did it to hurt me; you did a good job."

"Because you made it pretty clear to me that you wanted only so much of me and no more. I wasn't to interfere with you or crawl into your life. I was to be invisible."

"I was protecting my wife."

"Who was protecting me?"

He didn't say.

"I'm not saying you weren't considerate and kind in nice ways that I really appreciate. But when I was having a bad trip in Rome and wrote for some advice and understanding, you didn't even bother to be civilized. I felt pretty bad."

"That's what I was hoping."

"You got your hope."

"For your sake—"

"Whosever," Fanny said bitterly.

If it was only her body I wanted, why the long heartbreak? And if I was in love with a child how could I have been?

"Are you still sore at me?"

"I told you how I feel, I've lived the experience, lived through it."

"I don't bear grudges either," Fanny said quietly. "I don't have that kind of nature."

He complimented her on her nature.

He would give her, Dubin reflected, fifteen minutes, then walk her to her car and hit the road.

Fanny, her mood amiable, strode on freely. That she should now be walking by his side after the winter he had experienced seemed to him almost laughable, one of life's little jokes. Yet better so than having the memory of her as she was in Italy locked in the mind forever as his last view of her.

The biographer told her they were passing an abandoned orchard. "Nobody sprays the trees or picks the worm-eaten apples. They stay on the branches into winter, looking like red bulbs on a Christmas tree. I've seen crows peck at them through snow."

Fanny said she had never seen anything like that. "Why doesn't somebody spray the apples?"

"There was a house here belonging to the people who owned the orchard. When the man died the widow had it moved away on rollers. The land, I understand, later went to the county for non-payment of taxes."

They arrived at a clearing—before them in the long fields a spangling of wild flowers, soft islands of blue, yellow, white, violet in the hazy green grass.

He remembered Lawrence had said wild flowers made him want to dance. Dubin felt happy but kept it to himself.

The flower-stippled meadow extended to a crescent of oaks a quarter of a mile away.

"Do you know wild flowers, Fanny?"

"Just a few. Most of my life I've lived in cities, first in Trenton, and when I was seventeen we moved to L.A. I like the country, though, and have since I was small and was sent to camp. I once thought of majoring in environmental studies—preserving animals, forests, the land, you know."

"Why didn't you?"

"I got good enough grades but my heart wasn't in staying in college. I was restless with myself."

He pointed to buttercups, then daisies. "Those are oxeye daisies. Do you know what the word means?—the day's eye, Fanny—beautiful, the sun in a flower."

She fished a plastic case out of her bag—her contact lenses. Fanny wet them with the tip of her tongue, then pulled her eyelids apart and dabbed in each lens with her index finger. "Jesus, what pretty flowers!"

He pointed to a cluster of light-blue tiny flowers. "Do you know those?"

"Yes, forget-me-nots, I know them."

"Do you know the red ones there—trillium? They're also called red rooster."

Fanny clucked like a hen.

Dubin picked a flower and handed it to her.

At first she looked as though she didn't know what to do with it, then held it in her left hand.

"The bright yellow flat open ones are celandine," he said. "I once knew a girl by that name."

"Did you sleep with her?"

"I loved her."

"Is there a Fanny flower?"

"Not that I know but there is a sweet William."

"Male chauvinism," Fanny laughed.

Dubin chuckled huskily. He waded into the grass and plucked a white blossom. "This could be wild lily of the valley. I'm not sure, I'll have to look it up when I get home." He slipped the flower into his wallet.

"Do you have a flower book?"

"My wife has a dozen."

Fanny thought she would buy herself one next time she went into a bookstore. "It's about time I got to know some of them." Then she asked, "What about the blossoms on those bushes? Do you know the names of them?"

Dubin said it was odd about the shrubs there. "They're cultivated, not wild. The only way I can explain it—I figure this from the depression in the earth—is that once the house I mentioned stood here. The woman had shrubs growing around the place. That's bridal wreath you asked about. It's beginning to wither."

"How pretty some of those names are. What do you call those?"

"Mock orange. You have to smell the blossoms to be sure. There are others that look like them but have no scent."

"I can smell the orange," Fanny said. She had picked a blossom and touched it to her lips.

"It's mock orange."

"How do you know them all?"

Dubin said he didn't know that many. "Lawrence seemed to recognize every flower in creation. Thoreau catalogued anything he saw or met in the woods, literally hundreds of flowers. I know few."

"Man, you know all these."

"My lucky day. Some fields I pass I don't know more than Queen Anne's lace. My wife taught me most of them and some flowering bushes. When I forget their names I ask her again."

"How is she doing these days?" Fanny wanted to know. "Are her glands still bothering her?"

He said she was fine.

"You mentioned her yourself just now," she said slightly stiffly. "Roger happened to tell me she was good in her library work."

He affirmed his wife was fine.

"Does she still go around sniffing the gas burners?"

Dubin said he was used to the burners. "I try not to say anything when she smells them, and for that I expect her not to comment when I yell at myself in the bathroom mirror."

"She and I never liked each other much."

"Cleaning house wasn't your act, Fanny."

They were walking a few feet apart, Fanny kicking the flowers. "I'm not criticizing or anything like that but did you know she'd go around smelling the gas before you married her?"

"You can't know everything in advance or what's marriage for? You take your chances. Whoever marries you will be taking one."

"You can say that again. But I may not want to get married."

"It's not so bad. In a marriage, after a while you learn what's given: who your wife is and you are, and how well you can live with each other. If you think you have a chance you're married. That's your choice if nothing else was."

"It's not much of one."

"We met in a curious way," Dubin explained. "Once I said I'd tell you about it. It was like not really meeting until we were ready to. She had written a letter more or less advertising for a husband."

"And you answered it?" Fanny said in pretend-astonishment.

"I happened to read it, though it wasn't addressed to me, and another she wrote canceling the intent of the first. To make it short, I became interested in her. We corresponded until we had developed some sense of each other. If a man and woman stay around trying to define themselves, at a certain point they become responsible one to the other. So we met, looked, talked, and after a while arranged to be married."

"What do you mean 'arranged'?"

"That's how I think of it. Kitty may have a better word."

"Were you in love with her? Like with Celandine?"

"She was someone I wanted to love."

"Did she feel that way?"

They had gone through the flowers and were approaching a small wood of thick-armed dark-green oaks whose trunks were spotted with mold.

"I imagine there was an expectation of love. If you feel that, it doesn't take long to happen."

"Why didn't you live together first and try it out?"

"In those days," he explained, "few did that, Fanny. You got married. Those who didn't were rare birds and not always happy ones. Kitty was a widow with a child. I needed to be settled."

"Do you love her now? When I passed you on the road before I thought you looked lonely."

"Some are lonelier than others. My mother, in her sad way, was very lonely; my father had to be. I suppose I'm more than ordinarily a solitudinous type. It's not a curse if you learn what the pleasures of it are. But that's another story."

"I can't stand being lonely. There are no pleasures in it for me."

"You shouldn't have many worries, you seem to make friends easily."

She wanted to know how he meant that.

Dubin said he was not saying she was promiscuous.

"You'd better not because I'm not. If I was once I'm not any more." She looked at him intently. "Do you believe that?"

He wasn't sure but said he did. "What are your questions asking, Fanny?"

"About marriage. Everybody talks about it differently. I like to know what it is."

" 'Bear and forbear,' Sam Johnson defined it."

"That's not much."

"He was very sensible about marriage as he was in most things."

"What about you?"

"In the best of marriages you give what you can and get back as much or more. With the right people it's a decent enterprise. It gives pleasure."

"It sounds too much like work to me."

"Thomas Carlyle, who had an awful marriage, called it 'a discipline of character.' "

"I wouldn't want that kind of marriage," she said impatiently.

"What kind would you want?"

"I don't think I want to get married. It wore my mother out. She hates my father."

Dubin said he understood.

"What do you understand?"

"A little more about you."

"Maybe you do and maybe you don't."

"I think I do."

"What I mean is do you really understand what I'm like—what my needs are, for instance?"

He had some idea. "You've described yourself in your letters."

"I didn't tell you everything."

"I've seen you in action. Some things I can guess."

"I bet you'd be wrong."

"Possibly."

"Possibly," she mimicked him.

Fanny dropped the red trillium he had given her into her shoulder bag. "Did you ever want a divorce?"

He said he and his wife had discussed the subject more than once that past winter.

"What did you decide?"

"Nothing new. We were married, we stayed married."

Fanny reached down and plucked a blade of grass to suck on. "Like she expects you to go on forever protecting her?"

"Like she has character," Dubin answered. "Like I respond to it."

She threw the grass away. "Maybe I have character too."

Dubin hoped so.

After a wet morning and overcast late morning a warm sunny afternoon evolved. Large long clouds slowly sailed by.

"Oh, shit," the girl suddenly cried, hopping on one leg. "My foot is bleeding. I stepped on something."

She had cut the ball of her left foot on a piece of slate. Fanny sat down in the grass. The cut bled. Dubin got down on his knees to examine her foot.

"It doesn't look deep but it ought to be bandaged so you can get back to your car. The pond is close by. I could wet my handkerchief, wash the cut, and bandage your foot."

"You don't have to wash my foot, William. Just tie something around it so I don't get my sandal sticky with blood when I put it on. I just bought a new pair."

Dubin tried finger pressure to stop the bleeding.

"Here's some kleenex," Fanny said, pulling a wad out of her bag. "Use it and don't get your hankie bloody."

But he insisted on binding his handkerchief around her foot, knotting it on the arch. "The cut should be sterilized."

"I have a tube of first-aid cream in my glove compartment."

"I'll go get it."

"Not now," said Fanny. "I won't get blood poison. Or will I?" she asked worried.

"I'll get the cream."

"No," she said. "It's not a bad cut."

"Is the bandage too tight?"

"It feels comfortable."

With Dubin's assistance she got up. "Every time I see you I get some kind of free medical treatment. Did you ever want to be a doctor?"

"A lawyer," he said, "a drastic mistake."

The biographer suggested they turn back to the car but Fanny still wanted to see the water in the quarry.

"Can you go where it's rocky?"

"I'll take it easy. I think the bleeding has stopped."

They went on in the grass, Fanny hop-walking on her heel, and passed through the warm leaf-dappled mildewed oak wood; then ascended the sloping granite rock to look down at the green water in the jagged deep basin.

"It's a lot bigger than I thought. Do you swim here?"

"I come to look at the water."

"Want to try?"

"It's dirtier than I thought. Besides, we have no towels."

"You could dry yourself with your underwear."

"Why don't you go in yourself?"

"Never mind," Fanny said. "It might start my foot bleeding again."

They sat at the edge of the water, opposite them a palisade of earth and marble debris out of which some alders and white birch grew and many thick ferns; below, the granite wall was stained tan, gray, black.

The granite had been almost totally mined and the pit left to weather many years before Dubin came to Center Campobello. He had found the quarry in an adventurous jaunt with Kitty and still came every season to observe the reflection of the trees in the water. In the autumn Dubin watched yellow leaves floating in green water.

Fanny, piling her hair on her head, tried to see herself in the pond.

"Do you like my hair this way? It's not too short?"

Dubin didn't think so.

She let her hair fall and combed it, looking for herself in the water.

Fanny, with her bandaged foot and shorn hair, sat close to William Dubin as if they had no prior history. Her thighs were bare, bosom relaxed. The day was high and quiet.

Dubin recalled Venice dispassionately. Ah, William, nature's child, who would remotely have guessed you'd find your way to this spot in her company this day? He sat listening as the girl, her fingers interlocked behind her head, unshaved armpits visible, talked about her travail in Rome.

Harvey's death had seriously got her down. "He was always kind to me, sort of kidded me out of the blues I got into. I met him through his shmucky son Mitchell, who was an orthodontist in Jersey City. Mitch misused me when I was a kid and Harvey found out in a stupid letter I wrote that he had left around. I mentioned the sexual things he had taught me and told him those I liked. After he read the letter Harvey got pissed and warned him to leave me alone or I might get him thrown in the can on a statutory-rape rap, plus impairment of the morals of a minor. Harvey said if I or my father didn't bring charges he just might."

"How old were you?"

"Fifteen when I met him, sixteen when Harvey broke it up."

She said she had met Mitchell at her cousin Mildred's wedding. "He was built, with a good ass and strong shoulders. He had brown hair, reddish sideburns, and came on very macho. Anyway, he gave me a lot of attention and a wedding is where you want to feel good. He turned me on by talking about sex in a way that made me feel it was very mysterious and only he knew how to make it happen.

"I was having hot thoughts and went with him to his apartment after the wedding. Then for the next year almost, till Harvey found that letter, we were in bed or on the floor every Sunday afternoon. I took the bus in Trenton to Jersey City, then a cab to his apartment. He gave me the carfare. Mitchell taught me all the joys of sex and some that were kinky."

"Bastard," murmured Dubin.

"When I finally got away from him I was pretty much scared of sex for years. I bet you never guessed that? The best thing that came of my experience with Mitchell was that night Harvey called me when I was feeling low, and we got to be friends, and I have never regretted it."

"Why did you let the affair with the son go on so long?"

"Because I wasn't sure about it and thought the more I learn about sex the better for me. I thought everybody had to know what I learned from him. Besides, he said he loved me and I thought he really did. He even filled my cavities and straightened my front teeth. The first thing he did when I got there on Sundays was to take off my braces so that kisses wouldn't hurt."

"An ape," Dubin ventured.

Fanny said he wasn't such a bad guy. "I liked certain things we did. Outside of his habit of screwing whenever he wasn't working his heart was in the right place. He practiced a day a week in a free clinic and wouldn't charge poor people. Harvey said he was the narcissist of the family. When I understood his nature I felt sorry for him. He's been in psychoanalysis about twenty years."

Dubin grunted.

"I had a shaky time after we broke up. When I was seventeen I felt fifty years old. I wasn't getting much out of school but hung in because somehow or other my grades were decent. I went to college. About then I began to sleep around. I was afraid I might become frigid after Mitch, and was scared. I got anxious and slept with people I shouldn't have slept with. I was depressed and used to pray. Then one day I read a book by Havelock Ellis and it helped me orient myself differently. I also was seeing a shrink although my father begrudged every nickel. Anyway, by the time I was twenty I began to enjoy sex again and I want to go on enjoying it, like forever."

"Once you told me your sexual experience had made you a more moral person. Does that relate to the experience with Mitchell or its aftermath?"

"I said a better person." She looked him full in the face "I'll bet you thought of me as a hooker?"

"If I did, I don't."

"I'm not. I was ashamed of what happened in Venice. It was freaky, I was confused."

Fanny had opened her bag, found the trillium, and tossed it into the water. He asked her why.

"I wanted to see it float."

They watched the three-petaled red flower floating in the green quarry water.

Fanny, after a while, asked Dubin what his first sex was like.

"With an older woman," he replied, "doing a repair job."

"On you?"

He nodded. "She was married, a teacher of mine. I had read *Sons and Lovers* with her."

"How long did it last?"

"Not long. Long enough."

He asked her about Harvey. "Was he your lover before we met?"

"Not really. He was into marijuana and pottery, never quite putting it together. I stayed with him for weeks just to be with one man. There were times when we wanted to love each other but couldn't. I tried to help him keep up his confidence."

"You were kind to him?"

"We were kind to each other."

Fanny's arms were wrapped around her knees. She extended her left hand so he could see the bracelet he had bought her. "I wear it for luck."

"How so?"

"You let me keep it."

The light on the eastern hills was dark gold as the sun descended in the west.

"It's late," Dubin said.

"I'll bet you don't know why I first came to Center Campobello," Fanny said.

"Was there a particular reason?"

"I read your book *Mark Twain* when I was staying in the commune on Tupper Lake. The way he was at the end of his life after Susy died, and then his wife, and he also felt miserable for treating his epileptic daughter like an idiot all her life—that part wiped me out."

"At the end of his life he lived in a theater of shmalzy misery," Dubin said.

"Shmalzy?"

"He enjoyed cigars and being a celebrity. He was deteriorating physically and mentally, but maybe in the book I laid on his aging and loneliness a bit much. *Thoreau* is a better-proportioned, more objective work."

"I read it in Rome. Harvey bought it for me as a present when I was in the hospital. I like Thoreau but wouldn't want to live his kind of life, although I liked the way he felt about himself at Walden. What I mean is that after I finished reading *Mark Twain* somebody said you had a house in this town and I decided to see if you would meet me if I came here."

"Extraordinary."

"I hoped we could really talk, that you would want to. I wanted somebody other than a shrink to advise me about my life, how to get it together better than I did. I had the feeling you could tell me useful things about myself. I never thought we would end up going to Venice. When you asked me I felt let down."

"What did you expect after undressing in my study?"

"I don't know what I expected. I was afraid of you and didn't want to be, so I went with you."

"I'm sorry I didn't respond more appropriately to your needs."

"You did in your books. The only one I don't like is *Short Lives.*"

"Is that so? It's awfully popular in paperback."

"Oh?" Fanny said nervously. "I don't want to read about people ass backwards. I don't dig death hanging over everything they do or created. Are you afraid of death?"

"Not of death but maybe what leads to it."

"Doesn't life lead to it?"

"I'm speaking of sickness, accident—being incapacitated; unable to run my life; that can be worse than death. I'm afraid of the unexpected. What I expect I can deal with. On the other hand these short lives show how intensely and creatively life can be lived even when it is early aborted. In terms of years lived, they missed little; they weren't counting."

"If you're dead you're dead," Fanny said. "Nobody has to tell me what to do with my life, only how to get it together. I know all I want to about death. I don't want my nose rubbed in it."

"It's late," Dubin said after a minute, "let's go home."

She stared at him.

He helped her up, noticing she stood firmly on the cut foot.

Fanny promised to wash the blood out of his handkerchief and mail it to him.

He asked her where she had got the locket she was wearing.

She fingered it. "Harvey gave it to me about a week before his heart attack."

"A whole heart for a broken one?"

"He liked me a lot."

Fanny asked him whether Dubin would answer if she wrote to him once in a while.

He was not much a letter writer, he said.

Why waste what the winter had taught him?

As they were moving down the granite slope half a dozen black birds rose from the oak trees and flapped off toward the reddened sun. The dark rays of the dying sun touched the tips of the trees. Overhead, massive bronze clouds in long convoys were moving east. As Fanny and Dubin came out of the wood a softened early-evening light lay on the long field of wild flowers.

Fanny began to name them. "There's celandine, oxeye daisy, red rooster —what a ball those names are." Farther on she said, "There's forget-me-not, which I knew, and those bushes are bridal wreath."

She plucked a red trillium and thrust it into her shoulder bag, then began to collect a bouquet of daisies.

The clouds were crimson, those close to the hills were violet ships voyaging to black mountains.

Fifteen or more billion years after creation, the biographer thought, here's this sea of wild flowers on earth and amid them this girl picking white daisies.

"Look," said Fanny as they were walking in the grass, "there's wild lily of the valley, if you guessed right. I've learned the names of them all."

She touched Dubin's arm.

He touched the curve of her back. Fanny, letting her bouquet of daisies slip from her hand, turned to him.

The biographer, assailing doubt, took her in his arms. Fanny sank into the warm grass, arching her hips as he drew down her underpants.

This evens it, Dubin thought, for the cruel winter.

Six

Dear Fanny. In the movie that August night she reached for his hand and kissed it, a gesture that stirred him. Ponce de León had galloped in the wrong direction: the fountain of youth is the presence of youth. In her company he enjoyed the sense of fountain within, experienced flowers of splashing water.

He had seen her in the city twice in June and again in July; had come to New York for two-day visits. This time he arrived for a week one late afternoon on a Saturday in August, a warmish pleasant summer's day, Fanny's twenty-third birthday. She had written, "I want to spend my birthday with you." On the train Dubin had opened his paper, anticipating their meeting, going to bed with her. Soon a thin gloom stole over him and he lowered the newspaper to track down why. Easy enough: Kitty and Maud had driven him to the train station. There were kisses goodbye. He was on his way to the city, he had announced, to complete a contract for three articles he'd write to earn some needed cash; have a look in at the Public Library; maybe visit an old friend or two. "Have a good time," Kitty had said. "Lots of fun," Maud affirmed, not at her best that day. Her hair was still an unhappy mix of red streaked black. She looked as though she hated to see him go, and for a moment he wanted not to leave her. When he looked again she needed someone else and he thought that natural.

Everyone wants Dubin to enjoy himself. They were planning a few days on the Maine Coast. Maud, to tell the truth, was mostly bored, a summer at home less than satisfying as she dealt with an excitement within, now apparently on, now apparently off. Kitty had suggested a drive up the coast to cheer her up and Maud had consented to go if she did the driving. He wished, considering the circumstances, they hadn't insisted on taking him to the train, but they knew he disliked buses. Well, life isn't ideal. He loved them both and tried to put them out of mind. They returned at once through predictable doors and windows. One can't easily dispense with the actors of his personal history. The biographer, as he read the newspaper, hefted and measured guilt, yet managed to sidestep it: I'm not twenty, nor forty—I'm fifty-seven. Surely these years entitle me to this pleasure. In life one daren't miss what his nature requires. Only the spiritually impoverished can live without adventure. After a while the sweep of the broad silver-blue sunlit Hudson, from the window, the smoky Catskills in the distance, helped him cast off the subtle net on his spirit and he listened to himself thinking of being, soon, with Fanny.

Dubin, as the train sped on, reflected without nostalgia how it had been when he was a young man with a prearranged date—rarely with a girl one might meet by chance in park or museum, want to be with, and *is*. But prearrangement had the advantage—it seemed advantage—of buildup in imagination, anticipation of pleasure. As the time of meeting approached, nature improved, the evening expanded, stars were jewels in the sky. As he shaved, dressed, waited for the last minutes to go by before he left the house, enjoying reverie, expectation; he felt a sense of well-being so intense it could only taint, perhaps spoil, the experience: there were times the girl wasn't— couldn't possibly be—as much pleasure as his expectation of her. He would envision more than she was; wanted more to give than he ultimately gave. The occasion therefore became self-defeating, Dubin trying to squeeze out of prevision, desire, something it was not prepared to yield. He had expected more than reality entitled him to—defense against an ordinary fate: an extraordinary woman. Out of hubris, if not fear, young William Dubin had felt an unwillingness to risk himself with someone whose experience was too much like his own. When, years later, Kitty Willis appeared in his life, he felt he had met his equal in possibility, someone who could give him not only what he hadn't had, but hadn't thought of having; Dubin had then stopped sidestepping marriage.

Dear Fanny: He had told her when he was coming but hadn't expected her to be waiting for him when the train arrived. There she was at the rope barrier. Men looked at her as they passed by and she was modestly reserved although her body seemed extrinsic to her clothes, a natural gift Dubin approved in principle. Fanny had changed her hair style since he had seen her last, her thick hair now drawn above her ears and pulled through a silver ring into a loose light mane falling to below her summer-tanned shoulders. She wore a yellow skimp, her bosom snug in the fabric, her legs bare, always good to see in short dresses. She had put on a pound or two and was relaxed, her face womanly. Neither was on probation in the other's eyes. Dubin felt heartened to have recovered her. He felt himself a gifted man, an excellent biographer.

When they arrived in Fanny's apartment on West 83rd Street she unbuttoned his shirt and began quickly to undress. Dubin helped. In bed they loved each other generously. He, after a catnap, lay restfully on her pillow, gazing at a gardenia that looked like three gardenias in a water glass on top of her bookcase.

"I put it there for you to see because you like flowers."

"Dear Fanny."

The evening grew in pleasure, serenity, magnitude. She took ten minutes to brush her hair as Dubin watched each stroke. They dressed and hailed a cab to a bistro she knew on First Avenue. At a bar with its back to a curtained window, Dubin, man of the world, drank brandy and soda as he talked with the young bartender about the merits of Lawrence's early novels, and Fanny, sipping Scotch on the rocks, seriously listened, her warm side pressed to his. The bartender, when Dubin began to explicate D. H. Lawrence on sex— a much misunderstood question: "And I who loathe sexuality so deeply am considered a lurid sexuality specialist. Mi fa malo allo stomacho"—let his eyes rest seriously on Fanny's handsome bosom. Dubin felt expansive, amiable, personally wealthy. "Sex to him, you understand, despite his ideology of blood-being, was a metaphor for a flowering life."

The bartender gravely nodded.

Fanny, her arm around her middle-aged lover, nudged her head against his chest. Dubin kissed her ear. She had a gift of closeness, could almost not bear not being in contact with whomever she felt affection for. She touched, stroked, quietly pressed. Few men had it so good.

"Let's dance," she said. A combo of piano, bull fiddle, and drums in a far corner of the room had begun to play.

Dubin tried to beg off, swore he couldn't—not this new mode of dance. He had been brought up on fox-trot and waltz, could lindy a little, not more. "I don't know the steps."

"Make them up. Hop like a monkey. Peel a banana."

"Then what?"

"Climb a tree."

He did as he was told. Fanny danced to his movements in a way that made him look good. She danced deadpan with wide-open myopic eyes, inventing steps and graceful movements of her arms. When she came close he could smell her through her scent and felt he was dancing off the floor. A blonde of thirty or so dancing nearby with a man of Dubin's age winked at the biographer and told him to save the next one for her. Fanny laughed merrily.

After a supper of omelette, green salad, white wine, Fanny asked him where he wanted to go. Miraculous question: here's Dubin with nowhere to go except where he pleased. Nothing scheduled, appointed, expected. He was this evening, in truth, a free spirit. Dubin, the single. There were a dozen things to do and he might do them all.

"You name it," he told her.

"Disco? I know a good one."

"If you wish."

"Or we could see friends of mine in the East Village?"

"Young people?"

"About my age. They have two kids. Or we could go to a picture I hear is great."

"Fine."

They walked to a movie on Third Avenue. It was there Fanny kissed his hand in the dark and Dubin kissed hers. One did not have to guess with Fanny: she was there, gave instinctually; he easily gave in return. After the film he looked for a bookstore. Dubin remembered how happy it had made Kitty, one evening not long after they had met, when he bought her a book of poems.

Fanny had never read Yeats; he bought her the *Selected Poems*, exactly what he had got Kitty; and at the florist's up the block, a white rose. Fanny carried it and the book solemnly in one hand, hugging his right arm with her left as they walked on the Drive, refreshed by the cool air of the river. They walked until it occurred to them that the streets were no longer safe. Dubin felt a melancholy regret at the way the world had gone; and she, sensing his mood, fell silent.

At home Fanny put on the coffeepot while Dubin examined her bookcase and found in it hardback copies of each of his biographies. She had managed to get even the out-of-print *Abraham Lincoln*—probably had cost her twenty bucks. On the wall above the bookcase hung a medium-enlarged framed colored snapshot of Fanny, pigeons circling her head and shoulders, that Dubin had taken with her camera one morning ages ago—was it really less than a year?—in the Piazza San Marco. He remembered the picture of her in jeans and lank hair she had sent from Rome last winter and asked if he could have a print of the one on the wall.

"Sure, but suppose your wife sees it?"

"She doesn't poke into my things, and if she did she'd know who I was in Venice with."

"How is it you never told her?"

"An anonymous woman hurts less."

Fanny regarded him silently. She began to nibble the nail of her middle finger but there was no nail to nibble. Her fingernails were, as a rule, ragged. "Where does she think you are now?"

"Not where I presently am."

Dubin moved from the bookcase to get away from the thought. She followed him. "In one way I don't mind that hassle in Venice we had."

"Which way?"

"It made me feel closer to you than I might have if everything had gone right. Do you feel close to me, William?"

They kissed.

Fanny drew herself a vitabath. She got her diaphragm out of the bureau drawer and took it into the bathroom. She had been advised after her operation not to take the Pill, she had told Dubin. He was enjoying the thought of sleeping with her again tonight; it had been years since he had slept with a woman twice in a day. He undressed, glad he had slimmed down, tamed his pot belly, a shadow of itself. The telephone rang. Fanny got rid of whoever it was before the guy could seriously unburden himself. Dubin had heard a man's urgent voice; she didn't say who. He felt uneasy. As Fanny bathed he thought of her lying nude on her double bed and imagined a line of men coiled around it, a long line of types and ages extending into the hall and down a flight of stairs; from Mitchell the orthodontist to William Dubin the biographer. How many men had she had in her young life—fifty? eighty? —a hundred and fifty? How many diaphragms had she worn out in her comparatively short sexual lifetime? Did she have one on—was it possible? —when he took her amid the wild flowers? Or did she take me? He felt a momentary distrust of her; but as Dubin, lying on Fanny's sheets, reflected on the course of human lives—on desire, error, pain, understanding, change —he exculpated her in his mind; forgave Fanny her sexual past. And when they were lying in bed after her fragrant bath it seemed to him as if they had come together in innocence. He had re-created her virginity.

Fanny, with her nail scissors, snipped the thorns off the white rose and wound its green stem around his erect cock. She kissed the flower. Dubin wished her a happy birthday.

Kitty, before sex, lowered the shades; Fanny had none on her windows. She came out of the shower naked, dressed in the sunny bedroom and walked around with wet hair, barefoot in cotton underpants. Kitty sneezed when her hair was wet. She was trim. Fanny's rump was heavier than he had thought, her waist narrower. "Why don't you get yourself some window shades?" Dubin asked her.

"I have nothing to hide, do you?"

"What about the synagogue across the street?"

"That's on the second floor and even when I stand at the window with my clothes on nobody down there looks up at me. Even when I don't have any clothes on they don't look my way. Or if somebody does he's searching for God. I don't need window shades."

Dubin often watched the elderly Jews at prayer, or as they sat at study around a long table in a brown room on the left side of the synagogue. He bought two large white shades for Fanny's bedroom windows.

Her apartment, in an old six-story graystone, was not especially attractive, needed painting, bathroom repairs. Roaches haunted the area around sink and range. Dubin sprayed disinfectant liberally, diligently, until no limping survivor remained. Fanny had two medium-size rooms and a small kitchen but the windows, in heavy flaking frames, were large, the apartment light;

and she got it for two hundred a month. She had a new job that wasn't bad —the work interesting—as secretary to an executive secretary in a law office. She didn't like nine-to-five, found the hours restrictive, yet had time to think of herself, her needs.

During the week he lived with her, Dubin slept later than usual. Her alarm rang at 7:30. He awoke alert and began his modified exercises; Fanny, into Yoga when she came home, stopped to look on as she dried herself after her shower. Dubin fried an egg and made coffee to get her off on time. She ate slowly, hungrily. She was slow in the morning but not distracted. Fanny was clean but not, like Kitty, neat; he realized how alien to her nature it had been to houseclean for others last summer. It took her about an hour to shower, brush and fix her hair, then select and screw on earrings, a variety of single and double circles of silver mostly. She said, "I'll hit the can and be right out." As she slipped on her dress she seemed lost in thought. She left the house anytime from ten to nine to a quarter after, predicting she'd be fired by the end of the month. On his way to pick up a newspaper, he hurried her to the Broadway bus. She was usually in good humor, laughed when he was witty, kissed him slowly at the bus stop, to Dubin's self-conscious concern, because people were looking and he was embarrassed by his age; but he would rather be kissed.

Afterward he read the Watergate news with intense interest. Nixon had resigned. During the impeachment proceedings Dubin had trotted his walk holding a pocket radio in his hand. Fanny and he looked through the papers every night and talked about the case before going to bed. He wondered what sort of life one might write of Nixon, provided one could stand the monotony of his mind and character. The man made him uncomfortable. It occurred to Dubin how lucky he was to be working on someone of the rich complexity of D. H. Lawrence and felt affection for him, for his self-respect.

Dubin wrote on Fanny's kitchen table after he had cleared it off and washed the breakfast dishes. He put away the freeze-dry coffee and found a box of sanitary napkins in the food cabinet. In the bedroom he hung up her slight black nightgown on a hook behind the closet door. He liked the sight of her bright short dresses hanging in the closet and thought of buying her one or two on his own. He tossed her used tights into the hamper, gave up on the rat's nest of bottles, tubes, containers in the bathroom, but took a minute to mop the tiled floor. Dubin then put the plastic garbage bag out;

he had bought her a new garbage container. And he enjoyed the happy surprise with which she greeted the order he had made.

Once he had cleaned and straightened up the place—Fanny hastily made the bed before leaving—he was in a mood for work. It did not bother him that he was not in his study; this was, after all, a holiday, and allowing himself to work, gravy. He laid out his cards, jotted down notes, and began to write careful sentences. Dubin loved sentences. He worked all morning, getting up every so often to watch the elderly Jews reading or at prayer.

After lunch he rode the Fifth Avenue bus to the Public Library and read in the reference room. One day he took the train to Newark to see where he had lived as a child; he felt no nostalgia; but it occurred to him he hadn't visited his father's and mother's graves in years. Charlie Dubin had bought his wife's grave in a cemetery in the Bronx and his own in a huge graveyard in Queens. "I got a bargain for my plot." Most often in thinking of him Dubin saw the father of his childhood, younger than he himself was now. His mother he usually thought of as she had looked after she became insane. Only once had he been to his drowned brother's grave in Newark but could not bear to go that day. After the library, he usually walked home—up Fifth, through Central Park to West 96th, then back on West End to Fanny's on 83rd. That was almost the equivalent of the long walk in Center Campobello. He did not dwell on other equivalents of his New York experience.

Fanny lived in a walk-up graystone with a partly semicircular façade. A fenced yellow steam-stack on the far side of the street spouted a cloud of white steam all day and night. Diagonally across the street were a few stores; and above a florist's shop, the second-floor synagogue, under a roof with a raised skylight. It was not a hot August, and Fanny, if Dubin shopped for her, would rather prepare supper than go out. She fed him large quantities of food. Fanny wasn't a talented cook but she was not a bad one and dared cook fish, giggling and groaning. Dubin liked fish but Kitty rarely cooked it. Kitty loved snails, clams, mussels, and frog's legs; but Dubin did not. Fanny avoided snails and oysters but enjoyed lobster. Dubin had mastered shrimp and crabmeat and stayed clear of other shellfish. He had had none as a child. Fanny, one night in a fish restaurant, got him to share her lobster.

After supper if the apartment was stuffy they usually went out. They saw *A Comedy of Errors* in the park; once attended her weekly summer evening class in government at the New School. On Saturday afternoon Dubin took her to the Metropolitan Museum and told her what he knew about painting.

He explained what Kitty had told him about Chinese pottery. She listened as though memorizing. Her bookcase was varied: he noticed books on psychology, political theory, music, ecology. "Fanny," he said, "you're a hidden intellectual." "I'm smarter than I look," she answered, "but not always organized. I'm fairly well organized at work but not when it comes to making decisions for myself. That's where I am missing a cylinder. I wish you could help me make up my mind what I ought to be doing with myself." Dubin said he would. "I am better controlled when you're around," she said. "Do you know what I mean?"

On a framed bulletin board in the kitchen she tacked up snippets of sayings: "Be kind to yourself." He remembered.

"Morality begins when one can control experience."

He wondered if she had once that week thought of Kitty. Probably she would say that was his business. Dubin had attended to his business.

From his *H. D. Thoreau* she had copied this sentence: "There is no other land; there is no other life but this or the like of this."

He gave her credit

He was careful with her, considerate of her pace and qualities. He liked to do things she suggested. At twilight, one evening, they walked into Central Park and listened, amid a circle of people in a variety of dress, some standing there with their dogs, to the steel drums played by two West Indians who beat up high haunting melodies in their gleaming pots and let them flow into dusk. Afterward they walked to the east side of the park; there were lovers lying in the grass. Fanny slipped her hand into Dubin's back pocket and felt his ass as he walked. They wandered, as the street lights came on, up Madison, seeing themselves in store windows when they stopped to look. There was this fine-figured girl in a light-orange summer dress; and with her an erect slightly self-conscious middle-aged type, smoking a cigarillo, in bell-bottoms, blazer, and Panama hat. Each stared at the reflection of the other as though neither could believe they were together. They locked fingers as they walked.

She called him Bill, tried Will, went back to William. William could sound funny when she said it. When he read poetry to her she sat close in a chair, her bare legs resting on his thighs. She told him personal things: why her periods were late; confessed to occasional problems of constipation, for which he advised her to cook up a pot of prunes with lemon rind and have a plateful each morning. She wrote left-handed, he discovered to his surprise; was otherwise right-handed. She typed beautifully, retyped his Lawrence pages for him. Fanny created little favors for Dubin. At night she drew down the white shades and they turned to each other with passion. She slept heavily. He too slept deeply, lying against her strong young sweet-smelling body.

One night he woke from deep sleep to find himself being sucked off. The pleasure was all but unbearable. Fanny moved her moist mouth patiently until he came with a cry, almost of protest.

"What was that for?"

"I woke up and wanted to."

In the morning they woke making love. Fanny stayed home from work and they slept till noon. He had tried to break through sleep to get up but couldn't. Afterward they rose, showered, ate leisurely, went back to bed. Dubin loved her body, was conscious of her sensuality, aroused by the force of her sexual being. She was embarrassed by nothing, named her pleasures. He responded to her desire by running his tongue along her pudgy clitoris as she squirmed happily. A first for Dubin; he felt like a god.

Fanny asked if he had liked doing it. She was sitting cross-legged in bed. How intimate strangers can be.

"For the effect it has on you, yes."

"Don't do anything you are not comfortable with."

That night she massaged his back with lotions, unguents, kneading his shoulders, pressing her strong fingers into his flesh, working down his legs, rubbing, stroking. His heart beat like a drum. "Does your wife massage you too?" "No." "Never?" "Never." "Too bad," said Fanny. She was subtle, cunning, gifted in touch, wet him exquisitely. She seemed to watch her effect on him. Dubin cherished their intimacy.

But when he asked whether she was teaching him the orthodontist's repertory, Fanny denied it.

"What he taught me has got nothing to do with what I want to give you or want you to give me. One man is a hunk of wood in bed, another is a fire. At first I thought you'd be a loaf of rye bread but now there's something wild in you that I like."

"A wild rye bread or wildfire?"

"A wild flower," Fanny laughed. "I want you to have a lot of fun." Dubin replied it was what he wanted. He felt satisfied in a way he hadn't since early in his marriage. The intensity of pleasure, of possibility, was greater now. Live and learn.

I want her to teach me, he thought. I want to know everything she does. I'm more than twice her age.

Her orgasm, she swore, spaced her. "It's like coming full blast out of a cannon." She let go in surprise. "Will-yam," she sang as to a friend far away. His ended in a slow drop from the bursting sky; knowing it would end safely in a warm bed. He was fulfilled, relieved, as though he had feared what had happened to them might never have; then magically it had happened. Something good, fortunate, had come into his life. With this girl I know the flowering pleasure, heathen innocence, of the natural life. I live in her sun-strong garden. He was grateful to her; they held each other close and kissed affectionately.

As Fanny slept Dubin lay awake thinking of his *Passion of D. H. Lawrence*. He was glad the pleasures of this week had come to him as they had: this long careless giving of oneself in sex. His experiences with Fanny, in variety, intensity, excitement heightened by her watchful curious knowing, sureness of her sexual self, willingness to give, couldn't have come at a better moment. He understood Lawrence more fully, his religion of sexuality: a belief in the blood, the flesh, as wiser than the intellect. I think I know what he means by "the unknown God brought into consciousness"—"the slow invasion in you of the vast invisible God that lives in the ether"—"the old Pagan vision." "This is very important to our being, that we should realise that we have a blood-being, a blood-consciousness, a blood-soul, complete and apart from the mental and nerve consequences." I can't say I fully believe it, Dubin thought, but understand more clearly where it came from in his nature and why he said it in these words. I think—I feel I understand him.

Unable to sleep, he rose hyped up, his imagination pouring ideas like rain. He felt like working but had better not if he could work longer later. He stood at the bedroom window, one shade raised, gazing above the steaming smoke-stack at the synagogue. The building was darkened except for a small candle-lit room where a black-bearded black-hatted Jew, his white shawl glowing on his shoulders, bent back and forth in prayer. Once in a while Dubin prayed. It was a way of addressing the self; God had a tin ear. Who wanted to listen to human complaints within the heavenly music?

Whom shall I pray for?

He thought of Gerald and Maud but this time prayed a moment for

Fanny, then got into bed with the girl, who did not stir. He moved close to her sex-scented body, and as she sighed, fell into sleep.

He was awakened by the sound of rain, or a distant sobbing, as though someone was lost and he wasn't sure who. Dubin fought against waking but it sprang out of him like an idiot tearing at the roots of sleep. Protesting the task, he ascended a ladder, rising step by gluey step until he miraculously thrust his head through a foggy hole. In his confusion he called her Kitty. He lay with eyes open trying to understand what Fanny was complaining about. He felt her twisting in her sleep. With an effort he turned on the bed lamp. Her eyelids were twitching, arms moved in spasms, her mouth tormented; she seemed to be locked in a nightmare.

"Fanny." He shook her gently. "Take it easy." She whimpered yet drunkenly slept on. Dubin shook her again. With a groan Fanny quickly sat up, astonished to see him there. She fell into his arms in relief.

"Jesus," she shuddered, "I had this mind-blowing god-awful dream—it was one of those awful ones with blood and shit in it—that I'd been killed in an accident. I saw myself dead and couldn't wake until you made me." She wept in bed. "I don't want to die young. I hate that book you wrote. Why did you give it to me?"

"Forgive me," Dubin said.

Afterward she was depressed. Dubin got up to brew her a cup of tea. As he was waiting for the water to boil he looked uneasily out of the window for a sign of dawn. Wanting to sleep, he did not want it to be dawn; neither did the night—black, heavy, inert. Across the silent street the candlelight was out in the synagogue. Fanny sipped tea in bed. For a while they talked, then put out the light and quietly talked. She turned on her side, resting on his arm.

"I dreamed I saw someone with a crazy crippled face watching us from the fire escape."

"What fire escape?"

"I dreamed there was one. I feel scared about something, I wish I knew what it was. I'm afraid something bad might happen to me. I don't want to do the wrong thing with my life. Advise me, William. I'm afraid I'll be anxious again. Tell me what to do about myself. You're so serious about life, tell me what to do with mine."

He said it wasn't so simple, he didn't know her that well.

"You know me well enough," she said fiercely.

"You're a late bloomer, Fanny. I was too. Keep your eye on yourself. Find out who you are. Watch what you do and tell yourself why. Try to use yourself well."

"People have been saying something like that to me all my life. It drives me up a wall. Suppose I *never* find out who I am?"

"Then you'll have to find out why or pay for it."

"I don't want to go back to a shrink."

"I wasn't talking about shrinks."

"How did you find out you wanted to write biographies? If I knew what I wanted to do that would be half of it for me."

Dubin said trial and error plus good luck. "I was writing obituaries. Finally I read someone's life of somebody else and thought I could do better. My wife thought so too."

Fanny yawned and grew quiet. For a minute he thought she had fallen asleep. "What about her?" she asked.

"What about her?"

"Did she know what she wanted to do when she was my age?"

"At your age she was about to be a widow."

"I mean before that?"

"She was interested in music but not much came of it. She wanted to teach, she wanted to be a concert harpist, but she didn't do either. She met this doctor and he asked her to marry him."

"I don't want to get married—at least not yet."

"Not yet," Dubin agreed.

"When did she start being afraid she would die of cancer, or something like that?"

"Before I met her."

"Is that the reason she goes around smelling the gas burners?"

"I suppose so. It's a kind of ritual against death."

"Do you think I have one?"

"I don't know. Do you have many nightmares?"

"I used to have more when I was a kid."

"Maybe they're your gas burners."

"Maybe. What are yours?"

"I don't know."

"What about those long walks you always take?"

"I thought a walk was a walk."

Fanny was silent a moment. "Did Thoreau have a ritual? I don't remember whether you mentioned it in your book."

"His journal was his ritual. For all I know he may have thrown handfuls of snow over his left shoulder as he was walking in the woods."

"What about D. H. Lawrence?"

"Maybe his tuberculosis was psychosomatic, I don't know. He would never admit he was seriously ill till after he finished *The Plumed Serpent* in Mexico. He called his sickness catarrh, bronchitis, influenza, a bad cold, finally malaria—everything but the deadly thing it was. He used to say it wasn't his lungs, it was his bronchi; but his lungs were rotting."

"Are you afraid to die, William?" Fanny asked in the dark.

Dubin drew up his knees. "My God, Fanny, how many times are you going to ask me that? I don't want to talk any more. I'm worn out with all the sex we've had. I need sleep desperately. For God's sake, let me sleep."

"Are you sorry about us now?"

"No."

"Are you glad?"

"Yes."

"Is your wife good in bed, William?" Fanny then asked.

"Lay off, Fanny," Dubin said irritably. "She wouldn't want you to know."

"Oh, come off it."

"Obviously she's different from you."

"How different?"

"That's none of your business."

"Do you love her—this minute?"

"Yes."

"Do you love me?"

"Yes."

"Bullshit."

He waited for her to start punishing him but she had fallen asleep. Dubin couldn't till dawn.

In the morning Fanny apologized for having kept him awake during the night. She was menstruating heavily. "That's what gave me those lousy dreams," she said almost gaily. "I always have nightmares before I get the curse."

Sunday morning Dubin called his wife in Center Campobello from a public pay phone while he was out getting the newspaper. Kitty was angered.

"Where in Christ have you been? I was frantic. You weren't registered at the Gansevoort. They had no idea where you were."

Dubin said he was at the Brevoort.

"Why the Brevoort? You've never liked it there."

"For a change," he lied. "Were you calling from Maine? Is something the matter?"

"We never got to Maine. Maud couldn't make it. The night before we were to leave she got a long-distance call from a man she said was a friend, then asked out. She packed a bag and took a bus to New York. I can tell you she stopped being bored in a hurry."

Dubin was worried. "Is she here now?"

"I would imagine so."

"Where is she staying?"

"She hasn't called. I don't know where any of my family are."

"I'm standing here talking to you. Did she say when she'd be home?"

"Vaguely—about a week. She apologized for having to go. I'm certain she's having an affair."

"You don't know who he is?"

"No. Questions about her personal life annoy her."

"There are some questions one has to ask."

"Who she may or may not be sleeping with? You ask her."

"Maybe I will."

"When will you come home?"

"Tomorrow morning."

"I thought you said you'd be home today?"

"I want to visit my father's and mother's graves this afternoon."

"Yes, go," she said.

Dubin asked her to meet him at the train tomorrow noon and Kitty said she would.

He said he was sorry he had forgotten to give her the name of the hotel he'd been staying in.

"That's all right. Did you have a good time?"

"On and off." Hearing that, he laughed nervously. "Pretty good."

Kitty said she was glad.

After he had brought the paper to Fanny, Dubin hailed a cab to take him to the cemetery in the Bronx where his mother was buried. Her grave was overgrown with thick grass.

"Mama," he said, "rest in peace in your grave." Where else could she rest? He thought of her jumble of mad fears; of those he carried in his flesh. He wondered which of them Maud carried in her.

Dubin left a stone on the tombstone to let his mother know he had been there. Maybe it was to let himself know. The white stone he had left more than a dozen years ago when he had taken Kitty to visit the grave was still there, the color of rust. It had begun to rain. He stopped off at the cemetery office and told them to cut the long grass on his mother's grave.

Dubin then rode on the subway to Jamaica and at the station took a taxi to his father's cemetery. Charles Dubin had divorced himself from his wife in his grave. Let God take care of her now. His son carried a small leather-bound book and read from it a Hebrew prayer for the dead transliterated in English.

"Rest in peace, Papa," he said to the wet grave. "You did what you had to."

Dubin imagined nine other men standing at the grave with him, saying Kaddish.

He left the endless cemetery and rode the long subway ride back to Fanny's apartment. When she had returned from Rome she swore off smoking and had taken up Yoga. She wore black leotards with a run down her left thigh as she did her exercises. Fanny had got to a modified headstand, her head resting in a pool of her thick hair, when he entered the apartment.

She fell to her knees. Dubin pulled her up and they kissed with open mouths. Her breath was like the scent of a tropical flower. Her hand went to his fly.

"Not now," Dubin said.

"Because I'm bleeding?"

He said he was not much in a mood. He had just been to the cemetery.

"Did your wife ever want it when she was bleeding?"

"Ask her."

After a while Fanny said she was sorry she had asked. Her face was pallid and worried. "I was happy all week," she said to Dubin. "I don't want to spoil it."

He said he didn't want to spoil it either.

"Do you honestly like me?"

"Most honestly."

Her eyes softened. "I had a fine time, did you?" She touched his hand with her finger.

"Never better."

"Let's have more good times, lots of fun."

He said that was what he wanted.

"I will give you a key to the downstairs door and one for my apartment."

Dubin said he had better not take the keys. "If I left them around or they fell out of my pocket, Kitty would want to know what they were for."

Fanny reluctantly saw the point. "Anyway, when will you be back? I miss you already."

He promised soon.

"Oh, make it sooner. We're lovers now, aren't we?"

Seven

They made love on a sunny Sunday morning, the moving white curtains
enfolding warm light. Afterward Kitty, lying on her side, said the early-fall
anemones were especially prettily colored. It was a bright August day thinning toward autumn. He had made love with her, trying not to think of
Fanny. Dubin was conscious of himself lying beside his wife, his left arm
around her, hers draped across his belly. Kitty was slender, taller than Fanny,
felt lighter, weighed less. Her face was at peace and pretty. Her skin shone
in the morning light. He was glad she was satisfied; wanted her to have what
she was entitled to.

Forgive me, he thought.

"What for?"

He asked, after a minute, what he had said.

She laughed to herself. "What shall I forgive?"

"Who I am."

She had heard it before. "I forgive who you are."

Kitty ruffled his hair, yawned, sat up and reached for her robe. "Let's have
breakfast."

Sunday's was the breakfast they almost always ate together. On Sunday she fixed other than ordinary fare. Today she cooked an omelette aux fines herbes. The buttery golden omelette with greens looked succulent in the omelette pan. Biscuits were hot, creamy, coffee tasty. Mt. No Name, through the window behind Kitty, became more clearly visible as summer heat and haze diminished. There were a few yellowing leaves in the silver maples, not many. After a blow of wind a handful of dead leaves lay scattered on the grass. Dubin watched a single leaf, half-green, half-yellow, part from a branch and drift and twirl to the ground. He had always been affected by the sight. Now he thought of Fanny. He tried not to.

Kitty, after pouring second cups of coffee, asked him what his impression had been of Maud's summer. "What did you talk about with her?"

"Politics often. She was excited by the impeachment proceedings. We both were."

"I mean what did she say that was personal?"

"Not much about herself," Dubin told Kitty. "She wasn't giving much though there were moments she seemed to want to. Once in a while I said something that brought her close—not close enough—to saying what was on her mind. I had this sense, on her part, of gesture."

"What do you mean?"

"Her visit as a kind gesture to her parents."

"I hope to God she isn't having a bad time. If she's in love I'd hate it to be unhappy love."

"Do you think she's in love?"

Kitty said she thought so. "She's been reading Spanish love poems in her room. I hear her as I go up the stairs."

"Which poems?"

"One I asked about she copied out for me. It's Mother Juana Inés de la Cruz. She copied it and I learned it:

Al que ingrato me deja, busco amante;
al que amante me sigue, dejo ingrata;
constante adoro a quien mi amor maltrata;
maltrato a quien mi amor busca constante.

Al que trato de amor, hallo diamante,
y soy diamante al que de amor me trata . . .

When Kitty recited poetry her voice was sincere, soft, hesitant. Maud recited in a sweet emotional fluent voice.

"What does it mean?"

"She says she lovingly seeks the one who ungratefully abandons her; and he who lovingly pursues her she ungratefully abandons. "Him whom I treat lovingly I find to be hard, and I am hard for him who treats me lovingly.""

"It sounds rocky."

"It has a Spanish quality. Her voice sounds Spanishy."

"Castanets, black hair, and throaty voice?"

"She's a surprising girl."

"Has she said who the guy is—somebody Spanish or Mexican?"

"Didn't you ask?"

"No."

"He may be, maybe not, I'm not good at guessing. I hope she's happy with him. Being in love at her age was a happy time for me. When I woke in the morning I ran to see myself in the looking glass."

Dubin said it wasn't a happy time in his life.

"When I first met you, you said it was."

"In a way it was. I enjoyed hurrying to their houses with little bouquets of flowers."

"You haven't brought one home in years."

He said the garden was full of flowers. "I felt happy in love until I had to contend with feeling come back to earth. I was by then disenchanted with the one I'd been in love with and was waiting for the next experience. After a while I felt the waste of the affair."

"Why was it a waste?"

"Nothing had come of it."

"Does something have to come of everything?"

He said that was not a bad idea.

"What happened to the girl?"

"She went elsewhere."

"I sometimes am surprised that you wanted to marry me."

"I was ready for you. You were right for me with your kind of experience. I felt we were in the real world."

"I wasn't so sure of that in the beginning."

"I wasn't sure of myself as your step-husband."

"Oh, cut it out," Kitty grimaced.

Dubin changed the subject: "I sense Maud has a lot to learn."

"If I could she will, maybe Gerald will too. I hope he's happy someday."

"I doubt he thinks of happiness. I don't think it's on his agenda."

"What does he think of?"

"He does his tightrope."

"Where to?"

"To the next tightrope, from the one over rocks to the one over water."

Kitty's dark eyes showed concern. "I liked his last card. He seemed to be having a better time. But he never tells us what he's doing. I hate that kind of gap between son and mother. Do you think he'll want to come home soon?"

"It'll depend on what President Ford offers the deserters. He isn't a man with much moral imagination."

"Gerry Willis insists on an apology. He has an intense moral imagination."

"He's got the makings of a revolutionary."

"What a strange way for one's own son to be," Kitty said. "Before you know who he is he's someone other than you think."

Yet she gave the impression she might square things with Gerald if only he returned to the house for a visit. "I have a lot to say to him. I see things more clearly than I used to. I'm not as guilty as I used to be."

Despite the uncertainties of Gerry's life and Maud's, the worries they kicked up as they defined themselves, lived their experiences, mysteries, Dubin always enjoyed talking about them. Talk was a way of conjuring them up and bringing them close. He often thought of them without worrying about their fates, reflecting on the twists and turns their lives might take before they had settled into vocations—when one could see, if not a completely matured self, at least the self's direction. He wondered what they would ultimately want to work at, or work in. Maud was interested in many things, none strongly defined except her Spanish. Would she teach? Ask her what she hoped to do and she grew impatient. "I'll do something, don't worry. But don't expect me to get married after college or go to graduate school." "What shall I expect?" "Expect nothing and be surprised." Gerald, on the other hand, had always had strong specific interests—his math, astronomy, chess, music. Dubin could imagine him in a Swedish institute doing mathematical research. Or moved perhaps by some indefinable impulse, he might, like his father, become a physician.

They confided little and asked little, Dubin thought. I hoped they would want to know what I could tell them. I wish I had told them more about my life.

"Were we good parents or half-ass ones?" Kitty said. She asked it in a way that seemingly answered the question. She asked it often.

He thought they weren't bad parents but what seemed to count most was who parents were as people, not what they said they were. The more self-conscious or insistent or private they were, the quicker the kids made tracks into space.

"Who you are is the lesson they ingest, resist, live by."

"I can't do much about that," Kitty said, "but I do wish I had tried now and then to explain myself to them. I wanted to but couldn't freely. I hid my fears and they knew. But I love them and want their love. I know it's there, behind the clouds, but I'd like to feel it on me like the living sun."

"What's there will show as they come to terms with themselves."

"Let's not depend on them," Kitty said. "Let's depend on each other."

They went for a drive into the mountains that afternoon, Dubin driving. Fall was advanced there. Some branches of sugar maples had turned color from trunk to tip. In a few weeks trees would glow like jewels. He loved the softness, quietude, before the assault of color, the rage of winter. There were blue holes in the changing foliage—the sky flowing through trees. "Do you feel how sexy the mountains are as we drive through them?" Kitty asked. He said he knew what she meant. "Do you still think of me as sexy?" Dubin said she was.

That evening they had dinner at the Ondyks', with Oscar and Flora. Evan dug out his alto sax and played some songs of the forties. His eyes retained an almost expressionless quality—at most a fixed nostalgia—but the playing was lively. Kitty sang along with him. Then Oscar went to the piano and played Chopin for a while. He apologized for his piano playing. Flora, sitting close to Dubin, whispered she was sorry she hadn't brought her violin. "I sensed I'd want it with you here."

Kitty, when they arrived home, sat down at her harp and played intensely for ten minutes. In their bedroom she looked at herself in the mirror and said this had been one of their happiest days.

Dubin promised many more.

The biographer, while settling the business of his articles, had managed another short visit to Fanny at the end of August. He had registered at the Gansevoort and spent most of his time in her apartment. He would call the hotel for messages and telephone Kitty from a phone booth if she had called. She called once. Dubin and Fanny were immediately intimate. He was perhaps surprised at how quickly and comfortably they came together, as though he wasn't sure he had earned the privilege. He had and he hadn't, as when strangers become lovers they remain in part strangers. Or as when married men, having affairs with single women, expect less than total commitment. But Fanny had pronounced them lovers, and coming together in felt acceptance and desire was a happy circumstance. He enjoyed their familiar life together. They were friends, more to their relationship than sex; but happily there was sex. Dubin worried that he was seeing her so infrequently. How long would they go on being lovers if she had to wait for him to show up—with luck—once or twice a month? He knew she was seeing other men—how could he ask her not to? She had told him, "We go out but I honestly don't sleep with any of them. I pick guys who won't give me a hard time. One is almost your age, and reminds me of Harvey. I hope you don't mind? I also see women I know, one from work, if I feel lonely." Looking at him openly Fanny asked, "Do you believe me?"

Dubin said he did.

They squeezed hands and with serious faces kissed seriously.

She hesitantly showed him a term paper she had written for her government class and sat on the bed clipping her toenails as he read it.

Dubin told her it was informed and well written. Fanny respected facts and reasoned well. The term paper revealed qualities he had not often observed in her: of knowing more than she seemed to; of being organized as she thought things through. He said that to her.

"Are you surprised?"

"Only a little."

"Are you glad?"

He said he was.

"You like me to be a good student?"

"I like you to be a good whatever."

She laughed happily and offered to go to bed. When he asked her why, right then, Fanny said she felt sexy when he complimented her. They went out for dinner and for a while talked of courses she might take in the fall. She intended, she said, "really" "finally" to get her degree. Dubin ordered a bottle of champagne.

Champagne made her feel high, Fanny said. So did music, bright colors, a witty evening, a happy time. They hurried home; she loved hurrying home to make love. He did too. It was a good way to be.

Dubin left on Sunday morning, promising his earliest possible return, thankful she hadn't insisted on a secure date to write down.

"Let's say I'll be back the first chance I have, Fanny. It isn't always easy to get out but I'll manage."

"It's cool," Fanny said. She knew the game, the rules, the odds.

He traveled home thinking of her; putting her out of his mind when the train, its whistle like a sustained organ chord, approached the station where Kitty, sitting in her car, loyally awaited the bull's return. Dubin lifted his Panama, opened the car door; they kissed. As they drove home he had to restrain himself from talking about the girl, as if he were expecting his wife to appreciate Fanny's contribution to his well-being, good life. What "on balance" he owed his wife he would soon repay. He treated her tenderly.

These visits to Fanny sparked his work. Ideas swarmed in Dubin's mind. He was still writing of Lawrence and Frieda during their slow journey on the Continent after their elopement; their deepening love, celebrated in poems and letters written in Germany, Italy, Sicily, as they lived in a villino amid olive, almond, and lemon trees; or in a farmhouse on a mountainside.

> And at last I know my love for you is here;
> I can see it all, it is like twilight . . .
> Strange how we suffer in spite of this!

Dubin worked in the barn study, writing securely and rapidly. Kitty said she would rather he was in the house but would settle for a phone in the barn, "just in case."

"In case what?"

"In case I need you in a hurry. One never knows."

He had a telephone put in. She called rarely—once when the tree man wanted to see him: another elm was dying; once or twice when he had worked long past lunch and she was beginning to be worried.

He labored steadily. There were no serious distractions. Now and then he would put down his pen to pursue a thought of Fanny—usually to relive her looks or body; or simply enjoy the marvelous fact that William Dubin had, at his age, a vital vivid young friend. Sometimes he searched amid the papers in a folder on his desk for the picture she had recently given him—to contemplate Fanny. He kept it hidden in a box of photocopies of the Lawrence correspondence he had discovered in Eastwood, with her short affectionate letters beginning "Dearest William," and closing with four x's in place of love. Her handwriting slanted downward. A triangle of bare paper was left at the bottom. Dubin thought he could write a whole letter in it.

"When are you coming?" she wrote. "I am waiting in bed."

She mailed her typed letters without a return address, his name purposely mispelled; and varied the size and color of the envelope as if to indicate the letters were coming from different people in different places. Dubin remembered that Jonathan Swift had instructed Vanessa to have someone else address her letters to him; but the biographer wanted no part of that. He was surprised by Fanny's machinations; hadn't asked her to join the deceit; did not want to share it with her, nor be reminded or informed of her experience with other men.

"When are you coming? A lot is going to waste—I mean not using what you have is wasting it."

Once she wrote, "Suppose you got sick, how would I know? What could I do to see you? Sometimes I feel as though you aren't in my life."

He wrote her an affectionate letter. In it he said: "I'm happier now than I've been in years. There ought to be a way of having other selves to be with those we love."

Now was a new season, unfortunately without her. He would love to point out changes in nature, share them with her if only in Central Park; but he could not get off to the city. Kitty had insisted she'd go with him the next time round—they'd drive down together, as he had promised. She knew how thoroughly he had done his research; how trivial to voyage to New York to squeeze out a minor fact or two in the Public Library when there'd be many to check after he had completed a full draft. She knew he'd signed his contract for three long biographical articles. If he went to New York now it was mostly as a break; "for fun," Kitty said. She could use a little herself.

When she asked when he might be going he said he wasn't sure. She could go by herself if she liked—shop, visit friends, take in a play; but Kitty said she'd wait for him. It was more fun going together. Dubin waited: the work was flowing. And he was enjoying hoarfrost mornings before warm tangy autumn days; burning-leaf smell of trees yellowing in afternoon sun; a failing luminosity at twilight—most beautiful time of year. Melancholy too: signs of winter's fingers in woods and fields. Landscape as metaphor. Nature repeating the same old tale, usually with same effect; it plays in memory: what dies is present, what's present dies.

Although he missed Fanny he sometimes thought that so long as they cared for each other, admitted the reality and importance of their relationship, he did not always have to be with her. She was his in principle; he had somehow earned the privilege of her. The mild sadness that went with it— dominant emotion of his life, he often thought—touched but did not taint his desire for her. Unless it was the unyielding presence of Kitty in his thoughts that salted in the sadness.

Then Fanny drove up to Center Campobello one Saturday morning and called from her motel as he was working in the barn. There had been talk she might come up but Dubin had hoped he would bē in the city before that.

"I'm here," she announced, "to see the color and whoever wants to see me." Her laughter was strained and he imagined her sober expression.

Dubin had called her at the beginning of the week to say once more why he was finding it hard to get away; told her Kitty had insisted on going with him. "I'll have to drive down once with her and not see you. After that I'll try to come back alone."

"But couldn't we see each other for an hour after I get home from work? It's better than not at all."

"I wouldn't want to leave you with the evening in your lap after we'd been to bed."

"Let's take what we can get, William," Fanny had said. "I feel very generous after I've been with someone who means a lot to me."

He had said he'd tell Kitty they'd be coming down next week.

But Fanny hadn't waited. She had felt like driving up, she said. "Can't we meet tonight? I'd love to eat with you, then come back here. I have a nice room in this motel. They have cotton sheets on the bed. Some private people own it. It even has curtains and white window shades. I'll bet you like it."

He said after a minute he would try to arrange it. "One way or the other.

But I won't be able to see you tomorrow, Fanny. Don't plan on that. I'm usually home all day Sunday."

"Not even in the morning? I plan to leave by one o'clock. I'm having dinner with my friends in the Village who I told you about."

In the afternoon Dubin went for a drive and called Kitty to say the car had broken down. He was at a garage in Glens Falls and would have to wait until they got the part they needed from a neighboring town. "Don't wait for me. I'll pick up a sandwich across the street."

"I hate to eat alone," Kitty said.

Dubin felt shame; he said nothing.

"Maybe it's time to trade in this lousy car for a new one?"

He said they ought to consider it.

He met Fanny at the motel. They ate an early dinner in a nearby inn and returned to her room. She pulled down the shades and asked to be undressed. They made love impetuously, sensuously. She loved lavishly. He was excited by the aromas of her hair and flesh. She liked him to kiss the dark aureoles of her nipples. "William!" she cried as she came. Dubin fell through the sensuous sky into a mountain of leaves, bounced once, and fell peacefully asleep.

"Won't you see me for a little bit tomorrow?" Fanny asked. "Even an hour would be all right."

He promised he would.

She held up her hands to show him she was growing back her fingernails. He kissed both hands.

On Sunday Dubin rose early, left Kitty sleeping heavily and drove to the motel to have breakfast with Fanny. He had scribbled his wife a note saying he had written something that had come apart during the night and he had to puzzle out why. He was taking an early drive and would be back in time for lunch. He disliked what the note said but left it anyway.

After they had made love, as she was sitting cross-legged in bed, Fanny remarked, "I don't know exactly what we're doing, or what you're doing, but whatever it is hits me right. I felt this one today way up my ass."

"Bingo."

Fanny laughed. "We're good together."

"Is that what it is? Hasn't this happened to you before?"

"Not often. Only once or twice I can remember."

"I'm glad it happens when you're with me but I marvel a little."

"Maybe it's because of the way you want it. I dig the hungry way you go after me."

"You make me feel hungry. I have a long pleasure with you, on the edge of pain. Is it simply that we physically suit each other?"

"It has to be more than that," Fanny replied. "I think I come the way I do because I like myself better when I am with you."

Dubin kissed her knees.

"If we have it this good," Fanny said, "don't you think it's crazy not to see each other a lot more than we do?"

He said they would. She placed her warm palm on his.

He did not have to lie to Kitty when he arrived home shortly before noon. She hadn't seen the note and he tore it up. She had taken a sleeping pill in the middle of the night and was awakening as he came into the bedroom and raised the shades.

"Why didn't you wake me to eat with you?" Kitty said drowsily after glancing at the clock.

He said he had wanted her to sleep.

She shook him out of solid slumber. He woke with a long-drawn groan. She had had a mad dream—could not remember worse: She was a young woman with a baby in a crib. The crib was in flames. It had taken her an endless time to find the burning child's room. She had heard it shrieking and raced up the stairs. Kitty grabbed up the baby, its bedclothes afire, and ran to the bathroom to hold it in the shower, but the door was locked. William, let me in! She hastened from room to room, trying to find him, sick with fright. It occurred to her the child was Nathanael's and she ran to the telephone to call him but Nathanael was in his grave. Kitty had wakened, trying to remember whether she had fainted in the dream.

Dubin held her till she stopped shuddering.

He asked her what was worrying her.

"I don't know," Kitty said, "except a confusing lot of ongoing things. Neither of the kids is nearby or settled. I worry about them. I also worry about Vietnam. I hate the goddamn war. I think I will stop watching the news at night—those burning children running across the road. No wonder I have nightmares."

Dubin told Kitty in their austere high-ceilinged room at the Gansevoort that he would meet her for dinner at half past seven, or eight. Would she want to see a movie afterward?

"Make it half past seven," Kitty said, "I'm famished by eight. We'll see about the movie. We might want to do something else."

He told her he was having a drink with a biographer of Frieda Lawrence.

"Anyone I know?"

"Have you met Fritz Halsman?" He knew no Fritz Halsman and was surprised and irritated by the sincerity of his question.

"No. Why don't you invite him to dinner with us if he's free?"

"Maybe next time. He's not that interesting. I'm only checking a point with him."

Kitty was wearing a new fall dress with a cloche hat. She looked good in hats that framed the face. She had enjoyed the drive and said they ought to come into the city more often.

"Why bother living in the country?"

"New York was no decent place to bring up children. We both thought so years ago."

Dubin left quickly to say nothing else. When he lied he talked too much. In the cab he sat silent as the driver talked.

Dubin got to Fanny's as she was arriving in a taxi. They kissed in the street. "How much time do we have?" she asked.

"About two hours."

"Then we don't have to hurry."

She had her diaphragm on, had been wearing it since that morning. Upstairs she showed him a pair of lace-edged underpants she had bought during her lunch hour. "Let's get into bed," said Dubin. "I knew you'd like them," Fanny said.

Dubin was back at the hotel at 7:40, going on about the war ending soon. Then he warned himself to shut up. He had showered at Fanny's and was about to change his underwear when it occurred to him the shorts he kept in her dresser drawer were striped, whereas the pair he had been wearing were a solid blue. When he got back to the hotel he changed his underclothes and shirt in the bathroom to be sure Fanny's scent wasn't detectable on him. He used Kitty's soap.

Their dinner was excellent. He enjoyed his wife's wit and flushed good looks. She wanted to return to their room after dinner but he talked her into going to a movie that had just opened.

On their way home the next morning, Kitty driving, chatty, Dubin quiet, barely aware of scene or sight, he worried about the spreading dishonesty he was into. Awful, if you thought of yourself as an honest man. You spoke pebbles and pieces of metal and when you determined to say honest words you kept spitting out bits of brackish metal.

Since lying was beyond Kitty, or she beyond it, lying to her tainted his pleasure with Fanny, at least in afterthought. Kitty was trustworthy; Dubin hated to think he wasn't. Of course he could tell her the truth and hope for the best. Some men were able to inform their wives and still manage to carry on an affair. But Kitty wouldn't tolerate it; Dubin didn't see how they could go on living together if she knew. She wasn't constituted for an emotionally, not to say morally, ambiguous relationship. To protect her peace of mind he had to lie though he wanted to protect her from his lies. Nor did he intend, at least yet, to give up Fanny. At times he wondered if his deceit to Kitty might induce dishonesty in his work. The thought bothered him although he knew enough about the lives of writers to understand that even the morally deficient might write well. So he kept his sad secret, recalling that Freud had said no one could keep a secret forever. "If his lips are silent his fingertips give him away."

Yet he concealed his thoughts of Fanny; disguised details of other trips to the city; received letters from her in a post-office box he had recently rented. He called her once a week and she, him, more often, on his barn telephone; but there were times she would try to reach him in the house at night if she'd been unable to make a morning call. Dubin only rarely telephoned her at work. At night, if Kitty answered, Fanny hung up. Kitty reached for the phone when it rang. If he answered but couldn't speak to Fanny because his wife was there, Dubin hung up.

"Who was that, William?"

"Wrong number probably, somebody rang off."

"We've had a spate of hang-ups lately."

"They come and go. There seems to be a season for them."

He asked Fanny not to call him at home. "Then when can we talk?" she asked angrily. "If I can't get you in the barn in the morning because I am too busy to sneak in a call, that means I can't talk to you at all when I have something to tell you. I save most of my news to tell you. I'm taking environmental studies and psychology at N.Y.U. three nights a week. I wanted to talk about what I was writing in my psych paper and see if you like my ideas. I also think of us in bed. Do you suppose we could go to Europe again? I'm getting two weeks off this winter—they're not giving me a summer vacation, because I am new. But my boss says they like me and I make up time when I come in late. They like it that I'm going to school at night. I might get a raise the first of the year."

"Europe would be different this time," Dubin felt.

"If there hadn't been a last time there wouldn't be a this time," Fanny said.

He said he wasn't thinking of last time. "I was thinking we might go to Athens if I could come up with a good enough reason why, like maybe a cache of unpublished Lawrence letters had been discovered there—"

"Why don't you put your mind to it?"

He said he would think about it.

They arranged he would telephone her from the barn twice a week before she left for work, and she would not call him unless it was absolutely necessary.

When he phoned before eight she was usually alert, eager to talk, had much to say and said it warmly. Dubin would walk across the hoarfrost field to call her, then return for a second cup of coffee and to shave. He would afterward trot off to the barn to do his day's work. Fanny once in a while phoned in mid-morning to say a quick hello.

One early morning when he thought Kitty was sleeping, she was watching him cross the field to call Fanny, as a crow circled overhead cawing at him. At lunch she asked why he went to the barn so early, then returned to the house before going out again.

He said that if he first set up the day's work it made breakfast more serene.

Dubin groaned softly in her presence.

"What's up, William? Is something troubling you?"

He did not at once reply but, when he saw the worry in her eyes, shook his head, smiling, then dimmed the smile.

"I thought I heard you say 'deceit,' " she said.

"That was the word on my mind."

"Did Lawrence ever deceive Frieda?"

239

She often guessed where his thoughts were. Dubin told her that with Lawrence the deceit went the other way. "Frieda had deceived Weekley, her first husband, with at least two lovers. Lawrence she deceived mostly with Angelo Ravagli, their Italian landlord, who became her third husband. Once she traveled on the Continent with John Middleton Murry, but he said he turned her down because he didn't want to betray Lawrence. Some say they did sleep together. My own guess is they didn't while Lawrence was alive. I don't think Murry lied when he wrote he hadn't slept with her then because he didn't want to betray Lawrence."

"How complicated it is."

Dubin said it was.

"Do you think I might be deceiving you?" Kitty asked with a faint smile.

I wish you were, he thought.

Dubin was leaving, that end-of-October weekend, for New York, a year almost to the day when he and Fanny had flown to Venice.

"This is a quickie trip," he explained to Kitty. "I'll be gone Friday and part of Saturday. I should be back by early evening."

"Why can't I come?"

"I'll be going again in two or three weeks to attend other business. Come with me then, it'll be a longer weekend."

"Why are you going now?"

He said he wanted someone who knew wills to look at theirs and suggest changes. "We wrote it when the kids were young."

"Don't you remember enough law to read a will?"

"Not as much as you think."

"Why don't you do the will when you go next time? What's so important right now?"

"Offices are closed on Saturdays and Sundays. I can see someone late this afternoon."

"You could also telephone from here."

He didn't want to. "I've mailed the will out, a friend of mine has read it, I want to talk to him about changing it."

Her eyes were troubled. "Why are you suddenly concerned about a will? There's nothing wrong with you, is there?"

"No," Dubin said, sweating. "I happened to come across it in our safety deposit box and thought I ought to have it checked out. A legal instrument should be kept up to date."

She said talk of the will had worried her.

Dubin swore there was nothing wrong with him. He was irritated with himself for fabricating the will.

Ultimately he was able to lie with less guilt. He geared himself to it: had to protect his relationship with Fanny, at the same time not hurt Kitty. Still, he wouldn't eat his heart out over every fib he told. Not all evil is pure evil. Not all lies are forever.

When William Dubin returned from his youth-renewing short visit to Fanny, for which he blessed her, he felt a surge of love for his wife, followed by a saddening sense of loss—awareness of an illusion he seemed to favor: that as he fulfilled himself he did the same for Kitty. That was not true in any way. He had experienced pleasure he would like her to experience, dish her out a bit of pure lustful joy; but if another woman was the source of his pleasure—if you lived on her body—that diminished desire, affection— obligation—for the other, the wife. He continued to hide from Kitty his feeling for Fanny, his happy involvement with her; but it did not hide well. The Freudian fingertips showed: because of Fanny he was a different man, had grown new attributes, elements of a new self—how could you hide that? You pretended you were your old self, but the old self had changed. You pretended it hadn't, adding to pretense.

Kitty, he knew, sensed something. She had embraced him on his return almost with compassion, as if he had come back with a wound and only she knew it. She asked him again if he was well. Dubin said that next time a will or something of the sort came up he'd take care of it without mentioning it to her.

"No," she said, "you must tell me."

Nothing was wrong with him, Dubin insisted. "Don't worry about what doesn't exist."

"I won't if you promise not to hide from me what does." She laughed breathlessly, her eyes not looking at him. If she believed him with reservation, what, Dubin wondered, did she not believe?

Had she sensed some sort of withdrawal from her? Something more serious—of another kind than had happened last winter? It was months since Fanny and he had become lovers; doesn't an experience of love produce a newly experiencing self? All the exciting new sex diminishing the less exciting sex, the lesser pleasure? Something added, therefore something elsewhere subtracted? Kitty and her husband lived as married, but Fanny had joined the merry company. Dubin has two wives? Here's Kitty gazing out of a window reflecting herself, and beholds, in the wood in the distance, the shadow of a presence; aware of something not fearsome but a source of fear? Dubin, staring through the same glass, sees himself in view, Fanny, in white, standing dimly by his side, all but invisible. He searches the glass, amidst images of leafy trees and darkening shallow clouds, for Kitty, expecting her to be reflected nearby; but she stands alone, amid tall trees, in the deeper distance. What it amounts to, the biographer thinks, is that one may be able to mask dishonesty but not its effects: the diminution of libido, ebb of feeling for a woman, love for her. Deceit distances. He dreamed of Kitty pacing the black-railed widow's walk on the roof.

Dubin had caught a cold that became heavy bronchitis and he could not get to the city in mid-November. He called Fanny very early one morning, as Kitty slept, to say he couldn't possibly be going down this week. Fanny said she would drive to Center Campobello, but Dubin in his laryngitic voice told her he was reasonably sure he could make it to her after another week. Kitty then caught Dubin's cold, and since the trip was promised to her, he felt he oughtn't to go alone this time. It snowed a few days before Thanksgiving, a light snow that melted in a day as though a dropped handkerchief had been snatched up. Fanny urged Dubin to come by himself—he had a perfect excuse with Kitty ill; but he said it was getting more difficult to lie his way into the city so often.

"What's so often about coming here a month ago? I thought you had the excuse of talking to a lawyer about something?"

He said it wasn't a good one. "And it isn't like me to take off for New York in winter weather to talk to a lawyer when the woods are full of them here. I don't travel much in wintertime."

"Wouldn't it be groovy if we could fuck by phone," she said bitterly.

Dubin was silent.

"What I mean," Fanny said after a moment, "is I miss you. When I get lonely I feel like crawling up a wall. If you can't come here, William, I'll zip up there. I bought snow tires and I'd like to come up this next weekend."

"There's at least one dinner date this weekend. Could you make it the one after?"

"Are you sure you really want me to come? Sometimes I have the feeling you don't care all that much."

"You'd be wrong," he said.

"I'm ready to drive up any weekend if you can't come to me. If we don't get together one way we have to another or what's our life all about?"

"The experience of the absent loved one has inspired some beautiful poetry."

"I don't write poetry, I never could."

"Let's try to be together every third weekend or so, though please keep in mind I have no good reason suddenly to be out alone any given night of any particular weekend, let alone two nights in a row. It's not usual."

"I think you have a damn good reason."

"I know I have, but unfortunately not one I can give my wife."

"Unfortunately, old boy."

"I don't want to hurt anyone, little girl."

"I'm not your little girl and you are hurting me."

"I don't want to hurt you, Fanny."

"Other men get out from under their wives—why can't you?"

Dubin explained that he'd worked home for years. "It's hard to find excuses to get out alone when circumstances change. Though in a way it's mad, Fanny, what it amounts to is that one works in a room with the door shut and everyone knows where he is and expects him to be there for all time. Between biographies I am freer."

Fanny's tone softened. "Couldn't you please try to come here? You said your wife's cold is about gone. I'd rather have you come here than go to that lousy motel."

"I thought you liked it?"

"I like it when you're in my apartment with me—in my bed. I like to share my home with you as well as my ass. Why don't you move to New York so we can see each other easier and more often?"

"I've thought about it but it's not feasible right now. Kitty dislikes the city."

"Why don't you do what *you* want?"

"Some things you want to do you don't."

"I wouldn't live that way."

But she called him in the barn the next morning to tell him, happily, that she had got a week of her vacation shifted from January to December and had decided to spend the time in Center Campobello. "Can you swing that in mid-week for a day or two or three—not next week but the one after?"

"Make it for the one after," Dubin said. "We'll see each other as often as we can but I imagine you realize we won't be able to meet every day while you're here? I hope you'll be understanding and flexible about that."

"We could also meet in the afternoon. We can go on your walk together. I'd meet you at the bridge and we could walk together most of the way."

He said he would enjoy that. "But what about seeing each other intimately?"

"Couldn't I stay in your barn with you—not when you're working but at least part of the time?"

Dubin was about to tell her he couldn't risk it, then felt a frustrating sense of confinement; how tightly fenced in he was; could go nowhere without informing someone.

"Let's try," he said. "I've got a sofa convertible to a bed in my study. But we'll have to be very careful."

She promised she would be.

In the week she was in town Fanny and Dubin spent more time together than he would have predicted. She registered at the motel but at night would leave her car on the road to the old Wilson farm by Kitty's Wood. After Dubin had walked the snowy path with her once, she would go along it alone with a flashlight, to the field where the barn stood. He left the study heated for her and she waited till he had trudged back from the house after supper. They were happy to see each other. In dungarees, flannel shirt, boots, she looked like another Fanny, a young woman he had just met he was about to fall in love with. She grasped his hands; they kissed, fumbled with each other's clothes.

Fanny said she enjoyed the adventure of going through the wood, of being with him here. It didn't bother her to be near his wife in the house, although it worried Dubin. To get out tonight, he told Kitty he had reached a crucial point in the biography—he went into a discourse of how bad the marriage of Frieda and Lawrence was when they were fighting about her desire to see her three children. Lawrence jealously wanted her not to see them. They quarreled, were murderous to each other. Frieda broke a plate over his head. Lawrence smashed one phonograph record after another on hers. Dubin said it would be helpful if he could put in a few nights of steady work and knock off this chapter—write four or five pages a day instead of the usual two or two and a half.

"You're crazy," said Kitty, "to work all morning, then work again at night."

"Just this week—less than a week. I've done it before."

"But not every night. Please—it's mad."

"Why don't you pick a couple of nights for whatever you want me to do with you and leave the rest for me?"

"Have some nights," Kitty said. "I'm Queen of the Night and dispense them like peanuts."

"Don't get sore."

"Why don't you at least work in the house?"

He said she knew why: everything was in the barn—his books and notes.

Afterward Kitty quietly said she was sure she could find something to do with herself and Dubin thanked her.

He felt more daring than he'd been in years. One had to be daring before it was too late. He was almost fifty-eight hurrying toward sixty. Every year was a cheat, piling up age, reducing vitality. Still, he felt youthful and was sorry Kitty did not.

After Fanny and he had made love and had listened, as they lay warmly in bed, to music on her portable radio, or talked of their lives, she dressed and went through the woods to her car. Fanny said the woods scared her but she wouldn't let Dubin accompany her to the road.

"It's easier to spot two people than one."

"Nobody can see us walking through the woods from the house," Dubin said. "From the bedroom one can barely see the barn and not much of the woods. From Maud's room and my study you can see more."

"Can she see me leave the barn?"

"Not if you go out the study door. Certainly not in the dark."

"Let's don't take the chance," Fanny said.

After she had gone Dubin removed the bedsheet and reassembled the sofa. He looked for articles of dress or jewelry Fanny might have left behind, discovered her comb, hid it, and went back to the house. Before getting into bed with his wife he took a shower. Dubin lay up against Kitty's warm body, his arm over her hip, her back to him.

"What time is it?" she yawned.

"Toward midnight."

"Are you smiling?"

"No."

"I thought I could feel you smile on my shoulder. How did the work go?"

"Fine."

"Why do you shower every night?"

"It relaxes me."

"Do you want to make love?"

"Do you?"

"I will if you want to."

"No."

"You're not depressed?"

"No."

She fell asleep. In a few hours she would wake, counting the failures of her life. Holding her, Dubin slept. He felt her waken but slept on.

Fanny had arrived on Monday. He did not see her Tuesday but they talked on the phone. On Wednesday night Kitty went with Marisa Ondyk to a high school chorale, and Dubin met Fanny at the motel. They had drinks and later went through the wood to the barn and set up the sofa bed.

"Do you love me?" Fanny asked.

"You know I do."

"Why don't you say it?"

"Because you know."

"I like you to say it," Fanny said.

Dubin promised he would.

"Why do you love me?"

"Because you're a lovely lay."

"Is that all?"

"Because I love you."

"Why?"

"Because you're Fanny, named out of Jane Austen. Because of your affectionate nature. Because you want to make something of your life."

"You make me want to, William. You make me take myself seriously."

He said that was good.

"We are good together," she sighed. "Don't you think so?"

He said he did.

"But I'm not living my life to learn lessons," Fanny said. "Most of all I want to enjoy it."

He wanted her to.

"What are you thinking about?"

"You."

"Doing what?"

"Enjoying your life."

"Are you enjoying it with me?"

"All the way."

It was snowing heavily and when Dubin saw it come down he was concerned about her driving in the snow at night. He asked her to sleep in his study and leave early in the morning. "You ought to leave before seven. I'll drive around to the road and shovel you out if you're blocked in by snow after the road's been plowed."

"I can shovel myself out, I'm strong."

"Have you got a shovel?"

Fanny laughed to herself. "I'll bring one next time."

"I'll shovel you out at seven if you're blocked in."

Dubin slept badly. He worried about her but when he got up at six the next morning he saw through the bathroom window that the snow had stopped. Later he found Fanny's path from the barn and ran in it to the edge of the wood, kicking up her tracks in the snow. On the road her car was gone.

On Thursday it was snowing as they lay in the sofa bed. Lorenzo was with them. Dubin had him in the barn because some field mice had chewed up several of his note cards. Lorenzo lay on the bed, noisily licking himself. Fanny said she was leaving Saturday morning. He wasn't sure he could see her on Friday night but they would meet in the city in two or three weeks.

Their relationship had deepened. Each probed the other's needs. What he desired she gave him; she got what she seemed to want. After they had made love Fanny got out of bed and went naked to the sink. She drank a glass of water and brought him one.

"What for?"

"To drink, lover. Aren't you thirsty?"

" 'Lover' is an old-fashioned way of addressing a lover."

"In certain ways I am old-fashioned. Do you want the water?"

Dubin drank it. Neither Kitty nor he brought each other water after sex;

he got her a tissue. Kitty took a hot shower; Fanny drank a glass of water and used the wet corner of a towel to wash herself.

In the dark he thought of her as his wife. They'd live in New York. He would work in their apartment while she attended school. She could prepare for serious work of some sort once she knew what interested her. Maybe she could do something part-time if they were married. She could have kids if she wanted; he imagined she would. She had said she would in one of her letters. It might be hectic but she was a young woman and he would help where he could. Dubin wouldn't mind having young children again. He thought he'd be better with them than he'd been the first time. Children were strangers you loved because you could love. If they gave back love when they were grown you were ahead of the game. You had had them because you thought you could love. He felt Fanny would be happy with him, as happy as a second wife might be with a husband thirty-five years older than she. He would value her as she ought to value herself, perhaps help her unravel some of the distortions of her life. He imagined what she would look like at thirty, when he was sixty-five. Dubin liked what he imagined.

Lives ought to begin again around fifty, he thought. Middle age can stand new enterprises, new beginnings. Some marriages go on too long. If they ended by mutual consent after twenty-five years, or when the kids left the house, that might be refreshing for both partners. Getting into the world again to find out what was going on might do them good. Maybe Kitty would worry less about herself if she had to work; would sleep better; think less of illness, the garbage of the past. She'd get the house, of course. Fanny and he could live in Europe for the first year—maybe to try out living together. That might ease the transition into a new life for them all.

"What are you thinking about, William?"

"You are a loving friend."

"We are more than friends now."

"We are also good friends," Dubin said.

"We really could be," said Fanny.

"I thought we were?"

"If we were living together. I liked coming home from work and you were there."

"We can't now, I'm married."

She said after a minute, "Suppose you weren't any more?"

"But I am," Dubin said.

Fanny got up for a glass of water and did not bring him one.

He asked if she would care to see him tomorrow night.

"I thought you didn't think we ought to meet Friday?"

Dubin said he had changed his mind. "We can be together without going to bed."

After a few minutes Fanny asked, "Should we have another lay before I go?"

He didn't think so. Dubin kissed her mouth and she kissed his, then his eyes, and then again kissed his mouth.

Friday was a clear cold night. As they were comfortably together in bed Dubin got up to go to the toilet. Standing there, he saw through the freezing window a flicker of light amid the silver maples and watched with concern. The light disappeared at intervals and grew brighter as it moved in his direction.

"She's coming," he called hoarsely to Fanny, "Grab your clothes every-thing—get into the barn."

Fanny leaped out of bed, hastily gathered her clothes, boots, and portable radio, then hurried naked into the barn.

Dubin had his trousers and shirt on. He stepped into loafers, pulled the sheet off the bed, threw it into the barn after Fanny, slammed the door shut, and closed the sofa bed. He saw her sweater on his worktable and tossed it behind some file boxes on one of the bookshelves.

"William?" Kitty knocked on the door.

"Yes?"

"It's me. Can I come in?"

He took his time getting to the door to unlatch it.

"The furnace has pooped out," Kitty said, stepping into the study. "I was reading in bed, wondering if you'd ever come home and felt myself getting awfully chilly. When I looked at the thermostat it was fifty so I came to tell you."

"Did you call the furnace guy?"

"He comes faster for you."

"You could have phoned me from the house and not frozen your ass coming here in this cold."

Kitty looked around the room. She was wearing a heavy cloth coat, boots, and Dubin's red wool hat.

"Was your light out for a while? I was in Maud's room and could see no reflection of light in the snow."

"I had a headache and was resting my eyes in the dark."

"Why didn't you quit, for Pete's sake? It's mad to work as much as you've been this week."

"I've got only one paragraph to recopy."

"Can't it wait till tomorrow?"

"I want to get it done."

"What's that strange odor in here?" Kitty asked, breathing in, exhaling.

"I passed gas."

"It's not that."

"I smoked a cigarillo."

"It's not that either. The room smells sexy."

"I was thinking of Faye Dunaway. I was also thinking of Marilyn Monroe."

"Don't take your headache out on me, William," Kitty said. "It's your own bloody fault."

He said he was being funny.

The cat meowed in the barn.

"Is Lorenzo hungry?"

"I fed him."

Lorenzo meowed as though wailing.

Kitty pulled the door open and shone her flashlight in the dark.

"What's that sheet doing on the floor?"

Dubin tried to think but couldn't. He was watching Kitty's light move along the sidewall of the barn to the bolted double doors. She then shone the light on the clutter of garden tools, furniture she had discarded, tractor-mower, bags of peat moss. "Was that something moving?"

He didn't think so. "Lorenzo's been sleeping on the sheet. It needs washing. I was going to bring it home."

Lorenzo, eyes glowing, came running in the light. If he says anything, the biographer thought, I'll bash his head in.

"What's the matter with him?" Kitty asked.

"He wants company, he's tired of mice."

Dubin had picked up the phone and was dialing. He told the repairman his furnace had gone on the blink and he was afraid the house pipes would freeze if something wasn't done quickly. The man reluctantly said he would come over.

"He'll be over in ten minutes," Dubin told Kitty. "Please let him in. I'll knock off my last paragraph and go home."

"I'd still like to know what the smell in this room is."

"You know them all," he said.

"You're not exactly endearing tonight."

Dubin rubbed his eyes.

Kitty left the barn, slamming the door.

Through the toilet window he watched her going back in the snow until the light disappeared. He wondered if she had noticed Fanny's boot tracks.

Then he sat down on the sofa, sickened. He felt cold.

Fanny came into the room with her dungarees and bra on. She was barefoot and cold, her face without color.

"I was scared shitless," she said. "I thought I had broken my ankle. It hit something and hurt like hell."

He inspected her bruised blue ankle. "Does it still hurt?"

"It feels as if someone drove a nail into it."

Dubin said he was sorry. He still felt nauseated, half frozen.

"I don't want to have to do anything like that again, William," Fanny said. "I don't want to have to hide from her. Next time I swear I won't. I mean it, William."

"There won't be a next time," Dubin said.

"I won't hide from her again," Fanny said, her eyes taut.

He said he would see her in the city.

One Sunday Kitty rose early, dark-eyed and tight-lipped. She stretched her arms limply. When she had left the bed she removed her nightgown, slowly scratched her blemished buttock.

At breakfast he noticed her lusterless eyes and formal anxious altered voice. Her tight control tightened him. Kitty mulled over things till she had something: she put two and two together and usually came close to four. Had she now come up with Fanny in his life?

He asked if she had had a bad dream.

Kitty was gazing at the fried egg on her plate. She'd hardly touched breakfast. They were at the table together but she sat at the table alone.

Dubin spoke soberly: "Why don't you tell me what's bothering you?"

She said she hated to. "I really do."

"Then it's something physical?"

She looked at her plate. "I'm sure you'll say it's nothing."

"You think it's cancer?" he asked, beginning to eat his fried egg.

Kitty told him her left nipple had altered in size and she had found a mucus stain in her brassiere.

"Do you think it's cancer?"

"It could be," she said unhappily.

"What else could it be?" Dubin dipped his bread into the egg yolk.

"I don't know. For God's sake don't start preaching at me. I hate it when you righteously preach." She was frightfully tight.

He changed his tone. "Have you felt a lump?"

"No," she said tensely.

"Is the breast sore?"

She nodded, not crying, though her eyes were moist.

He sipped his coffee. Dubin then put his cup down and got up and kissed her. He said he was sure it wasn't cancer.

She studied his face to see if he thought otherwise. "What makes you say so?"

"No lumps." He said she ought to see the doctor anyway. "Once you're on a cancer kick, it's wise to."

Kitty said she would, then confessed that even the thought of a mammogram frightened her.

"I'll go with you," he said.

"No, I'll go alone," Kitty said. "I always have."

On Tuesday she visited the surgeon in Center Campobello, who said it was not cancer. He said it was a papilloma, a nodule he located close to the surface of the breast near the nipple.

Kitty afterward told Dubin that the surgeon had said a papilloma was usually benign and he thought he could treat it in his office. A week later —she had been calm since seeing him—he made the incision. After a biopsy, which revealed no sign of malignancy, Kitty gave out a sob of relief. Later she bought a new dress. Arriving home, she embraced Dubin and said she loved him very much. She moved gingerly but freely, as though she was free of dread yet was worried for having once more tried her fate. How many more times could she do it and still escape cancer?

Dubin, as he combed his hair before the mirror, said he was glad it had come to nothing.

"It wasn't exactly nothing," Kitty said. "He removed a nodule that was blocking the duct. That wasn't nothing, and it wasn't my imagination."

He admitted it.

"You look critical?"

"I'm not but it wasn't cancer. The average is still in your favor."

"I'll bet you weren't in the least worried," Kitty said, brushing her eyelids with a tissue. "You didn't seem to be. I'll bet you were thinking about your friend Lawrence and the mystique of the female breast in Indian cow worship. Or maybe you were thinking of Lady Chatterley's handsome ass and well-shaped healthy teats."

He'd been thinking mostly of Fanny.

"That was your sixth or seventh cancer scare since I've known you," Dubin said. "I expected nothing serious."

"My mother had cancer. You may be wrong someday."

He said he hoped he wouldn't be.

Kitty that night suggested making love "in celebration," and he offered the next night, said he was worn out.

"My problems?"

"Mine."

In the morning she seemed distant to him. He felt distant from her. It seemed to Dubin he felt more affection for her when Fanny was around. When she was, Kitty was often in his thoughts, tenderly at times.

With Fanny gone he was constantly thinking of her. That he was working well was not surprising because his mood was good. He lived much in his thoughts of his developing work and in long reveries of Fanny. Dubin invented and discarded reasons to take off for New York. It irritated him that he had to go through so much fantasy to experience the girl.

The next night he made love to his wife. She hadn't wanted to, but responded to his impulse. He was careful not to touch her healing breast. To heighten their pleasure Dubin tried one of the things Fanny had taught him.

"Where did you pick that up?" Kitty wanted to know.

"Do you like it?"

"I'm not sure. I think so."

"Do you object?"

"No."

Afterward she asked, "Where did you pick up that little adventurous bit you tried tonight?"

"From a book I read."

"What made you read that kind of book?"

He was about to say he was human. Dubin said, "To bring something new to our sex lives."

"Do you have any complaints about me?" Kitty asked.

He said he hadn't.

"I'll bet you do. Nathanael thought I was pretty good in bed. He thought me a passionate woman. I *am* passionate."

"One responds differently to different people," Dubin said. "He was your first husband. I'm your second and for too long I was your step-husband."

"If you say 'step-husband' again I swear I'll leave you." Her voice quavered with anger.

He pictured her leaving; probably she would ask him to leave.

The next day Kitty, as she was dressing, quietly asked Dubin if he wanted a divorce. "I don't think you want or need me any more. I sense it. If something has gone wrong why don't you tell me? Have you met someone you'd rather be with?"

Dubin said he hadn't.

"Is that girl you went to Venice with still around?"

He said she wasn't.

"Who was she?"

He would rather not say.

"Do I know her?"

He would rather not say.

"Then I do and she's around," said Kitty.

"I sleep with her twice a day."

"Then what *is* the matter with you. What's made you so unresponsive these last few months? Are we about to go through another awful winter? Why has my husband become my second cousin once removed? Removed is the word. We never talk any more. I don't really know what's happening to you. Tell me what's happening to you? Have you been sleeping with Flora?"

He said that had happened once.

"Then what's eating you, for Christ's sake?"

"Maybe it's marriage. Sometimes I feel boxed in, unfree."

"Boxed in, how?"

"A long marriage gets hard to take. You must feel it yourself."

He was thinking of her sameness, dissatisfactions, eccentricities. He was bored with her fears, her unforgotten unforgettable past.

"What do you mean 'unfree'?—unfree for what?"

"To forget for ten minutes that I'm married."

"That sounds like more than a whim. You must have a reason to want to feel unmarried. What is your need?"

Dubin didn't say.

"Wouldn't a divorce make you feel happier, freer?"

"No," he said, but his heart was gladdened by the thought.

Kitty criticized his nature—Dubin's sobriety, sameness, inability to enjoy life. She said she enjoyed life. "Until we met, you lived on romantic dreams, on nothing really. Now your devotion is work. Your work is all you think of and then you complain you aren't free."

Kitty spoke bitterly, her hands nervously in motion. She had slept with a bracelet on he had once given her. She had dressed and looked good though her eyes were angry.

Dubin, raising his voice, accused her of having depreciated his love for her. "You weren't satisfied with what I had to give—what I gave you. You had to define it to death. The day we were married you began to educate me. You defined love. You defined marriage. You insisted on telling me what I was giving and what I wasn't. I gave with feeling and you gave it a name."

"I wanted it to be a strong enduring love, in and of this world. I had experienced a strong loving love. I wanted what I needed. I had to tell you."

"Love was love to me. It needed not defining but nurturing. It wanted a life of its own. It didn't need Nathanael for company or comparison, or you dissecting it."

He wasn't certain what he was saying, that he was telling the truth about the past. He was trying to but it seemed, in their quarrel, impossible to recall exactly; to say what had truly happened to them. Or exactly what was happening now. How can you define the truth if you can't tell it? How can you tell the truth if you begin with lies?

Kitty said, "I wasn't doubting you—for the sake of doubt—or comparing your love to Nathanael's. I was trying to understand your feelings, your nature, my own. I wanted deep whole lasting love. I can't keep myself from analyzing or defining. I am not Frieda Lawrence. I am not your earth mother."

She wept copiously, in a low wail. "You'll leave me, I know in my heart."

Dubin told her not to cry. He racked his brain thinking how not to fail her yet go on with Fanny.

Then he put his arms around Kitty. "Let's get into bed."

She raised her tear-stained face. "Why?"

"I want you."

"I just got dressed." She slowly removed her clothes. He tried not to notice her aging body, tried not to think of Fanny's youth.

In bed Dubin's flesh failed him. He was unable to perform. He lay back frustrated, told himself not to be alarmed.

Kitty, lying on her pillow, wondered if it was her fault. "I mean maybe all this talk of divorce upset you?"

He said it wasn't her fault, yet hoped it was.

"These things happen. Don't be upset."

"It hadn't happened to me before."

"It's an incident, it's not for all time."

He said he hoped not; he was too young for that. "Lawrence was impotent at forty-two, but he was a sick man."

"Don't think of it."

Afterward Kitty told him she'd been seeing Evan Ondyk again, and Dubin was sorry for her and for himself.

"I was thinking of going away for a while," she said. "Maybe for a week —at the most, two. I'll go see Gerald in Stockholm."

He thought it would be a good thing for her to do. "I should be myself when you get back."

"Don't worry about it," Kitty said calmly. "You've been ever so much better than Nathanael that way. It started with him around thirty-eight, yet on the whole he functioned well."

Dubin said he wasn't worried.

The cold rose in an almost invisible haze from the icy ridged road. The low still polar sky was white as far as he could see. A light snow had struck the hills and whitened the surrounding fields. Nature shrouded, playing dead. Dubin, as he walked, lived in his frozen thoughts. Was that Oscar Greenfeld ahead, plodding past the abandoned farmhouse down the road? The biographer walked on, heavily clothed, not attempting to catch up with the flutist. Dubin wore two scarves, his tan-and-black over a thick black scarf, waffle stompers, earmuffs under his red wool hat.

He tried to think what he'd been thinking of but now and then his thoughts froze. The shrunken afternoon was already into dusk on this Saturday in a below-zero January. Dubin was fifty-eight. That was not Oscar ahead, no wooden flute he held in his hand. It was a man with a double-barreled shotgun resting on his forearm as he trudged on in the dusk. He wore a plaid hunter's cap, heavy sweater, sealskin Eskimo boots. Dubin lingered to see what he shot at from the road but the hunter, from time to time stopping to survey the field, shot at nothing.

The biographer made up his mind to pass quickly and the hunter let him hurry by. A minute later he called his name: "Mr. Dubin?"

It was Roger Foster.

They walked together, Dubin at a loss for something to say. Roger embarrassed him.

"What's the gun for?" he finally asked. "I thought the hunting season was over?"

"Not much really, Mr. Dubin," Roger said. "I thought I'd like to take a potshot at a rabbit or two but haven't laid eyes on one. You can hardly see them this time of the year but sometimes you can spot a cottontail against a tree or rock. No harm done because I generally miss when I shoot. My heart's not in it. I guess I went out with Dad's gun because I felt sort of down. Thought I'd stir up a little excitement for myself but haven't so far."

Dubin grunted.

Neither spoke as they walked on, then Roger said in a tone of regret, "I don't guess you like me all that well, Mr. Dubin. I really don't know why. I grant you're a good biographer, but so far as understanding live people, I honestly don't think you know the kind of man I am."

Dubin nodded. Who knows the passing stranger, or the stranger you pass, he thought, even if your wife in a desperate moment aberrantly falls for him.

"I'll bet you still think of me as a sort of stud because I had that reputation in my early twenties, though I am honestly not that way now. Give me credit for growing up—people do."

"Roger," Dubin said, "I admit I don't know you very well although every

257

so often you unexpectedly enter my life. I have no plans for you to be in it, but now and then you suddenly are—as though you'd stepped out of the pages of Dostoyevsky and begun tracking me. I've come across this fateful phenomenon more often than one would think in biographies I've read or written. Somebody looks around and there's this guy tailing him, for good or ill. I suppose it's different when it's a woman—it's as if you'd been expecting her. Anyway, when you least anticipate or want it, a stranger appears, generally an unlikely person, who for one or another reason attempts to define himself to you, and against every expectation, not to mention your resistance, insists on assuming a role in your life. I have no idea what yours is in mine, but I don't want you to feel I am antagonistic to you in principle or that I am angry about something I am not at all angry about. The older I get, the less I hold people's pasts or past relationships against them—or, for that matter, against myself."

"To tell the honest truth," Roger said, "I made no reference to anybody but myself, but since you might be thinking about the time Mrs. Dubin, who I happen to greatly respect, was working in the library, all I want to say is that if there's anybody I was interested in, and still am, it's Fanny Bick."

Dubin blew on his icy gloved hands, his breath pure white. How much does he know? He thought: I will tell him nothing.

"The fact of it is, Mr. Dubin, I happen to love Fanny and hope to marry her someday."

"Ah?" said Dubin. "And does she hope to marry you?"

Roger laughed throatily, wryly, his moody eyes drawn to the white field. "I've asked her at least four times, including when she was visiting here in December, but she told me she was interested in somebody else, and though she honestly didn't mention your name, the message I got was whoever he was is you."

Dubin did not for a minute speak. "What makes you think so?"

"I know Fanny admires your biographies and yourself. Also I sort of know that you helped her put herself together after she had a shaky time in Europe last year. She has a different emphasis than since I first met her. She's a lot more serious about herself in a way she didn't use to be. I also know you have this mutual friendship that means a lot to her."

"Did she tell you that?"

"Not in so many black-and-white words but it's what I guess. At first I thought it might be something sort of non-sexual, only now I don't think that any more, if you don't mind me saying so, Mr. Dubin. I don't think of you as that kind of a person."

"What kind of person am I?"

"I wish I really knew."

"What do you want from me, Roger?"

They had stopped walking. Each peered into the other's face.

"I admit you've been helpful in advising Fanny, but otherwise the fact is you're married, Mr. Dubin, with two grownup kids and a wife who happens to need you," Roger said, looking down at Dubin's galoshes. "What's more, you're a good thirty or more years older than Fanny. When we first met she liked me an awful lot, and I honestly and sincerely think she still has a real affection left that might get to be permanent under different circumstances. I figure if you weren't around I might stand a good chance to marry her, although I also admit she has this affinity for older men. Mr. Dubin, I'm speaking to you as if I were your own son—I'm not proud. I thought I would respectfully tell you how I feel about her, hoping you might make some decision that would give me a fair shake, or at least a halfway decent chance in the future."

"To marry her?"

"To marry her if I could—if she wants to get married. Not everybody does nowadays, though I and both my sisters honestly do. What I'm trying to say to you is I love Fanny very much." His voice shook.

"So do I."

Roger, to Dubin's embarrassed surprise, sank down on one knee in an awkward gesture of supplication, or despair. In his left hand he still held his shotgun.

Dubin walked on, then broke into a trot.

He hadn't seen Fanny in weeks, felt inertia, lassitude, stasis, wanted not to see her. Was he therefore feeling less for the girl? Less what? He had got used to her, knew her too well? Some of the excitement, the surprise, was gone? Only her presence, in truth, surprised and she was not present. Though Kitty and he had resolved his temporary mishap and were again comfortable in bed, Dubin felt he wasn't that much interested in the sexual life. She had postponed going away because of him. She didn't seem to understand how much he wanted to be alone, left alone; he wanted to be, at least for now, without challenge to emotion, attention, thought; if possible, also, without desire. Who needs that forever goad? Fanny seriously complicated his life. Having one major problem was enough for him—the Lawrence biography. That continued to go well: at times it carried Dubin aloft as if he were in a balloon with a spy glass surveying the floating earth. It was the "complication"—the task he wanted most to be concerned with. Gerry and Maud were an ongoing other; he was used to their problems, and to Kitty's tangled skein. But Fanny was a complication coming on too fast and strong. She was, in his life, unique; still he didn't want her pressing him to go abroad with her, urging him to move to New York; he didn't want her suggesting they live together, implying divorce. It was all right for Kitty to bring up divorce but not Fanny.

Was what he felt for Fanny love? It wasn't the way he had felt toward women in his youth. Do men of more than fifty love less keenly than young men? He thought the opposite was true: the years deepened the need, the force, the channel of love. At fifty there had to be more at stake: love as a breakwater against age, loss of vital energy, the approach of death. Dubin enjoyed the girl's feeling for him but how much was he offering in return? Obviously not too much at the moment although they shared a real enough friendship. He sometimes felt as if he was waiting for her to say it didn't seem to be working and why didn't they simply call it quits? There were moments when he thought breaking it up now might be a relief—a lot less to worry about; he'd be freer to concentrate on his work. Maybe she was expecting him to make a decision—more Fanny, less Kitty; or vice versa; or simply no Fanny at all? There was a real problem, did he have a real choice?

She hadn't telephoned lately, nor he her. He thought she might still be annoyed by the barn incident with Kitty though her two or three short letters hadn't mentioned it. He had more than once expressed regret. Her letters outlined what she was doing, reading, experiencing; they made no request nor persuasion. She was, she said, "tired," but not of what. What good am I for her? the biographer asked himself. Her letters were contained, muted, saying nothing very personal. She did not say, lately, that she loved him. He wrote innocuous replies. Let's be friends, Dubin thought, and from time to time, lovers. That would diminish complication and make life easier to manage. He never broached this to her. Lawrence had distastefully spoken of "merely companionate sex."

But with the change of season Dubin was glad he had made no serious negative statement to Fanny. Winter broke, retreated, cold waning although greedily lingering; spring was immanent—tied hand and foot but softly exhaling its herbal breath; mysteriously freed, spying out—stalking—the land as well as memory. Spring lights spring within. My spring gives birth to yours—to you. The girl blossomed, bloomed, in his thoughts. Dear God, what have I done? Why have I allowed myself to doubt my true feeling for her? He missed her company, easy laughter, warmth, intimate voice—whatever it said was intimate—her touch, vibrance, their acceptance and enjoyment of each other. He missed her desire, giving, the flower of their embrace in bed. He thought of her, trying not to, between stitches of biographical sentences; on his long and short walks; as he lay in bed with his wife. He thought of their best times, joyfully together. He wanted, he spoke it aloud, to be with her; but heard no sound. He did not visit her in the city; she did not come to him, one way or another, in Center Campobello.

As the season advanced Dubin grew restless, irritable; life was unchanged, confined, reduced. He tried unsuccessfully to hide his mood from Kitty "You aren't with me," she chided him, "you are elsewhere. Where are you?" He didn't say; flipped his fingers as if there was no answer, why ask? He wanted her to sense his abstinence; instead she sensed his absence, still said they seemed to be drifting apart. It took two to drift together; Dubin was in no mood to. They disagreed, argued, sometimes bitterly over trivialities: he had forgotten to remind her, though he had promised he would, when a television program began; she had sent out special delivery a letter he had wanted certified. He did not listen when she talked, Kitty complained. She could not follow directions, he said. He listened, Dubin responded, past all possible listening. "Who the hell are you to give *directions?*" Kitty said. She walked out with her fingers in her ears.

She accused him of destroying their social life by turning down every invitation; he accused her of not offering any. She did little entertaining. They went at each other face to face; but Dubin noticed she no longer threatened divorce, as if she had sensed it was now, for him, a viable option.

His sleep became surface-thin; he dreamed endlessly: how can one swim in shallow water? One night Kitty woke him out of a dream of Fanny to say she smelled something. Was it a fire? Gas escaping? Had she left a burner on?

Half asleep, he sniffed the air and smelled nothing.

"Are you sure, William?"

"What can I be sure of?"

Barefoot, he plodded dully through the house but could smell no smoke nor locate any. Dubin, muttering, sniffed at the burners in the kitchen, bitter to be awake at this miserable hour engaged in idiotic sniffing. A mad woman makes a man mad.

Kitty was standing at the bedroom window in her nightgown, inhaling the night air. It had rained.

"It was the wet earth I must have smelled—it's so refreshing. Forgive me, it waked me out of sound sleep. How fresh, how fragrant the earth is."

He got into bed, chilled. Fanny did not reappear in his dreams. In the morning they quarreled over what he called her punitive sense of smell. Kitty said she thought a vacation from each other would do them both good. She'd been thinking of Stockholm again, wanted to see Gerald. Maud was writing more often lately, but from Gerald, during the winter months, had come wintry silence. She was worried.

Later, her eyes uncertain, downcast, Kitty asked Dubin, "Would you care to come with me?"

He had expected it. "What's the good of it if I go with you? We need time away from each other."

He had had, that morning, a loving note from Fanny: "Lover, father, friend—love me, I love you." The self-conceived defensive ice had broken; the river of feeling flowed.

"I'll go alone," Kitty said.

He approved, shame contained. She had rarely, since she'd married him, traveled by herself. It would do her good. What if she were widowed again and had to travel alone?

He knew she'd go—felt admiration for her, affection. On Friday of that week—the first in April—Kitty packed a suitcase and flew to Stockholm.

There were green shoots in her garden, shades of yellow and green, flowers to follow. He waited a day, called Fanny at 8 a.m., on Saturday. She was at once alert, had been expecting a call. Dubin told her Kitty had gone to Stockholm. "Your note meant a great deal to me."

"I'll bomb up there right away."

Fanny arrived shortly after twelve, expansive, happy, vital. Every time he saw her, especially after weeks gone by, she seemed more womanly. She stepped out of her Volvo, carrying a tote bag, her purse slung over her shoulder. Fanny entered the house unself-consciously. "I know this place like the palm of my hand." It excited Dubin to have her with him where he had first desired her. He said they would sleep in the guest room on the third floor.

"Should we go up now?"

"We've got two days together, Fanny. Let's eat first."

"It's just that we haven't seen each other so long."

He put his arm around her. She nuzzled close, reminded him this was their first spring together. "And not our last."

He had prepared lunch—asparagus, a salmon salad, white wine. They ate at the dining table, knees touching. Afterward she rinsed the dishes as Dubin stacked the dishwasher, conscious of her in Kitty's kitchen, domain. Having her in the house was part of the adventure.

"Don't sweat it, William," she said, sensing something. "I've handled nearly everything in this kitchen and will put everything back in place."

He trusted her instincts. They went outside. The silver maples were still leafless and the grass hadn't come to green life but the blue-skyed day embraced the earth. They went through the field into the warm wood. Dubin pulled down branches of opening tree buds. They found white hepatica in bloom and full-grown purple and gold crocus and one paper-thin narcissus amid last year's dead leaves. He thought of the wild flowers they had lain in.

"Come on," Fanny said, taking his hand. They left the woods and she began to run ahead of him on the path. Dubin trotted amiably after her. In the house she ran up the stairs. He followed, thinking she was heading for the third floor. Instead she darted into the master bedroom.

He called to her. "Not in that bed, please, Fanny."

"Why not?" she laughed, her face flushed, eyes very green.

"Kitty wouldn't like it. Come upstairs."

"I want to sleep with you in your bed. You sleep with me in mine."

She tugged down the bedspread. Dubin grabbed and held her. Fanny, twisting in his arms, pulled down the zipper of his fly. He drew off her shirt. She had nothing on under her jeans. Dubin undressed. Fanny, naked, flipped down the blankets on the double bed.

"I said no." He pulled her to him, holding her tightly. She struggled forcefully but he maneuvered her away from the bed. Fanny tried to shake him off. She was strong, sweated. Dubin, enjoying the struggle, forced her to the floor, lowering himself on her on the rug. Fanny squirmed, rocking from side to side, trying to fend him off with her knees.

"Get off me, you ape."

Dubin froze. Her body smoldered under his. Neither of them moved. As he was getting up, Fanny, grasping his shoulders, pulled him down. They kissed to their teeth. She bit his lip, drawing blood, then as he cried out, yielded—he felt her thighs grow soft, part. Dubin went in hard; she received him gently.

Afterward when she asked if she could lie—simply lie—in the bed he permitted it. He slid under the blanket with her, lying on Kitty's side as Fanny lay in his place.

They lay together, palms touching. Dubin felt a great gratitude to her— to life for all it offered. He tried to think of a gift for Fanny, something durable, valuable, beautiful. He wished he had a ring to give her. Perhaps he would have something made. Fanny slept heavily; Dubin slept with her.

In his dream a storm woke them. They woke in a thunderstorm. Through the east window they could see lightning streak through massive clouds, bathing the black sky in forked flickering light. Thunder rumbled, ripped through the cloud mass, crashed over their heads. Fanny clung to him.

"Are you afraid?"

"I would be if I were alone."

The white curtains were blowing, whipping in the wind.

"Jesus, the windows!" Dubin hopped out of bed. He ran to Maud's room to close hers and was about to race upstairs but remembered those were shut. Naked, he hurried down to the living room to close the open window there. Dubin wiped the sill and wet floor with a kitchen towel as thunder roared overhead. Excited by the storm, the biographer watched through the window as lightning flared in a circle. He saw himself pursuing the storm to catch it in a basket.

Rain hissed in the fireplace. He shut the vent and ran up the stairs.

Fanny was not in the double bed.

"Are you in the bathroom?"

She was not. A crackling explosion lit the bedroom. Dubin waited for thunder to crash but heard it rumbling in the distance.

"Fanny, where are you?"

No answer. He pulled open the door of Kitty's dress closet and found the girl, in his wife's African robe, crouched against the wall. Dubin offered his hand but Fanny refused it and rose awkwardly, her complexion pale. "Please don't ask me any questions."

"I won't except are you all right?"

"It's a question."

"Come to bed."

Fanny stepped out of Kitty's robe and slipped under the bedcovers. She was shivering. Dubin held her. As her body grew warm a calm settled in him.

It rained steadily, heavily, still poured. He listened to the water gushing from gutter spouts. Soon it rained lightly and as the storm departed he listened to it lessening; then to the raindrops dripping from the eaves of the roof and to the plop-plop of drops from the chestnut tree in front of the house.

"Are you feeling better?" he asked her.

"I want you to know I don't hide in a closet every time there's a storm."

"Why did you now?"

"I don't know. Let's don't talk about it."

Her hand caressed his thigh. "I'm in the mood, are you?"

"I could be but upstairs—not in this bed."

"You can have the sheets laundered. Also the rug cleaned where we fucked on the floor, and her bathrobe dry-cleaned."

"Don't be angry, Fanny. I never mentioned the robe."

"Scared as I was, I could see you didn't want me to wear it."

"Kitty's senses are sharp. She might know if someone had worn it."

"I never heard of anyone who goes around smelling everything."

"You have your thing, she has hers."

Fanny, after a moment, in a quieter voice spoke of Athens. "Do you think we can go there this month or maybe in May, William? I have another week of vacation coming to me. They might give it to me in May."

"Don't push it. I'll go if I can—it's on my mind."

Fanny sat up in the dark. "I really can't understand where we stand," she said angrily. "We have been through a lot together—some of it wasn't so good but a lot has been fun for both of us. We're happy when we are together, natural, relaxed—we really are. And we get along swell in bed— we enjoy each other in good ways. Sometimes the sex is fantastic. Then why do you let so long go by before we meet again, William? There are times I think all you want is a lay every couple of months or so, just to change the scenery."

Dubin denied it.

"Don't you love me?" she asked.

He said he must.

"What do you mean by that word?"

"I do."

"Then how can we go on like this? I had to hide from her in the goddamn barn, and now I can't even love you in your bed. Why are you so tight-assed?"

Dubin didn't say.

"When do you think you will leave her?"

He said, after a moment, that he had no plans to.

"What plans do you have?"

"Mostly to get on with my Lawrence."

"You expect us to go on as we have been—as we are right now?"

"If possible. I confess I worry about you. I have more than once asked myself whether I ought to let you go—for your sake."

"What do you answer yourself?"

"I honestly don't want to."

"Are you afraid to leave her?"

"It's not fear I feel."

"Then why do you stay with her?"

"There are commitments in marriage. It takes a while to reconsider each."

"I don't think you reconsider anything," Fanny said. "You may want to but you don't. You keep what you have and use anything else you can get."

Dubin said he was not only for himself. "My dear Fanny—"

The telephone rang shrilly.

He grabbed for it in the dark.

"Hello, dear—" Kitty was on the phone, her voice affectionate. Though he had been expecting her call Dubin was displeased to have it come as he was lying in bed with Fanny.

His wife sounded distraught. "Gerald has disappeared. I spoke to everybody I could locate who might know him, but nobody would say where he is now. I can't tell you what yesterday was like. Finally I met a young Swedish couple who said he had joined the Communist Party and gone into the Soviet Union. I'm told other deserters have. I feel desolate."

She wept on the phone. His teeth were on edge.

"It's so dreary here," Kitty said. "It's been raining since I got off the plane. I've had almost no sleep. The hotel room is drafty. The Old City is beautiful and I was hoping to see it in the sun with Gerald, but he's not here."

"Why don't you see some of it yourself, anyway, by bus or launch? See something, for Christ's sake. Gerry may show up if you stay around a few days."

"I'm going to the American Embassy Monday morning to talk with them about how to get in touch with him, although I imagine they aren't much interested in deserters. I wish you had come with me."

Dubin said he hadn't been able to.

"What's the matter with your voice?—You sound as though you'd got a cold."

"I haven't."

Fanny coughed; Dubin cleared his throat.

Kitty worriedly asked, "Should I go to Moscow? I don't really know what to do next. Will you come with me? Shall I wait for you here?"

He advised her not to rush it. "We'd better go to Washington first. After we talk to a lawyer we may want to see someone in the State Department. Find out all you can about Gerry, then come home. Could he be in another city? He told me he liked Uppsala."

"Nobody I talked to seems to think he's in Sweden."

Dubin doubted anyone knew with certainty. "He may write soon. He could be with the Eskimos in Lapland. Better come home."

She said she'd fly home Tuesday, and Dubin said he'd pick her up at the airport.

"Goodbye."

He turned on the light. Fanny had got out of bed—he thought to go to the bathroom but she had pulled on her underpants and was buttoning a blouse.

"Good God, Fanny, what are you getting dressed for? We've got the whole night before us."

She sat at the edge of the bed. "Listen, William, I've told you how good I think we are together and I mean more than in bed. I want you in me but I also want you by me. I feel happy when we're with each other, sometimes like we were blessed. I know I am good for you but not on the run."

Dubin said he was sorry Kitty had happened to call just then. "I'm worried about Gerry but that doesn't mean we can't go on with our plans to enjoy ourselves alone here. She won't be back till Tuesday. We've got two and a half days to ourselves."

"I've been thinking about us and still can't explain what's happening," Fanny said. "One thing I do know is I'm not someone who's around just to keep your mind off old age. I have got to be more to you than a substitute for your lost youth, whatever the hell that is. If you want to know something, William, everybody feels they have lost some part of their youth. I know I have, and maybe that's what it's for. Maybe if you lose it you make up by learning something you have to know—the way I imagine you have, and the way I'd like to. But I have to be myself, Fanny Bick, a woman living with or married to a man who wants her—wants to live with her and enjoy their life. I am sick of hiding myself, of not being who I am. It drives me up a wall. I am entitled to an open ordinary and satisfying life of my own."

She stepped into her sandals.

Dubin urged her to stay. The storm had swept the clouds away. A wet sunset hung in the trees. "Tomorrow will be a lovely day. We'll walk in the woods; we'll do anything we please and we can talk out our problems and see what they add up to."

"I know what they add up to and what they will go on adding up to if you don't make a decision. Besides, you will be edgy about where Gerald is and that's not what I want to deal with when I spend a weekend with you. Not this weekend if I can help it."

She had collected her underclothes, diaphragm box, toilet things, and dropped them into her tote bag.

Dubin, barefoot, in striped pajamas, followed her downstairs. "At least stay till Sunday. Let's have breakfast together. Fanny, it's obscene for you to be going off like this. We mean more to each other than that."

"I don't want to be in this house any longer," Fanny said. "I feel your wife's presence all over the place. I really don't like her. I don't think you do either."

"How would you know?"

"I know what I feel in my gut."

He grabbed her arms. "Fanny, you've got to stay. We're friends—genuinely friends. That has to mean something, no matter how our friendship is limited. We have to yield to circumstance for the time being."

"I can't any more."

"I beg you—"

"I can't," Fanny said gloomily.

"When will you be in touch with me?" Dubin asked as she slipped into a raincoat. "When shall I come to the city?"

She didn't want to think about that now.

"You're making a mistake," he told her.

She studied him solemnly without replying.

He put on the driveway light and watched her back her car out and turn on the road, eyes fixed before her. She had barely returned his wave.

Dubin watched till Fanny had gone.

"Maybe I've done her a favor to let her go." He listened to himself talking to himself. He heard himself groan.

Eight

Dubin and his daughter walk the wet strand of dark shore. A fast step or two and she will lose him in the fog. He hears the mewling of invisible gulls.

A droning wind blowing from the dunes of this sliver of San Francisco beach had driven them from the cold sand where they had tried to picnic, then from the rocks. They shared a sandwich and gulp of tepid coffee and wandered along the gray shore. Long white-capped waves, flowing from the mist-hidden swelling sea, broke in froth at their feet. Hers were wet, slender, rosy; his corded, purple-veined, sticky with sand. Dubin, in green sweater and dark trousers rolled to his knobby knees, trailed Maud in the thinning rising fog. Years ago, in Cuernavaca, he and Kitty had got her the off-white peasant dress she was wearing; it looked like a wedding dress but she did not look like a bride. In the wind it clung to her back and wet legs. Her shoulders were thin, hair brownish-red. She had snipped off most of the edge of streaky black. Maud as they walked seemed, in Dubin's eyes, to be looking through shadows. Her face had spilled its bloom; she was twenty and seemed thirty. Kitty, after rereading her last letter, had announced the end of an affair.

Dubin had said he must go see her.

"Yes, do," Kitty said. "I can't, I've had one very long trip this spring."

On the beach they walk apart.

270

He asked her to tell him what had happened.

Maud spoke a Chinese poem: "I am not disheartened in the mindless void. / Wheresoever I go I leave no footprint. / For I am not within color or sound."

"I asked a simple question."

"My response is not hard to understand."

"Are you into Zen?" her father asked.

"If Zen will have me" . . .

After Fanny had left he waked, that Sunday morning without her, to a cardinal's shrill whistling. Dubin at length got out of bed, drew up a shade, and peered into the trees. The red bird, at his glance, flew off. After a woodpecker had stopped rattling away—he often ticked when Dubin typed —the biographer listened to another birdsong: wood thrush warbling a fluting melody. Does the bird hear music or does it hear noise? Will I ever hear a nightingale? He went back to bed and tried to sleep, remembered it had felt late, and at once rose. The clock said past noon. He hadn't slept so long in years. Had it coming to him.

He had liked that day alone: the company of Wm. Dubin, who'd been with him all his life—nobody's father, husband, or lover. He was a man in a house getting himself breakfast; enjoyed scrambling an egg. He thought he'd skip the Sunday paper—too heavy, too long—and drew out of the bookshelf *Far from the Madding Crowd*, had liked it when he was seventeen. Though Lawrence had called Thomas Hardy "a bad artist," Dubin tended to favor his work and the kind of person his fiction seemed to say he was. Lawrence had had his Frieda; he bedded her and yawped. His passionate love for a woman had sprung his ideology of wise blood, as though passionate love could be thus contained, reduced. Hardy, although strongly moved by a variety of women, had flitted from one to another, not daring much. For years he'd been sexually attracted—one after another—to three female cousins, "lower-class" women, none of whom he had appeared to have had an affair with. Then he contracted an essentially loveless marriage to a tough overweight childlike woman, who ultimately freed him from their prison by dying. Hardy was of course of his late-Victorian time; but time or none, he was not as frank or honest about himself as the miner's son. Hiding his knocked-up cook of a mother, and his unaccomplished simple relatives, Thomas Hardy fabricated a "biography" "by" his second wife and former secretary, Florence. "If I get you here," he wrote her after the death of his wife, "won't I clutch you tight." The book for years had misled its readers about his nature and experience. Lawrence, though he admired Hardy's sensibility, and his "instinct," could not stand the way the sexually repressed characters in his novels maimed and ultimately destroyed themselves; failed "life's plenitude" by succumbing to the stupid blind power of the community. Yet Dubin, sympathetic to the older writer, considered he might someday write a biography of Thomas Hardy. He wondered why he wasn't doing it now instead of the one of Lawrence.

Hardy and Dubin both had blue-gray eyes.

Flora had called. She had seen Kitty at the airport the day she delivered Oscar to a flight for a concert in Salt Lake City.

"If you're free, come over."

Dubin, after a moment, doubted he could make it.

"Have you given me up, William?"

"I find it hard to poach in Oscar's domain."

"I am my own domain." She hung up.

He had decided on a bath for a change. Lying, afterward, in his bed, he fell asleep. When he awoke it was night, a crescent moon in the lit sky. He lay in bed wondering if he was lonely.

He ate supper out of a sardine tin with a squeeze of lemon and a sliced tomato. After rinsing spoons, forks, and cup he put in a long-distance call to Maud. The girl who answered said she was in San Francisco. He sat down and wrote her a letter; he owed her several. And he was glad Kitty was getting back Tuesday. He worried on and off about Gerald; but in bed at midnight, when he thought back on the day, it hadn't been a bad Sunday.

After a good morning of work Dubin had driven into town for a paper, conscious that he had dreamed heavily during the night, though he could remember nothing of his dreams. He tucked the newspaper under his arm and experienced something stronger than an impulse to walk a few blocks to Roger Foster's house, although a hand in his head was waving him back. Dubin hurried on, possibly to see what he hadn't come here yesterday for fear of seeing. "What's fate for?" He had thought while shaving: if she went to Roger's house after leaving me she'd be gone now—has to be at work today. If for some reason she's still with him, I don't want to know.

Yet here's Dubin spying her out; and as he had imagined he might, without surprise, came upon Fanny's white Volvo parked in the street in front of Roger's house. His reaction was quickly to flee; instead he circled her car to be certain it was Fanny's; and on the back seat spied a yellow apple and her sandals. It was as though the apple bled. Wait up, Dubin, a hoarse voice advised, but his thoughts raced on. He pictured clearly and in living color a scene from the past: Here's Dubin and Fanny at odds in Venice though he had left it for good a year and a half ago. When the performance was over he was convinced he had made a mistake in letting the girl go. How could he, in his right mind, have done it? He ought by some means or other to have persuaded her to stay. His legs wobbled.

Dubin had considered going for a drive to mull over what to do but couldn't bear to leave the spot without having talked to Fanny. He felt he had misplaced something, an arm or leg. Let me be sane, the biographer thought: nothing very serious has happened. There's been no irrevocable break—of course we'll meet again. We are important to each other. Why should I think she's slept with Roger because she may have stayed the night in his house?—perhaps slept in a room there as she'd done when she first came to this town. Even two nights. How unkind I am to her. Suppose she did sleep with him—hadn't she every right to, given the situation and how I mishandled her? Besides, they're friends: the guy loves her, wants to marry her, and Fanny's warmhearted response to feeling is one of her talents. I mustn't think of it as another betrayal. If anybody's to blame it's me.

He'd gone home thinking he'd telephone Fanny and ask to see her. The phone rang for a full five minutes. He then called the library, asked for Roger, and when the librarian said hello, Dubin remained silent. Roger hung up. Still, he was at work, not in bed with her. Dubin then picked up his Hardy novel but reading it felt unreal. Boldwood's morbid jealousy of Bathsheba embarrassed him. He drove again to Roger's house, went up the porch steps, rang the bell. No one came to the door. As he was driving home Dubin turned in mid-block and rode back to town. It was now almost five o'clock. He waited fifteen minutes under a locust tree up the street from the red-brick library building. When Roger came out and locked the door Dubin trailed him from a block behind, then lingered in his parked car, hoping Fanny would come out of the house—if she ever did—and drive off to New York City. He'd follow and signal her in her mirror to pull over so they could talk.

An hour later, Fanny, in skirt and red blouse, left the house with Roger. She was not carrying her worldly goods, not even the shoulder bag. Roger double-locked the front door as she waited on the porch—they looked like a young couple on their way to dinner out. They went down the steps, Roger's face lit by a happy smile, Fanny talking animatedly—no mourner she —and got into his Chevy. Was her car out of commission? Was that why she had stopped off momentarily, and then it grew to a visit? Dubin swiped at this straw—wanted it to be so; but her car was in the street—not at the garage. Not very likely. They drove away—where Dubin could not know unless he took off after them. The thought was degrading though he favored the action. Where would it get him? He did not follow them.

Instead he drove home; he'd considered Flora's but quashed that. He felt like a man trying to keep something evil, indecent, from breaking out. This will pass, he promised himself. Don't go on reacting like a child to a threatened loss of affection. I've had my morbid little experiences—no more of that. If I have to give Fanny up I will. This is as good a time as any—better, in fact: I'm into the act. But when he thought of her bestowing on Roger that warm affection she had so often expressed for him, those intimate pleasures she had shared with William Dubin, the floor under him seemed to sag. A spurt of jealousy spread like acid in the blood. He resisted the feeling, as if it was a wild animal he was giving birth to. My God, why is this happening to me? Why should it be? In the shower he thought: she's had Roger before and nothing came of it. He can't give her better than I gave—give. She's bound to come back if I'm patient. Just don't do the wrong thing. The wrong thing is to suffer needlessly.

So Dubin informed himself, but his thoughts did not appease or console him. He was heavy with desire of her, his penis as if salted, swollen. "Control yourself," he warned himself, and didn't like the sound of it. Could Fanny have planned this: had guessed he would check her out at Roger's—had foreseen his reaction, possibly to force him to define his commitment to her; decided once and for all how genuine, compelling, it was? That wasn't much Fanny's way, yet who knew for sure? Whatever her way was he had to have her back—at least till he could sanely reason it out and come to a sane decision.

Reason's the word: see the situation as is—no one had said goodbye forever, so why jump the gun? Of course Fanny would call him—a question of time. This self-created crisis—his sense, surely illusory, of their affair having ended badly, had hit him in the head upon discovering her car at Roger's curb. He had once more to contend with the shame of supposed betrayal: Fanny reacts to frustration by sleeping with the nearest guy in sight—had the bitch learned nothing? No, Dubin thought, this is something else again, in truth more serious. Roger is not the gondolier; he wants to marry her, an altogether ultimately more perilous situation for me. This fear tips Dubin's unsettled self and jealous bubbles bubble forth. My God, what else am I capable of that I didn't know? How many more hollows will I uncover in myself? How can this sort of thing, not at all admirable in youth, go on happening to a grown man? The biographer warned himself: It's one thing for a man not to know, not to have learned; it's another not to be able to live by what one does know. That's sure danger.

The next day Fanny's car had disappeared. Dubin had discovered this on his way to the airport to pick up his wife. He'd felt a short-lived relief, until he learned in a long-distance call he made later that Fanny wasn't at work; was not expected in until Wednesday morning. Roger, he then learned, wasn't at the library. Where in hell were they?

Kitty's plane was delayed several hours. Dubin had to return for her that evening. Subdued, worn dark with fatigue, she embraced her husband. On entering the house Kitty cautiously sniffed the burners, interesting reversal. After he had poured her a cup of tea she talked at length of her search for Gerald, ending with her litany of regrets. He observed her carefully, after a while excusing himself to sneak in a call to Fanny via the phone upstairs, leaving Lorenzo to comfort Kitty. No one answered at the girl's apartment. He wondered where she was and what they were doing. The original misery played its dirty little tune. That night he persuaded Kitty, despite her fatigue, to make love, exchanging an overwhelming desire for momentary release—the small brain of the shmuck was without conscience. But the act eased the acid-eating self: Fanny, wherever she was, Kitty's grace kept at bay.

Let her go, he told himself as his wife slept. It wasn't meant to be more than an affair, a short adventure and quits. I've had a good time with her. She isn't the kind of woman I would have thought to marry, although people do change: we aren't who we were; she is matured, shows more control, wants better for herself than she's had. And we've seriously affected one another. Obviously she means more to me than I'd supposed. I've learned that in winter and summer, at home and abroad. She lives in my blood and neither will nor reason can wring her out. Myself, my self's heart, aches for her, for

275

a glowing fundamental pleasure that comes with and from her, an easeful enjoyment of life.

That night the biographer loved and violated her in sensual and perverse ways. He tore at her every sexual stirring, gratified every fantasy. In steaming dreams and torpid reverie he sought satisfaction on her now familiar, though always surprising, pleasure-yielding body. When at last he fell into a grating half sleep he spoke her name aloud.

Kitty abruptly awoke. "Fanny who?"

"Fanny," Dubin confessed, "must be the girl who worked for us summer before last."

"Why are you dreaming of her now?"

"What shall I tell my dreams to dream?"

Kitty yawned. "She must have caught your fancy."

She got up to go to the bathroom. Dubin waited for her to come out and then went in; he fumbled in his pajamas for the offending member.

In the morning a letter had come from Fanny: "Once you said be kind to yourself. I am trying to be. That's why I think we ought to stay broken off. For about a week I didn't think we really were but now I do think so. You wouldn't have let me split that night if in your heart you weren't glad I was going. Maybe you didn't actually want it to happen but you took the out I gave you. I gave it to you to be kind to myself. I was tired of the punishment I was taking. I want someone who wants me. I don't care if we get married or don't but I won't live alone, it hurts too much. I can't see any future for us the way things have been going—sometimes I think you're blind, William—so we'd better not see each other any more. I appreciate certain things you have done for me—some my father might have done but didn't—although with one hand you take away what the other gives. I hope you know what *I* have done for *you*. Sincerely, Fanny."

Dubin wrote an impassioned plea: "Dearest Fanny, Let's not make a hasty mistake. Let's not end what may have barely begun."

Such was the biographer's commitment. He had mailed his letter and also called her from the barn but now her home telephone was disconnected; and at work they said Fanny had quit.

"If she really hasn't, kindly tell her it's William Dubin on the phone, with much good will and an expectation of kindness."

"Why would I want to lie to you?" the operator asked. "I've often been in love myself."

Dubin had then telephoned Roger Foster, with a wretched stirring of jealousy, to ask if he knew where Fanny could be found; and Roger said, without sorrow or laughter, he thought she'd gone back to Los Angeles.

"Do you happen to know her address, Roger?"

"I actually don't, Mr. Dubin. Not that I didn't ask her, but Fanny wasn't all that certain where she was heading. Maybe L.A., or to San Francisco, and she said she'd send me a postcard once she knew for sure."

"Would you kindly let me know where she is when you get that card?"

"I will if she doesn't object."

Dubin had felt an irrational impulse to tell him to stay the hell away from Fanny but had no right to say it.

A few days later he had made up his mind to go to New York to see if he could find her. Kitty, alternating worry about Gerald with a nagging concern for Maud, who seemed to have stopped writing or calling, said she was in no mood to be left alone in the house.

"The house won't hurt you," Dubin said.

He had thought of telling her he was intending to get legal advice about Gerald's case but ultimately said nothing. She hadn't asked him why he was going to the city. Kitty hadn't offered to drive him to the station, so Dubin drove himself. He parked at the depot and boarded the train before realizing he had left her without a car.

In the city he went at once to Fanny's apartment. The door stood open. The flat was empty—the floor covered with paint-spattered drop cloths. The landlord and a painter standing on a ladder were talking inside.

"Excuse me," said Dubin, "do you happen to know where the young lady who lived here has moved to?"

"Who knows," said the landlord, "where they go."

"Where they want," said the painter, "they go. These are different times."

Dubin, at the window, gazed down at the synagogue. An old Jew was praying. Where they want they pray.

At the Gansevoort he sat at the desk in his room and wrote Fanny a note, to her at the law office—to be forwarded. "My dearest Fanny, I wish I had done it better. I wish I were a single man—or perhaps more daring. I wish . . . Life is so varied, sweet, sad. Think of me thinking of you. Surely we'll see each other again? My sense of it is that you're handling your life with purpose. Go on as you are. Ever yours, William Dubin."

As he addressed the envelope he was running through his mind the winter without her.

The morning in San Francisco he met Maud in the hotel lobby and drove in her VW to the beach. Maud is drawn, distant, lonely. He is tormented to see her so . . .

In her last letter she had said she wasn't intending to return to college for her senior year. Her father was at first angered, but rereading her several letters of the past year had filled him with regret: she had been signaling something less than the joyful life. He had let her down, Dubin had felt, in not more insistently trying to discover what was eating her. He had asked superficial questions and accepted casual replies. In one letter she had spoken of an interest in Eastern religions, not before a serious concern of hers. With Maud much happened in little time. In another letter she wished she had her life to live over. "Before you've begun to live?" No response to speak of. He tried it on the telephone: "Before you've begun to live?" "Who's to say how much anybody else has lived?" Fair enough, though not enough. Kitty still theorized that Maud was having her ups and downs in love. Dubin hoped it was that simple. So did Kitty.

Two weeks ago Maud had telephoned and asked not to be called by them.

"Why not?" Dubin asked.

"I need time to think things through."

"We won't interfere with your thoughts."

"I'm asking a favor," Maud wept.

Granted.

Last summer when she was home and bored, beyond occasionally asking her out for lunch or a drive, or to walk his walk with him, he felt he had given her not much. Yet she was, after all, home: they talked at the table; had shared the drama of Watergate—it was interesting to see Nixon, perennial loser, like a magician fabricating his losses. Maud read, played tennis, backpacked with the couple living on Mt. No Name; but it was obvious the focus of her life was elsewhere. Dubin and she seemed to resist each other —no explanation he could think of except they were interested in others. His thoughts had lain in Fanny's lap. One would think that if a man loves, the fountain flows: all may drink, no limit. But in truth the feeling of love for those one has loved was not boundless—it was bound. One loved according to his capacity but capacities differ. If you loved someone with deepening passion the love of others was effectively reduced, perhaps even paid for the passion. No, love was not boundless—not more than a pailful—barely enough for one at a time. You pour love out for a single self: in theory, no; but in practice other selves get less.

Not that Maud had wanted more from him than he ordinarily gave of affection. She had seemed, last summer, to want less; but that he hadn't offered more in a time of need bothered Dubin. It worried him that he never really had known what was going on with Maud once she was past sixteen, as if this fact, natural enough, embedded in their history, was itself the major cause of what was presently lacking in their relationship. He had thought of telling her about Fanny—being honest—but hadn't because he didn't want her to think of him as her mother's betrayer. Reasoning it thus was how Dubin balanced the construction in his mind: in loving Fanny he withheld love from his wife and daughter.

Fanny had, on her last birthday, waited for him at the train; he searched for her face in the crowd awaiting arrivals at the San Francisco Airport. Neither she nor his daughter appeared.

On the beach he impulsively drew her to him. Maud, shivering, stooped to pick up a shell. Dubin thrust his hands into his pockets. "I remember," he said, "when you were a little girl. Once you asked me to marry you."

"Oh, Papa," she said with an impatient gesture.

"Sentimentality has its moments."

"Not just this minute, please."

"Maud," Dubin said, "Why don't you tell me what's going on with you? Are you in love? Is it going badly?"

"I'm always in love. Sooner or later it goes badly."

He did not know what to reply.

Maud then said she wouldn't be going back to college in the fall. "I've had it with school. I want something else—something more satisfying."

"Like Zen?"

She wiped her eyes as though she were wiping away tears. The wind blew her hair into her face. Heartache, he reflected, became her age, not his.

"Why don't you call it a day here," Dubin advised, "and do your senior year in the East? You've never greatly liked California."

"I don't think so. I'm tired of intellectual studies, tired of intellectuals."

"Who in particular?"

"No one you know."

"You've always had intellectual interests."

"They're not very relevant to my life any more."

"It's a temporary feeling, believe me."

"Maybe. Maybe not. Buddha gave up books entirely at a critical time of his life."

"Lawrence never did, although I suppose it could be said he was an anti-intellectual natural intellectual."

"I wouldn't mention them both in the same breath."

"What makes you think so? In Sicily, when the peasants saw him with his red beard they cried out, 'Look! Jesus Christ!' "

"What are you trying to prove, Papa?"

"I wish I could tell you what I know about life."

"Don't get on that kick, please, not now. I've read your books."

Dubin, after a while, asked her if she wanted to try psychiatric counseling.

"I've had six months of that at Berkeley. It leaves me cold."

He laughed dully, looked at the ocean, looked away. "I've made the traditional suggestions. What I'm really saying is trust me, confide in me."

She said she had been talking to a Zen Master in South San Francisco. "When I came into his house he said he'd been waiting for me to appear. I'm thinking of entering a Zen commune if they consider me worthy. I've met some of his disciples. People in serious meditation have such clear luminous eyes. I'd like to be one of them. I expect to become a Zen disciple."

Dubin said he understood the rules were strict and the formal training no picnic. "It takes, I understand, years of disciplined effort. I'd like you to enjoy the youth of your youth."

He had read in Zen after rereading her letters.

"I'm not out to bliss it, Papa. I want discipline."

The word drew a tear to his left eye. He felt a sorrow of sorts for what she had of him in her.

Maud said she expected first to be instructed in meditation. "During the formal training I'll support myself by working in the commune—whatever they want me to do is worth doing. I want to live on my own labor, not yours. Please don't send me any more money, though I'm grateful for what you've done for me. I'm fed up with my ego. I want, eventually, satori—true enlightenment, an end to confusion and pain. I'd like to be different than

I've been. I'm not looking for, quote, happiness. I want to be in the *Is*ness of the Great Self. I will begin with emptiness."

"Emptiness I know about. It's nothing. Take something, you're only twenty."

"Twenty-one."

"Twenty-one," he said hastily.

"My age makes no difference. I feel like forty. I'd like to step out of time."

"Maud, come off that goddamned fantastic horse."

"That will get you nothing."

"My child," Dubin urged, "take your clear luminous eyes in your hand, as my father used to say, and look through them to see life clearly. In life fulfill yourself."

"I want fulfillment in Zen."

"Why don't you come home and think things through before you make your next move?"

"What's home?" she asked. "Two lonely people trying to get along."

"Use us, for Christ's sake, we'd be less lonely."

"I have my own life to live."

"Then *live* it. Don't be a nun, Maud. You've always called yourself a Jew. Jews live in the world. Don't hide from pain, insult, fear of failure. Don't expect perpetual serenity. It's not that kind of life or real world."

"How do you define the real world? All things share in the Buddha nature if one can find it in herself. I want to live in Buddha, that's where it is for me and I wish you wouldn't try to dissuade me now that I know where I want to be. Frankly, Papa, Zen would be good for you too."

She was walking in the surf.

He followed her along the ribbed hard sand. The wind was down; the fog had lifted but not the fog in Dubin. Of himself he had said nothing; she hadn't asked.

Maud strode on; Dubin followed. He was tempted to say, "My child, I understand your pain. I live with my own. Let me tell you about it." He didn't say it; he was, he thought, the father.

She walked on, eyes in the distance. My daughter, the stranger. He looked back: the waves washed the smooth shore and flowed into the sea. When he looked again their footsteps had reappeared.

Maud walks in Dubin's dreams.

It was a quiet long summer, two alone in a big house. The weather had turned humid-hot, and in the evening they sat on the porch facing the long-trunked graceful silver maples. Kitty's garden showed bunches of red phlox within a border of late-blooming yellow lilies. She served salads in white bowls, or cold sliced meats and cheeses they carried out on earthenware plates, with brown bottles of Alsatian wines. As they ate they watched the reflection of dull-gold sunsets on the heavy hills. The grass yielded light at dusk. Swallows darting in broken circles above the trees swooped low over the green lawn. Lorenzo, after long watching the birds, slept on the warm planks by the porch rail.

"He sleeps his life away," Kitty said.

"It's his to sleep."

At dark she lit a three-candle candelabrum he had bought her in Venice their first time there. Kitty smoked to keep the mosquitoes away. The biographer would watch the candles melt until the stars appeared. Afterward they read downstairs until their bedroom had cooled off, and then read in bed. Kitty was into Lawrence's poetry again.

"My God, listen to this—he's talking about his lonely erect phallus: 'How beautiful he is! without sound, / without eyes, without hands; yet flame of the living ground. / He stands, the column of fire by night. / And he knows from the depths; he quite / alone understands.' Isn't it just like D. H. Lawrence to write that?" Kitty laughed.

Dubin said he knew the poem. "He loved his thing."

"Don't you?"

"Yes."

He was reading the *Confessions of St. Augustine*, often putting the book down when he could not concentrate. "Love means that I want you to be," Augustine had said. As Dubin read he heard the *ping* of the moths hitting the window screens and saw lightning bugs flash in the trees in the outside dark. There was no breeze through the open windows; the curtains were limp. Kitty lay with her eyes shut, fanning herself in long strokes with a magazine.

"Lord, it's hot."

"Not that hot."

"I feel hot. Don't tell me it's only me."

"It's cooling now," Dubin said.

It was cooler at midnight, but they were restless in bed. Kitty said it looked like another uncomfortable summer. "Whatever's happened to Northeast weather? Where are the east winds and cool summers?" Dubin didn't know. In the warm dark when they moved apart to try to sleep, Fanny crept close to him, Dubin lay close to her.

Sometimes as he wrote he felt lust arise from nowhere, tempting him at his task. That morning he had gored Fanny on his horn. Fanny pressed her fleshy firm breasts to his lips, caressed his buttocks. Her experienced tongue traveled up his inner thigh to the head of his cock. She dipped it again and again into her mouth. Then she rose on her knees, placing herself above his erect flesh and locked it in her moist vagina, riding rhythmically, enacting an ancient legend in sweet time. Seizing her, he held her motionless, pumping upward until she burst into flame. William, she groaned in silence. He came, at length, extravagantly.

Dubin felt the shame of lust at his age.

"Clouds arose from the slimy desires of the flesh and from my youth's spring. They clouded over and darkened my soul, so that I could not distinguish the calm light of chaste love from the fog of lust."

Augustine's youth's spring; Dubin's late wasteful autumn. Not that flesh is slime, but some emotions are outworn. The expense of spirit: not because he had had her in his wife's company, but because he had had her when he hadn't; when she was no longer his to have.

He turned to Kitty. "Will you sleep with me—make love?"

"In this heat?"

"It's cooler now."

"All right." Her arms were warm, bosom soft.

After a while she asked, "What's the matter?"

"I don't think it's going to work."

"Are you sure?"

He said he was sorry.

"It's too hot," Kitty said. "I wouldn't worry about it."

Better this way, Dubin thought.

She fell asleep. He slept an hour and awoke, indecently mourning the girl. He had done it badly. They'd been friends, better friends than he'd had any right to expect, given the restrictions he had laid on her. With Fanny he had felt a dozen years younger, had acted like a young man, a young woman's lover. Not having her increased his not having. The mourning was harder to bear than the lust. They were two faces of the same loss, not having her you wanted most.

Dubin slept through the ringing alarm, aware of Kitty trying to rouse him and then letting him sleep. He woke heavily, with an increasingly burdensome sense of having mishandled the girl. He felt a gross hollow rooted in himself. The biographer played back the loneliness of his youth. There was more to their lives than he had allowed to happen. Out of the confusion caused by Kitty's call from Stockholm, Gerry's disappearance, his own guilt for being at that moment in bed with Fanny—he had botched it with her; had—without thinking it through—let her walk out of his life.

Perhaps he had allowed it to happen because it had momentarily seemed to simplify life. Dubin felt he had blown it finally when he went looking for her car, expecting to find it where he had found it; to feel justified in letting her go; to be betrayed again so that he could blame her rather than himself. He had indulged in jealousy to re-create the wound of mourning, lust, loneliness. What he ought to have done once she left and he regretted it was to get into his car, drive to New York, and there await her return even if it meant living a few days in a hotel and working in his room. He could have wired Kitty he would pick her up at Kennedy instead of Albany and then stayed with her at the Gansevoort until Fanny had come back and they had talked. I'd have promised her more. More what or more how he couldn't say, but more better. If he had been there waiting for her they would easily have made it up. Instead he had allowed himself to be eaten, undermined, by his jealousy.

He sent off another letter to Fanny via the apartment on West 83rd Street. It was returned in two weeks. He mailed the same letter in another envelope to the law office and then had a very good day. By the end of June he had heard nothing from Fanny yet went on writing to her. It was not a bad way to keep her present: about to reply; therefore in his future. It was a good way to keep his mind at peace and protect his work. He felt so until, one by one, his letters came back stamped "Return to sender." They hadn't been forwarded; she must have requested that: "Don't forward anything return-addressed Center Campobello, I want to get rid of that shmuck." Dubin worked at forgetting. No sense trying to kick the corpse of farewell into life. She left me before and I beat it out of my system. It shouldn't be so hard to do again in summertime. The season is easier, gentler—in my favor. There are green-leaved trees and many flowers around. Yet he had a self-conscious intrusive sense of himself abandoned by a girl, left exposed in his emotional long underwear, if not bare ass. He was embarrassed to have intruded on her youth. Dubin's nose twitched. He felt less vital than a year ago. His face was smaller, wrinkled, pouched under the eyes. He was losing hair, hated the sight of his comb after combing. His belly was expanding— if not in cubits, in eighth-inches; but growing in the long haul. His thick toenails were hard to cut. He had one pink foot and one white. He was adamantly a late-middle-aged gent. One paid for the pursuit of youth—from Faustus to Wm. Dubin. Wanting that much to be young was a way of hurrying time. The years ran forward backward. He counted on two fingers the time to sixty, obscene age. They say an old man dies young, back-slapping myth.

Dubin recomposed the old diet; rising at daybreak; water therapy; jogging the long walk in rain or shine, principally humid heat. Nothing to celebrate but discipline as evasion of a larger pain—ducking from that before it laid on with a bludgeon, insult he was sick of; indulged in to protect the self, self that lived the Lawrence. The dieting was strict, a pleasure-denying effort he was in no mood for. He came to the table with small appetite and left hungry. As in a former time he gobbled squares of chocolate hidden in a drawer. In bed hunger burned in every capillary. Not to brood or tear at himself he went quietly down the creaking stairs to the kitchen. Dubin made himself a liverwurst sandwich on rye, then one of cream cheese and jam smeared on white bread; he devoured both and still was hungry. He ate, he figured, Fanny, her live flesh. He drank wineglasses full of heavy cream—her breasts vanished. He ate her bare-boned; she no longer tempted. No aphrodisiac skeletons. Afterward he savaged himself for her hold on him.

But as the weeks went by his painful discipline fed him. It compels order; is order, he thought. I wish I could do it more easily, but if I can't I will do it this way. If, as in the past, he went into the bathroom to rinse his mouth after eating, he cut out desire for chocolate, feasting at night. If he still felt hunger he drank a glass of skim milk, sometimes two. Dubin lost weight without gaining virtue. Kitty wanted to know how much more he intended to shrink. He said he felt better: loss of flesh lightened the mind.

"You're not depressed again, are you?"

He was trying not to be.

"Then what's eating you?"

285

He felt her eating him and rose from the table. "I don't want to account for every move I make. Stop asking so many goddamn questions."

She studied him impassively; then Kitty got up and stalked out of the room.

His heart sank. Cutting off contact with her, such as it was—as he had caused it to be—punished him most. Not that he blamed her; it was an effectual defense. Dubin considered apologizing but decided not to. It would be a relief if she didn't talk to him for a few days.

He walked-ran day after day although it was a living bore, the sameness, the ritual. This extraordinary world—is this how life wants me to live it? But he ran to keep himself on keel, to wind himself into work the next morning. Dubin arose at the alarm ring, strayed into the bathroom, stepped blindly into the shower. Hot water poured on his head. He modified it to tepid, cold, colder—till it attacked and he gasped, ran in the tub. He held his head in the cold spray until he was numbed; then toweled himself at the open steamed window, feeling wet when dry. He exercised in his underpants in Maud's room, bent touching toes, pedaled on his back, pulled his knees into his bulging gut, willed pushups, other self-savaging. If the day was hot he exercised just out of bed, then showered, and went down to breakfast at least awake. He heard Lawrence scream *murder*.

The biography was going comparatively well, considering that Fanny, a more accomplished sexual person than Connie Chatterley, haunted his thoughts, rode like a witch astride each sentence he wrote. If the afternoon was impossible he jogged at dusk, at times having to rest against a tree, or lie on his back in the warm grass in the shade of maples grown thick with summer leafage. Dubin began in a walk then upped it to a slow jog. The idea was not to think but let momentum carry him. His spine loosened as he moved, hips and shoulders relaxed, bound energy came unbound. Going uphill in the heat, sweating, breathing laboriously, he stared at his feet as he plodded on. Downhill, he gazed into the shimmering distance. Sometimes a ring of gnats circled his head. Fanny floated in and out of the mind, invisibly kept him company. A short affair and long mourning. Having gone, why didn't she go? What kept her imprinted like a burn on the brain? Yet his sense of loss was more than loss of Fanny. What you dug out of left a hole deeper than the hole. He disliked himself for having twice succumbed to her, and twice to this self-inflicted punishment.

One Sunday morning as he was backing up on the driveway to get the car closer to the house so he could hose it, Dubin heard a savage yowl, hiss, scream through the window. He jammed the brake and frantically hopped out of the car. He knew what he had done. The wheel had crushed Lorenzo lying asleep on the warm asphalt. The cat vomited his tongue, his legs twitched as he died. Dubin, moaning, hid his eyes in his hands. Ten minutes later he furtively entered the house, stole a bath towel from the linen closet, and wrapped the remains of Lorenzo in it. He carried the bloody bundle to the barn, found a shovel, and buried the dead cat in Kitty's Wood. He remembered secretly burying Maud's black-and-white kitty there many years ago. Why does every misery happen twice? "Forgive me, Lorenzo," but the dead cat had nothing to say. Dubin buried him in a hole three feet deep, then returned wearily across the field, hoping Kitty hadn't seen the accident; but when he approached the house she was standing at the window observing him; her face dark, mourning.

The old house gave forth sounds at night—more, recently. It groaned, banged and creaked, without apparent cause. The biographer had long ago heard that the man who had built it had killed himself in the barn. Were his miseries adrift in the house at night? Was he? Dubin had never told Kitty about the suicide.

Kitty, one night, sat up suddenly in bed. "What was that?"

"What?"

She had heard gnawing scraping noises in the ceiling above their bed. He thought a field mouse or chipmunk might have come up inside the wall.

"If only Lorenzo were alive."

"If only."

That night Dubin listened to slow steps on the driveway, but when he got up to peer out of the window, could see no one, nothing in the pitch-dark.

"Should we call the police?" she whispered.

After a time he realized the "footsteps" was water dripping, after rain, from a leak in the gutter.

"What was that?" she whispered as he was falling asleep.

They listened sharply.

"Nothing. What did you think you'd heard?"

"Nothing."

"It was nothing," he said.

Sometimes when the furnace, heating water, rumbled, an upstairs door near the chimney shook.

Once Dubin woke to lonely secret steps coming up the stairs, but as he strained to hear, heard only his heartbeat drumming against the mattress.

When the wind blew, the house sighed, moaned, made sounds like living presences. One summer night Kitty, waking in fright, said she had heard a window slowly go up. Dubin listened sitting up, then pulled a sock on, and dragged himself throughout the house from floor to floor, turning on lights, inspecting window screens to see if one was slashed or missing. All were intact.

"It's mad to get up," he told her. "If I met someone I'd be a dead duck if he hit me on the head. We're safer putting the light on but not getting out of bed."

"I'd never get back to sleep," she said, "if someone didn't check the house."

When he returned to bed after his ritual exploration Kitty locked arms around him and fell asleep. Dubin, his senses alert, lay awake listening for noises in the night.

The window shades rattled. A door slammed in a cross-draft.

"What was that?"

"Nothing. Go back to sleep."

"If I can."

When he urinated, the toilet bowl sounded faintly like a ringing bell.

"Is that the phone?"

"What phone?" she wanted to know.

He was tired of the house—of living in the country. He'd had his fill of housebound cold Northeast winters; of short savage springs; increasingly hot humid summers. Kitty was right, the weather had changed for the worse: cold was colder, hot hotter. He wouldn't mind once more living in the city, chancy as the city was. Millions lived there in peace; millions who hadn't been insulted or mugged. One day on a bus, or as he walked along Madison, he might meet Fanny.

Dubin worried about Maud, chaste in Zen: and Gerald, in the Soviet Union—to what intent, purpose, future? They were into fates he couldn't have foreseen. He felt at times embittered by his worries about them. And he was fed up with his work; of the endless effort it took to keep going.

And tired of living with Kitty. He was bored with the bounds of marriage;

would like to be free before he was too old to enjoy it. Sherwood Anderson had one day escaped from his paint factory, left one or another wife to go to Chicago and write in a rooming house. Gauguin, taking years to sever himself from wife and children, frantically traveling wherever he could, at last made it to Tahiti. Could Dubin do what they had done?—take off and live as he pleased? He preferred, at his age, more solitude, time to himself. When he said something of the sort Kitty's knee-jerk response was: "If you want a divorce you can have a divorce. Don't stay for my sake." He would have to take off before pity restrained him; pack some necessary things and go to New York. One day while she was out of the house he would drive up in a van to collect his clothes, papers, books, and the pine table he liked to write on in the barn. Kitty would get along one way or another.

She now worked two afternoons a week at the Youth Opportunity Center. She saw Ondyk once a week and stayed on after their session for a drink. Considerate of Evan, the biographer thought. Kitty had returned from Stockholm muted, nervous. She wrote long explanatory letters in behalf of Gerald to the State Department and a letter of inquiry to the American Embassy in Moscow. She wrote she had heard that her son, a deserter, was in the Soviet Union—where she couldn't say—and would appreciate it if they tried to find him and put him in touch with his parents. She received official letters in reply—they were looking into the matter—from Washington and Moscow. She wrote every week to Maud in her commune in South San Francisco. "What ails my children?" Kitty asked. She stood at the edge of her garden, regarding her flowers. She rarely played the harp—now and then for five minutes. She had again taken to reading her *Handbook of Psychiatry*, the second volume. Her or me? Dubin thought. He expected, if he looked, to find his name in the index. She seemed forlorn, abandoned by her second husband, such as he was. Her voice was dry; she was thin, distant, out of it somehow. She would look long at her extended legs as she sat in a chair. Whatever she had bought to wear lately seemed wrongly styled or colored. She had bought a fall hat with a bright green ribbon and returned it the next day. "I thought you didn't like green?" Dubin said. "I wondered if it might work this time." She needed, she said, a pair of reading glasses. Lately as she read she had seen floating black spots, but would not go to an eye doctor. "I'm not in a mood to tempt fate." "What do you get out of waiting but anxiety?" "I dislike running to doctors." "Do you think you're being brave?" "Oh, let up, William, I'm being myself."

One evening she asked, "Don't you think it's time we had sex?"

He said perhaps it was.

"You never court me any more."

It's because in a long marriage your wife becomes your sister, he thought. Dubin asked her why she didn't court him.

"You never exactly encourage it."

Kitty brushed her teeth and got into a nightgown he liked. Tonight she lay in bed, waiting for him to begin. He asked her if she was tired and she said she wasn't, was he? He wanted, after Fanny, Dubin thought, someone like Fanny. With her the sexual act began long before the sexual act. Dubin was in his wife when to his surprise his penis wilted like a plucked flower. That hadn't happened before during intercourse. He withdrew and fell back in bed. She tried to bring him to life but he did not respond.

"Had you come?"

He said no.

"Do you feel all right?" she asked gently.

Dubin said he had up to then.

"Well, don't blame yourself. Let's try tomorrow. I'm tired myself."

"Then why did you suggest it?"

"It's been a long time."

They tried for three nights but he achieved no erection. He felt his fear on her body.

"Don't be worried," she urged. "I'm sure it's temporary. Maybe the poor thing is bored. I wish I could plant it in my garden and let it grow like an asparagus."

"I wish you could."

"Are you scared?"

He said he was.

She kissed him. "Let's not make ourselves tense. We'll wait a week and try again. Why do you think it happened in medias res?"

"Maybe because you think of it as in medias res."

"Oh, cut it out."

"One day it happens," he said.

"It shouldn't to you yet. Some men even go on into their eighties. One has to stay with it."

"I'll stay with it if it lets me."

"Is it my fault? I haven't felt much like sex since I came back from Stockholm." She looked at him hopefully, then uneasily.

He asked her if she had been reading about impotence in men.

Kitty confessed she had recently read a chapter in a book.

"Maybe that did it. I respond as you expect me to." He felt he was going after her unjustly but couldn't stop. "If you define me from the book maybe that's the kind of man you get."

She said that was totally irrational.

"All I'm saying is if I'm spinach in your thoughts that's what you'll get when you open the can."

"If you're spinach to me it's because you think of *me* as a vegetable."

"You're reading the book, not I."

"It could be physical," she said earnestly. "Diabetes, for instance, can bring it on. Have you had a blood-sugar test recently?"

He said he hadn't.

"Maybe it's something else—I don't mean to wish diabetes on you," she said with an uncertain laugh, "but something seems wrong. You blame me—that's what your wisecracks and ironies amount to—but you've changed in a way I can't really understand. Have you been sleeping with someone?"

"Do you mean Flora?"

"Her or whoever?"

"You're the only one I sleep with."

Dubin wondered if lying, or the habit of lying, could make a man impotent. You lied to someone and could not lie with her.

"You might have no trouble with another woman," Kitty said.

"I might not."

"If you're sleeping with someone and it's working with her when it's not with me, maybe we ought to think of parting."

He felt his nose twitch.

"Unless"—she hesitated—"would you want to go to Evan now—for advice?"

"You go to him. I wouldn't want to."

"There are other therapists not too far away. There's a new man in Winslow I hear is good."

"How do you know who's new in Winslow? How do you know these things?"

"Evan told me." A moment later she said, "If you're thinking of divorce you ought to let me in on it."

"I think of it often," Dubin said.

Kitty, sitting on the edge of the bed, slipping on her mules, turned to him grimly.

"I wish you'd tell me the truth. Do you have a girl in town?"

"Neither in or out of town."

"*Did* you have during this past winter? I had the feeling you did, when you brought those sex-goodies for me to try with you. I'll bet you had a girl then."

He admitted he had.

"That's what I thought," Kitty said with satisfaction. "Who was she?"

"Nobody you know." Dubin was lying back with his eyes shut.

"You can go to her if you like. Why don't you just go to her?"

"She's not there to go to."

"Then find yourself someone who is," she said angrily.

He said he had no plans to.

"Are you ashamed you'd be impotent?"

"I am ashamed. Your question deepens my shame."

"You deepen your shame."

Afterward they were uneasy with each other. In her presence he lacked; because he lacked she lacked. For each negation or strangeness there is an opposing negation or strangeness. They had got into bed as though they were fragile; as though neither thought it would work. When it did not they looked at each other in loneliness and embarrassment. Neither suggested trying again the next night, or in the foreseeable future.

He thought of himself as crippled. Dubin imagined going to New York to look for a hooker on Eighth Avenue to test his virility. But even reverie didn't work. The hooker said she couldn't take him on because she was overbooked; but she offered him a remedy for his trouble:

"You got to boil it in salt water to clean out the pipe."

"Why don't you blow it out?"

"I couldn't," she said. "I have this sore in my throat."

Dubin didn't think he would go to the city.

Kitty suggested a vacation.

"Not just now," he said.

"Then when?"

"I'm not sure, but not now."

"How's the work going?"

"Surprisingly well."

"What do you think we ought to do?"

"Give it time. Wait and see."

"Wait and see what?"

"If we should seriously be thinking of separating."

She turned away from him, her eyes bruised.

"You'd rather think of divorce than therapy?"

He said he would rather work it out on his own if he could.

"How do you expect to do that?"

"I wish I knew," he said, trying to be conciliatory. "You might walk into the room and pick up a pin. The thing might rise and salute."

They laughed, Dubin wheezily; then looked at each other sadly.

"One feels out of it," Kitty said.

He went on working in the barn, living with the slug of impotence in his mind. But as long as he wrote he felt he was not impotent. Kitty tried to arrange her time so she was doing something gainful almost all day. She went to bed early. When Dubin got into bed she stirred but did not waken. If she was awake she did not say so. He was afraid to touch her or himself. He felt for her a terrible pity.

"Oh, come on," Kitty said, awaking happily one morning. "We haven't been hit by the plague. Let's not give in to our moods. Let's have some parties. Let's see friends." Dubin said it was a fine idea. She made breakfast singing, "We'll sail the ocean blue." In the afternoon she persuaded him to help her bake bread. "We haven't done that since the kids were little. Do you remember how it excited them?" The day went well.

She telephoned friends, who immediately accepted her invitations. She'd been, as Nathanael's wife, a less than accomplished cook, but as Dubin's, Kitty cooked well. They entertained at one dinner party the Greenfelds, Habershams, and Morphys. Morphy was an internist, their nearest neighbor before the covered bridge, who grew small evergreens on his farm for the Christmas tree trade. At another party the Ondyks came with Ossie Lapham and his wife. Ossie was an ornithologist and she, Renata, a twenty-eight-year-old pretty American type who was reading Colette for the first time. She told

Dubin Colette had changed her life but didn't say how. Later she asked him if he had ever wanted to have an affair. He said he had. "So have I." "Don't fall in love with him," Dubin advised.

Kitty had a sound instinct for parties of whatever sort and people enjoyed them. She was, at the beginning of the first dinner party, constrained with Flora, but carried the evening off well. Oscar wasn't drinking that night. He seemed to be brooding, looked pale, strained; he volunteered no information and Dubin asked nothing.

After dinner he danced with Flora. Neither mentioned her last phone call or his non-response. "I wear my sleeve on my heart," said Flora.

"In regard to what?"

"In regard to my heart."

He regretted not having gone to her when she had phoned that Sunday morning, after Fanny had left. It might have lessened the effect of her departure if he had spent the day with Flora. In Oscar's presence Dubin felt little guilt; he attributed it to his affection for him, and for having been punished enough also to have been punished for betraying a friend. As the guests were leaving, Kitty stood at the door with her arm around her husband.

In bed they kissed affectionately. "We used to fall asleep in each other's arms," she said. Soon they were exploring their familiar bodies, hesitated, pressed on, trying to invent strategies to outwit the failed flesh; failed.

"Would you still rather wait and see than do anything about it?"

Dubin said he had been to a doctor.

"Why didn't you tell me?"

"I wanted to go without fuss."

"What did he say?"

"It's not diabetes, or the Lariche blood-vessels business, or anything like that. He couldn't say what it was."

"Now that we know that," she said quietly, "maybe this would be a good time to talk to a psychotherapist?"

"Whatever I feel I don't feel impotent," Dubin said.

The point seemed important to make. He said he wanted to wait a while longer to try to figure out what was happening. "It's my life, I want it to tell me what it knows."

"Mother of God," said Kitty, "the way you complicate everything twice

294

over. What happens in these cases has been determined. It's cut-and-dried. You can read about it in books. I imagine it would be very difficult, if not impossible, to cure yourself."

"That's a strange tack for somebody who's always trying to cure herself. This may be a temporary thing. I want to try to work it out."

"Don't be a fanatic," Kitty said. "What happens to me while you're working it out? What happens to *my* young life?"

"I can satisfy you in other ways."

"I don't want a satisfaction, I want a functioning husband."

Afterward she told him to work it out anyway he pleased. "I don't want to discourage you."

She tried not to appear worried, though her eyes and mouth worried. She watered the garden for half an hour, and holding the dripping hose, studied it for another half hour. From afar she contemplated Dubin reading on the porch, glancing away when he looked her way. She had probably told Ondyk about his present incapacity. It was her prerogative though he hated having Ondyk know. He hadn't earned the right,

Dubin had avoided him at their last dinner party. He had talked at length with Marisa, an insecure self-conscious woman. She often blew her nervous nose. Marisa spoke of her husband glowingly in his presence, but he did not mention her in hers. Kitty had talked seriously with Evan more than once that night; she seemed uncomfortable without him. If she had discussed Dubin with him, she did not admit it. "I don't want to tell you what I talk about with him," Kitty said. "He is now a member of the family," the biographer said.

"Would you like me to leave him and find someone else?"

"Whoever you find, don't bring him into the house. I don't want to treat as a friend anybody whose business it is to look up my ass, or yours."

She walked away. Kitty seemed to retreat inwardly. She had stopped playing her harp. They ate in silences. When they walked she went ahead of him, as she used to at times when they were first married. She developed a cough and coughed heavily at night.

"Why don't you do something about it?"

"Why don't you?"

He slept in Gerald's room; she slept in Maud's.

They argued as they hadn't in years, nasty arguments, each topping the other in accusation, neither able to forgo having the last word. Kitty needled him; Dubin shouted. The windows vibrated, his force alarming him.

One morning he gave her a list of things he needed from town: "newspaper, typewriter ribbon, stamps, cigarillos." At the door she turned. "I hate your fucking little lists, I've always hated them. Hereafter *tell* me what you want. I won't look at a list."

When she returned to the house to smell the burners he said, "I put things down on paper because you don't. If you hadn't forgotten to buy a quart of milk that day, I wouldn't have hit a tree and broken my bones. Make your own list, but for Christ's sake make one."

The door slammed as though it had exploded. A window shade snapped and rolled upward.

The front page of the newspaper she brought home was torn, and Dubin mended it with diaphanous tape.

"Why bother?" Kitty asked. "Isn't it to show me up? That I haven't the sense to pick up an untorn newspaper?"

"The wire they bale them with tears them," he said. "I don't mind mending the paper. If I pay for it I'd like to be able to read what it says."

"You explain everything—absolutely everything."

"What we're really arguing about is my sexual inadequacy, and that I haven't taken your advice."

Getting into bed that night after he had gone downstairs to make sure he had locked the front door, as Dubin lay back his head cracked against hers. Kitty screamed. He bellowed: "How the hell did I know your head was on my pillow!"

"I wanted to be affectionate." Tears flowed from her eyes.

He sat in the kitchen at the table where she had piled three pounds of ripe tomatoes in a glass bowl. Dubin bit into a blood-red tomato, hungrily sucking its meat and tepid seedy juice. He devoured two large tomatoes seasoned with coarse salt, then went to bed.

Kitty was awake. "What's that rotten smell?"

"My thoughts."

She rolled over on her side.

He fantasied himself on his walk. He tried to see what he always saw, but this time a stranger with dirty eyes sneaked out of the wood and struck Dubin on the head with a lead pipe. The biographer lay bleeding in the road. The man removed his wallet, counted five singles, and again struck Dubin with the pipe.

"Is that all a man's life means to you?" muttered the bloody-headed biographer.

"Fuck you," said the stranger. "I don't owe you a thing."

Kitty came by. She wept aloud for what she had not done with her life but not for what she had done with it.

"Shush," she said the next morning as he growled at himself in the mirror. He knew he frightened her but could not stop talking to the suffering man in the warped glass.

What if I am impotent forever? Suppose it goes from the cock to the brain? What shall I do? What can I do?

The fanatic regime of two winters ago that Dubin had revived to prevent a great misery happening, he continued to practice in order to change the heartbreaking fate that had befallen him.

One night the ghost of the old man who had hanged himself in the barn tramped across the field to the yellow black-shuttered house and trod up the stairs. Opening the creaking bedroom door, he flung his bloody noose on their bed.

"I am not going to be left to Frieda's tender mercies until I am well again. She is really a devil—and I feel as if I would part with her for ever—to let her go alone to Germany, while I take another road. For it is true, I have been bullied by her long enough. I really could leave her without a pang, I believe. The time has come to make an end, one way or another."

Kitty mourned the dead cat. "He liked to keep me company. I loved the way he stretched out on the kitchen floor with the sun on him." After supper she cut up meat scraps for Lorenzo before remembering he was no longer there to eat them. She hid the cat's dish in a drawer. Thinking it might relieve her to know where Lorenzo was buried, Dubin showed her his grave one evening and Kitty planted an iris bulb in it. "We found him and we lost him."

As they were walking across the field she said, "William, let's be kind.

Let's not be nasty. I'm not blaming you for the cat's death or anything else. Let's be considerate and kind."

He put his arm around her, wanting to suggest going to bed, not daring to.

They slept badly in the heat although they slept alone. Dubin wore himself out trying to sleep. He could barely drag himself to the shower. August caught fire from July. At 7 a.m. the thermometer showed seventy-four; at noon it boiled at over ninety. The sun for days flamed. The woods were dry. Trees in the morning mist were like gloomy sculptures: a drunken slanted maple; thick-armed oak; bushy orange-berry mountain ash. Crows barked in the tops of furry pines. Dubin, on his way to the hot barn, cawed at the crows.

Although he had a box fan there he decided to stop working in the barn. The sun beat down on the roof, and by mid-morning the heat lay on him like an overcoat. He had considered putting in an air-conditioner, but in this climate it seemed an obscene act. Maybe next year if the summer started hot. The biographer returned to his cooler study in the house. He hung on the wall his Medal of Freedom and framed picture of Thoreau. With the fan on, the room was bearable, though the muted rattle of the vibrating blades was no help. In Kitty's garden wheelbarrow he trundled back boxes of note cards, folders of manuscript pages. He left the barn reluctantly, imagining the telephone ringing, no one there to answer.

Dubin began to write one of the articles he had contracted for. It was hard to write with his mind on Lawrence; he was impatient to be back to him but was worried about money. He worked on the biography for two hours each morning and then for two wrote the article. Each sentence was like lifting a rock. Exhausted, he went downstairs to make himself iced coffee. Kitty, her hair up, hot face glistening, was sitting on the porch reading the paper as she fanned herself with her left hand. She seemed not to know he was there. Renewed energy lasted perhaps twenty minutes. Dubin tried another shower, dried himself, returned to his desk. When he read what he had written that morning he laid down the pen. Lassitude came over him. If the weather was minding its business this should be fall beginning. Against the will he felt he ought to lay off a few days. I will write faster once it gets cool.

From his bookshelves he plucked an armful of lives and letters he knew well. Dubin thumbed through lives of Jung, Freud, Swift, Samuel Johnson, Chekhov, Goya, Montaigne, Ruskin, Darwin, Hardy, Mahler, Virginia

Woolf. On August 21, 1581, Montaigne, after a night of torment, had passed a stone, "having, to tell the truth, exactly the shape of a prick." "My thoughts have been clouded with sensuality . . ." Johnson lamented. "A strange oblivion has overspread me." "I wind round and round in my present memories the spirals of my errors": Augustine. "Why is it so dull here?" asks Chekhov. "It is snowing, a blizzard, there is a draft from the windows, the stove is sizzling hot, I had the thought of writing, and am not writing anything." "I am sometimes so agitated that I can no longer stand myself," Goya told a friend. "I lack force and work little." Freud devastated Dubin: "Anyone turning biographer has committed himself to lies, to concealment, to hypocrisy, to flattery, and even to hiding his own lack of understanding: for biographical truth is not to be had, and even if it were it couldn't be useful." "I shall be like that tree," said Swift, "I shall die first at the top." "But really, for me," Lawrence wrote in a letter, "it's been a devilish time ever since I was born. But for the fact that when one's got a job on, one ought to go through with it, I'd prefer to be dead any minute." Dubin read to learn what he didn't know or might have forgotten. He sought insight as if hunting for burning bushes on Sinai: how men hold themselves together. But the biographies reminded him of the life he wasn't writing; the life he wasn't living.

Lawrence had become impotent in his early forties—what a terrifying loss to a man who writes poems to his erect phallus. Someone had theorized that his condition was related to tuberculosis, which it took him many years to admit he had; but who is to say what pure Greek fate he had wrought for himself in the labyrinth of the Lawrencian mind, in the recesses of the blue-black blood? Frieda had whispered the sad news around, possibly to justify an affair or two. How curious it is, Dubin thought, as you write a man's life, how often his experiences become yours to live. This goes on from book to book: their lives evoke mine or why do I write? I write to know the next room of my fate. To know it I must complete Lawrence's life. He died at forty-four. I'm fifty-eight but if I die now I die young. My concern with aging has made me conscious of death. William Dubin's in his last life, no longer those one lives to learn with—if he learns. In middle age some degree of accomplishment kept me young, aware of youth in me. The future was my next biography; now it's age. Subjectivity sickens me. I fear myself fearing.

Dubin had taken the measure of himself and measured less.

Almost as he was thinking this, the rains swept summer aside and autumn flowed in. The muggy heat evaporated: weather turned crisp cool; sky cold blue; air transparent. Whirring flocks of birds settled on the lawns, pecked in the dying grass, and flew off in rushing flights. The yellowing trees giving off yellow candlelight turned dull-gold.

He went back to his work, pushed on, wished he was writing in the barn.

As he jogged the long walk one wet late-afternoon, Dubin slipped on a stone, fell heavily, and lay in the road in torment. He felt he had broken his ankle. After excruciating minutes the pain let up and he managed to hobble on. He arrived at the highway, where he was able to hitch a ride in a pickup truck to the hospital emergency room.

Kitty came for him in her new apple-green Toyota. They had traded in the Ford; she would not drive the car that had killed Lorenzo. The swelling was reduced with ice and the strained ankle bound with an ace bandage. Dubin was advised to stop walking for at least a week. The effect was depressingly confining. He had given up the article and gone back entirely to the book. Money was becoming a problem, but if he had to borrow he'd have to borrow. Kitty wouldn't like it. He'd try the article later at a chapter break.

The biographer had to cut out calisthenics and set aside his diet. Immediately he gained weight, felt leaden, heavy, unfocused. In the cellar he located Maud's old bike, cleaned and oiled it, and with Kitty's assistance got it up the stairs. He pedaled the bicycle to the bridge, but the ankle was not that much healed and the pressure of pedaling became painful. The next day he was at a loss what to do for activity. He was restive, nervous. When Dubin stopped running he ran within—a running runs within. To catch up with himself he got into the new automobile.

Dubin went on his long walk in Kitty's car. It took not more than fifteen minutes to drive the route slowly, so he drove it several times. He drove at twenty an hour, puffing a cigar, though not much tasting it; trying to see what he usually saw when he was walking: the seasonally changing landscape —rumpled yellow autumn hills and darkening orange mountains. Close by, eternally a scattering of stiff farmhouses, weathered barns, squat and tall silos, cows in spongy pastures. As he drove his route he was surprised by the narrowness of the road he usually walked. It reminded him of the thin long hallways of the railroad flats he had lived in as a child. Ahead the light receded; the road was shadowy, empty. Dubin drove the emptiness. What am I afraid of other than myself? At the highway he turned left instead of right, and in a burst of speed was halfway to Winslow before returning. The next day he repeated the drive until he had lost count of the number of voyages he had made, and a fog descended on the deserted road.

He could think of nothing that was working as he wanted it to. He had returned the biographies and letters to their proper places in the shelves. Dubin thought of all the lives he had hoped to write that he never would. His nose twitched like a rabbit's as he flipped through Kitty's *Handbook of Psychiatry,* Vol. II. He read in it nothing that gave him pleasure or relief, and hid the book in a closet. Dubin, weary of himself, wanted to be better than he was, free of twitches, tics, compulsive gestures. He wanted to be self-sufficient, in control, good to others, good to his wife. He wanted to breathe in the purity of fresh morning. He was disheartened by his monotonous days and nights. I'm like a rock with an iron fence around it. I'm not doing anything for anybody. He got into the apple-green Toyota and drove to the green bridge.

Dubin journeyed the usual way, not seeing much, head constricted, attention wandering. It began to drizzle and he automatically flicked on the wipers, trying not to think though his mind steamed with thought; and when he lit a cigarillo, his hand trembled. On the wet road close to the path to the quarry Dubin passed a man squatting by his car; he had just changed a rear tire and was lowering the hydraulic jack. The biographer passed him in a spurt of speed. A quarter of a mile farther up the road he pulled to the side and shut off the ignition, tensely trying to think whether to turn back, struggling to control the rush of fear he felt at the thought. The man he had passed in the road was Evan Ondyk. Maybe I ought to talk to him? Dubin touched the starter, turned with difficulty, and reluctantly drove back. He felt shaken, unwell. A vital self had walked out of his life, leaving this old bag.

Lowering his window, he gravely hailed Ondyk. "Need any help?"

"I thought it was you, William. No, thanks, all's done." He lifted the flat-tired wheel, then the jack, into the trunk of the car and slammed down the lid.

Dubin parked on the left side of the road, ten feet beyond Ondyk's Buick on the right. He turned off his wipers but left the motor running. He was still in flight.

"Evan," he said with an effort through the half-open window, "I'm not in the best of shape. In fact I'm not feeling at all well. Would you mind getting into the car with me and talking for a minute? Or I could get into yours?"

"A minute is all I have," Ondyk said, his eyes darting at Dubin's. He hesitated. "Oh, what the hell, talk away, William. But I can't get into the car with you. This flat tire has made hash of my schedule. I'll have to skip something. If it's lunch with Marisa she'll be sore as hell."

"You'll get wet out there."

"I have my rain hat in the car."

The psychotherapist was standing in the road in the drizzle, his hair covered with droplets of rain. His damp brow glistened and blond mustache drooped. He was a heavy-shouldered handsome man with a slender nose, cleft chin, moody eyes. A familiar stranger, Dubin thought. Confiding in him was difficult.

The biographer caught a glimpse of himself in his mirror—shock of recognition: eyes tight, shifty, fearful—mouth compressed, uneasy—complexion gray. He heard his own frightened breathing, felt ashamed of what he was into—consulting a man he had never much liked, a psychotherapist—embarrassed by his embarrassment. There were, among recurring others, two known Dubins: the man sitting in the car and someone within writhing in shame.

"How's Kitty doing?" he heard himself ask. The question seemed strange, imperiling, as though he'd left her and had to ask a neighbor for news.

Ondyk, in the drizzle, smiled slightly. "Ask her, William, don't ask me."

"Of course. I'm sorry."

He cursed his nose twitching spasmodically. Ondyk sneaked a sidelong look at him. Dubin forced himself not to avert his glance.

"I'm not myself," he said with a hollow laugh. "I'm feeling off-center, off-base—as if I have two left sides and nowhere to take them. I work little, without concentration. I'm full of odd crawling fears. I may need an assist, Evan. Has Kitty told you?"

"She didn't put it to me like that. She sort of indicated your book on Lawrence might be doing you in."

"Was that what she said?"

"Something like that."

"What else?"

"That's her business. Listen, William, you and I aren't great friends, but

it mightn't be a bad idea if I speak to you as one. I'm no literary critic—
that's not my specialty—but I could never figure out why a man of your
disposition and temperament would want to get so many years of his life
involved with a tormented semi-narcissistic figure like D. H. Lawrence.
Thoreau I can understand for you, but not this fellow. Not all of us are
congenial with each other, as I'm sure you'll agree. I'm thinking of the wear
and tear in the long run—what a ball-breaking strain it must be to have to
identify with someone whose nature is so radically different from yours. Isn't
objectivity breached by his constant bilge?"

Dubin did not resist the man's approach. It was easier to reply to than
something directly personal.

He answered, lowering his eyes, forcing himself to speak: "He's a strange
mindful but essentially a meliorist. He wants a better world but on his own
terms: reform sex—the passional lives of men—and you reform the world.
But he had very little faith in mankind and allowed himself some destestable
beliefs. One critic said his philosophy might be that of any thug or moron
if separated from the warm intense articulate being he was. He could be a
forthright detached critic of his work. He knew and did not always approve
his nature. And whatever his excesses he remained an artist. His fiction,
though not always successful, was the work of a man of genius."

Dubin, clearing his throat intermittently, said he took no great pleasure
in Lawrence's religious primitivism and anti-democratic fantasies. Or in his
view of debased social body with its law-oriented degenerate Jews, weak in
maleness, leading in the race to total corruption. Or in his hatred of women
whose evil power over blood males emasculated them. "He called the public
'stinking humanity' and equated socialism with syphilis. He was engorged
with the rage of a failed prophet.

"On the other hand," he said to Ondyk, "I can't say I'm much upset by
his hatred of capitalism and outraged sense of the perversion of human life
by technology. Finally, he brings his destructive impulses to a life-enhancing
end in his books. He lived in a vast consciousness of life. At his best he wants
man to risk himself for a plenitude of life through love."

"Why not?" Ondyk asked.

"Why not?" Dubin hoarsely echoed.

"He sounds better than I thought."

"When you write biography you want to write about people who will make
you strain to understand them." Dubin said it was like chasing a runner you

would never catch up with. "But the game is, I suppose, to make the reader think that's exactly what you have done, and maybe in a blaze of illumination even have outdistanced him. It's an illusionary farce that holds me by the tail."

The biographer tried to laugh but nothing came of it.

"Still and all," Evan said, continuing to observe Dubin, "though I know I am technically out of my depth, you and he are two radically different types, and living every day with the anger, spleen, and hostility of this enraged man is bound to exacerbate your other day-to-day problems."

"He's hard to take when I'm taking myself hard," Dubin admitted. "He's hard to take now, but I've worked on him for years and have to finish the job.":

"You have serious problems."

"I know, but if you don't mind me saying so, Evan, I wish you'd drop this approach. If I give Lawrence up I give up a book, and the thought of that —I confess I've thought of it—makes me feel shivery and sick. I don't want that kind of failure to contend with at this time of my life. I would have no confidence in anything I went to next."

The drizzle turned into rain. Ondyk got his porkpie rain hat out of his car, lowered the brim all around, and placed it on his wet head. He flipped up his jacket collar. In the rain he stood patiently at the window observing the uncomfortable biographer. Dubin's motor was still running. He fought an intense urge to step on the gas and bolt.

"What did you mean before when you said you needed an assist? Were you thinking of consulting me professionally?"

"Kitty said it might be a good idea."

"What's your view?"

Dubin scratched himself nervously. "I'm of two minds. I have my reservations."

"I've heard you on that subject," Ondyk said, wiping his wet face with his wet handkerchief. "In any case it doesn't make much difference because I can't take you on, William. Kitty's my patient and though there are therapists who do marriage counseling with husband and wife it's not my dish of fish, so I regret I have to say no." He smiled moodily. "I know someone in Winslow I could refer you to."

Dubin didn't think so. "I respect what you do or I wouldn't be encouraging my wife to see you. But I'm not so sure it's right for me at this time of my life. Maybe when I was younger, but I couldn't afford it then."

"If you had needed it seriously, you'd have found a means to afford it."

"I assume I needed it. But that was long ago and I found another way. What I'm saying is I think I understand what's happening to me. I've been there before."

"And you may be there again if you don't do something about it. Simply understanding isn't what it's about, William, you know that. Cure is process —working it through is the only way."

"The unconscious," Dubin heard himself hesitantly say, "is not unavailable to those who study themselves."

"So you intend to continue with your Teddy Roosevelt regime of exercise and calorie counting?"

Dubin laughed unhappily. "It keeps me going."

"In your wife's car with your bad ankle?"

"Till I can figure out a new move, or find myself making one."

"In the meantime undergoing a lot of useless suffering. It's pure waste; so is self-obfuscation."

"We judge ourselves, we take risks," Dubin told himself. Staring uncomfortably at Ondyk standing in the rain he felt wet. The psychotherapist sneezed.

"You're sure you won't get into the car with me, Evan?"

"This will take one last minute. I hate to breach confidentiality, William, but you know I know you have a very serious problem."

Dubin knew.

"Impotence is no joy."

"I don't feel impotent."

Ondyk stared at him in disbelief. "Can a man who writes biography afford to delude himself?"

Dubin, after another miserable moment, thanked the psychotherapist for his advice. "I regret you got wet on my behalf."

"No sweat." Ondyk, in his damp clothes, got into his car.

Dubin, releasing his brake, headed north as Ondyk drove south. For twenty minutes he felt intense relief. Had St. George slain the dragon? He drove the circle backward, but could then not think where to go. His relief evaporated. On awakening that morning he hadn't known what to do next; nor did he now.

That evening the phone rang. "It's Evan," Kitty said. "He wants to talk to you."

"Tell him I'm out."

He had been reading in Lawrence: "We ought to dance with rapture that we should be alive and in the flesh and part of the living incarnate cosmos."

"Speak to him out of common courtesy if for no other reason," Kitty said. "You haven't a friend in the world."

"Only you," Dubin, on his third drink, said. "Tell your friend I'm out."

In the night he would regret it. He was alone in the cosmos and desperately needed anyone, even a friend.

As Dubin slowly drove the ascending road a gaunt runner in a gray sweatsuit, wearing an electric-red safety bib, came loping down toward him. He was an open-mouthed jogger with an awkward gait, who looked as though he hated every step he ran. Sweat streamed down his glistening face, drawn, bony. Dubin, recognizing Oscar Greenfeld, had in astonishment braked the car.

"Holy cow, is that you, Oscar?"

The flutist flatly ran on six or seven steps before wearily halting. He was reluctant to. Dubin backed up the car. He knew the feeling: if you stopped you'd never start again.

"My God, Oscar, what are you doing in that sweatsuit and red bib?"

Greenfeld, pressing his hand to his left side, drew two long noisy breaths before replying. Gasping, he spoke: "Have to. Doctor prescribed—de rigueur. Don't know whether you heard—I had a heart incident this past winter. Have been doing three miles every day since I got back on my feet. Run everywhere—drive to a road whose view I like, then go. Used to walk, but now I run. Run for heart and flute. Running, as they say, makes wind."

Dubin moaned in dismay. "Heart attack? Last winter? God in heaven, Oscar, why didn't you tell me in all this time? Have we become such poor friends? I feel dreadful. Why didn't Flora call or at least say something when you came to dinner? You looked awful, I was afraid to ask. I find the whole thing hard to believe."

Oscar smiled wanly. "I was in Prague for a concert when it happened. Flora flew over and stayed a month till I could leave. I had the attack on her last birthday, about the time you were fucking her in my house. She told me after we last saw you and Kitty. She felt she finally had to."

He glowered at Dubin, his white face dark, jaw trembling.

"Oscar," Dubin, anguished, cried, "believe me, I regret it."

"William," Greenfeld said, raising his breathy voice, "I don't pretend to be innocent of evil to others. I've screwed around in my time, but what I wasn't prepared for, nor will I ever be, is that my former best friend would betray me in my own house, where he had always been a welcome guest, with my wife. Hypocrite! Fool! I detest you!"

Oscar, resuming his run, disappeared down the road.

Dubin could not for a while remember how to start the car.

A horseman in overalls appeared on the downsloping curved road, a thick-bellied unshaved man wearing field boots, his legs dangling down the flanks of a white heavy-hooved workhorse. Dubin had more than once seen them on this road, wondering where he led the horse or the mare took him. A quarter of a mile up, past acres of unharvested corn, they usually disappeared into the fields. Neither Dubin nor the man had ever so much as nodded to each other when they met. It was that kind of world.

But today as the overalled horseman plodded by Dubin's car, he reined in the white mare and in anger and agitation pointed to the glowing hills under light-shedding seas of autumn clouds.

"Look there! Them Jews are crucifyin' the earth!"

Smacking the horse's flank, he darkly trotted away.

Midway up the nearest hill, a long low one to the north, Dubin beheld an earth-colored savage slash through the foliage where half a dozen twenty-ton yellow bulldozers were shuttling and darting, undercutting and uprooting hundreds of ancient trees.

A deep unyielding pain overwhelmed the biographer as it occurred to him this was part of a highway cloverleaf being built to divert traffic from town. Dubin had been hearing about it for a dozen years, but had never expected to see it built. He looked with heartache at the long ragged gash where the trees had been torn out of the sides of the living hill. Nature itself, inevitably necessary to his sense of who he was or could be, was being disgraced, destroyed. "Willie," he warned himself, "our natural beauty—inspiration, joy, precious possession, goes gurgling down the drain while you sit in your room writing a life of D. H. Lawrence, of which there are presently too many.

Awake, you stupid prick. Stop wasting life's sweet time. Do something to preserve the natural world! Do what has to be done before it can't be any longer!"

Struggling to restrain the dimming that assailed him; to cling to his shaky balance, Dubin, for the first time in his life, fainted away.

A riderless white horse galloped by.

The woman with the broken face, her wasted body swathed in voluminous skirts, pursued him heartbrokenly. Dubin, running for dear life along the rocky shore, his heart pounding beyond belief, sank in exhaustion to the ground. With palms clasped he begged mercy; but it was not the pursuing bitch who'd caught up with him: it was a panting sad-eyed man with a hole in the middle of his face. Now the hole slid across the face, now down. But Dubin glimpsed, through a haze of webbed purple capillaries within, a potato nose and downturned stained mouth from which an ancient rotting voice spoke:

"My name is Richard M. Nixon. I am well-acquainted with your distinguished biography of Abraham Lincoln, my fellow Republican, and I offer you a substantial sum to write one of my life, Mr. Dubin. I've got to get the shit scraped off of my good name."

"And who will scrape it off of mine?"

Kitty, for no reason she could relate, unless it was a hopeful letter she had recently received from the State Department, was sleeping better; but Dubin had caught from her, abetted by the breathless summer, the ailment of sleeplessness. Those you live with teach you. Sometimes she woke and asked him in a whisper if he was sleeping. Knowing that the sound of the human voice invariably set her talking, he stayed silent. Kitty fell back to sleep.

The little Dubin slept each night savaged him. Anything woke him if he momentarily dozed. Any new sound in the night. Or her impassioned breathing during dreams. Or the hint of whistling in his nose. Or his heartbeat drumming in his ears on the pillow. Awake, he feared not sleeping. It took him hours to sleep again, as though for not sleeping the magistrate fined you hours of sleep. He slept a ragged dream-macerated sleep. To break the long wakefulness, Dubin read in the middle of the night. He walked miles in a small room. He took long showers in the dark. If he slept afterward he slept on the knife edge of waking. He must sleep or he couldn't work; wouldn't have the energy even not to work. He feared he would never sleep again. Many were thus afflicted. If he tried pills, although Kitty said he wouldn't, he felt stupid in the morning. The drugged sleep wasted the rest of the day. He would rather be sleepless and work a clear hour or two before his eyelids descended like heavy curtains.

One morning after his alarm had rung, Kitty urged, him, "Sleep, William, I'll take care of you."

He had to get up.

"No you don't. Stay in bed, it's Saturday."

"I've been in bed all fucking night."

He drew on a sock and after five minutes pulled up his pants. Kitty catnapped for a minute, then got into her robe and followed him downstairs.

"Would you like me to scramble you an egg?"

He tried to think.

"Forget your goddamn diet." Then she laughed. Dubin was standing at the kitchen window. Kitty went over to him and said, "Why don't you laugh? She tickled him under the arms. "Where's your funny bone?"

"Not there."

She said she wanted to cry. Resting her head on his shoulder she said she loved him.

After a while he put his arm around her. "I'm a pain-in-the-ass, but try to be patient."

"I can be patient, but how much longer?"

Dubin couldn't say.

"Do it your way," Kitty said, "but *please* do something."

He said he would; she did not ask what.

She hadn't said whether Ondyk had told her they had met on the road.

Dubin saw himself sleeping in a single bed in another house. He slept well there. Would he write better? Would his single life be freer, more varied, joyful? He thought it might in the long run. When he felt better he would ask her to divorce him. Not now but when he was himself once more. Or when he could sleep no longer in this house. That would be a clear sign. He would say he had to leave her because he could not sleep in her bed.

He went relentlessly to his work. Nothing happened. Dubin sobbed noisily.

Kitty knocked on his door. "Can I help?"

He could think of no way.

He wept because his memory was bad. He had at first almost not noticed, or tried not to notice. Recently, forgetting had laid hold hard. It didn't help that Dubin knew Montaigne had complained of a slow mind and incredible lack of memory, despite which he wrote works of genius. Emerson, at sixty-five, was closer to how Dubin felt at fifty-eight: the old man complained of a tied tongue; he said he was "wanting in command of imagery" to match his thought. You had this thing to say and the words would not come; butterflies appeared and flew around the thought. Dubin, against the will, actively forgot names, details, words. He was losing them as though they were coins dropping out of holes in his pockets; or out of his raddled brain. They fell like raindrops into a stream—go find them. Usually when he forgot words he would wait for them to seep back into consciousness like fish drawn up to the hungry surface of a stream. He would remember the initial letter of the forgotten word or sense sounds in it; soon the word reappeared in an illumination. Now words rarely returned when Dubin needed them. He concentrated, trying hard to conjure up a word he could not repossess. It had teased him with its closeness, then burst like a bubble. It was not his to have. He couldn't say what he wanted to; he remained silent.

Dubin forgot what he told himself not to. I'll remember it, he thought, but it hid from him. When he went to bed with a sentence to remember, or one that had come to him as he was trying to sleep, although he kept it alive during the night—unless he wrote it down it had disappeared from his memory by morning. And when he wrote down a sentence, to preserve on paper, it seemed to him he at once forgot a dozen germane to it. As if one sentence is all you are allowed—one to a customer. Or as though someone recites an evil incantation, and therefore a potential paragraph turns to dust. Where are the associations of yesteryear? It was a game of disappearances. Here's this man walking on the road but when you meet up it's his shadow; or it's another man on another road whom you don't remember or even want to know.

Dubin forgot what he read as he was reading it, and much of what he had recently read. Books fell apart in his head; or went up in smoke. He could not repeat, step by step, a long argument. He remembered only the bare bones of what he must know to keep working on his biography. He had notes in place of memory; had to reread often to recall what he had forgotten. He forgot the contents of some of Lawrence's novels; he forgot the arrangement of his Trinitarian metaphysic in the novels. He forgot how important things had happened to him, though not the stations of his short life. When he reread what he had written about him, it seemed to Dubin that someone else had written it. Instead of a chisel he had a hammer to cut stone. I am barely a geographer of D. H. Lawrence. How can my small mind encompass his? *He* forgot nothing.

Augustine had discovered God in his memory: he had left Him there, abandoned Him, and there God had remained. "I recall Thee to my remembrance." God had returned. Dubin discovered realms of space in his memory. Am I forgetting life, or is life forgetting me? He feared telling Kitty what was happening to him, although she sometimes looked as if she knew. Had guessed? What are you forgetting? her eyes seemed to ask. You, Dubin thought, I am forgetting you. What one forgot conceived a further forgetting: a hole unraveling. Unweaving Fanny, he had unwoven the tapestry of their experience. His rotting bones lay amid skeins of memories. Memory cannibalized past experience. It was a maw that ate itself.

He had felt there was much purposeful forgetting in his life; now it *all* seemed purposeful. The purpose was to diminish displeasure, or suffering, or mourning; or simply not to live in active remembrance of the sadnesses of the past. Associative links between one unhappy experience and another had expired in pain and humiliation. He remembered comparatively little of his poor father and crazy mother. His dead brother was drowned in his mind. That had happened almost a half century ago. Dubin had misplaced— displaced?—most of his childhood; he often felt he could replay it minutely; but when he pressed himself to, all he could recall were the bare bones of things. He could remember the color of his mother's eyes, but not their true expression. He remembered only vaguely her features, not the sound of her voice; yet he remembered things she had said. He had once, as a child, noticed menstrual blood on her petticoat and she told him she had had a nosebleed. "There on the back, Mama?" "I turned my head to look for something." After school she gave him a peeled apple with a slice of buttered white bread. When he was sick she mashed a plateful of potatoes in hot milk. One day he had asked her to take him to the movies and she had promised. In those days a child had to ask an adult to take him in and Willie didn't like to. He waited all afternoon for his mother to come down and accompany him to the movies. She came down wearing an old hat. They walked half a block, and then she said she couldn't go, and wept, and went back upstairs. He remembered her grief when her young son was brought home dead. He remembered her thereafter as an insane woman with an altered face and voice, although not much of that time of her life because she was dead before he was fourteen. Once she was in the kitchen, talking sanely to him, when on hearing footsteps in the hall she had with a fearful glance put on her insane face. "Don't go, Willie, out in the rain." She entered his dreams sane and left mad. She began with words of love and ended with sounds that frightened him. He loved and feared her. He forgot words, to forget her; but she, with her fears, lived in his flesh.

When she was dead and he and Charlie Dubin were alone in the house sitting shivah, the waiter sat soaking his purple-veined feet as he read his newspaper. William had felt shame for his father, for his ineffectuality, unwillingness to try to be more than a poor waiter—for hiding his crazy wife in the back bedroom. Without knowing why, as he looked at him, he felt then a sudden keen compassion for the old man. It seemed to the son that whatever else Charlie could or couldn't do, he had done what he had to. The boy was ashamed of having been ashamed of him. Years later he forgave his mother for having lived her insane life in his presence. It was the only life she had to live.

He had told his children little about them, because Charlie and Hannah Dubin had never been present as grandparents. Kitty knew them only as legend. She had met Charlie once and he had tried to please her. Only when Maud had said she wanted to know more about them had Dubin told her at length what he remembered. When he tried to write down what he recalled of their lives, he was surprised at how short an account it had come to. His memories of them had fused into few memories. He had once left himself a week to write about them, but had written all he could in less than two evenings. Where was it all? Where had that part of his life gone? Dubin shook blots out of his fountain pen but could not turn them into words.

Forgetting dimmed the remembering self: kept it in hiding. Often he took in experience, half forgetting. He was not always present in the present; was not always attentive to what was there to be experienced, kept in mind, recalled, remembered. Dubin followed his thoughts where they went, elsewhere. He used to warn himself to observe and remember. He listened carefully to what Kitty said she saw, or had seen: color in colors he hadn't noticed; sounds he hadn't heard. Gerry observed interesting odd combinations of things and events. Maud, in any given experience, saw more details than Dubin saw. He thought he saw whole forms better than they, but wasn't sure. Perhaps he had taken to writing lives in part to teach himself what others saw better. Thoreau looked with eyes, ears and hands, wrote down what he saw, afterward reinvented the world out of his journal. Lawrence observed with genius—a dozen eyes in each eye; saw everything at a glance, retained it, had the language to describe, now or years later, whatever or whomever he had looked at. Kitty, too, saw quickly who was who, though not always what was what. Dubin was a slow study: it took him years to understand who any given man was, including some he thought he had known well; for instance Oscar Greenfeld. He honed his observations in nature on Wordsworth's, Thoreau's, Hardy's; now on Lawrence. Eventually he saw better than he had seen, including inscapes of the self. Dubin sensed what he had forgotten, remembered having lived much in reverie as a youth. There were times he had hidden from life; felt himself, after all these years, doing something of the same now—was walking backward; away from living. He feared the consequences; thought, I must stop that. I must change in some serious way or come to grief.

Kitty put her garden to bed. October was cool sunny warming in the afternoon. He watched her from his window, on her knees, cutting perennial stalks, pulling weeds, pruning, transposing plants. She sprinkled pine needles around rhododendron roots, azalea, mountain laurel. The mountain laurel had done well that summer. Something had done well. A boy she worked with at the Youth Center raked dead leaves. The garden was now for next year. She had complained about autumn flowers, said they didn't grow well for her. Even chrysanthemums, usually an easy flower, had not flourished for her. He imagined the garden under snow.

She came into the kitchen as he stood there with his cup of cold coffee and tiredly washed her hands at the sink. Neither spoke. She opened drawers, looked in them for a while, closed them. She put things away, tidied up mechanically. When they passed in the hall Kitty smiled vaguely. She seemed to be elsewhere; he wasn't sure where she was. Dubin was elsewhere. She was listless, scattered; he hardly recognized her. He hoped someone might help her; he couldn't. One morning she entered his study without knocking and seated herself in the armchair. She had come in, Dubin figured, because she knew he wasn't doing much, as if that made the work interruptible. The thought angered him. She never sat down when he was working well; she'd come in for a stamp or something she had run out of and duck out. Now her presence irritated him, her determined unhappy face, her wilting shoulders. He didn't like the greenish pants or brown blouse she wore. They were colors she punished him with.

Kitty seemed not to know how to begin, then began, sitting stiffly upright, her dark eyes excluding him. This isn't how I want to talk to her, Dubin thought. She ought to think of a better way than to come barging in. It takes two to talk at ease.

"I know who the girl is who was with you in Venice," Kitty said.

"Do you?" Once he hadn't wanted her to know, now he didn't care.

"Fanny Bick," Kitty said coldly. "I don't know why I was so dense in guessing it. I could feel you come alive while she was in the house the summer she worked here. Once I heard you talking together in your study as though you were lovers. They sound like lovers talking, I remember thinking, but I forgot about her when she left. Recently I remembered the airmail letters you were getting from Italy after you came home, then I remembered thinking I'd seen that handwriting before."

Dubin admitted it was Fanny.

"Why didn't you tell me when I asked you?"

"I wasn't out to hurt you."

"It doesn't hurt any the less now."

"I told you I'd had an affair. I didn't say who with."

"Were you ashamed of her?"

"No."

"You took up with her a second time," Kitty said angrily.

He said she had nothing to worry about. "I don't see her any more."

"Did you use to see her in town?"

He said he had.

"Weren't you also seeing her in New York? I suspected you were visiting someone."

He said he had seen Fanny in New York, but that was over now.

"You lied to me?"

"Many times."

"Do you still love her?"

"Still?"

"I assumed you loved her?"

He said he had put her out of his mind.

Kitty's voice wavered. "Why don't you go back to her? Maybe you'd be better off."

She wasn't there to go back to, Dubin said.

"I'll bet you wish she was."

"I wish you'd let up. I wish you'd get out of here."

"Think it over," she said coolly. "You're obviously not getting much from me or giving me very much. If I'm the cause of your discontent, and/or sexual problem, I'm willing to let you go. Some men are impotent only with their wives."

"And some with their mistresses. I read the same chapter you did in that goddamn book."

Though he felt any change would be helpful now, he didn't say it.

"You can leave or I will if you'd rather," Kitty said, seeming to pretend detachment. "We can make the other arrangements later." Her eyes were listless, bruised.

Dubin said if anyone ought to go it should be he.

"Then go," she said bitterly, rising, standing by the chair. "Go today if you want."

He said he couldn't go then. Circumstances weren't right.

"It's your own damn fault. You're crippled out of pride."

"Does Ondyk say that?"

"*I* say it," she shouted. "I also say you can be an awfully stupid bastard. Ask Oscar to toot that in your ear." Kitty slammed the door.

One of his problems, Dubin thought, was that he too often saw himself with her eyes.

He stared out of the window at her shorn garden. He saw her buried in it.

Although his ankle was healed he had not resumed his walk-run on the long road. He had given up losing weight; hadn't the strength to go on with it. Dubin was eight pounds heavier than he'd been early that summer and it was a tight fit into his clothes. He'd had two suits altered by the tailor. "You're bulging," Kitty said. "You ought to go on with your long walks." She piled concern on concern. The husband of a full-time wife is an overworked husband. Whatever she noticed she named. He ate what she fed him —more when she wasn't there: cheese, cake, chocolate. He ate in a hurry, hardly tasting what was in his mouth. It came to nothing: repletion, shame of gluttony. What was happening in his life, the world, in this cursed house, rose to his throat.

Dubin tried sleeping in Gerry's room, in Maud's; it did no good; he could not sleep in three rooms. Kitty asked him to return to their double bed. "What for?" "I sleep better with you there." She seemed newly frightened, as though for her life. She no longer sniffed the burners before going to bed. Her harp rusted. At night Dubin poured himself half a water-glassful of brandy, sipping as he tried to read. Kitty stared at him. Was he saying his thoughts aloud? He asked her and she smiled vaguely. Dubin went to bed drunk, then woke at two. He changed beds, not to awaken her by his restlessness, whispered lamentation. If he woke her she talked. He left the bed at 5 a.m. and dressed in the bathroom. The sky was night-dark, the light of the town rising like silver fumes. There were black trees, then the silver bowl of town, then dark hills. At seven the red sun had burned through the morning mist. His hangover nauseated him. Dubin made coffee. Kitty came down in a gray robe. "It's going to be a beautiful day." He carried his dishes to the sink, trod upstairs to work.

"Fanatic," she cried from the bottom of the stairs. "Fanatic!"

He worked without energy but feared not working. He labored, striving not to forget. He must hold on to the facts and to language. He must keep the right thing in the right place. The facts could be preserved by often studying his note cards, thousands of them. My notes are good, he muttered. I must go on stringing sentences. If I put them together in the right order I can rewrite later, when I feel myself; make what I've written come to life. Breathe into dead words. But the wrong words were coming up too often. When he tried to think of a distinctive synonym of a noun or verb he was down to a rare one or two. He felt for words in a fog, so busy trying to remember that he failed to think. He read the dictionary, then shoved it aside. Language is not life. I've given up life to write lives.

The past when he reached for it was not there. It was hard to sustain that illusion, a colorless weightless fabric that dissolved as he felt for it. He forgot Lawrence's past, did not always remember what went where, came first. Was he seriously sick before his mother died, or sick after? A confusion of villas, countries, complaints. But he lives in his work; who needs me to record how or where he lived outside it?

He searched his files for correspondence with old friends, some who'd been dead for years, to recall who they'd been. What his experience with them had been. He reread Kitty's long letters to him and his to her. Marriage had diminished their variety: one moved to monochrome. Forgetting was without color. He wanted to forget they'd been married as strangers holding to strange pasts. In a sense they were afraid not to be strangers. He wanted to forget that love hadn't come to full-flowering sensuality, as Lawrence had preached it, whatever else it had come to. They had been happy but never sensually so, one with the other. He wanted to forget he did not now love her.

As the days went by, the depression he had held off with upraised hands, as though it was a poisonous cloud, slipped through his fingers and smote him with suffocating force. It fell on his head like a smothering garment. To breathe he pounded his chest, bellowed his name. Dubin felt the entrapment, experienced dullness, nullity. He lived within six sheets of glass, shouting soundless pleas for freedom. He could feel himself cry out but was encased in glass to his head. I am distant to all that surrounds me but my dwarfish scaly self. In reflexive defense he read for the thousandth time: "A grief without a pang, void, dark, and drear." He recited Coleridge's pain to lighten his own and sank into the poet's pit, sipping brandy as the melancholy Coleridge savored tincture of opium. Lawrence, in sickness and depression, lay in bed coughing all night as he stared at a black window. Samuel Johnson sat on a three-legged stool in a tiny room, gazing into a vile abyss. He prayed to God and it came back nought: "My memory grows confused, and I know not how the days pass over me." Dubin knitted and purled the fabric of nothing, entirely nothing. His head shrank as he monotonously recited his name. He went through the movements of life but it was like inching forward on a bed of coals. He could not escape the imprisoning consciousness, the fixed self nailed to its past. He sat alone in a drafty house, forgetting.

A shocking multitude of single hairs appeared in his comb. His chest hair was turning gray. A rotting tooth had to be pulled. He held a book two feet from his face to focus the words. His handwriting grew in size: he'd been avoiding glasses. His haggard face was slack, faded eyes furtively hiding. He looked straight at no one. If he slept he was awakened by cramps twisting his feet. In the dark of night Dubin hopped on the floor to unknot his muscles. Kitty prescribed bananas to supply missing potassium. She knew what was missing. She made banana pudding, baked banana bread. He suffered indigestion, feared an ulcer, eructated, farted. He pissed in a limp stream dribbling in his underpants. Dubin had discovered his prostate. St. Paul might have wished it on fornicators. He had entered the age of aging. I shall never recover what I have lost. He feared illness, immobility; the disgrace of death.

Yet he worked. It was not impossible: the movements of life. He moved his fingers, watched them move. The moving fingers wrote sentences Dubin hadn't invented. He copied them from cards. It meant little but he worked. In the window, the sky was heavy with streamers of moving blue-gray-black clouds blown high from the northeast, eerily, mysteriously floating with outstretched wings, not east but west. A flock of honking geese headed not south but north. He feared their voyage. An avalanche of slashing rivers of rain poured into a forest of raised spears of light. In the dark distance stood winter with its white sword. Dubin shut his eyes not to see what he dared not confront.

Time timed; crept faster. He slept with his watch in his hand. Time tightened its iron fingers around his throat. He turned the clock away, struck it, blinded it. If he thought of tomorrow today withered. Time ran in Dubin; he ran in time. Time excoriated the man from his toenails to the hairs of his head. Stuck its dirty fingers up his old ass. Time preached dying. Life was a trace of dark light in a gaseous entity, a darkly glowing sail in an irradiated universal sea of loss.

Dubin feared ineptitude, imbalance, disorder. The sameness of each boring day slowed the effort to go on. Whispering, sighing, moaning, he raged against the yellow mirror: face of cast-iron gravity; against the crackbrained psychic homunculus. He had done it wrong, made the wrong choices: ought never to have married her; ought never to have let the girl go. In one place he found himself in another. In the bathroom in the cellar. Lost self, selves. Dubin feared his mother's fate, saw her go mad in his looking glass. When had not wanting to live occurred to her?

Or should he burn the book? Free himself from dead life.

A spectral face glowed like a candle flame; waxen, with red beard and rancid enraged ice-blue eyes; he cursed in an agitated high-pitched voice: You rat-faced Jew, I am unknown to you—as Christ is Who was born to the Spirit, Word, the Man, the Male. Your Jew mind is antagonistic to the active Male Principle. You dare not live as man *ought*. Sex, to you, is functional, equivalent to passing excrement. You fear primal impulses. Work which should be an extension of human consciousness you distort to the end-all of existence. You write muckspout lives because you fear you have no life to live. Your impotence is Jewish self-hatred. I detest and loathe you! Mudworm! Dog! *Stay yer bloody distance. Th'art blind to the joy of my life. Tha s'lltna touch me. Burn yer blahsted book for s'lltna live t' see it done!*

Dubin waked running, fearing what he might do. He ran to Gerald's room, pulled up the window, called his name. Gerry, come home. No one in the night replied. He heard Maud whisper to a whispering voice. Her room was empty, white shades drawn. My children, help me—remember the hours I sat by your beds. Kitty lay heavily asleep, openmouthed. He must not wake her, she mustn't see who he was. Downstairs he dialed Ondyk—twelve rings and no reply. Dubin cursed him for sleeping with his phone jack disconnected. I'll go to his house and pound on the door. He ran into the night, feared he would destroy himself or his book.

He drove the circular route backward, his lights plowing the moving haze. At the bridge he turned into a curved lane, then skidded along it into a dirt road, and from there to the other way to the bridge. A dozen times he passed Ondyk's white-framed dark-shuttered house and each time warned himself against his own dreadful pride. At the edge of town he crossed a railroad track against a swinging pendulum signal, as a black locomotive dragging a single freight car loomed out of the churning mist and rumbled by. He drove watching his reflection in the windshield, the overhead light on. A stranger sat in the lit car gloomily crouched over the wheel, driving in the circular dark. Whoever saw him would know he was breaking—had broken—down. Hastily he flicked off the interior light, backed up the car, and drove the opposite way, past Kitty's Wood, the deserted Wilson farmhouse, on the long lonely country road. Here I will live out my days and nights riding forever.

The motor *ping*ed, gave out on the descending road. Dubin jammed his shoe on the gas but nothing came of it. He coasted as far as he could, until the car came to a tedious stop near a dead spruce at the side of the level potholed roadway. He inspected the gas gauge with a lit match. Empty. Kitty clung to his every move. He had asked her to get gas. He turned off the headlights and switched on the flasher. Its orange blinkings lit the heavy-shadowed road. His watch had stopped at one minute past three. Dubin waited in the car, fearing to return home; detested being where he was but did not know where else to go. With both bony hands he fought panic.

The moon rose in a glowing saucer of light in the indigo sky; under it the mountains shone luminously black. In the haze of moonlight on the night field a farmhouse was visible—a light in a window, or perhaps in front of a barn. Dubin's fear of himself rose like a river about to flood. Shoving the car door open he plunged into the rutted field, running in the soft earth toward the farmhouse, skirting a section of withering silage corn. Nearby stood a grove of trees. Approaching them, he lost sight of the light. He was not sure where the trees were in relation to the farmhouse, if it was a farmhouse. Then he spied the light through the trees. Dubin trod on dead leaves in the dimly lit wood of maples and oak wearing tatters of brown foliage. If it was a farmhouse he would watch a minute to see if anyone was up before he went to the door.

He would knock, he thought, and tell whoever answered that his car had broken down. He would ask to use the telephone and try Ondyk again. He would rather call Oscar Greenfeld but felt he couldn't. He did not want to go home. He did not want to be near the manuscript. If he called Kitty he would ask her to hide it. Dubin thought that if the farmer would drive him to the bus station he would take an early bus to New York City. There he would phone Kitty and tell her where he had abandoned her car, but not where he had holed up. He would say he'd get in touch with her when he felt himself again, whenever that was. When he had been away from her for a while. He could not imagine what he would do with himself in the city. He wondered if Maud would leave the Zen commune to come see him in New York. He did not think she would. He did not think he would ask her.

He heard a growling bark of a dog and retreated into the wood. His testicles shrank. The thought of a dog to contend with was more than he could bear. Why hadn't he waited in the car till morning, or got a hitch on the highway and tried Ondyk again? What farmer in his right mind would open his door to a stranger's knock at this time of the night? I'd better get out of here before the dog sniffs me. Was the animal leashed? He listened for the clink of a chain but heard none. Nor did he hear a barking dog. Dubin moved stealthily back through the trees. When he came out of the wood he saw no cornfield in the darkened moonlight. It would have to be on the other side of the wood—a larger wood than the grove of trees he had imagined. He must go carefully not to alert the dog, chain or no chain. Once he got to the cornfield and saw his flasher in the road he'd know where he was, at least for the moment.

The moon slowly moved behind a darkly glowing white cloud mass, and Dubin saw by the light of a cluster of bright stars that he was standing in an unfenced small graveyard, perhaps a family cemetery. He sank down to see who his company was. He touched the nearest stone slab with his fingers but the carved limestone letters had been eroded by wind and rain, the snow, the seasons. Whoever lay dead there was not saying who he had been. Crawling to the next grave, he felt the slender long headstone above it, and found it too was effaced. He rose to his feet, and as the clouds broke and moonlight flooded the graveyard, he discovered to his horrified surprise that the stone he had touched had been erected before an open grave. Dubin ran.

As he came into the moonlit wood to try to find his way back to the cornfield, he heard what he thought was a rushing wind and listened in fright as it became the sound of an animal coming at him through the spattering dead leaves. Dubin stood momentarily immobilized, then with a choking cry tore his belt out of his pants, and as the dog hurtled up at him, swung at it in panic with the belt buckle. The silver buckle struck the dog's skull with a thud-like crack. The animal yelped, withdrawing with a whimpering snarl. Dubin, dropping the belt, rushed to a tree and jumped for a low limb. He lifted his leg over it as the dog with a snarling growl flung himself up at him, fastening its slobbering teeth into his right shoe, as he tried in terror to drag himself up the tree. He was unable to move. The dog, its eyes glowing yellow, clung like a deadweight to his foot.

"Help," Dubin cried. "Help me!"

The door of the farmhouse, twenty feet away, shot open, and through the trees he saw a somber oblong of light as a burly man with a rusty pistol appeared in the lit doorway. The man raised the gun and fired into the wood.

"Git 'im!"

The dog quivered and fell to the ground at Dubin's feet, growling throatily, threshing its legs as though running a race it had long ago lost.

Dubin dropped from the branch and ducked through the brush. With a cry the farmer holding his smoking pistol came charging into the wood. A moan of deep-boweled lamentation rose like slow smoke. Dubin heard a bullet thwack into a tree as several dead leaves fluttered down on his head. For a minute he ran in a circle, then stepped into the crotch of a two-trunked oak with ragged low boughs. Catching one, he managed to pull himself up into the oak's bare crown. He shinnied and climbed, straining, writhing, until he was fifteen feet above the ground, where he watched through the branches the white-faced farmer hunting him with a gun.

"I'll git you for murderin' my dog, you homusexual bastard!" He was a large-faced gray-haired man in a white undershirt, dirty work-pants, earth-stained leather boots. His face poured sweat as he wandered in the gloomy wood. He seemed dazed, frightened, mourning his dog.

Dubin shivered in the cold tree. He was moved to call out—beg the man's pardon, explain what had happened tonight, perhaps tell him the story of his life—why it had brought him at this moment to this wood. But he dared not utter a sound—felt the farmer would shoot at his voice. He'd be dead before he could identify himself—a madman hiding in a stranger's tree.

The farmer sank to his knees before his dead dog, its head and neck dark with blood. He lay with his cheek on the dog's flank, his shoulders shaking. Dubin, watching from above, thought: At midnight I was in bed unable to sleep, and a few hours later am up somebody's tree after causing him to kill his dog. He regretted there wasn't time to live more than once and maybe do things better another time.

To his dismay, the burly farmer, rising, began to shoot into the trees. He would stand under one, grimly shoot a bullet into it, then pass to the next. "I'll git you, you-Jew-son-of-a-bitch, one way or t'other!"

Dubin, on the verge of calling out who and where he was, held back, fearing the man would fire before he had two words out. He saw himself fall to the ground like an ungainly huge bird.

The farmer aimed his pistol and shot into Dubin's tree. The bullet broke a branch over his head; it brushed his face as it cracked through others on its way to the ground. To keep himself from falling, he clasped the trunk of the rough oak with both arms.

The gun banged twice more as the man aimed at nearby trees. When the pistol was empty, he stumbled into the house, probably to reload. Dubin began hastily to descend, but before he could get halfway down, the farmer reappeared with a quilted blanket and tenderly covered his dead dog. Lifting the animal as if it were a child, he carried it into the wood. Dubin knew an empty grave where he could bury it.

It had begun to rain. The moon had gone; the wood was pitch-black. He slid down the tree, his raw hands bleeding. Avoiding the wood where the farmer had disappeared, he ran in the brush through the trees into the open.

Skirting the lit narrow farmhouse, Dubin ran in the wet dark, expecting a bullet in the back of his head.

Then he saw the cornfield. In the rain he trotted alongside the rows of silage corn, the stalks sighing in the wet. As he turned the end of the sloping field, he beheld through trees the blinking orange light of Kitty's car on the road. In a few minutes he was in it, drenched to the flesh, his teeth chattering. His watch read a minute after three.

Dubin sat exhausted in the freezing car, waiting for morning. He tried to sleep but his consciousness was lit like a lamp. He could not put out the light in the dark. When the sky turned gray he staggered out of the car, came back to lock it, and in the misty drizzle headed toward the highway. As he walked the wet road Dubin thought of the long night. His panic was gone. He knew where he had left it, but not where it would find him again. He promised himself to send the old farmer a dog.

I've had it with testing myself, he thought. Du bist Dubin. I know who I am—well enough to take the next necessary step. I learn best when struggling with the work—with the lives I write. Tomorrow I'll go on with it or I may find myself up another tree, trying to change my life. I must stop running from Lawrence dying. I must act my age.

A dog barked shrilly in the nearby woods, and Dubin began to run. He ran poorly, hardly a trot, came to a stop in a few paces, hobbled on. Until this night he hadn't run in an age. He could not run now. If a dog appeared out of the trees he could do nothing but cry murder. He was holding his pants up with his hand. Blood oozed from the toe of the shoe the dog had torn; he was limping.

As he crossed the wet highway in predawn traffic, a car with blazing lights bore down on him. Dubin waved both arms, crying out a warning. The lights dimmed but the car, after hesitating, again came at him. With a cry he broke into a limping run, holding his pants. A horn honked. The auto stopped with a clonk abreast the biographer running in the highway, a door fell open. "I thought it was you, get in, William." She was wearing her blue-tinted glasses. The car was warm. He slid in with relief and gratitude. Fanny, calling Dubin lover, said she had come back to stay. Was it this, he wondered, he had earned tonight?

Nine

He remembered Dr. Johnson in the marketplace at Uttoxeter, standing bareheaded in the rain where his father's bookstall had been. Years before, the old bookseller, ailing that day, had asked his son to go there in his place and the son had refused. "Pride prevented me." Fifty years later Samuel Johnson, an old man, laboriously journeyed to the market and stood an hour in the rain by the stall his father had once used, to do for the dead man what he hadn't done.

Oscar Greenfeld appeared in the hospital room.

He had come to see Dubin because his own brush with death had revived in him a sense of their old friendship.

The biographer, recovering from bacterial pneumonia, thanked him; pointed to a leather chair. He was lying on a raised pillow watching the green-streaked short November sunset. Each was moved. Each tried not to notice how old they were becoming. Both for a while sat in silence.

Greenfeld then told Dubin the joke about the rabbi who when his shammes prayed, "Dear God, I am nothing, you are everything," remarked, "Look who says he's nothing."

Dubin laughed fruitily.

Oscar placed on the bed the book he had picked up on the chair: "I'd have thought Lawrence."

"Montaigne," Dubin said, "premeditating death as premeditation of freedom."

"Why bother?" The flutist coughed raucously, wiping his mouth with a handkerchief. "Not to worry, I am not contagious."

Dubin said that sometime after an accidental foretaste of death in a collision on horses with a servant riding forth to greet him, Montaigne had concluded that death was of minor concern to him. "He felt if we don't know how to live it's wrong to teach ourselves to die and so make the end inconsistent with the whole."

"He's got his nose in his belly button," Oscar said in irritation.

"He had no belly button," Dubin snapped.

"He sounds like Buddha."

"In the end the great sound alike."

"Are you afraid of death?"

"No more than ever."

"After my heart attack I got fed up with the way it buzzed in my mind. To save my sanity I stopped thinking."

"I have to know."

"So much is evasion, illusion. How often do we truly know what is? Do I know you? Do you know me? I thought you and I agreed on that?"

"It's a practical thing," Dubin said gloomily. "I'm tired of the number of times I make the same error. One fails at a certain point when he continues to fail."

"My sense of it," Greenfeld said, "is that there is little serious changing of self in life, no matter what one knows. Who knows how to change? It comes or it doesn't. I don't say one mayn't try to make the wrong thing harder to repeat—sometimes he succeeds, usually no. I'd rather concentrate on improving my fluting."

Dubin said he wanted to know what a man his age ought to know.

"Wasn't it your friend Lawrence who insisted there's no knowing one's way through life?"

Dubin admitted it. "He lived in his own personal mystery, infinitely expanded. I won't relinquish for myself what he failed to know about himself."

"Forgive him: he wrote well and died young."

325

Oscar had brought with him his leather case and began to assemble his silver flute on the chair he'd been sitting in.

Dubin, as he watched, mused: "I thought biography—the thousands of lives I've read and the few I've written—would make the difference between badly and decently knowing. I thought I would know, at my age, what to do when I had to."

"Still into knowing? Your friend says in an unforgettable passage you read me once to let life invade you. Don't prejudge a flower or the blue sky. Here, William, let me play you, please, a song of Schubert's I've just transcribed —"Seufzer," a good word for "Sighs.""

Wetting his lips, he played the lied with silvery intensity, moving his head as he moved his fingers. The notes were light clear liquescent.

In the growing dark Dubin listened to the fluting melody of unfulfilled wanting: *"Denn ach, allein irre ich in Hain."*

"Not me," the man in the bed insisted. "I've had it with loneliness. I've had it with youth. I'll take only what I'm entitled to."

"A ripe old age?"

"I'm an odd inward man held together by an ordered life."

Oscar unscrewed the flute and placed the parts in its velvet-lined case.

"It's a song, a short song, all I can offer."

He was, at that time of his life, a thin man with saddened eyes and a hacking cough, except when he played his flute. When he played he was a young man with a silvery voice.

Sunset had turned the clouds light-green streaked with charcoal. When Oscar left it was night.

"Will you want the light on?" he asked as he was going.

"It's mad to die," Dubin passionately cried.

"Flora," said Oscar, "sends her best."

"Please give her mine."

They kissed in the dark and parted.

"Can't we go on being lovers?"

If it was the wrong question how do you know till you ask?

Fanny and Dubin were standing at the long narrow window that Myra Wilson used to call "the west parlor window," where she had often watched sunsets; often with Kitty Dubin, who afterward described them to her husband. Kitty collected sunsets. Fanny's hair was loosely braided into a pigtail halfway down her back. Both were wearing coats and wool hats—Dubin his red, Fanny a beige hat pulled down over her ears—in the cold farmhouse as they gazed through the slightly distorted green glass at the long stretch of weedy snow that went on for miles to the dense gray forest rising beyond the fields of Fanny's farm. She had bought it with her inheritance. Her mother had died of a stroke that past summer. "I got half of what she left, my sister the other half. My mother is the only person I feel really loved me."

Dubin did not protest nor deny.

She told him that her father, recovered from his recent illness, had gone with a chick to the South of France. "Don't expect anything more," he had said to Fanny. "Whatever you're getting out of my pocket you got from your mother."

"I don't expect a thing from you, you ape," she said she had said.

Dubin, as father, winced.

She had soon thereafter driven across the country to Center Campobello, not exactly sure why. "Except that I like small Northeastern towns, even if they are too freaking cold. But I love to live in the country and already have friends here. A lot of young people are coming into the area, buying farmhouses, some doing marginal farming as well as things of their own." Not long after her arrival she had seen, bargained for, and bought the Wilson farm.

That's for a long time to come, Dubin thought.

He asked Fanny why she hadn't been to see him at the hospital after delivering him there the rainy morning he became ill. Their present meeting, as they gazed out of the window, one overcast frozen day in December, was their first since he had left the hospital.

"I phoned but wouldn't go because I didn't want to walk into your wife."

Her plain face was serious, light-green eyes distant, calm as they talked; but she hadn't once laid a finger on his arm in the intimate way she had. There was no more than an inch between them where they were standing. It was that kind of window: to see out of it together two had to be standing close. Dubin did not touch her because he sensed she wasn't about to touch him. It was a game of losses: probability annulled possibility.

"About that question you asked me," Fanny at last said, "I don't think I ought to go on sleeping with you as we used to, William. I have my own life to live."

It was the wrong question: he oughtn't to have asked, at least not now.

"I know the good things about you," she said. "And I know you understand me. I even feel you love me in your way but I still can't sleep with you. I have to look out for myself and you're not free to be with me. But I would like to be friends, William, if you want to be mine if we don't go to bed any more. I came back here to find something different for myself, something that might last—which doesn't mean going on sleeping with a married man. I have to be careful of my future. It's my life and I have to respect it."

He nodded sagely, as though he had put the words in her mouth.

"Still," Dubin said, "if it was over between us, past redemption, what drew you back? Was it Roger?"

"Not really," Fanny answered with a quivering yawn, "although I'm glad he's here just as much as I am you are. I'm not sure why or when I made up my mind to come back. Part of it was because I went to U.C.L.A. last summer and got enough credits for a B.A. degree, which N.Y.U. says it will give me in January. I finally got that done partly because of you—because I wanted to show you I could—but most of all because I want to go on to the next step of my life. I think I have got my head together by now. I wasted all I want to waste of life. If I waste more it's cutting my bone. I feel this is the right scene for me. I've always had a nice feeling about being in the country, as if something good might happen to me here."

"Did you foresee a farm in your life? I never heard you say so."

"Not necessarily a farm but something to do with the earth—with having land. I don't know much about nature but now I would like to. There are new things in my thoughts that tie up with some that are old."

Dubin, in a stray thought, remembered her lying receptive to him in a field of flowers.

"I had this shrink once," Fanny said, "who said because my father was so flighty and unconcerned I had this image of myself with roots in the earth. I've often felt I wanted to dig my hands into soil and make something grow."

Dubin wondered if she felt the sexuality of the earth. "You're a vital sexual creature, Fanny—in a good sense."

She laughed breathily. "Anyway I'm not oversexed, although I think my father thought I was."

"I never thought so."

"I liked it when you once said I celebrate life with my sexuality."

He said so had he with her.

"Craig Bosell's brother-in-law," Fanny went on, as Dubin in silence lamented his loss, "wants to rent twenty-five acres of my land to put in corn and soybeans. I will plant a vegetable garden next to the house and besides that I already have six goats in the barn and a dozen Rhode Island Reds that I handle myself. I had a course in animal husbandry last summer and it's not all that hard if you have patience and don't mind getting your hands in animal shit. I think I can support myself with what I grow and earn on this farm. I'm sure I will get along although all I have left in cash is six thousand of the forty-eight I got from my mother."

"Why did you buy the farm outright? Why didn't you take a mortgage and leave yourself more cash?"

"I felt I wanted to completely own my property when I moved in."

"Fanny Farmer," Dubin said with a limp laugh this winter's day.

She tittered.

Lifting his hat, he said he had to be going.

Raising her arm, she showed him she still wore his bracelet.

Fanny then embraced Dubin and he was about to pull her into a desperate clinch until he realized she was hugging him formally, as if he were her cousin Alfred if she had one; and Dubin felt this was indeed the coup de grace—their affair had run its course.

He trotted all the way home but had to walk back for the car.

That night after supper, Dubin, repossessed by desire, waited in the auto, parked without lights beyond a stand of sugar maples fifty feet up the road from Fanny's farmhouse. The biographer had sad thoughts of free will; of functioning and failing at this time of his life. Greenfeld was right about significant change in a man's life: as you were grooved so you were graved. He berated himself for spying on the girl, fried himself alive. He could not justify his renascent jealousy; lived badly with it. It had, against his will, boiled up, monotonizing feeling, wearying, irritating him; but there was no escaping it. You fled; it grabbed you by the cock and swung you round. Why be jealous now they had formally buried the corpse of their intimate relationship? No rational answer to an irrational response; yet he waited to see if Roger Foster showed up, not knowing what he would say or do if the youth did. Would a fistfight settle anything more than Dubin's hash?

The light went out in the farmhouse kitchen, then bloomed upstairs in Fanny's bedroom. The girl didn't know that Myra Wilson had died in that room or would she have slept elsewhere? Yet there was something chaste about a young woman sleeping alone in a room where a courageous old woman had died. Dubin, when the bedroom light went out, drove home.

That was Tuesday. He waited three more nights before Roger appeared on Friday after eight, in his father's one-ton truck. The biographer ducked the truck's brights, fearing he would be spotlighted like a hooked fish on the front seat; but the road curved where he was parked and the lights lit up several sparse elms on the other side. Roger drove into the farmhouse driveway and rang the rusty bell on the door. Dubin kept himself out of sight as Fanny's dog, Snowdrop, a golden Labrador that looked almost white at night, came woofing out of the house as she, in calf-length yellow boots and padded jacket, held the door open for her guest.

The dog sniffed at Roger and was let loose. Snowdrop, frisking through the snow, his tag tinkling, found Dubin's car, where the driver sat motionless on the qui vive, ready to turn on the ignition and take off if the beast barked loudly. Snowdrop, instead, sniffed at the left front tire, pissed a steaming stream on it, and trotted up the road. Dubin waited five minutes, then got out of the car and approached the house.

What were they up to in Myra's old-fashioned parlor? He trod in the soft snow around to the back of the farmhouse, sinking to the tops of his carefully buckled galoshes; listened at the narrow window, his cold ear pressed to the side of the house where he could see an avocado plant Fanny had in a white wooden tub a few feet behind the windowsill. She had kept Myra's worn leather armchairs but had replaced the stuffed velveteen sofa with a slim tan one along modern lines.

It was that they were no doubt occupying. He strained to see. What a base thing to be doing, Dubin—at your age a Peeping Tom. He observed himself staring at them through the avocado leaves, a gray-haired old man with thick salt-and-pepper sideburns and jealous eyes. What if they spotted him spying, to his eternal humiliation? His heart raced but he remained rooted there, ears straining, and heard Roger ask, "Are you still seeing the guy?" Fanny replied, "We're friends but nothing more. I told him so the other day."

There has to be more to it than she says, the old man thought.

The Labrador ran up to Dubin with a throaty growl.

"It's me, Snowdrop," he whispered, experiencing excruciating déjà vu. We met Monday. You sniffed me up and down."

Fanny appeared at the window, shading her eyes; peered out. After a minute she left. Would she go to the door? My God, what will I say?

Dubin walked backward, the dog persisting, harrying him, growling, now and then letting out a sharp bark. The biographer instinctively moved toward some trees. The dog, snorting, snapped at his sleeve. Dubin tore it free. The animal jumped for his face. He forcefully shoved it aside, fearing exposure, disgrace. Fanny hadn't yet come out. Dubin was about to make a run to his car but the hound was being playful, so he stopped in his flight to rub its head, and Snowdrop licked his gloved hand. In another minute he had made it into the auto, slamming the door and pressing down the lock button. Saved by Fanny: her affectionate nature conditions the likable hound. If it weren't hers the dog would have mangled me. Snowdrop raised his leg, wet the other tire. Dubin started the car after Roger left the farmhouse. He drove for a while, returning to see Fanny's orange light go on upstairs. He rode home, more or less content.

Two days after, the evil effects of his nature caught up with him. Fanny had seen him through the window. "I know that was you spying on us last night," she wrote. "Please don't come here any more. I don't want to have the shame of seeing you do anything like that again."

Barely able to stand himself, Dubin drove to the farmhouse. Fanny was in the barn feeding a pregnant Nubian goat. Bosell had built stalls for the goats and repaired the henhouse for the dozen Reds.

She stared at a panful of brown eggs she had collected as Dubin apologized. "To tell the truth, Fanny, I was a victim of a fit of unreasoning jealousy. Forgive me, my feeling for you is immense."

"What would you say if I told you I'd had an abortion last summer?" she asked wearily, grimly.

"I'd regret it."

"I don't. I never really cared for the guy."

"I regret that too."

"What else do you regret?"

"That I wasn't single and closer to your age when we met."

"What are you really saying?"

"Let's go on for a while. Let's see what happens."

"I can't," she said flatly, nasally, her stiffened eyes fixed on his face. "I wish you wouldn't ask me that any more."

"I won't," he said compassionately. Dubin hurried out of the barn and drove at once to Winslow. After searching through a tray of rings at a jeweler's he found one he liked, a hammered gold band with six glowing rubies. He wrote out a check for $450.

Dubin picked up a hothouse gardenia for Fanny and peacefully drove back to Center Campobello. He would give her the gift and depart. At the barn door he met Bosell, who said he thought Fanny had gone into the house to nap.

He tried writing her a note on the parlor table. Dubin wrote two: "From a former lover who never made it as a friend." And since that didn't say much, tried "Goodbye, dear Fanny, with thanks for all *you* gave me." He left neither. He left the ring in its blue velour box and the gardenia in a glass of water. He hurried up the driveway to his car.

A window was noisily raised at the front of the house. "William!"

Dubin trotted back.

Fanny had come downstairs after her nap. Her face was refreshed, softened, flushed by sleep. She was standing at the parlor table, wearing Dubin's ruby ring and holding his white flower.

"It looks like a wedding ring. I feel like a bride."

The flickering red candle Fanny had left on the bookcase gave forth a darkish private light.

She had put on Bach: *Ein feste Burg ist unser Gott . . .*

They had eaten in the parlor and were now in her bedroom, deceptively small in the shadowy light. Fanny, in her see-through caftan, wearing white bra and black underpants, pattered in bare feet from bathroom to bedroom, watering her potted plants out of a drinking glass.

The bedroom was furnished as her city apartment had been, with the exception of Myra's standing lamp with its large orange shade: the same chairs, pictures on the walls, even the colored snap with pigeons in San Marco, the same books in the bookcase; almost everything but the single bed —double in the city. What this meant he seemed to think he knew. Dubin, listening to the choral bang of the cantata, sat in striped boxer shorts and undershirt, his clothes piled on a straight-back chair, black winter shoes stuffed with black socks tucked under it. In the bathroom he combed his gray hair with her slightly soiled bone comb and rinsed his mouth. Fanny had once instructed him to urinate before getting into bed. "You'll come better." She educates me. He was grateful.

Wohl auf, der Bräutigam kömmt . . .

She glanced at him momentarily anxiously as he took the water glass from her hand and held it as they kissed. Their first kiss, after a season of separation, loss, before renewing joy, hurt. Dubin set the glass down and began to unbraid Fanny's warm hair. She shook it out, heavy full. Her shoulders, breasts, youthful legs, were splendid. He loved her glowing flesh. Fanny removed her heart-shaped locket and his bracelet, placing them on the bookcase near the dripping red candle. She kept the ruby ring on. Forcefully she pulled his undershirt over his head; he drew down her black underpants. Fanny kissed his live cock. What they were doing they did as though the experience were new. It was a new experience. He was, in her arms, a youthful figure. On his knees he embraced her legs, kissed her between them.

So geh herein zu mir,
Du mir erwälte Braut!

She led him to bed, flipped aside the blanket. He drew it over their hips.
"Hello, lover."
"Hello, my child."
"I'm not your child."
"Hello, dear Fanny."
They wrestled in her narrow bed, she with her youth; he with his wiles. At her climax Fanny's mouth slackened; she shut her eyes as though in disbelief and came in silence.

Mit harfen und mit zimbeln schön.

Dubin slept with his arms around her; she with her hand cupping his balls.

When he awoke that Christmas-day morning he felt, as he stared at the bedroom floor, that weeds were growing between the boards. Kitty, awake, said, "If I am born again I hope it will be with B-cup breasts."

"Don't get up," she said. Sitting, she drew off her blue-flowered nightgown and moved toward him. Dubin lay back. Though he willingly embraced her warm familiar body he felt no stirring of desire. She held his phallus but it lay inert.

Kitty, lying motionless, her head on his breast, shifted to the edge of the bed and lay looking out the window.

Dubin said he was sorry.

"You're doing this to punish me."

"What for?"

333

"For being who I am. For having married you. Because you lived your life with me."

"I lived with you willingly."

"I think you willed it."

"I will waking up, for Christ's sake. I will my goddamned work. There are times I will living."

"Love can't be willed."

"There is a will-to-love."

"The thought depresses me."

"Don't let it," he shouted at her.

"Oh crap," said Kitty.

"Don't piss on the past. Don't deny the love I felt for you because you don't think I feel it now."

"I know you don't."

"I'm saying not to deny I loved you."

"What good is that to me now?"

"It preserves the past. It keeps you from making something into nothing."

"When I was a little girl I used to fantasy a church bell tolling when someone was advising me to count my blessings if I was feeling loss. I remember the sound."

"Why bother?"

"Don't feel superior to me. You're the one who's impotent."

He didn't say whom he was not impotent with.

You tell the truth, Dubin thought, it stands erect, finds the well. You lie as I lie to her it plays dead. She gets no use of it.

Kitty, on her back, monotonously recited complaints he had heard many times in many voices:

"We were never passionately in love. I suppose it was a mistake to have got married. I should have waited. We had the best of intentions, and hopes, but it was surely a mistake. What you lack of love in marriage, of true passion, if you're me, you never make up. You miss it always, even when, I suppose, you oughtn't to. I went through my young married life telling myself the good things I had—my home, children, hardworking faithful husband—a decent life, surely—but I missed something."

"The bell tolled?"

"Often."

334

"Tough," Dubin said. "Whatever you missed you'd have missed with any man. Marriage doesn't make up for what life fails to deliver."

"With some it does, the right marriage."

"Yes, for a while, but a time comes when you miss what you've always wanted more of. I would have lacked something with any woman I married."

"We missed more, married to each other. The kids missed something too. They sensed our lack of deep love for each other. Both of them sensed it and I'm sure it bothered them."

"People bother people. If it was there to sense I'd want them to."

"They were hurt by our tensions, irritations, quarrels. We pretended a better relationship than we had."

"Doesn't everyone? You put it together as best you can. You protect it."

"It was not the best of marriages." Kitty wept briefly into the pillow.

Dubin lay on his side, his back to her, trying to tote it up as a fairly decent marriage. Not in this mood.

She blew her nose. Shifting into dispassion, she told him she had dreamed that she had bought a plane ticket to Amsterdam to see the spring tulips but had landed, instead, in Newark, New Jersey, where William Dubin lived with his parents.

"I went up a couple of rickety flights of stairs in a broken-windowed tenement, but when I got to your door I was afraid to ring. Finally I had to. I was a widow with a child, who needed help. I'd been told you were looking for a wife. The door opened, and a woman ran down the hall and hid in the bathroom. I came across you in a small room at the end of a hallway. You were a man with earlocks and dark lonely eyes. You were wearing a yarmulka and studying a book in Hebrew. The letters looked like broken bits of a puzzle. This man is a rabbi, I thought. It would be a mistake to marry him."

"Marry a Jew?"

"A rabbi. Someone who, for obvious reasons, would never be devoted to me."

"What brought you to a rabbi?"

"My peculiar fate. He knew about me when I arrived and said he would marry me. I wept."

"Why would a rabbi marry you?"

"I don't know."

335

"Why didn't you go home and marry someone else?"

"I couldn't."

Afterward, Kitty said, "I'm sure I failed you more than I thought, but that's just the point—I would have done better with someone more like myself. You should have married a Jewish woman who was better put together and needed less attention, someone who slept nights and wouldn't keep you awake. You'd have waked fresh as a daisy, running to work."

"Who would you have done better with?"

Her eyes were moist. "If Nathanael hadn't died."

"I wish to God he hadn't."

After a long hesitation, Dubin, turning to her, said their talk was self-defeating.

"I'm not afraid of the truth, are you?"

"What truth are we telling each other?"

"That we live side by side but not together. We live in the same house, but I can float around for days yet not make contact with you. After your affair with Fanny in Venice, the feeling we had for one another that we'd kept more or less intact, began to unravel. You speak of a will-to-love. If what I get is what you've willed there's not much to sustain me."

"You make it sound more negative than it was, or is. Will or no will, I've always appreciated you as a woman."

"I want more than appreciation."

"So it was a bad marriage?"

She was observing him gravely, uneasily, sadly. "It's not much of one, I'm afraid. Not any more. I have to be honest."

He damned her honesty, felt at a loss, had not wanted to fail in marriage. "Then I owe you an apology," Dubin said.

"I admit we tried, but we aren't sufficiently suited to each other or there'd be less holding back, much more giving. That has to be said."

"Who I am is not Nathanael?"

"He was in love with me when we got married. I loved him. He wanted me close by. He did not resent me for needing him. He wasn't cold to me, even when I made the mistake of being cold to him."

"Nate the saint, except when he bopped you in the eye?"

"He was dreadfully sorry for that. He was a good man. He gave affection easily."

"Once I had the impression I was giving you love," Dubin said. "It felt

336

like love, but maybe less came across than I thought. Maybe at most I was thinking I was giving love, a rationale or self-deception suiting your needs to my ethic or aesthetics, or both."

He had thought this before but had never said it to her. Kitty listened as though she had often heard it.

"I don't suppose it's very hard to fool yourself about loving," Dubin went on. "It isn't easy to give if you're anchored in an involved subjectivity. Some people complicate their feelings in self-protective ways. I must be one of them. You think you're sailing with a cargo of love, but never deliver because you haven't hoisted anchor, although you have the illusion you had."

"You're erecting a monument to impossibility— Why I never really loved my wife."

"I'm trying to respond to your argument. On the other hand, not all are receptive to those who've taught themselves to love a little. I imagined love for you. To me it felt like love. I thought you could feel it coming from me —I think you did, but maybe less than I imagined, as though I'd set the thermostat to warm but you, with your nature, never got over feeling chilly in our house."

Dubin said he regretted that. He regretted Dubin, the lacking man. "I regret he comes out meager when he means to be generous, potent, large in love."

"You're not large in love."

"To be honest," he confessed, sitting up with the force of his insight, "William Dubin, the biographer, is grateful to you for having through the years described to him what his lacking love, lacking nature, come to—for having kept him up with himself so that he could be a truthful measure, as well as recorder, of the lives of those he writes about, and therefore a better biographer."

Kitty got out of bed, tight-jawed. "It's more of the same, another denial of me. Everything sooner or later goes back to your biographies. That's your grand passion—if you could fuck your books you'd have it made."

"I'd rather do the same for you."

"No, you wouldn't," she cried. "You could if you wanted to. Your explanation of your rationale is itself a rationale. I sense something unsaid, as though you were evading truth in pretending to tell it."

It's a way of life, the biographer thought. I must stop thinking of myself as a truthful man.

As they were dabbling at breakfast, Kitty, struggling for control, said as she tremblingly poured his coffee, "I hear someone has bought the Wilson farm."

He said he hadn't heard about it.

On New Year's Day night, Dubin trudging up the snowy road to the farm, was caught in the flaring lights of a truck that had backed out of Fanny's driveway. He'd been thinking of his desire for her; it was sometimes only desire. Was it, too, a lacking love?

The driver brought the truck to a stop. "Is that you, Mr. Dubin?" He had poked his head out of the window.

"Dubin," said the biographer, shielding his eyes in the light, as he stood by a snowbank.

The truck lights went off. "Roger Foster here. I want you to know I intend to wait you out for Fanny. I got a long life ahead of me."

Dubin said his father was a waiter.

He jogged past the truck.

Roger drove on with his lights off.

One winter's late-afternoon Maud Dubin arrived home with her large suitcase and duffel bag and went at once up to her old room to sleep. "For a visit?" Dubin asked his wife when he returned after a quick hour at the farm. "She's pregnant," Kitty said unhappily. He was overwhelmed by a long sense of loss. He had been concerned with Maud rarely lately and castigated himself for it.

"How many months?" he afterward asked.

"Probably two." Kitty paced around the room with her hands clasped.

"Has she spoken of an abortion?"

"She wants to have the baby." Her unhappiness yielded a tender smile; she loved little babies.

Maud slept fifteen hours and in the early morning appeared in her father's study in bathrobe and boots. She laid down on his desk a pack of cigarettes and book of matches. Her face was fresh after sleep and a shower, her eyes trying to be calm.

He knew she had never liked talking to him in his study—he was, she had said, *always* there. "Would you rather talk in your room," Dubin asked, "or maybe go for a walk later?"

She said she would rather talk now.

He thought of the child she had been and was once more aware of loss. Of what? That he hadn't married her? That his love could not control her fate? He hid from her his sense of desecrated life.

Maud lit a cigarette, her hand trembling. "Mother said she's told you? Not much of an annunciation, I'm afraid."

"I hate accidents determining people's fates," Dubin said.

"I've made my peace with it."

He advised her not too quickly to make peace. Maud smoked silently.

He wanted to put his arms around her—his daughter, who ran through experience as though she was slicing bread—but sensed she would rather he didn't.

"It's hard to believe. I pictured you chaste in Zen."

"Believe," Maud said dryly.

"This is what satori came to?"

"Do you really want to know?"

He nodded, wanting to know but not to hear.

She said a letter had come after she'd been four months at the commune —"from a man I've had a long affair with. He asked to see me. I thought I wouldn't—I was the one who had broken it off but maybe the Zen hadn't taken—I was finding it hard to concentrate. And I kept on thinking of you telling me to remember I was Jewish and live in the real world. Anyway, I saw him again and got pregnant."

He sighed. "So I helped initiate the conception?"

"Don't be ironic, Papa."

"I'm bitter."

"Don't be, I'm not. The Zen Master asked me to stay in the commune. He said I could have my baby there and the commune would help me to take care of it. They are incredibly kind people but I felt I had no right to stay because I had failed their teaching. So I went home."

"Does the man know you're pregnant—the father, or whatever you call him?"

"You call him the father, he's a fatherly man."

"Does he know?"

She shook her head.

"Why haven't you told him?"

"It wouldn't do any good—he's married."

After a while Dubin asked, "Any chance of his divorcing his wife?"

Her complexion reddened. "I wouldn't say so. He's about your age and has been married thirty-five years."

Dubin broke into a sweat. "My age?"

"Sixty."

"My God, he's older than I."

"I've often told myself that."

"How in Christ did you ever get involved with an old man at your age?"

He had trouble with the question, thought of himself as hypocrite, except that Fanny, when they had met, was an experienced woman.

"I don't think of him as old."

That drew a mist to her father's eyes.

"Sixty is the age he happens to be," Maud said, rubbing her cigarette out. "For a while I was frightened about the difference in years—that he was three times my age. Then it became a sort of mythic thing in my mind that he was more than lover—he was father, friend, and lover—that there was something extraordinary in our relationship, that it had been happening since man appeared on earth. I stopped being afraid. His age made little difference to me—although it did to him—because in his heart he was young, because he loved me. He seemed to know everything I wanted to know. I valued myself better when I was with him."

"I always valued you highly."

"Too highly, I bet?"

"I never thought so. I thought you valued yourself?"

"I do but with doubt. He was my Spanish teacher in my sophomore year. In class he couldn't keep his eyes off me. When we talked I could see his love. Once he poured a paper cup of water for me in the hall and his hand shook. We began to sleep together. He never asked, it happened when I realized I was in love with him."

She said they saw each other seriously from then on. "Finally his wife found out and had a breakdown. I felt I had to leave college. I joined the Zen commune in South San Francisco but still missed him. When he wrote to me we got back together for a few days and when I woke up in the motel room the morning he left, I knew I was pregnant."

"Didn't he ask if you were protected? What sort of ass is he?"

"If I had slept with a fifteen-year-old boy I still would have got pregnant,"

Maud said. "I was stupid about my diaphragm. He had no reason to think I didn't know what I was doing. He's a gentle and courteous man. He taught me an awful lot about poetry. We read the classic Spanish poets together. I was happy with him. What's wrong with happiness?"

Dubin didn't say.

"Was he the man you went to Venice with?"

"I don't know how you know that. I never told you or Mother I went to Venice with anyone. We weren't there when you were, without Mother."

"How did you know I was there without Mother?"

"You all but confessed it the winter I was here for a week."

Dubin got up as she rose, kissed her hair, drew her to him. He could feel her pregnant frame trembling. "I'm glad you're home."

"I suppose you feel betrayed?"

"I feel a lot but not betrayed. You're the one who's betrayed."

"I don't think of it that way."

She went to the window, raised it, breathed deeply. "I need a breath of air."

"You won't get any air through the storm window. My God, you've forgotten you ever lived here." He opened a window with a ventilating slot at the bottom of the outer frame.

Maud was sitting again, smoking. He advised her not to if she was pregnant but she continued to smoke.

"Maud," Dubin asked, "what is your life trying to prove?"

"Why do you ask me that kind of question?"

"I wouldn't if you asked yourself."

"I'm trying to live my life without you."

He said he desperately wanted her to.

"Pay attention to your wife," said Maud, rising. "She's not a happy woman." She left the study.

At supper when they glanced at one another they looked away. Kitty served Maud's vegetable casserole. Maud ate poorly, diddled the baby carrots to the side of her plate. Dubin ate hungrily.

"It's not the world's greatest tragedy," Kitty said, looking out of the window.

Maud stared at her.

"I'm sorry, I didn't mean it that way," her mother said. "But I can't help wishing it hadn't happened."

They talked about Gerald. Maud said they had to do more than just write letters to make contact with him.

"Your father has promised to go to Moscow with me," Kitty said to her.

"We'd better know what we're doing," Dubin said. "We can't just pitch a tent in the middle of Red Square."

Chewing listlessly, Kitty asked Maud her plans.

"To have my baby. To support myself with her/him. To make the least do. To live a simple decent life."

"You ought to finish college," Dubin said.

"In time she will," said Kitty. "The baby comes first."

He pictured his daughter as a young widow with a child. What else were you with a fatherless child? They had tipped her life in some odd way.

Maud's eyes would still not meet his.

"What will you do with a little baby to take care of?" Kitty uneasily asked.

"What I have to do. Many women do it nowadays. There are ways of getting together for everyone's benefit."

"Living alone with a child can be trying," her mother said. "I won't deny its pleasures, but it can be quite sad putting a baby to sleep without a father there. It's a double loneliness though the child won't know for a while, a fate I would gladly have spared you. Maybe you ought to consider abortion?"

"You've taught me to value life. I value life. How can I have an abortion?"

If she marries someone to be a father for her child, Dubin was thinking, he will someday hunger for a lover.

"What kind of work do you think you can get?" he asked Maud.

"I have no idea."

"Would you want to consult a psychiatrist?" Dubin then said to his daughter.

"What for?"

"To loosen your fate a little."

"My illegitimate baby isn't my fate."

"Insight may come faster with some help."

"I want it to come slow."

"Leave her alone," Kitty told him.

"Leave *me* alone."

Maud said she'd live in New York City with her baby.

"Why there?" Kitty asked.

"There are more opportunities for a single mother."

"You could live here. I'd help with the baby. You'd be a lot freer."

"I don't want to live here."

"What kind of opportunities?" Dubin wanted to know. "Welfare? Food stamps?"

"That isn't what she means," Kitty said with irritation.

Maud said she would take welfare if she had to. Dubin said she was not being wise.

"Maybe I will be someday, who can tell?"

"I'd expect to help you," he offered. "But things are tight with us now. Inflation isn't helping. I'm worried about money."

"I don't want to be helped," Maud said.

"You ought to notify the baby's father about your situation. He has some obligation to you."

"I will when I feel like it."

"Maud, be reasonable," Kitty said

"I am reasonable, Mother." She flung her napkin on the table and ran upstairs.

"Be careful with her," Kitty said to Dubin. "Don't be insensitive."

"Tell her not to be. An unwanted pregnancy is no privilege."

They had raised their voices, began to quarrel. Above their heads Maud thumped on the floor with her boot.

They stopped shouting.

The next afternoon Dubin and his daughter walked in the snow to the covered bridge. Maud took his arm. Usually he asked her to walk with him; today she had suggested it. Dubin thought he would say she could rely on his support. She was wearing the antique gold earrings he had bought her in Stockholm. He was moved by them, by her.

He pointed out how many blue jays were around that winter. They counted eight in the snow at one spot.

At the bridge she nervously said, "Papa, my lover was a black man. I may have a black child."

Dubin, even as he was touched by her, groaned aloud.

"Jesus, how you mess up your life, Maud."

"Be gentle, please." The girl looked as if she were drowning. He felt he must keep her afloat, yet could not restrain his anger. "Not only an old man but black in the bargain. Not only a single mother but white with a black baby. What kind of simple life can you have when you complicate yours so incredibly?"

"I happened to love a certain man."

"There are times when love is impossible."

"I never thought of it as impossible."

"Now I understand why you came home that winter with your hair dyed black."

"You understand nothing." Her face was stiff, eyes motionless.

"I understand the misery you're heading into. You'd be better off aborting."

"No one's going to make me abort my baby," she wept.

When they had returned to the house she packed her suitcase and duffel bag and ordered a cab to take her to the bus station.

Kitty canceled the cab. "If you insist on going I'll take you."

Dubin asked Maud not to leave. "I'm sorry I lost my cool. Stay, let's talk it over calmly."

Kitty said stay for her sake.

"I can't, Mother, I'm miserable here."

Her father carried her things out to the car. His breath misted as he kissed her cheek. "We'll be in touch, my child. Things will be better."

When Kitty came back from the bus she accused him of having driven the girl out of the house.

Dubin got into the car and drove quickly to the bus station. A bus had just left and he followed it to Winslow until it occurred to him that wasn't the way to New York.

One night as the telephone rang while Kitty and Dubin sat in the living room, each looked tensely at the other; neither moved to answer. The ringing went on and ceased. They watched it ring and listened to an aftermath of ringing silence.

"Why didn't you answer it?" he asked.

"Why didn't you?"

"It might have been Maud. I thought you would. You usually answer the phone."

"You'd have been embarrassed if it was your girl calling long-distance."

"I have no girl calling long-distance. It might have been Maud."

"She wouldn't hang up after five rings."

"Has she called?"

Kitty shook her head.

"Do you have her address?"

"She said she would write."

"I asked her to stay in touch," he said.

The next day when the phone rang he picked up the receiver and heard it click off after he and Kitty simultaneously said hello. Dubin wondered if it was Fanny signaling him to get in touch with her but when he rang her up from the barn she said she hadn't called.

"Why would I if I promised not to call you at your house any more?"

"Something might have come up so that we couldn't meet."

"I'd leave a note for you on the table inside my front door."

He would rather have her do that than call, Dubin agreed. He hadn't yet told Kitty Fanny had bought the Wilson farm. She'd find it out soon enough herself, but whatever time he had before that he wanted to have. Sooner or later time would evolve a course of action. He wanted it to be the right one; he wanted time on his side.

The next day when the phone rang Kitty answered it in her husband's presence. After listening a minute she seemed puzzled. "You must have the wrong number." She hung up slowly.

"Have you noticed all the wrong numbers?"

"Sometimes the circuits get screwed up."

"It puts me on edge. I mean when there are so many."

"I noticed it a couple of weeks ago but not lately."

"I guess you're right," Kitty said.

She was sleeping better, gaining weight. She complained that flesh was hitting her on the hips and belly. She was having trouble getting into her best dresses, would have to diet. Knowing how intensely she worried about Maud, not to speak of Gerald, Dubin thought that all in all she was in good control. Seeing Ondyk obviously helped her. So did her work in the Youth Opportunity Center; there she could do for others what she couldn't do for her elusive children. At night Kitty carefully creamed her face and hands. She had got a short haircut and looked pretty.

"Do you want to go to bed?" Dubin asked her one evening.

"Let's give it a little longer," she hesitantly said. Her dark eyes were sober.

"Are you afraid?"

"Yes."

He said they could wait a while longer; he felt bad saying it.

She hadn't complained lately about his problem. She seemed calm about it, objective, patient. She treated him, Dubin thought, as if he was someone convalescing; or she hoped convalescing. Kitty would glance into his study or wherever he happened to be when she was on her way out, and ask him how he felt. "Fine," Dubin said. "How's the work going?" "Fine," he said. She smiled and left quickly, returning to smell the burners casually, as though she had really returned to look at the clock. She reminded him a little of the woman she had been when they first met. She seemed more independent lately, able to get along without consulting him. He put her out of his thoughts, yet found himself thinking of her. He sensed her secretly eluding him. He felt some regret, but did not worry about it—wanted her to be on her own, free of him.

Dubin could not recall when he began thinking of her diary. It seemed to him he had lately become curious to have a look at it. It had been around so often he was surprised when it was no longer in sight. When Kitty left the house one morning, he stopped work to search for it. Dubin went from room to room, looking in dresser drawers, amidst her underwear, on closet shelves, behind books in her bookcase, for the worn hardbound blue spiral notebook she wrote in every so often, sometimes late at night—her intense outpourings in thoughtful passages. The tone of the book was self-critical, but often she said things about life that made him reflect on life. He had guessed she might be writing in the diary lately and searched for it continually, half disgusted with what he was doing; yet he felt there had been a change in her he had to understand.

Dubin wanted to know how she defined herself now; and what her degree of feeling or non-feeling for him was. Maybe he had become curious to read the diary when he realized she was no longer leaving it around like yesterday's newspaper. He had often seen it on her dresser or his; or downstairs on a kitchen chair; or in the bathroom. Sometimes it annoyed him to come across it if he thought she had placed it where it would be at hand, his hand. He hadn't wanted to read what she feared or was bored with; or how William Dubin had once more failed her. Why bother reading it when she would sooner or later say openly what she had written? On the whole he knew how she measured him. Too bad he hadn't kept a journal of his own for her to read, though she would never read it without asking if she might. Tolstoy and his wife let each other read their diaries and were both wounded. Total confession was not necessarily pure honesty. There were mean ways to confess whatever one was confessing. However, in Kitty's present mood, whatever it was, Dubin felt he wanted a glimpse of her mind. He had to know what he could freely do next. He wanted to do it the way it would hurt least.

He searched under their bed; through a pile of unanswered correspondence on her desk; in her desk drawers. Nor was there a letter from a lover, if she had one. Dubin had been incredulously wondering if she might be having an affair. With whom? This would be tricky terrain for Kitty. She had more than once remarked she had no objection to extramarital affairs "for some women," those, Dubin gathered, who could find little relief from meager marriages. "But I doubt I'd want to get into that act," she said. "I'm not made for it." Kitty laughed breathily as though she had confessed a serious lack.

"How would you know till you had tried?"

"I know myself," she had said. She spoke with doubt, looking at him as though expecting him to deny the doubt, which he did not do.

She said then with more certainty, "I'm not saying I wouldn't want to try an affair. I've thought about it, frankly, though I don't know who'd be interested in me at my age. I'm not a young woman any more."

He said again, hesitating to say it, that she was, nevertheless, attractive. "Stop remembering when you were born."

"I wish I had been more adventurous when I was young—more daring. I wish I could have let go—I'm a passionate woman—but I wouldn't have been comfortable with an affair while Nathanael was walking the dog, or you were picking flowers. And I don't think I'd care for the concealment and dishonesty that goes with an affair, though my grandmother told me my mother was very good at it, could do it all without blinking an eyelash. But I am not my mother. Somewhere along the line I think I bored her."

Dubin gave her credit: Kitty knew herself not badly, and lived with it, not badly. He thought of her as comparatively untried. Life had fallen on her once like a tree that had cracked and been blown over in a storm. She had crawled out from under a ton of broken branches, shocked, bleeding, traumatized; but after that, life had more or less let her be. A little crippled was fine with life. So long as you're wounded you know you're alive. Yet he felt the more experienced he became, the less she seemed to be. Though Kitty

347

called herself passionate there were areas of sensual experience she had made no attempt to know. She did not play with what might explode in her face. One tree falling on you in a lifetime was enough forever. She seemed always self-protective; had a quality of that kind, therefore that kind of innocence. Besides she couldn't lie. Perhaps he could teach her?

Was she changing—might she have changed? Had she thought it over, decided, at her age, because of her age, to take a chance—in protest of his neglect of her? If she were into an affair now had he forced it on her? But an affair with whom in Center Campobello? Oscar—perhaps evening the score for Flora and Dubin? Not likely: if he'd allowed himself to be attracted by Kitty he'd have gone after her years ago. Only once had he persuaded her to play the harp to his flute. Evan Ondyk? She had said he would not appeal to her as a lover. Roger Foster?—the desire for a young lover revived? Given the failure of their former attraction, Dubin doubted her interest in Roger now. Still, he couldn't say for sure. Women of Kitty's age could be desirable to younger men. She might be willing if he was. But Dubin thought if she was into an affair it would probably be with a stranger to him, possibly one of the psychiatric social-worker types she met at the Youth Center. Kitty admired people who advised others about their lives.

Dubin had noticed a leak in the hot-water tank and one morning went down to the cellar to see how bad it was. The water was dripping steadily. He hurried upstairs to call the plumber and when he picked up the receiver heard Evan Ondyk on the phone. He was about to hang up when Evan quietly said, "We can have lunch and be together."

"Is someone on the telephone?" Kitty asked loudly, nervously. Dubin could hear her voice on the phone; at the same time he heard it coming from upstairs. His heart hammered; he didn't speak and could not hang up lest she hear him.

Ondyk after a long moment said he didn't think so. "Where's William?"

"I think in his study. Let's not talk any more now, Evan. I'll meet you— you know where—and please don't call me here—I get anxious when the telephone rings."

"Kitty, you called me."

"So you wouldn't call me."

He insisted he was being careful. "How else can I reach you when time unexpectedly becomes available?"

"Smoke signals," she said.

They laughed.

"I look forward."

"I too." She hung up.

From therapy to bed with the psychotherapist, an easy next step. The bastard probably tells himself he's doing me a favor—filling in for a friend with a soft cock.

Dubin waited in the cellar till Kitty came down for breakfast. He entered the kitchen, saying there was a leak in the hot-water tank. She said she would call the plumber. Neither of them looked long at the other.

In mid-morning, as she was taking a bath, he left the house and walked to town to rent a car. Dubin parked it on a nearby road on an overcast February day. Before Kitty, wearing flushed-pink stockings, left the house shortly before noon, she said, "The plumber will be here in the morning. I may do some shopping. There's a hamburger for you defrosted in the fridge if you want one for lunch. Coffee is set to boil."

She paused trying to think whether there was something else to say but there wasn't. Kitty did not return to dip her head over the burners. Now she knew what an affair might do for one.

Dubin followed her at a distance in his rented car. She drove to a motel a few miles away, her apple-green automobile turning into its driveway. As he rode by he observed his wife enter the cabin where Ondyk's Buick was parked. Fair is fair. It was the same motel Dubin had been in with Fanny.

He arrived home nervously excited. He felt, too, nostalgic regret. He felt relief accompanied by an oppressive surge of energy. Sitting at his desk with a sheet of paper before him he listed the steps of a divorce. He remembered more law then he had thought. It occurred to him that he had kept up with recent changes in divorce law in New York State.

In the weeks that followed Dubin pretended to know nothing about Kitty's affair. He sometimes felt an embarrassed self-punitive regret when she went off to be with her lover. When she went to meet him she wore the silver bracelet Dubin had got her in Stockholm after he had bought the gold one in Venice for Fanny. And lately Kitty also wore an old locket she had, a medallion of Mary the Mother. She usually left her wedding ring home when she went to see Evan. Dubin pretended not to notice, or seem suspicious. He doubted she could have carried on an affair when she was a young woman. The years, her need, made the difference.

He still kept his eye open for her diary. What was she writing about her affair? He felt a desire to know. In her clothes closet he came across her blue gardening sneakers. They were long sneakers, split at the toes, comic. Her droopy faded orange straw hat looked as if it belonged to somebody's grandmother. He thought of himself and her, a generation ago, as a young man and woman who had just met, and moved by mutual respect and the magic of possibility, were willing to try to know and love each other. It was, in this world, a brave thing to do, and they had for a while done it. There was indeed, Dubin thought, a married state; and if you had lived in it for years with someone who had treated you considerately you wanted to go on thinking of her as the considerate woman she was. You wanted to go on respecting her whether she was still your wife or not. He hoped she would not spoil that for him.

One afternoon Dubin discovered Kitty's diary in the kitchen oven. It had been elsewhere, but now it was in the oven. Kitty sometimes temporarily shoved things in it to get them out of the way. He had asked her not to, but she said she had never in her life caused a fire. Dubin riffled through the last pages of the notebook. She had written little about herself recently, not a word about Ondyk, nothing directly about Dubin. He discovered, not without surprise, that she had been reading biographies of accomplished women. Four she mentioned were Charlotte Brontë, Rosa Luxemburg, Jane Welsh, Eleanor Roosevelt. She commented on how they had fought for strength and resisted the tyranny of lovers and husbands.

Most of her notes in the diary were about Jane Welsh, Thomas Carlyle's wife, a woman of exceptional intellect, character, wit, with vivid powers of literary expression, who might have had, Kitty wrote, "a remarkable writing career if she weren't enmeshed in a miserable Victorian marriage. What an age!" Carlyle, though he could at times be a tender and affectionate husband, especially when he was miles from her, in Scotland or elsewhere writing letters to her, was an almost totally self-centered man of genius; for years bound to, and groaning in his bowels over, the multi-volumed lives of Cromwell and Frederick the Great it took him forever to write, while his unhappy wife was sometimes suffering from illness and neglect in the next room. Once after she had been seriously hurt in a street accident she wrote in her diary, "Oh, my husband! I am suffering torments! Each day I suffer more horribly. O, I would like you beside me. I am terribly alone. But I don't want to interrupt your work." Though Carlyle depended heavily on her, he was all but blind to her loneliness; he gave her little emotionally and nothing sexually. Like Ruskin he seemed to have been impotent throughout his married life. When she died in London, he, in Scotland, dreamed she had died. She was buried in her father's grave and Carlyle's remorse began. For fifteen years he mourned her. "Oh that I had you yet for five minutes beside me, to tell you all."

"About time," Kitty wrote. Her last entry on Jane Welsh read: "She waked between thirty and forty times a night, averaging three hours of sleep, 'all in fractions.' But she was not a defeated person, a victim, thanks to her talent for friendship, writing, self-preservation. She felt marriage was a 'shockingly immoral institution.' And 'an extremely disagreeable one.' " Kitty called Carlyle "a narcissistic, nervous, *obsessed, impotent biographer.* " Dubin noted the emphasis.

The entry after that in her diary was a despairing one about Gerald. Dubin tossed the notebook back into the oven and seriously considered turning the gas on.

One night she came to Maud's room, where he was sleeping, and standing by the bed in the dark, told him she had had a terrible dream about their daughter: "She had given birth but wouldn't let me see the baby. Then a black man went into the room and stabbed it. I sank into a faint so deep I don't know how I managed to wake up and come here."

"Do you want to get into bed with me?"

She said, after momentary silence, "Would you mind first going down to look at the burners? I meant to but forgot."

There's this hissing open burner in her head, he thought, and I live with it as though it were real.

Dubin got up as she slipped into Maud's narrow bed. Stepping into his slippers he went down to the kitchen to sniff the gas. First he tightened the knobs, then breathed over the burners to make sure no gas was leaking. He felt he had to smell them if she asked him to. It was a responsibility: you lied about your girl but not about the gas. He tried to estimate how often he had smelled the burners since he had married Kitty. How many cubic feet of gas had he inhaled in the hundreds of times he had bent over the burners for her? One married her wounds with the woman. One ingested them. And it worked the other way, he supposed. His wounds had wounded her.

What would I smell for Fanny? Only her body. Her breasts smell like flowers and her cunt like the salt sea.

The bed lamp was on when he returned to Maud's room. Kitty's head lay on the pillow in darkish light.

"Is there something I can do for you?" she asked.

"Nothing," said Dubin, "except please let me sleep if I fall asleep. You stay here, I'll go to our bed."

"Are you sure?"

"Nothing at all."

As he was becoming sleepy, Kitty slid into their bed with him. "William," she said, "I have something to tell you: I've been having an affair with Evan. It started a couple of months ago, and you know why."

"That horse's ass," he said dully.

"No, he isn't. He's considerate and appreciative and a lot wiser than you think. He asked me to go to bed with him and I did. He's not very happy with Marisa, and I was hard up and disgusted with you. But what I want to say now is that I've broken it off. I don't regret what I've done, but I didn't do it easily. If it weren't for you I don't think I would have done it."

"Is he still your therapist?"

"I don't think we'd better. I'm sorry because he was good with me. I don't know what to do about that."

"Would you want a divorce?" Dubin asked her.

She said bitterly she no longer knew what she wanted.

Winter

Dear William, Dear Mother—If this ever reaches you it will be through a contact I had with a friend in the French Embassy when I first came here. I'm in her room writing this as she packs. She's leaving the Soviet Union to marry a medical student in France and has promised to try to sneak this letter out. If she does you will get it from Rouen but won't be able to answer. I have no address to give you. I am in serious trouble— which won't surprise you. I sleep in a freezing shack. I have little to eat. I am worn out and sick.

Here's what happened—I was recruited in Stockholm by the KGB into Soviet espionage. I wasn't sure I wanted to accept but finally talked myself into it. I think I thought I was being true to myself. I was flown into the Soviet Union from Finland after a boat trip across the Baltic. In Moscow I was trained to work with coding and code-breaking electronic equipment.

Colonel Kovacol, in charge of my unit, twice cited me for excellent work. As you might expect it didn't take me long to fall out of favor. Whatever reasons I came here for, I didn't come out of a love for communism, and I underestimated the effects of totalitarianism. Men *are* superfluous in this society. The worst things in American life are all here, derived from a terrifying materialism. Everybody eats now but few think independently and those who do and say so usually end up in prison. It depressed me that I always go one worse when I hope to go one better. Finally I made up my mind to ask out, I requested to be sent back to Sweden. That was, of course, a stupid mistake. I should have waited until they had some reason of their own to send me out of the country.

Kovacol told me there was no way out for a foreigner who knew the secrets of their coding computers. He asked me what I thought I was accomplishing by quitting and I said I wanted to rectify a serious error. I didn't say my life was full of them. He said the fate of a bourgeois humanist was bound to be narrow. He said I was lucky he didn't shoot me on the spot and then discharged me from the unit without pay. The friend I had come with from Stockholm, the one who had given them my name originally, wouldn't see me again.

For a few weeks they let me alone, then began to tail me to see if I had any contacts. I had one a short while, a man I met one night in a park. At first he didn't trust me but then became sympathetic. When he told me he was a Jew I said you were, William, and told him about my situation here. Arkady Davidovich turned out to be a dissident. For some weeks he and his wife helped me with food parcels they hid in various spots I had been told to look in, but I stopped picking them up when I realized the secret police were tight on my tail. Arkady and his wife have two kids, a boy thirteen and a girl nine, and I didn't want them to get into worse trouble because of me. We don't meet any more but sometimes they manage to slip an envelope with a couple of rubles to me. I walk into a crowd and when I come out usually there are two or three rubles in my pocket. Lately—now that I am being followed day and night—that happens rarely.

I've tried to get into the U.S. Embassy, but the Soviet guards recognize me and won't let me in. If I wait for an American to come out they shove me along with their nightsticks. I don't know how they do it but when I call from a public booth the call is jammed. I hear a buzz and when I talk my voice breaks into noise. It's as though your self had destructed.

I don't know how much longer I can last. I'm on the move and they are generally close behind but not making the arrest, though I've begun to hunger for it. If I'm lucky I'll end up in a strict-regime labor camp in the Gulag. Frankly, it would be a relief. I wouldn't have to scrounge for bread or try to hide where they watch me hiding. I have a croupy cough and almost constant diarrhea. Maybe that's the punishment they've arranged till I collapse.

I'm afraid of my fate. I'm afraid of myself for the fate I've created. Right now I'd give half my life to be free the other half.

I wish I could say there was something you could do for me. Maybe talk to the press? But if you do they might shoot me at once. I've blocked my exits. All my life I've been walking in a tunnel believing I was out in the open. The only really generous thing I ever really did was to stop taking food from a dissident Jew and his family.

Tell Maud I think of her a lot. My mother is my mother, and you are my father, William. Some simple things take a long time to get thought out.

Gerry.

Dubin mourned D. H. Lawrence.

In a letter to his sister-in-law Else, he said: "It is very lovely, the wind, clouds, the running sea that bursts like a blossom on the island opposite. If only I was well, and had my strength back!

"But I am so weak. And something inside me weeps black tears. I wish it would go away."

Frieda held his ankle as he lay dying. "I held his ankle from time to time, it felt so full of life, all my days I shall hold his ankle in my hand."

After Lawrence's death, Middleton Murry, the ex-friend he detested, came to stand at his grave; and soon thereafter Frieda and he became lovers. Murry later wrote in his diary, "With her for the first time in my life, I know what fulfilment in love really meant."

Kitty could not sleep. Dubin woke and saw her not sleeping.

"Haven't you slept yet?"

"No. When will we leave for Russia?"

"When the visas come."

"What will we do when we get there?"

"Cry out his name."

"Maud hasn't called."

"I know."

Kitty slept, snoring lightly. She spoke in her sleep, "Nat, dear Nat."

Dubin, with sweet pleasure, remembered his mother covering him with a second blanket on a very cold night.

He lay awake, recomposing a letter to Gerry he carried in his head. Then he got out of bed and went upstairs to sleep in the boy's bed.

A breeze blew up in the late afternoon, making sea sounds in the tops of leafless trees; at night winter dipped its cold hands into the wind. But a half-moon brightened the night-blue sky, lit, softened, as though spring might begin as moonlight, a not bad idea in a cold climate.

Dubin again worked in the barn study. Kitty hadn't asked why he worked when or where he worked. He wrote there mornings and returned after supper till almost midnight, except those nights he left the light on and went early to Fanny's farm. If the phone rang, he had told Kitty, he would not answer, wanted no interruptions.

The biographer, carrying a heavy birch stick, trotted through the woods and up the road to the farm. The snow had melted but at night the dirt road hardened and was ridged. In a few weeks it would be mud season. He had given up his afternoon walks and this was his new route, from house to house by way of his barn, Kitty's Wood, the farm, then back to the barn study to be alone a few minutes before he went home. In bed, awake as Kitty slept her early sleep, he considered fasting a day a week.

Dubin ran, this windy pre-spring night, to Fanny's. Where else? The wind buffeted him and he ducked behind trees to catch his breath. On the road the going was easier with the wind blowing behind him. Fanny's large barn was dark and silent. Her kitchen light was on. Through the window he saw her sitting at the table in her padded jacket and beige wool hat, reading the local paper. Snowdrop yawned at her feet. Her boots were muddy. She looked dismally tired. Dubin, concerned about her, knocked the clapper and entered, using the key she had given him. The sink was full of dirty dishes he quickly washed for her.

The farm, Fanny confessed, had seriously been worrying her. She hadn't wanted to give it this much time and labor. Craig Bosell had fallen off a ladder in his cellar and broken his right hip; he was in the hospital. She could not replace him at the modest salary he accepted. The day after he left, one of the Toggenburgs was killed in the goat pasture by a dog that had burrowed under the wire fence. He had torn her udder and chewed off an ear. Fanny had chased the hound with an ax as Snowdrop yelped but the bloody doe was dead. Bawling, she dug the goat a grave. Dubin helped bury her.

The goats weren't easy to handle. The pregnant doe, Trudy, a large-eared black-and-white yammering Nubian that Fanny had bought bred, was a neurotic beast. Left alone in the dark she trumpeted in fear until she learned to flip the light switch with her nose after Fanny had left the barn. The barn light burned all night and she had to fence the goat into another stall. Trudy bleated throughout the night. Fanny returned her to her former stall and let her turn the light on when she wanted to. "I was afraid of the dark myself when I was a little girl." She loved the pregnant goat. "She's about to kid and I almost hate to see it happen she's so satisfied to be a pregnant goat."

She shoveled the goats' hay into the overhead manger and filled with warmish drinking water their rubber buckets hooked to the wall; she also cleaned their stalls, carried out manure; laid new sawdust, and spent an hour every day brushing their coats. Later she collected the warm newly laid eggs from the hens' nests, sold or bartered them in town; had a dozen other tasks that kept her busy till dark. Although she complained she was dead-tired she seemed always to have energy for sex. "Or what's it all about?" In her bedroom she changed into a sheer nightgown before Dubin came upstairs. In bed she was adventurous, exciting, even wise. Afterward they quietly talked, affectionately, honestly. Then Dubin showered, dressed, and trotted back to his study, sitting there contemplatively ten or fifteen minutes before going home.

"How did it go tonight?" Kitty asked.

He told her fine.

One night in February when the temperature had fallen below zero, Fanny's pipes froze and it cost her seventy-two dollars to repair the one that had burst in the cellar and thaw out the others to get the water running. In a driving storm a week later the roof leaked around the chimney. Patching that cost another fifty. She worried about the rising cost of services; Dubin worried with her. She said she didn't know how she would go on doing all she did, plus milk Trudy twice a day after she had kidded; and that summer take care of the vegetable garden she wanted. "Besides that I would like to plant some flowers to look at when I feel like it." Dubin said she had to have help and suggested, to begin with, hiring a high school boy part-time. He offered to pay his hourly wages. "I've lectured twice lately for good fees."

Fanny said no.

"Why not?"

"I'm not your goddamned wife—I don't want your money."

"What can I do for a friend?" he said after a minute.

"I will pay my own bills."

He sometimes came over in the afternoon to work at whatever he could. Dubin sawed wood for the kitchen stove. Once he replaced a broken window. He fixed an electric light socket—little jobs he hadn't done for years. And Roger Foster, Fanny informed him, came on weekend mornings. "He helps me clean my barn."

Though her hips and bosom seemed fuller, Fanny said she had lost weight. Her face was thinner. One night as she unbraided her hair he found a strand of gray in it; and Dubin noticed that the four or five darkish hairs under her chin had once more sprouted forth. Fanny, hopping out of bed to look in the mirror, was incensed. "I spent over a hundred bucks on electrolysis and injections. I thought I'd got rid of them forever." She said angrily: "Even if they grow seven feet long I will never cut those hairs again."

"Lady Bluebeard," he teased.

"Don't you call me that," she yelled at him.

He begged her pardon.

"You also call me Kitty, in case you don't know it."

"Often?"

"Once in a while."

Dubin said he was sorry.

Crawling back into bed she complained about her life: "Nothing is going the way I hoped. I haven't had any time to myself since Craig broke his hip. I have no time to read. I feel flaked out when I look at a page of print. Sometimes the feeling that my life is not turning out right floods over me."

"Do you think taking on this farm was a mistake?"

He disliked his question because he feared her answer, but Fanny said after a pause, "Not actually coming here but maybe my idea of having a barnful of tender loving animals welcoming me with yaps of joy in the morning was out of my childhood books. Still this place is right for me, and I love the house and have been fixing it up, little by little, the way I want."

357

Dubin said it was tastefully done.

"I wouldn't think of leaving it. My main gripe is I am tied down too much. Everything I do I *have* to."

"Not everything."

"You'd be surprised." Smiling in afterthought she said, "Not everything."

Fanny said she had been thinking a lot about the future.

"Relative to what?"

"To myself—that I still find it hard to zero in on what I want out of my life."

"You know yourself better than you did, not a long time ago."

"Yes, but I am still not sure what I want to do—what I want to work at. Sometimes I say, the hell with that, I'd rather get married. I want to have a baby before I am too old. I want to get settled. I don't want to be a single woman forever."

He said she was entitled to these things.

"With you?"

"With or without me."

Fanny let it slowly go at that, then said, "Other times I think I'd rather stay single and in some career I respect. I honestly think that. I want to work at something worthwhile that I could do well. I want to do something really well, not get lost in the shuffle. I want to like myself up to the hilt sometime in my life."

He asked her what she had in mind to do.

"I've thought a lot about that, and have even thought of selling antiques in my house," Fanny said. "My mother did that once, and I have taste but it doesn't take much of a brain. I thought of teaching but don't want to. I don't feel I have the right to—everybody knows what I know. I've also looked at veterinary-medicine catalogues but there I am fantasizing. What I keep going back to in my mind—ever since I worked as a secretary in a law office—is to study law and practice it. But the trouble is I don't think I can handle law school right now, though I think I could get accepted if I applied. They're taking more women nowadays and I have good grades even if it did take me six years to knock off my B.A."

They had talked before about studying law and talked of it now as they lay in bed. Dubin had told her about his own disappointing experience as a lawyer. "I got little pleasure out of it though perhaps the fault was mine for not being more patient. I could have changed the nature of my practice if I wasn't so anxious about making a living. I lived on cases involving small finaglers and found myself engaged in pisher dishonesties. I told myself the law is not perfect and neither are men, but I couldn't stand what I was doing. Montaigne wanted to get out of public life so he could stop lying for convenience' sake. I wanted to stop lying, period."

"Law doesn't have to be only that way," Fanny said. "What I think I'd like to get into is the law protecting the environment and dealing with women's rights. I'd also like to represent poor people in court. I like that pro bono stuff."

"You'd have to do more than pro bono to make a living."

"I could grow most of my food here and work in the legal-aid office in town. Or if I couldn't get a job there I'd do half of make-a-living law and half pro bono, once I passed the bar."

He asked her if she would go away to law school if she was accepted. "There's an old established one in Albany and a new one in Royalton."

"In the first place I couldn't afford that. In the second place I want to live here."

"It isn't that you're without potential funds, Fanny. Real estate keeps going up. You could sell this farm for a good profit."

"I told you I don't want to sell my farm," she said, sitting up. "I expect to go on living here."

"Don't get angry in bed."

"Stay the night," Fanny said. "I feel lonely."

He said he couldn't.

Kitty, when Dubin got home, was awake, reading. She no longer set up his breakfast dishes for the morning. She no longer paired his washed socks; she dropped them in a heap on his dresser.

"Do you think I could find work as a secretary?" she asked him. "I'm a good typist, all I need is shorthand. I could pick that up in an extension class at night, but who would want to employ a woman over fifty as a secretary?"

"Some people would."

"Not many."

He thought she could make it.

"That won't absolve you from supporting me."

He was not expecting absolution.

"It'll be an empty life," Kitty said.

He said nothing.

After a while she said, "I'm smoking too much. Sometimes when I take a deep breath my lungs seem to be burning."

"Cut down," he advised.

She said her sleep was dreadful.

"Why don't you try a sleep-disorder clinic? There are many now. Maybe they can help you."

She said she just might. "Will you come with me?"

He said he would.

After a restless night Dubin made several morning calls to attorneys in nearby Vermont. He took a tablet for heartburn and drove to Arlington to see two lawyers who had said they could see him that morning.

Dubin returned to Fanny's a few days later—that windy pre-spring night in early March—to tell her it was possible to study law by clerking in a law office and thus not have to go to law school.

"You'll have to decide pretty quickly because the State of Vermont isn't permitting this procedure much longer."

"I'd want to start right away if anybody wanted me," Fanny said in excitement. "What do I have to do?"

"You'd have to be pretty sure of it or it would be an awful waste of time for you and the attorney who had taken you on."

"I *am* sure, William. I know I am."

Dubin explained he had been to see Ursula Habersham, a friend of his wife's. "She's a State Senator who's giving up politics because of her husband's poor health. Now she's trying to revive her law office. When I told her about you out here on a farm, wanting to study law, she was interested. I recommended you as a responsible person with a B.A., who by now would have fulfilled the residency requirements. She said she might take you on as a clerk if you were as apt as I said."

Dubin told her she would read law with Habersham and after four years under her tutelage would take the bar. "If you pass you can practice. There's no salary while you're learning. What you learn is what you're paid."

Fanny hugged him. "It's what I want to do. I will be a good apprentice. It's just the kind of thing I need."

"Four years is a long haul."

She said she wasn't going anywhere.

Dubin said, "I've got you an interview for Monday afternoon."

Fanny said her mind was made up. "Except what will I do with my goats?"

"Sell them."

"All but Trudy and her baby. I can take care of them. Jesus, I'm excited, William. My father will fall on his face when he hears I am studying law. Do you think she will take me on?"

"She liked what I told her about you. She liked the fact you had done secretarial work in a law office. I think you stand a fair chance. I praised all your talents but one."

"I think you like me, lover," Fanny said.

In her bedroom Dubin gave her a packet of notes he had saved from law school. "These are my old notes on contracts."

She promised to read them. "If I get into the law office I will throw a blast to celebrate. I've never had a party in this house."

"Who would you want to come?"

"People around and whatever friends of yours you invite."

As they were undressing in the bedroom—she kept an electric heater going on nights Dubin appeared—Fanny said she had run into Kitty at the grocery market that morning. "We were both picking out loaves of bread and then recognized each other."

White or rye? he wondered.

"What did she say?"

"Only what was I doing in town. I said living on a farm. She has bigger feet than I remembered. I could feel she didn't like me though she was polite. I felt sorry for her. She looks mousy and sort of sad."

"Did you say anything else?"

"She looked at the gold bracelet you bought me in Venice but didn't say anything although she looked as if she had guessed you had given it to me. Then we went our different ways."

Fanny suggested Dubin ought to stay three days with her and four with his wife. "She could have Thursday to Sunday. I'd like you to be with me Monday to Wednesday. There's a nice warm room with a desk for you to work in downstairs while you're here. I'd like to have that to look forward to. It would be less lonely those nights you aren't here."

Dubin said he didn't think Kitty would agree to that.

Fanny smiled vaguely. "Try it and see. I bet she would now. It's only fair."

He said he might.

"I don't understand why you stayed married to her."

"It wasn't so hard," he explained. "I'm a family man. We had kids we loved. I had my work to do. Conditions were good. There are other things."

"But do you love her?"

"I love her life."

"Do you love me?"

He said he did.

She put on softly a Mozart flute concerto. They embraced in bed. "God bless you, dear Fanny." She wet his flesh with her pointed tongue.

Dubin soon heaved himself out of bed, stumbled into the bathroom, got into pants and shirt.

As he came out of the farmhouse Fanny's window went up and she leaned out in the orange light, her hair flying in the pre-spring wind.

"Don't kid yourself," she called.

Roger Foster waited in the shadow of a long-boughed two-trunked silver maple as Dubin ran up the moonlit road, holding his half-stiffened phallus in his hand, for his wife with love.

Works by William B. Dubin

SHORT LIVES

ABRAHAM LINCOLN

MARK TWAIN

H. D. THOREAU

THE PASSION OF D. H. LAWRENCE: A LIFE

THE ART OF BIOGRAPHY

ANNA FREUD (WITH MAUD D. PERRERA)